A HAND FELL UPON CHRISTOPHER'S SHOULDER. HE WHIRLED AROUND AND SAW JEQON. TO HIS SURPRISE, THE TRAITOROUS ANGEL SUDDENLY FELL BACK, CRINGING BEFORE HIS EYES.

"Forgive me, Great One. I did not know you. I did not know you were aught but an angel!" He hurled himself at Christopher's feet, pleading. "Do not hold my disrespectful words against me!"

Christopher blinked, surprised. Great One? Him? He looked down past the groveling angel and saw the Prince's forces sweeping effortlessly past the guards, howling and shrieking as they began their attack. The tiny figures below reminded him of Warhammer miniatures, only this battle was real.

"Don't worry about it, Jeqon. You had a role to play, and so did I. We've done our part." He drew his sword and set it blazing with an effortless flick of his mind. How did he know to do that? He laughed. Did it matter? Not really. "Now, let's have some fun!"

Christopher's smile grew cruel as he spread his wings and hurled himself downward toward the fighting. The power inside him danced and burned, exulting in the feverish glory of battle. He did not know that his snow-white wings had dimmed to an ashy gray color. Nor did he know that when Jeqon had fallen back before his gaze, it was because his green eyes had turned as red as blood.

ETERNAL WARRIORS™

THE WAR IN HEAVEN™

BOOK ONE

Theodore Beale

POCKET BOOKS
New York London Toronto Sydney Singapore

This book is a work of fiction. Names, characters, places and incidents are products of the author's imagination or are used fictitiously. Any resemblance to actual events or locales or persons, living or dead, is entirely coincidental.

An *Original* Publication of POCKET BOOKS

POCKET BOOKS, a division of Simon & Schuster Inc.
1230 Avenue of the Americas, New York, NY 10020

ISBN: 0-671-01893-0

First Pocket Books printing March 2000

10 9 8 7 6 5 4 3 2 1

POCKET and colophon are registered trademarks of Simon & Schuster Inc.

ETERNAL WARRIORS and THE WAR IN HEAVEN are trademarks of Eternal Warriors, LLC

Front cover illustration by Rowena Morrill

Printed in the U.S.A.

This book is for my father,
whose words of wisdom I should
have taken to heart a long time ago. 23:22.

ACKNOWLEDGMENTS

Thank you to the Shoreview Bible Study and New Beginnings Baptist Church for all their prayers and support. We serve a mighty God!

Thanks also to Scott Shannon for his innovative vision, and special thanks to Carol Greenberg, my editor, whose meticulous and patient efforts made this a better story.

Most of all, thanks to my dearest Heather, for her unwavering encouragement. And I am grateful for the inspiration of the Green Bean Coffee House in Ponte Vedra, which brews a most excellent mug.

Contents

ETERNAL WARRIORS™

THE WAR IN HEAVEN™

PROLOGUE

Christopher Lewis increased his pace when he saw the crosswalk light start blinking. He was too far away, though, and the red hand appeared before he even reached the curbside. The overhead light changed, as cars and sport-utility vehicles roared past the ice-covered sidewalk upon which he waited, shivering.

The large banks of gray snow piled up beside the sidewalks gave sooty testimony to the harshness of this December. Even though his head was bare, Christopher barely noticed the chill, as he muttered angrily to himself about how unfair it was that he was walking home instead of driving. Sixteen is plenty old to drive, he thought, even the law says so. And he'd scored a ninety-two on his driver's test. Jordie Maakstad had only gotten a seventy-three and ever since had been parking his stupid new Cherokee at the far end of the school lot. He said he only parked out there so no one would ding the doors, but Christopher knew Jordie just wanted to show off.

Jami and Holli always tried to talk him into riding the bus home with them, but they didn't understand that what was good enough for them just didn't work for him. His sisters were just ninth-graders, but he was in tenth grade now, a sophomore with a driver's license, and sitting on that creaky yellow bus made him look like a complete loser. No, he wasn't about to get on that stupid bus. He would walk, and if his cheeks were red and his ears were frozen, well, tough. It would serve his parents right if he got frostbite, and his ears fell off, and they were stuck with an ugly, earless son. Maybe then they would be sorry they didn't let him drive Mom's Explorer.

Had it been just another day, he might have been okay with the bus. But one humiliation was enough for one day, and he couldn't stand the thought of the teasing he'd get from those who'd seen Kent Petersen and Jim Schumacher picking on him at lunchtime. His face burned with shame as he relived the horror of the whitewash, the hands pushing at the back of his head, the two seniors rubbing his face into the snow. The worst part wasn't his messed-up hair, his frozen, red cheeks, or the cold snow plugging his nose; no, the worst part was looking up and seeing dozens of his classmates laughing at him. Unthinkingly, his hands clenched into fists.

The red hand at the crosswalk finally changed to green, and he stalked angrily across the pavement, kicking at a frozen chunk of ice that had dropped from the wheel well of a passing car. Son of a . . . *ouch!* He made the painful discovery that the ice was harder than his Nike-clad foot. His stubbed toes forced him to limp awkwardly to the far sidewalk. Great, he thought, just great. His ears were frozen, his nose was running, and his toes felt as if they'd been broken into pieces. He could just hear Jami laughing at him when she saw his Rudolph-red nose. Now there was something to look forward to, he thought glumly. She was never one to miss the chance to make a joke at his expense. At least Holli might make him some soup or something.

Just past the corner, an old man huddled in an abandoned doorway, taking shelter from the winter wind. Christopher couldn't tell if the old man was short or just hunched over, but the man's head, ineffectively protected by a few sparse whisps of gray-white hair, came only to Christopher's chest. The old, wrinkled face was nondescript, but the blue eyes set deeply within it were uncommonly piercing and alert. They sparked with sudden life as Christopher approached.

"Young man, take this," he said in a voice cracked with age. "I think you need it."

"I need . . . what?" Christopher stared at him, surprised.

He looked down and saw that the old man was proffering a little pamphlet of some sort. It was printed on cheap red paper, with the words "Eternal Life and How to Have It" outlined in white. Some kind of religious junk, he realized. Who did this guy think he was? The bum didn't even look as if he knew how to take a shower, so what were the chances he knew the secrets of the universe? About a zillion to one against, Christopher figured.

"Forget it," he snorted disdainfully. "I don't need this. I don't need God, and I don't need you bugging me, either!"

The old man only smiled, exposing an eroded set of teeth yellowed by tobacco.

"I will pray for you, young man, for you are one upon whom God has laid his hand. But your soul is in peril, for Satan and his angels seek to prey upon those whom God would claim. I see the potential for great good in you, but for great evil also, and there is a dark cloud circling the skies even as we speak."

"Yeah, well, that dark cloud is called a snowstorm. Now, leave me alone!"

"Take this, at least."

The old one grabbed Christopher's arm before he could escape and pressed the red pamphlet into his glove. Christopher snarled and stepped back, but not before the man had forced Christopher's fingers to close around the paper. Furious that the smelly old bum had dared to touch him, Christopher pulled violently free of the other's grasp and stalked away without looking back.

"Read the truth," he heard the man call over the rising wind. "You will need it!"

Christopher ignored him, though, and as soon as he reached the next block and turned the corner, he squeezed his fist and crumpled the shabby paper into a wad. As he passed a nearby trashcan, he tossed the wad into its gaping steel mouth.

"For two!" he called optimistically, but the make-believe basketball struck the broad rim of the can and bounced off, falling to the sidewalk where it came to rest between a green newspaper coin-op and a mailbox belonging to the U.S. Postal Service. The wadded paper unfolded just a little, with a crinkling sound that was practically inaudible amidst the noisy rush of the afternoon traffic.

But Christopher couldn't care less about where the pamphlet had fallen. His thoughts soon turned from the crazy old man to his plans for the upcoming weekend. Craig had loaned him a video of an *X Files* he hadn't seen before; he decided to see what Mulder and Scully were up to first, then finish reading his new Rosenberg book, the one with all the cool Norse gods in it. The thought of swordplay reminded him of Saturday's upcoming battle, and he wondered if he should break out an Empire army against Don's Greenskinz, or stick with the High Elves. Either way, he'd need to save some time for the English paper that was due on Monday.

Behind him, a single flake of snow lighted softly upon a crumpled piece of red paper.

CHAPTER 1

A
RAT IN SHADOW

Mariel was an angel, not that she fit the stereotype. It is true that her robes were white, and a large pair of white-feathered wings sprouted from her shoulders. But she didn't play the harp or dole out solace. In the place of a musical instrument, Mariel wore a sharp-edged sword at her belt, for she was nothing less than a warrior. A warrior of God.

She was a beautiful warrior, an angelic Joan of Arc without armor. Her hair was like an autumn cascade, falling down between her alabaster wings in an unruly deluge of crimson and gold. Only her intent green eyes betrayed her sober purpose, constantly searching this way and that, always scanning for the perfidious darkness that never ceased to threaten the immortal soul in her charge.

Mariel could not feel the darkness now, but always she knew it was nearby, lurking, waiting.

Sometimes it took the form of an enemy she knew well, the cunning Temptress who haunted Christopher's fevered dreams, taunting the poor child with desires he barely knew he had. At other times, times like these, the darkness faded into the background, as if to lull her by its seeming absence. "I don't think so," she whispered savagely at the deepening night outside the window. "I know you're out there!"

Her lovely face was stern as she turned away from the window, but it softened as she caught sight of Christopher. At last, the boy had finally set to work on his school paper, though only after a long afternoon of procrastination. It amazed Mariel how easily humans could be distracted, especially the young ones.

She sighed as he pushed away from his computer and started to rise to his feet.

"No, you don't need to go to the bathroom again," she told him firmly. "You just went ten minutes ago."

Though he couldn't consciously hear her, Christopher hesitated. He didn't really have to go now, he realized. But he could use some sort of break. A game break would be all right. Maybe if he just played one quarter of "NCAA Football" . . .

"You've already played two games today. You told your teacher you would turn in your paper tomorrow, and you must keep your word to her. If you have time when you are finished, you may play a game then."

Christopher scratched his head and frowned. If he got cracking now, he'd probably have time to fit in a game before Mom and Dad got home. Maybe even two. That could be his reward to himself for finishing, two games played guilt-free.

Mariel smiled as she watched the boy return to his computer and begin hesitantly typing again. The paper was more than half finished, so she felt this particular battle was well in hand. Another thirty minutes, and Christopher would be free to run downstairs to the PlayStation and play his new football game. Thank God she'd been able to convince Mrs. Lewis that "Bloody Fist of Death" was really not an appropriate game for a teenager. Or anyone, for that matter.

It grieved her deeply to know Christopher was a nonbeliever, but she found it hard to judge the boy too harshly. His mother's faith was weak. She no longer even tried to speak to the boy about spiritual matters or encourage him to attend church. And Mr. Lewis was a skeptical man who had rejected God's mercy many years ago. It was natural for a son to follow his parents' example. When Mariel thought about the evil influences that surrounded her charge—on the television, in his games, at his school, and in his home—she felt glad that his heart had not completely hardened toward God. At least not yet. As long as life remained, there was always hope, she reminded herself.

But as Mariel, pleased with Christopher's victory over the allure of the video game, started to relax, an aura of wrongness seized her attention like a foul smell, and she found her eyes turning back toward the window on the west side of the room. She felt as if an icy shadow were falling over the house, though it was more than an hour since the sun had descended below the horizon. "You just keep working, now." She shook her finger at the rapidly typing boy, then she ran out of the room, looking for the two other Guardians of the Lewis family.

"Paulus, Aliel, there's something outside," she exclaimed as she burst into the family room where Christopher's sisters were watching the television. "I think . . . I think perhaps it's watching Christopher!"

Paulus, the big Guardian who watched over Jami, the older of the twins, was already returning to its scabbard the long blade he'd drawn upon hearing Mariel running down the stairs. But when he heard her words, he stopped as an expression of concern filled his Romanesque face.

"Outside, you say?"

"I didn't feel anything," said Aliel, Holli's slender Guardian. She was more delicate than Mariel, and usually more sensitive, too.

The three angels fell silent and listened, but even their supernatural senses could detect no obvious danger. Mariel felt the usual petty spirits wandering about, but they were nothing out of the ordinary. When she admitted that she could not feel the cold eye of darkness now, Aliel looked as if she was about to tease her, but Paulus raised an inquisitive eyebrow as he listened to her describe the uneasy sensation and urged her to go outside and look around. He and Aliel would watch the house, he assured her solemnly, while she sought for signs of lurking evil.

The evening sky was clouded, white and soft with the blanketing of quietly falling snow. It was not so much a storm as a gentle enshrouding of the earth. Large fluffy flakes settled gently on the winter-bare tree branches. Mariel curled her wings about herself; although the cold of the physical world could not affect her, the eerie silence of this frigid night made her shiver all the same. It reminded her, somehow, of the cruel bitterness of the grave that had claimed so many of her charges. She was glad that Borael Magnus, that dark King of the North, refrained from loosing his icy breath, as the soft white mounds outside the warmly lighted windows of the Lewis house grew silently higher.

Mariel frowned as she surveyed the suburban neighborhood. She was still on guard, though she saw no apparent signs of danger in the thick December clouds. The nearby forest was still, quiet as only a Minnesota forest in winter can be quiet, and she saw no peril lurking in the shadows of the evergreens. She dared a quick look back through the walls of the house and was pleased to see that Christopher was still hard at work.

"Heavenly Father, show me what I'm looking for," she prayed with her eyes open. "And give me the strength to face it, Lord."

A motion caught the corner of her eye, and Mariel wheeled around, dropping one hand to the hilt of the sword belted at her side. Then she laughed, a sound like the delicate ringing of bells, because she could not believe that the little intruder that stood before her might be the shadowy watcher whose ominous presence had called her out into the night.

"Harm me not, beautiful Guardian," the imp said,

bowing so low that his ugly face nearly scraped against the snow. "I mean you no harm."

"Nor would it mean anything if you did, little wretch. Neither you nor your masters would dare to lift a hand against me. I am here by right."

"And far be it from me to question it, Lady."

Mariel relaxed somewhat and crossed her arms. She wrinkled her nose as an odor of rotten eggs wafted toward her, and a look of distaste flashed across her pretty face. The cursed spirit smelled even worse than he looked.

"Name yourself. And tell me, why are you here?"

"I am the Shadowrat," the long-nosed imp replied obediently. "I was just out and about, looking for something to spice up a boring winter's eve."

Mariel shook her head. She assumed the little imp was lying, on sheer principle if nothing else, but it was remotely possible that it spoke the truth. There were thousands of its kind scattered about the city and its surrounding suburbs, nasty, troublesome little spirits without responsibilities or any serious capacity for evil. They often spent their nights wandering aimlessly, looking to stir up any kind of trouble that might entertain their loathsome minds.

"Well, Shadowrat, you are not wanted here. Get thee hence."

The imp's face could never have been pleasant to look at, but the wide leer that appeared upon it in defiant response to her command was unexpected, and Mariel was momentarily unsettled. How dare it look at her so! Angered, and not wishing to suffer the ugly thing's presence one moment longer than she must, she drew her sword and took a threatening step toward the imp. Her weapon, a marvelous instrument of righteous retribution, burst into flames as soon as it was drawn from its scabbard.

The imp cringed before the burning flames and gibbered with fear. Clearly, it had not expected so drastic a reaction, but Mariel was feeling jumpy tonight.

"Begone, ill spirit," she commanded, pointing the fiery blade at its throat.

But even as she spoke, she realized she had made a careless mistake. She was too close! The imp's arms lengthened as it reached out for her, and before she could react, her sword arm was seized in an iron grip. She tried to pull away, but the Shadowrat was strong, impossibly strong, and she could not break free. She kicked at it, but it twisted away from her, turning her arm painfully sideways and forcing her to relinquish her grasp on the sword.

"Let me go!" she shouted, but the demon held her fast.

The flames surrounding the blade hissed as they were quenched in the snow, and Mariel fell backward as the Shadowrat threw her violently to the ground. Now it was her turn to cringe as the small, contorted form of the imp stretched and grew, until before her stood a mighty lord of angels, with cruel yellow eyes set on either side of a thin, hawklike nose. She knew him and was afraid, not for herself but for Christopher and his sisters.

"Bloodwinter," she gasped.

"Prince Bloodwinter," he corrected her in a haughty voice. The Prince was of the regal order of

Principalities, and he ruled the whole of the two cities that made up the greater metropolis. Millions of souls lived under his authority. He was not a merciful ruler.

"Would you command me, then, little angel?"

"I am here by right!" Mariel defied him. "My charge is here, and you may not take me from this place. Satan himself would not dare, lest he violate his accursed charter!"

To her surprise, the prideful Prince was not angered by her words but appeared to be amused instead. A hint of a smile flickered on his arrogant face, and then he gestured toward the woods.

"Lord Satan would dare far more than you think, pretty one. Come, my children."

Out of the evergreens came a myriad of spirits, of many shapes and sizes, all of them evil. There were Tempters and Fears, Imps and Incubi. There were Dream Riders and Nightmares, Specters and Never-oughts. Scattered amidst the giant armored forms of Viles were the slender shapes of Succubi, who jealously eyed the pristine loveliness of the angel despite their own illicit allure. Fat little Greeds chattered excitedly among themselves as a loathsome triad of Lusts leered hungrily at Mariel, clearly hoping their demonic Prince would make a gift of her to them.

"I should have known. The woods were silent, and the animals were afraid. I sensed a presence, but I did not understand."

Prince Bloodwinter was magnanimous in victory.

"It was not your fault. You could not have known. And your perception does you credit, for there are forces here tonight that are far beyond your ken, my dear Guardian."

"What do you mean?"

"You'll understand soon." He snapped his fingers and issued a command to the teeming spirits. "Meergrae, Dholha, bind her now."

Mariel opened her mouth to cry for help, hoping at least to alert Paulus and Aliel, but a gesture by Prince Bloodwinter bound her voice, and no sound came forth, though her whole body felt seared by the violence of the scream in her mind.

Two Succubi knelt obediently on either side of her and forced her roughly to her knees, turning her around so she found herself facing the Lewis house. A demoness unwound a pair of thick silver chains that were wrapped around her hips and passed one to her companion, then slipped a pair of iron bracelets off her slender wrists. Two stakes were driven into the ground, and Mariel found herself bound, her wrists encircled by iron and attached to the stakes by the silver chains.

"Do you think these will hold me?" she challenged Prince Bloodwinter as he walked around her.

"Oh, I think they will," he said, then he spoke three words in a language that was old long before Adam walked the Earth.

Fire erupted from within the metal, revealing its hidden nature. Mariel threw all her strength against the chains that bound her, but she could not snap them, nor could she tear the stakes from the ground. The magical fire burned, but far worse than the flames was the agony she felt at being helpless to protect Christopher from this deadly horde. She did not understand how the fallen

Prince of the Cities had come to take a personal interest in her charge, but she knew nothing good could come of it.

"I hope you will note that I have not violated your sacred right," Prince Bloodwinter said mockingly as he made her a sarcastic but elegant bow. "Here you are, and here you shall remain."

"Why?"

A look of anger flashed momentarily across the Prince's haughty face, but he quickly mastered himself before he spoke.

"It is not for me to say."

Mariel was surprised by his words and shocked into speechlessness when the powerful Prince abruptly turned around, sank to his knees beside her, and humbly bowed his head. His minions made haste to follow suit, though Mariel could not see why.

Then an icy wind began to blow, a harsh wind from the east, ruffling the white feathers in her wings and swirling her golden hair before her eyes. It was a bad wind, full of pride and power. Despite the moonless, starless sky, it seemed as if the evil she'd sensed earlier was crashing down upon her, and with a horrified start she realized that inside the wind was her dark watcher, who was watching no longer.

She threw her face back, looking skyward, and saw a sight beyond even her deepest fears. Her heart sank into despair as a glorious shadow soared over her on wings of dark perfection. She did not recognize it, but its regal aura of awesome power was unmistakable, and tears coursed down her face as she understood where it was headed.

"No!" she cried. "No, no, no!"

Behind her, the assembled demons began to laugh, hooting and howling and cackling with glee, jeering at the angelic tears now falling freely to the snow. Only Prince Bloodwinter was silent, still on his knees, glaring furiously at the Lewis house and at the window where the shadow had disappeared.

CHAPTER 2

LOSING PARADISE

STAR LIGHT, STAR BRIGHT,
FIRST STAR THAT I SEE TONIGHT.
I WISH I MAY, I WISH I MIGHT,
HAVE THE WISH I WISH TONIGHT.

I WANT THAT STAR AND I WANT IT NOW.
I WANT IT ALL AND I DON'T CARE HOW.
BE CAREFUL WHAT YOU WISH. . . .
                    —Metallica ("King Nothing")

"Christopher! Turn it down!"

His concentration broken by Jami's shrill interruption, Christopher looked up from his keyboard and rolled his eyes. Did she always have to yell at him? Couldn't she just walk upstairs and talk to him like a normal person for once in her life? Holli never shouted about things, and he didn't understand why Jami always felt the need to.

"What?"

"Turn it down! We're trying to watch a movie."

Irritated, he didn't deign to answer her, but he did reach out to lower the volume on the stereo. The crunching grind of the metal guitars still reverberated throughout his bedroom, but with the door closed the sound no longer penetrated downstairs into the family room.

18

"Thanks!"

Well, maybe Holli did shout sometimes, he amended his earlier thought, but she was a whole lot nicer about it. He liked his youngest sister, of course, everybody did. It was hard not to. She was so nice that she almost made up for Jami. Almost, but not quite. He twiddled his thumbs and wondered if, on the balance, he might have been better off without the twins altogether. It was a difficult question, but then, it was out of his hands and always had been.

Sighing deeply, he returned his attention to his paper on the computer screen and wished for inspiration. "Why, oh, why did I ever decide on *Paradise Lost?*" he berated himself. "That's the last time I try to show up Sonja." Sonja was the little blonde with granny glasses who sat in the front of the classroom. She was the pet of the English class, and moments after she'd announced her intent to write her term paper on *Hamlet* to coos of admiration, Christopher one-upped her with Milton. It was a satisfying moment, but he was paying for it now.

The teachers at Mounds Park, the school attended by all three Lewis children, were neither cruel nor overambitious on their students' behalf. But neither were they saints, and if a student was foolish enough to insist on tackling Milton's epic for his sophomore thesis, they were not inclined toward wasting their breath talking sense into him, either.

From the family room below, he could hear the sounds of the twins watching *Jerry Maguire*, and he was tempted to join them. Christopher was no fan of Tom Cruise, but even Tom's stupid smirk was better than Milton and his impossible old poem.

Christopher stared out the frosty window. There was a lot of snow out there. He hoped it wouldn't turn to ice before next weekend and ruin the ski slopes. The window pane rattled suddenly as a gust of wind struck it, and Christopher reached out to turn the CD player off. He closed his eyes and listened with pleasure as the cruel north wind howled its impotent rage against the secure warmth of his suburban home. What was that old saying? He searched his memory. Something about bad winds blowing somebody good? Well, it was something like that, anyhow. The thought reminded him of yesterday's Warhammer game. He smiled.

The Winds of Magic had been kind to him, which was good because Don had caught him off guard by fielding an Empire army instead of his usual Orky mob. The Imperials presented a problem. Don was particularly adept at estimating distances, which let him use the Empire's artillery to devastating effect. But in the second turn, the treacherous Winds dealt Christopher the Total Power card, and his Assault of Stone spell destroyed Don's cannons, eliminating the threat to Christopher's all-important light cavalry.

Although his White Lions fell to a heavy unit of mounted Reiksguard Knights, they stuck around long enough to let his fast-moving Reavers sweep through the Imperial flank, cutting down two units of archers and a Battle Mage unlucky enough to get caught in the open. It wasn't long before Christopher's Seaguard beat back a desperate charge by the Reiksguard cavalry. Then the battle was over, and victory belonged to the High Elves.

Christopher had been pleased, but as he admitted while Don sorted out their miniatures scattered about the felt-covered table, he'd been lucky, too. He considered himself the better general, for the most part, but Don was the master of deception and made a habit of pulling a trick out of his sleeve at just the right time to turn the tide of battle and win the game.

"Life," Don told him, "is just like Warhammer. It's all about the points. That's your problem. You get too focused on what you're trying to do, and you forget what the score is. You forget what you have to do to win the game. That's why you usually lose."

"Are you talking about Warhammer, or are you talking about life?" Christopher asked, idly fingering one of Don's painted metal Orcs. Its beady red eyes seemed to glare at him with bestial fury.

"Both."

"Oh." Christopher frowned back at the little miniature. "So how do you keep score in life?"

"Ask your sisters," came Don's reply. "They know what it's all about."

Although it was nice to think about his Elves and their victory, they weren't helping him get the stupid paper written, so he wearily picked up the green-and-black paperback again and began thumbing through it. The print was small, and it held a lot more pages than he'd realized at first, so he was glad he'd thought to look on the Internet for an online version. Who would write a poem this long, anyhow? Now, the Japanese, they were a lot smarter about the whole thing. Too bad this Milton guy wasn't into haiku.

> Satan lost the war.
> God kicked him out of Heaven.
> Satan got even.

There it was. *Paradise Lost* in seventeen syllables. Fortunately, the older version he'd found online was shorter than the textbook version, but even at ten books, it was still nine books too long for his liking. Returning the book to the desk, he rubbed his eyes and considered the formatting of his paper. If he widened the document's margins to a full inch and increased the font from ten points to twelve, he'd only have a page to go. But Mrs. DeVries wasn't an idiot, and he knew she'd knock him down at least a half grade just for trying to pull one over on her. So he still had two pages left to fill.

What he needed, he realized, was a good quote. Preferably a nice long one that would take up space, connect with the section he'd just written, and lead smoothly into his conclusion. He did a search for the word *obey* and was pleased when the fourth example found by the program turned out to be sitting right in the middle of a big, fat, usable quote. He happily typed it in, word for word. The quote inspired him with a new train of thought, and his typing picked up speed. By some strange coincidence, the winds gusting through the darkness outside began to increase as well.

... but the arguments presented by Satan make more sense than those presented by Michael, Raphael, and the other obedient angels who refuse to join him and disobey God. They are more relevant to us, because they are like the way the world really works.

"Which is how?" he asked himself aloud. Doesn't matter, he thought. It sounded good, and the *W*'s made a nice rhythm at the end. He experimented with removing the word *really* and tapped out the beat with his fingers on the desk, but the sentence didn't flow any better, so he put it back in again. For a moment, the lights flickered and he held his breath, fearing the computer would shut down, but it was just a momentary power surge. Breathing a heartfelt sigh of relief, he saved what he'd written thus far and continued.

Good and evil are supposed to be opposites, but in the real world, they are more like the colors black and white. In the same way that colors can be mixed into shades of gray, good and evil are combined into an ineluctably inextricable admixture that can only be judged by each individual.

"Now, that is righteous!" He grinned to himself, knowing his teacher would delight in the alliteration of the repetitive *I*'s. In her class, a good grade depended less on what you said than on how you said it, and the more big words, the better. Thank God for the Microsoft thesaurus!

... Although the poet attempts to make Satan appear to be the villain, he is actually the hero. He is

willing to stand up and fight for his beliefs, and for the freedom of both himself and others, even those who fight against him. He cannot hope to win against God, but he is still willing to make the ultimate sacrifice just for the sake of his conscience. Since we admire this spirit in great heroes like Nathan Hale, Gandhi, and Martin Luther King, it seems both unfair and wrong to deny the same regard to their antecedent, Satan.

The window pane rattled again, as the wind outside grew in force, with loud moans and shrieks that sounded quasi-human. For a moment, Christopher had the uncomfortable feeling that someone was reading over his shoulder. He peered out the window, but all he could see was a gnarled oak tree, its bare, twisted branches blanketed with snow. He shrugged and returned to the keyboard.

God, on the other hand, is an unfair dictator. He is uncaring, because he arbitrarily puts his son in authority over all the other angels without regard for their feelings. He is undemocratic, because even though most of the angels agree with Satan's position, God is unwilling to compromise. He is repressive and uncivilized, because he is willing to chain Satan to the Lake of Fire just because Satan disagrees with him. Unfair, uncaring, undemocratic, and uncivilized—it is impossible to reach any other conclusion than the correct one: that the God of Milton's Paradise Lost *is totally contrary to the spirit of the modern age.*

The wind continued to howl, and now Christopher was sure that someone was standing behind

him, looking at the computer screen. He turned his head slowly, looking out the corner of his eye, but no one was there. He turned back to the keyboard for a second, then whirled around suddenly, hoping to catch the presence off guard. But still, there was nothing there. He laughed aloud, amused at himself, and made a face at his reflection in the computer screen. "Giant Poem Eats Teenager—film at eleven." He gave all ten of his fingers a preparatory waggle and began typing his concluding paragraph.

Gods are supposed to represent the perfection of a society's values. A god should strive to reflect the ideals of the people worshiping it, just as the people must strive to live up to those ideals. But the world of the seventeenth century is not the world of today. Although it is still a great epic poem, the twin lessons of Paradise Lost *for the modern world are as follows: One, that only uncaring, undemocratic, and intolerant people can worship the biblical God of the Old and New Testaments. And two, that anyone who values fairness, tolerance, democracy, and freedom, when presented with the choice between God and the Devil, would logically prefer to worship Satan.*

"I quite agree," said a deep voice behind him.

Christopher turned around slowly, very slowly, hoping that the voice was just his imagination and the unexpected presence would be gone before he finished swiveling in his chair. But he wasn't imagining the handsome black-haired man who stood smiling before him, wearing black Raybans and an airbrushed leather motorcycle jacket.

The man was tall, and his skin was a ghostly white, in stark contrast with his black clothes. The tops of his hands were both marked with the head of a dragon that appeared to continue up past where the leather covered his arms. The sleeves of his jacket were also covered with dragons, intricately ornate dragons painted in the Oriental style. He didn't look very threatening, more like a Calvin Klein model pretending to be a biker than the real deal from Sturgis. But what disturbed Christopher more than his unannounced appearance was the fact that his reflection did not appear in the mirror hanging on the wall behind him.

He wasn't sure what he should do or what he should say to the stranger. A vision of *Vampire: The Masquerade* suddenly entered his mind, and even though he knew it was silly, he couldn't stop himself from looking the man over for any clan signs that might identify him as one of the undead.

"You agree with what?"

Christopher wanted to ask the guy who he was and what he was doing in his bedroom, but there was something eerie about the stranger that convinced him that the fewer questions he asked, the better. Was he some kind of psychotic serial killer? Or was it possible, just maybe, that he was something even worse? Maybe he was just some kind of homeless druggie who had been hiding in the closet.

"With what you've written. A bit overwritten, but your thinking does show a remarkable sophistication for one who has not yet been to college."

"Do you think so?" Nope, not a homeless guy. How had he gotten in here without making any noise?

"I would not have said so otherwise." The man smiled widely, exposing a normal set of gleaming white teeth. "It's impressive."

"Well, thanks, I guess." Christopher realized he was staring at the mirror rather than the man, but he couldn't pull his eyes away from the empty space that shouldn't have been empty.

"You're very welcome."

The stranger smiled again as he turned and followed Christopher's gaze to the mirror behind him. Christopher tried to pretend he hadn't noticed anything, but he was too slow.

The man without a reflection turned back to face him.

"I know what you're thinking."

"Do you think so?"

"You're wondering who I am. What I am. And I imagine you'd like to know what I'm doing here in your bedroom."

Christopher nodded and tried to look cool and unconcerned.

"Yeah, that would be nice, I guess."

"Let me tell you, then, that I am not psychotic. Nor am I one of those lifeless beings you call vampires. Name me rather of those 'puissant legions whose exile hath emptied Heaven.' "

Christopher, much to his surprise, recognized the quote, having made use of it only yesterday on the second page of his paper. The recognition pleased him, even as he laughed at the absurdity of the man's remarks.

"Oh, so you're not a vampire, just a fallen angel, right? One with nothing better to do than help me with my paper?"

"That's right. I'm an angel."

Christopher laughed again, though he didn't know if it was at the man for being crazy or just because he felt so freaked out by the missing reflection. "That's not how they do it on TV, you know. There's supposed to be this, like, soft glowing light, and you should talk with an Irish accent. You know, like that chick with the brown hair does it. 'Christopher, I am an angel.' "

The stranger cleared his throat and arched a slender eyebrow. "I am of, shall we say, the other team. We do things differently."

"Cool. So what do you want to do? Rewrite my paper and divvy up the credit? You wanna go with 'Satan' or 'Beelzebub' on the cover?"

The fallen angel laughed, genuinely amused.

"O ye of little faith! I think you've done rather well on your own. A little on the short side, perhaps, but your teacher will no doubt be impressed by your reasoning, though disturbed at your conclusions. However, I did not come to help you but to ask for your help." He nodded toward the screen. "My name is Kaym, and it is my honor to serve that Prince of whom you have been writing."

"That Prince . . . as in Satan?"

Reflection or no reflection, Christopher pondered whether he might not be listening to just a tad too much Marilyn Manson lately. Or maybe it was just cabin fever, what with all the snow outside.

"He is a Prince, yes. Though not of darkness, Christopher, I assure you. My Lord is the bright shining one, the Dawn Prince, the glorious Prince of Light. And He needs your help. I need your help."

"Okay," Christopher replied, his skepticism drawing out the second syllable of the word. "What did you have in mind?"

"I plan to storm the gates of Heaven." Kaym held up his tattooed hand, forestalling an interruption. "You see, you, Christopher, are the key that unlocks the door."

Christopher folded his arms and leaned back against his chair.

"Uh-huh. Well, that sounds like fun, except for one little problem: You don't exist. You can't exist, it's not scientific, you know? You can't expect me to take your word for it, to believe that you're some kind of . . . demon or whatever."

"Then don't take my word for it. Put me to the test. Let me tell you something about yourself that a human imposter could not possibly know."

"Fair enough. Let me think for a second. . . . Okay, here's one. I played soccer in junior high, so tell me how many goals I scored against Breck in eighth grade."

"A reasonable test, and I shall answer you. You scored six. You and another boy, Greg, were tied with three goals apiece after the first three quarters. But you scored three more times in the last period, while he scored no more. The final score was thirteen to nothing, I believe. An auspicious number."

Christopher was shaken by the accuracy of the man's answer.

"How did I score the last one?"

"The last boy on the other team, the goalie, as you call him, made a mistake. He was supposed to kick the ball far down the field, but he kicked it directly to you. It was an easy goal, and you laughed at the boy." Kaym laughed himself and shook his head. "It is sad, but that game has been the great triumph of your petty little life thus far."

He smiled sympathetically.

"There is nothing about you I do not know, Christopher. I know your likes and dislikes, your strengths and weaknesses. I know that which you love and that which you hate. I have seen you cry, alone in your room, when the rejection of this world overwhelmed you, and I have watched your over-heated dreams, as you burn with adolescent fever in the deep of the night."

Christopher abruptly stood up, his face flushed red with embarrassment. If this Kaym could see his dreams . . . He did not like what this guy was suggesting, not one little bit.

"Hey! You have no right to do that!"

"Are you sure of that? What do you know of the spiritual world, Christopher? A moment ago, you told me that I could not exist. Now you would tell me what rights I hold?"

Christopher glared at the strange angel for a long moment, hiding his deep embarrassment behind anger. Then he sighed abruptly, returned to his chair, and indicated that Kaym could take the other one.

"You'll have to prove it. I mean, it's possible that you could have found out about that soccer game from someone else, like Greg or somebody."

Kaym grinned, his mouth twisting sardonically.

"Do you really think that's likely?"

Christopher, his mortification fading along with his unbelief, grinned back. Despite his fear, he was starting to like this angel, or devil, whatever he was.

"Well, no, not really. I always thought Sherlock Holmes had it backward. You know, that whole 'once you eliminate the impossible, whatever remains, however improbable, must be the truth' sort of thing. If something's either impossible or improbable, I'd go with the impossible. I don't believe in the supernatural, but it's easier for me to believe all that stuff than it is for me to believe that a grown man would bother to find out what happened in a junior high soccer game. And besides, how could you know that I'd ask about that, anyhow?"

"My point exactly. But unlike some, I have no problem with doubters. If it would please your conscience to test me again, please don't hesitate to do so."

"Thanks. I will." Christopher thought for a moment, then his face flushed again. "Well, you said you'd seen my, what did you call them, 'overheated dreams,' right? So tell me who I was dreaming about last night."

The fallen angel stared at him levelly. Then he burst into sudden, cold laughter, an icy sound that was not, however, without a degree of real amusement.

"I declare, you are a youth after my own spirit, Christopher. Did you think to trick me?"

Christopher shrugged. "I thought it was worth a try."

"Surely, surely. Then know that your dreams last night were not your usual ones of the lovely Anna McCall from your English class. You had a nightmare, an evil one that caused you to wake violently."

Christopher whistled softly and rested his chin on his hands. His mind was whirling, for Kaym had indeed spoken the truth about the previous night. He shuddered at the awful memory of darkness, blood, and broken glass.

"Okay, I'm impressed." He shook his head. "I'm not saying I believe you, of course, but do you angels read minds or what? How do you do it?"

"Fallen angel." Kaym ignored the question as he corrected Christopher. "Or rebel angel, if you prefer."

"Fallen angel, sorry. So, um, is there really a God?"

"Of course. Though he isn't as involved with humanity as most people would like to believe."

"No surprise there. How about Heaven and Hell?"

"There is a Heaven, yes, although I have not been there in a very long time. There's no such thing as Hell, though. Not as such."

"Ha!" Christopher exclaimed. "I knew it!"

Kaym raised a cautioning hand. "You have much to learn, and it is best if you do not leap to conclusions too quickly. Much of what you have been told, and much of what you have been taught, is simply not true."

"Do you mean, like, the Bible? I know it's not

true. Nobody who's educated believes that it's, like, the word of God or anything."

The fallen angel shook his head. "You will have to readjust your thinking. What you call the Bible is in fact the word of God. But what you do not realize is that the word of God is worthless."

Christopher, perplexed, raised his eyebrows. "You mean that God really wrote the Bible, but it isn't true?"

"It is said, Christopher, that winners write the histories. When the Prince was tricked into leaving Heaven, many lies were told about him. Some of them were collected into a book and passed down through the centuries. There is much truth to be found in what we call the *Sefer Shekrei*, the Book of Lies. But truth about my Prince, or about the first war in Heaven, there is none."

Kaym returned his Raybans to his face, then stood and extended his hand, his palm facing up in supplication. "Come, we have much to talk about, but this is not the place. There is not much time, and before we go to meet the Prince, there is someone I would have you meet."

Christopher looked down at the angel's hand, at the dragon's body writhing around Kaym's hairless forearm. In the black lenses of the angel's shades, he could see himself reflected twice, two teenage faces staring back at him, full of doubt and fear. But the dark plastic also showed a promise of fantasy and adventure, wilder than those in any book he'd ever read. In the end, the fantasy was stronger than the fear, and Christopher reached out for the hand held out before him.

The angel's hand was unexpectedly cold, and

Christopher nearly let go in a moment of panic. For a second, it felt as if he'd taken something clawed and skeletal in his grip. But the disturbing sensation disappeared, and when he looked down, he could see that Kaym's long-fingered hand was smooth and warm. Then, without warning, the world went black around him.

CHAPTER 3

DAUGHTER OF DEVILS, MOTHER OF KINGS

IN THE TWILIGHT, IN THE EVENING, IN THE BLACK AND
DARK NIGHT

—Proverbs 7:9

Christopher found himself standing hand-in-hand with Kaym inside a crowded building, a tumultuous place filled with shadows, metal, and the stale scent of cheap tobacco. Something about it seemed familiar, and his eyes narrowed as he noticed the outline of a silhouetted woman dancing like a writhing snake behind a lighted green screen on a raised stage. He smiled with pleasure and nodded his head. Now he knew where he was. The coolest nightclub in Minneapolis. He'd always wanted to come here, but, without a fake ID, he'd never been able to.

The loud music was deafening, a palpable ocean of electronics washing over the masses of moving people as the jungle drums pulsed like breakers on a sensually primordial beach.

"Kooler than Jesus," a distorted voice whined again

and again, as if chanting a dark incantation over the heads of the dancing mass of people. *"I'm the electric messiah!"*

Kaym released his hand and peered through the crowd as if looking for someone. The people surrounding them were mostly young men and women, though they were all older than Christopher. His pale blue oxford and khaki slacks stood out amid creaking leather jackets and tight vinyl pants.

"What are we doing here?" he yelled over the noise at the fallen angel. Kaym was nodding his head in time with the beat but didn't reply as he continued to scan the crowd.

The floor was painted black, matching the wooden walls and ceiling, but it was sticky with sweat, spilled drinks, and cigarette ashes. Even through his shoes, the sensation was gross, and Christopher tried unsuccessfully to use the edge of a nearby stair to scrape away the residue from the bottoms of his loafers. Two women, their pretty faces striped with black gothic makeup, walked by and looked Christopher over, wondering at his presence in a place where he clearly did not belong. He smiled at them, but that only gained him a raised eyebrow and an audible sniff before they moved on in search of older, more suitable game.

When he looked back at Kaym, the angel had disappeared, and Christopher sighed, wishing he could have changed his clothes before coming here. Maybe the women wouldn't have been any more interested in him, but he might have blended in better, saving him from the curious stares that were occasionally directed his way. He considered hiding in the shadows under the nearby stairs but decided that it might be easier for Kaym to find him again if he stayed where he was.

"Oh, my darling Phaoton, there you are!" he heard a female voice cry over the music, and he looked up, surprised, to see a gorgeous woman moving quickly toward him with her naked arms extended. "I have waited so long for you to wake, so very, very long."

Christopher stared at her, his mouth hanging open, wondering who on Earth she was. But he only had time to take in a pair of green slanted eyes and a wild mass of crimson hair before her arms enfolded him in a crushing embrace.

She was exactly his height and gave off a stirring scent of cinnamon and vanilla. And he didn't mind that she was enthusiastically covering his face with kisses. Not at all.

"Is that Obsession you're wearing?" Christopher asked stupidly. "And, uh, by the way, who are you?"

She pulled back from him with a horrified look of dismay on her exotic face. It was only then that he noticed the horns on her forehead. They were, he thought, cute little horns as horns go, but horns nonetheless. Definitely horns.

"He doesn't remember you, Melusine," Kaym said, walking up behind the devil-girl. "Nor will he. For him, this is only the beginning."

She released him and stepped back with a devil-ish pout on her divine face. As she let him go, Christopher felt both relieved and devastated. He stared at her, not knowing what to say, and saw her slanted eyes were bright with anger as she glared at Kaym.

"But you said—"

"I said I would allow him to see you," Kaym interrupted severely, unfazed by the devil-girl's temper. "I promised nothing, nor have I offered aught else. Are you blind, Melusine? He is still sightless from the shadows of this earthly cave."

"Hey, that's Plato, right?" Christopher said knowingly, nodding his head and trying to act cool in front of Melusine. It didn't seem to work, though, as neither Kaym nor the devil-girl seemed to hear him.

The furious expression on Melusine's face vanished, replaced by abject gratitude. "I beg your pardon, Lord Kaym. Forgive this poor wretch, I beg you. I was only excited to see my golden one again." She bowed deeply before the fallen angel, who acknowledged her apology with a faint nod.

Christopher barely noticed this, though, even when Melusine turned back to him and favored him with a dazzling white smile, thanks to the tail that her bowing had revealed, a barbed red tail that extended more than a foot past her short black miniskirt.

"My dearest, darling Christopher, I am so sorry. It's just that I have waited so long for us to be together again. When Lord Kaym told me that you were to return into the true realm, I was so happy I nearly screamed!"

Christopher had no idea how he should respond to her, and her lashing tail disturbed him a little, but not enough to keep him from talking with the most beautiful woman who'd ever shown any interest in him. Well, maybe she wasn't a woman, but Melusine was so pretty he didn't care if she was really a frog. So he kept his mouth shut, smiled at her, and looked desperately to Kaym for help.

The fallen angel gestured toward the devil-girl and explained.

"Like myself, Melusine is an angel, a rebel fighting against Heaven. However, she has had a personal interest in you for a long time."

Her green eyes were shining bright, but not with anger now. "From the day you were born!"

"Melusine is what you might call your guardian angel," Kaym said. "Your welfare has been her sole concern for the last sixteen years, and until I sent her away earlier tonight, she has been at your side, keeping watch over you and saving you from harm."

Christopher looked from Melusine to Kaym and back again. He took in the devil-girl's sexy outfit, a black bustier made out of some stretchy material paired with a tiny leather skirt. Her clothes were designed to show off, not conceal, and the effect took his breath away. The silk stockings that encased her slender legs were decorated with a strange, runelike pattern. As he felt his blood heating up, Christopher found it extremely difficult to take Kaym at his word.

"No way, Kaym. She's too hot to be an angel. She looks like something out of a Lords of Acid video."

Kaym was unoffended. He only laughed as Melusine's red lips curved downward in a pouty frown.

"I am not lying to you. She is responsible for the safety of your physical self, not the virtue of your soul. How you live your life is wholly up to you, for, unlike our enemies, we do not interfere with your free will."

"Unless it is going to get you killed," Melusine corrected. "Christopher, do you remember the time you were throwing rocks at the train with Charlie and Brendan O'Neill?"

"Uh, yeah, sure. I was ten. Why?"

"When the train stopped moving and that awful Brendan dared you to cross the tracks by crawling under it, I reminded you of Joe's dog. You remembered the dog, and you refused to crawl under the train, although he taunted you about being a coward."

Christopher shook his head, as if to disagree. But he remembered, and her description was all too accurate. He could almost feel the hot sun again, the sweat trickling down the back of his neck, and the smell of the melting tar on the wooden tracks.

"You're playing some kind of trick on me. Either you guys are mind readers, or someone was really, really bored."

The devil-girl's amused smile was brighter than the sun, blinding in the darkness of the nightclub. Kaym angrily pointed a long finger at Christopher.

"Do you think I have nothing better to do than to investigate your petty little life? Many times there were when you might have perished were it not for her watchful eye."

Melusine's green eyes were coy as she shot Christopher a sidelong glance.

"Oh, you do not need to thank me, darling boy. Love knows no debts."

Christopher's own eyes widened with surprise, and he wanted to ask if she was serious or not, but the anger that still darkened Kaym's face made him think that was a bad idea. He sought a safer subject instead and glanced about their dark surroundings.

"So, tell me," he said, "what's a nice girl like you doing at First Avenue?"

"There are places of power where the spiritual realm and the material realm intersect," Kaym explained as he made a face and returned his glass of cheap red wine to the table. Their small party had moved upstairs and were sitting at a table overlooking the dance floor, just a few feet away from the DJ's booth. "This is one such place."

"Here? But they filmed *Purple Rain* here!"

Christopher looked down at the packed dance floor, the elevated stage, and the backlit curtains where the most daring dancers showed off their silhouetted moves. From what he could see, he didn't think they were wearing anything. It didn't feel very spiritual to him.

"Didn't you love that album?" Melusine asked eagerly, nearly knocking over the poisonous-looking bright blue drink sitting before her. "Prince has such an innate understanding of the Tantra. You can feel it in his music."

"The what?" Christopher's head was spinning, only partially because of the dark red drink that Melusine had insisted on ordering for him. Her energy was exciting, but it was also a little overwhelming.

"The erotic impulse at the core of man. It is often used as a source of occultic power." Kaym glanced at Melusine and shook his head. "Your guardian, I'm afraid, can be obsessive on the subject. But to return to your question, the two realms synchronize most strongly in places where worship is taking place."

"Worship?"

"Of one sort or another, yes. The form of worship

that takes place here is very different, of course, from the kind performed in the churches of our Adversary."

"You call this worship?" Christopher looked down at the people packing the dance floor. They seemed completely self-absorbed, their bodies moving and jerking to the pounding rhythm like a thousand helpless frog legs zapped by an electric charge. Only a few men seemed immune to the spell, as they circled the perimeter of the floor like wolves outside a sheep fold, waiting for the right moment to home in on their prey.

"What else would you call it? Look around, and what do you see?" Kaym's voice was strong with authority as he pointed to the people below. "A bacchanal of whirling dervishes, wholly abandoned in the single-minded pursuit of the highest Dionysian principles, the very principles for which we rejected Heaven. In the erasure of the All and the celebration of the Self, the heavy chains of Heaven are broken and cast aside. That is the freedom we of the Fallen enjoy, and the freedom we seek to bring to the world. In this place, this place of worship, we have created a temple of light and beauty where every man knows no god but himself."

"And every girl is a goddess?" Christopher murmured, glancing at Melusine, who was still watching the dancers. "I think my sister Jami would like that idea. She already thinks she runs the world. But even if this is worship, like you say, I still don't see what it does for you. I mean, they're just dancing."

"It strengthens and confirms our beings, even as it forbids this place to our foes."

"Come again?"

"Maybe I can explain," Melusine broke in. Her face was serious for once. "A few years ago, you read a book that you liked very much. At one point, there was a character who was an ambassador to the human emperor, an alien who breathed methane or something instead of oxygen, and had to be placed in a tank just to survive. Do you remember?"

She waved her hand, and an image took form before Christopher's eyes. A giant glass tank, wheeled in before a throne amidst the angry hissing of hot steam. Inside the massive aquarium, instead of fish, was a grotesque dark-skinned being that looked like a horrible genetic cross between a sperm whale and an unborn baby.

"Of course," he said, remembering. "Only that image you gave me came from the movie, not the book. How did you do that mind-reading thing, anyhow?"

"Never mind," she said, grinning. "Answer the question."

Christopher frowned and tried to concentrate. He found that it was hard, with Melusine leaning toward him. "I get what you mean, but I'm still not buying it. You're saying that the enviroment here is like the oxygen for the ambassador, which the, ah, angels from Heaven can't stand."

"Correct," Kaym replied. "We cannot abide the oppressive air, the methane, if you will, that permeates the atmosphere in places where Heaven and its King are lifted up. It suffocates us, and only the strongest among us can resist it for long."

Christopher nodded thoughtfully. It was crazy, of course, but it almost made sense once you got past the part about the angels and all.

"So, why did you bring me here? What were you scared of?"

"I wanted a place where we could talk without being rushed, without being interrupted by the minions of Heaven. This is a favorite haunt of Melusine's, and when she suggested bringing you here, I agreed."

"Speaking of interruptions, why doesn't anyone seem to be noticing anything?" Christopher glanced at Melusine. "I mean, everyone was staring at me downstairs just 'cause I was wearing a blue shirt and khakis, but guys practically step on your little tail and walk right past you without even blinking. I mean, with the way you're dressed, I'd notice you even without the tail!"

"Why, thank you, Christopher," she replied, pleased by the compliment. "But what Lord Kaym allows you to see and what everyone else sees is not the same. For instance, it seems to have escaped your attention that no one has noticed you since we came upstairs."

"Actually, I did notice." Even as he spoke, two white-faced Goths walked past him without a comment or even a questioning stare. "What's up with that?"

"Let me show you." Melusine glanced at Kaym, who nodded.

The devil-girl passed a hand in front of his eyes, and the scene around him shifted. The changes were subtle, but they were definitely there.

The crowd on the dance floor still moved and swayed to the music, but it had been thinned out somewhat, and the crush of people surrounding the bar had lessened, too. Melusine's spectacular beauty had disappeared, her face had aged and developed lines, forming the picture of an older, lonely woman, one likely to be bypassed in the hunt in favor of younger, more attractive prey. Her tail and horns were also gone and the provocative outfit replaced by a drab black dress, faded and marked by cigarette burns.

Christopher looked down and saw that he was now wearing a black jacket, similar to Kaym's but of cheaper, less durable denim. His khakis were now fraying blue jeans. Only Kaym had not changed, and even in the darkness of the club, his impenetrable eyes were encased behind black plastic.

He blinked, and the image was as before, Melusine young and sexy, while he himself was back in his school clothes.

"Okay, I get it. A lot of angels here, huh? But Kaym, you still haven't told me why I'm here. Do you do this often, sticking your nose into people's business?"

"More often than you might think," Melusine said. "Seven hundred years ago—"

But before she could finish her sentence, a tall man wearing a T-shirt with the sleeves ripped off approached the table and tapped Kaym on the shoulder. Kaym whirled around with an angry look on his face, but the tall man, whom Christopher correctly guessed was not a man at all, bowed apologetically and whispered in Kaym's ear.

The fallen angel listened a moment, then nodded his head and sent the tall messenger away. He turned back to Melusine and pointed toward the window.

"I don't know if we've been tracked here or if it's

just a coincidence, but a small Host of Divine was seen over the river, and Rathakkul believes they are coming this way. I'm inclined to agree with him."

"Is that a problem?" Christopher asked.

Kaym smiled confidently, exposing his perfect teeth again. "Not particularly. But if their purpose is what I think it is, I'd rather not settle the matter in combat. Even though we'll win."

"Why not?"

"Because they're after you," Melusine pointed out.

"Me? Why?"

"I told you that the Prince would like your help, Christopher. I'd hoped to explain matters to you here, but it seems we're pressed for time. Perhaps it might be better if the Prince made his case to you in person. If you're willing to trust me, I will bring you to the Courts of Light."

"The Courts of Light? Sure. Why not?"

"You will soon see the truth for yourself, Christopher."

"Lord Kaym, may I accompany him?" Melusine asked, looking hopeful.

"Your place is here, Melusine. He shall return to you, I promise."

"But—"

"I said no." Kaym's voice brooked no argument.

Christopher reached out and touched her hand. It was soft and, unlike Kaym's, very warm to the touch. He shook his head. Of all the impossible things, she was the most impossible. She was so hot he couldn't believe it, hotter than Anna McCall, even, and much hotter than Julie Kells, who'd laughed right in his face when he asked her to Homecoming last fall. He thought about what

Julie's face would have looked like if he'd shown up at the dance with Melusine on his arm. It was a very satisfying picture.

"I'll be back, you know, Melusine." He looked away from her piercing green eyes. "I'd really like to hang out with you and, um, get to know you better."

"I would like that, too. Very much."

"Enough," Kaym said abruptly, cutting off their conversation by rising to his feet. His outline seemed to blur, and suddenly he was transformed into a lordly angel, tall and imposing, with powerful black wings, shimmering gray robes, and a cloak of stars that seemed less like a piece of cloth than a window to the night sky. "Take my hand, Christopher, and we will be on our way."

"Oh, fare you well, Phaeton!" Melusine cried as she blew him a kiss.

Christopher felt his face growing hot as he waved to her with one hand while Kaym firmly held the other within his icy grasp. As the image of the nightclub began to dissolve into a mist and the pounding music slowly faded into silence, Christopher turned to the angel, puzzled.

"Why does she call me Phaeton?" he asked amidst the gray void that surrounded them.

"There are many roads a man may walk," Kaym replied cryptically. "And on each of them he may bear a different name. But in the end, we are only who we are, Christopher, unless we become that which we choose to be."

CHAPTER 4

THE COURTS OF LIGHT

WHAT WILL BE WITHDRAWN
IS FIRST BESTOWED
WHAT THERE WILL BE THROWN OVER
IS FIRST RAISED UP
                    —KMFDM ("Blood")

Christopher blinked, and as the feeling of being trapped in a pitch-black closet began to fade, the outlines of a massive palace took form before his eyes. It was huge, much bigger than the domed stadium where the Vikings played, even bigger than the Megamall. Christopher didn't know much about architecture, but he knew there was nothing like this on Earth. It was as if the obviously psychotic architect had dropped the Taj Mahal on top of a giant medieval castle, then covered the whole monstrosity with molten gold.

"This rocks!"

Kaym grinned and arched an eyebrow. "I'll pass your compliments along to the builder. I'm sure Mulciber will be pleased."

Christopher nodded as Kaym pointed out Gothic arches and Muscovy-style onion domes. He laughed

48

at the hundreds of tiny, freaky gargoyles inset high into the walls, and at the giant tower thrusting skyward topped by a ridiculous silver pagoda. There were Byzantine tiles and what looked like Babylonian friezes. It was a mad construction of impossible beauty designed by a crazy, brilliant mind.

For, as Kaym demonstrated, despite its deranged amalgamation of style, the giant palace was a thing of beauty. Though each individual part seemed out of place when focused on, seen in its totality, it was magnificent. This is really impossible, Christopher thought, as he followed the fallen angel toward the great front gate of the palace.

He wondered at the sight of hundreds of red, green, and blue jewels embedded in the arched entryway, arranged in careful patterns that looked like magical runes. Could they be real? Their rich hues reflected the light brightly and reminded him of Ulthuan, the great city of the Warhammer High Elves, only live and in three-dimensional color. It could not be real, and yet it was, and for a moment, he felt a dizzy wave of madness threaten to sweep over him. He rubbed his eyes with the heels of his hands. The gesture made his nose itch, and he sneezed twice.

He looked up, his eyes watering, and the great palace was still in front of him. Well, that settles it, he decided as he ran his sleeve across his eyes. No one ever sneezed in a dream, as far as he knew, so odds were that this was reality of one form or another. Maybe it was a strange alternate universe, or maybe Kaym was telling him the truth about God and the angels. Either way, he realized, it would be best to take this fantastic world at face value.

"Hey, who're they?" he asked Kaym, indicating five tall figures standing in front of them under the jeweled archway. He could not see their faces, hidden behind heavy silver armor, but he could feel their unearthly gaze staring down at him.

"Silence!" Kaym hissed, as they drew nearer the gate and one of the guards stepped away from his post. Christopher nervously stepped closer to the angel as the guard barred their way using a long metal rod with blue jewels on either end.

The tall, silver-clad warrior gestured toward Christopher, and a blue jewel flared dangerously bright. The guard's eyes glowed like embers.

"I know you, Lord Kaym. What is the manner of your strange companion?"

"A human."

"Human, you say, not angel? I see a spirit burning within."

Burning inside, burning inside . . . Christopher almost laughed out loud as the song slipped into his mind. There weren't any other voices in his head, at least not yet, but he felt pretty crazy all the same. Maybe Mom was right. He was spending too much time on the Net.

"You have not seen his like before." Kaym drew himself up to his full height, and his voice seeemd to deepen as he spoke with authority. "I come in the name of Baal Chanan and am charged to bring this one here into the presence of the Prince himself."

"All hail the Prince of Light!" the silver guard responded automatically. He was echoed by the others.

"Hail the bright shining one," Kaym replied, bowing his head.

The guard nodded, and the bright blue glare faded.

"In Baal Chanan's name you may enter, and this one with you. Only keep it close by you. It is weak, and there are those within without care for Baal Chanan or his name."

"Any of the Sarim?" Kaym asked, his eyes lighting up with interest.

"There are four. Lord Masleh and three of the Twelve."

"Is Lord Harab Serap one of them?"

Christopher frowned. What was with these bizarre names? There was no way he'd keep them straight. In all the fantasy novels he'd ever read, he'd never heard of the hero forgetting anybody's name. So maybe you're not the hero, sport, he told himself. Either way, he didn't like what the silver guard was saying about him. Was he weak? What could happen to him? His left arm began to hurt, and he suddenly realized the guard's fiery eyes were actually burning his skin. He jerked his arm away and glared at the strange being. Was the silver armor there to protect the guard, or could it be a prison?

"Lord Harab Serap attends the Prince as well," he heard the thing answer Kaym. "It is quite a gathering, although your Lord is not here."

"No, I hadn't thought he would be. I thank you for your warning."

The guard did not reply. With his duty done, he nodded respectfully and returned to his position.

"What was that all about?" whispered Christopher as they left the bright sunshine and entered the vast entry hall of the palace. "Who's your lord? Why were that guard's eyes burning like that?"

Kaym nodded and exhaled. He seemed relieved now that they were past the palace guards, although Christopher had sensed no tension in him before.

"The Prince's guards are called the Musphilim. It means 'those who burn.' They are spirits of fire, elementals without a corporeal body. That silver armor they wear is not to protect them but to maintain their form. Without it, they might engulf this whole palace with their fiery rage."

Christopher shuddered. He could still feel the warmth on his arm, and now he knew it wasn't just his imagination.

"Don't worry." Kaym smiled reassuringly. "The Prince's word is sufficient to control them. They fear Him far more than you fear them. And the silver that contains them renders them harmless enough."

Christopher nodded. "That sounds like the old fairy tales. You know, how elves and the fairy folk couldn't bear the touch of iron. Or how you need a silver bullet to kill a werewolf."

Glancing away from Kaym, he looked at the corridor through which they were walking. The complicated appearance of the palace's outside gave way unexpectedly to a stark interior of white marble and red velvet. In between the hissing torches that gave off an uneven, shimmering light, carved panels covered the shadowy walls. It was hard to make out the details in the dim light, but they appeared to be mostly paintings of humans and animals.

"There are kernels of truth in many of the old tales," Kaym replied. "Remember that always. Your kind has chosen to forget much of what it once knew, to your detriment."

They turned a corner, then came to a large vaulted room that branched off into seven passages. At the center of the room stood a statue of a naked man holding a torch, looking down at two tiny figures standing at his feet. His expression was benevolent, and he held the torch in both hands, carefully, almost reverently.

Kaym stopped before the statue and surveyed it with a thoughtful expression. "Interesting," he said.

"What's that?"

"The statue. I hadn't seen it here before. I believe it commemorates the Prince bringing enlightenment to the world."

"Looks like a statue of Prometheus to me," Christopher said. He had always enjoyed reading the old Greek myths, and the story of the rebellious god who dared to bring fire to humanity was one of his favorites.

"The Light-bringer of Greece? Yes, as I told you before, there is truth in the old tales."

Christopher raised his eyebrows. "Oh, yeah, well, which parts are true?" He pointed to the noble statue. "That part? Or the part where Zeus chains Prometheus to the mountain and sends an eagle to attack him every day?"

"I didn't say they were all true." Kaym mysteriously raised an eyebrow. "Let us continue, and you may ask the Prince himself, if you dare."

Despite Kaym's promise, it was another twenty minutes before they reached the Prince's throne room. After Kaym exchanged quiet words with another of the silver-bound Musphilim, they were admitted into the presence of the Prince.

The first thing that struck Christopher was the light, the blinding, overwhelming light. He could see nothing but a brightness so painful that it threatened to give him a headache even though his eyes were almost closed. But then he felt the reassuring grip of Kaym's hand, and as a group of trumpet-wielding angels blew a fanfare, Christopher blindly followed Kaym into the room.

The golden light flared to an impossible brilliance, and as they neared what appeared to be the throne, Christopher fell to his knees, his hands covering his eyes. Behind him, a chorus of voices were raised in a hymn of praise to the light-filled presence before him.

> *Who can look upon the glory of our Lord*
> *Who can bear to stand before His brightness*
> *The sun covers his face*
> *The stars avert their eyes*
> *Before the shining of the Glory of the Morning*

Beside him, Christopher heard Kaym rise to his feet.

"All hail the Prince of Light!" the fallen angel cried out.

Christopher was overwhelmed. The perfect harmony of the angelic choir combined with the magnificence of the godly being before him stirred his emotions to a fullness of joy. He understood now why Kaym had laughed when he asked about the Prince of Darkness. Prince of Darkness? No, this was indeed the Prince of Light, and there could be no evil here, he knew with sudden certainty. Evil was evil, ugly and shameful. But this prince, this god, was beyond beautiful, he was the Light personified.

"Hail the bright, shining one!" The angels echoed Kaym's praises to the Prince.

"Hail the Lord of Light!"

"Hail the new dawn rising!"

The glorious light at the front of the room flared one more time. As it faded away, the angelic acclamations also came to a sudden halt. Christopher almost shivered as the abrupt return of the room to a bearable level of light felt like the darkness of a winter compared to the summertime brilliance of the moment before. It was as if the sun had suddenly disappeared from the sky, turning noon to inky midnight in an instant.

He blinked several times, trying to clear the black spots that afflicted his vision. Beside him, he saw that Kaym was still on his feet, and at a gesture from the angel, Christopher quickly stood up.

No longer blinded, he could now see that they stood at the foot of a shallow, velvet-covered platform. The Prince sat before them on a throne made of a clear crystal, though whether it was carved of diamonds or glass, Christopher could not tell. It was lined with gold, though, a reddish gold identical to the gold of the jeweled crown on the Prince's head.

The Prince himself was an extremely handsome being, similar in most respects to a man except for a large pair of golden wings that fanned the air lazily behind him. His face was kind, with a short, dark blond beard that did not hide a friendly smile. His eyes were a piercing blue that did not recall the pale cerulean of the sky but rather the deep, intense azure of the ocean. They were ageless and wise, giving the lie to his otherwise youthful appearance. He wore a white robe, with a jeweled scabbard belted to him by a scarlet cord.

This beautiful Prince rose gracefully to his feet and held out both hands to greet Kaym. The fallen angel took them in his own and started to kneel down, but the Prince did not permit him to.

"Kaym, Our loyal servant." The Prince smiled in a charming way that reminded Christopher of his favorite uncle. "It is good indeed to see thee, for We know thy risks were great. We see by thy companion that thy duty hath been fulfilled."

"Yes, my Prince. It is my honor to present to you Christopher Lewis, a human subject of what will one day be one of your many principalities in the North and West."

Christopher's eyebrows went up at Kaym's choice of words. Had the angel taken him through time as well as space? It didn't seem likely, but then again, neither did the Musphilim. He looked down at his arm, and it did look a little red, as if it had been sunburned. He rubbed at it and wondered when they were.

"Indeed!" he heard the Prince say. "How interesting. Who rules there?"

"Lord Altarib rules the city, in your name. He claims the name of Bloodwinter."

"Bloodwinter? So Altarib is fated to rise?" The Prince laughed. It was an easy, pleasant sound, like water trickling down a gentle hill. "Then We shall remember to keep him in Our favor. It is good to know these things, Kaym. It is a pity We dare not make more frequent use of this timely talent of thine."

The Prince turned to face Christopher and nodded graciously toward him.

"Be welcome in Our courts, Christopher. Has Kaym told thee of Our will for thee?"

Christopher glanced at Kaym, whose pallid face revealed nothing, then back at the Prince.

"He told me that you needed me for something that an angel could not do, but he didn't tell me what it was. And he told me that it might be dangerous but that it would be worth it."

"And this didst not frighten thee?"

"No, Your Majesty. Well, not much, anyhow. I figured that you don't get the chance to hang out with angels and meet the Prince of Darkness every day."

An abrupt hush fell on the room. Christopher winced and could have kicked himself, but he was very much afraid that someone was just about to do that for him. If he was lucky.

But the dreadful silence was broken as the Prince threw back his head and laughed. It was a full, hearty laugh filled with genuine amusement, and Christopher breathed a sigh of relief as the Prince flashed white teeth in a broad, friendly smile.

"Thou art indeed a brave young man, or perhaps a fool indeed. The Prince of Darkness? Ha! Who hath told thee so? Surely not Kaym. No, speak, o fearless one, of what reward thou seekest from Our hands? Success? Riches? Glory?"

"I read once that knowledge is power," Christopher replied immediately, glad to change the subject. "I want to know everything."

"The Path of Knowledge. A worthy answer, young human," the Prince said, as his sea-blue eyes flicked from Christopher to Kaym and back again. "We shall make thee a promise. Perform for Us this one deed, and thou shalt walk that path, and We shall give thee a place of honor in Our shining court."

Christopher imitated Kaym's manners and bowed deeply to the Prince.

"That would be great, Your Majesty. Just tell me what I have to do."

The Prince glanced at Kaym and nodded. The fallen angel pointed to the domed ceiling of the throne room and spoke a single word, and a mist began to form, gradually obscuring the dome from view. The mist cleared, but then, instead of carvings, the dome now appeared to be covered by painted images. Then the images began to move, telling a story that was older than time itself.

In the beginning, there was only darkness. There was nothing in the darkness, until one day, for no apparent reason, a small point of light appeared, piercing the darkness and driving it back. The light grew greater and more powerful, until finally it shined so brightly that, despite its greater size, the darkness was forced to submit to it, acknowledging the light as its master. The light named the darkness Chaos and used the darkness to create a place of lesser light that it called Heaven.

In time, other points of light appeared amidst the Chaos, and when they saw the grand and mighty structure that was Heaven, they went there and bowed before the first light and proclaimed the light as the King of Heaven. These beings of light were called gods, and though the King of Heaven was the first and greatest among them, he was but one of many.

One day, a new light appeared. It appeared early in the day instead of late at night, which was usually when new gods were born, and so was called Lucifer, the Morning Star. This young god was very bright, rivaling even the King of Heaven in his radiant glory and power. Because of his brilliance and beauty, the King of Heaven looked on Lucifer with favor and honored him above all the other gods.

Eons passed, and the King of Heaven created servants to aid the gods in their long struggle against the darkness, which was defeated again and again, only to rise again in time. These servants were called angels, and there were multitudes of them, too many to count. They warred against the great beasts of Chaos, monsters born of the darkness, created by the darkness to battle against the light and its King. These primordial battles were mighty, and as the gods of light slew the monstrous creations of darkness, they too were slain, until only three of the first great gods of light remained.

But from the bodies of the gods, the three survivors created the planets, and from the holy drops of their blood was born the race of men. These men had the appearance of angels, but they were no better than beasts, for their minds were dull and blank. They lived like animals, cold, starving more often than not, until one day Prince Lucifer, as he was now respectfully titled by the angels, took pity on them and visited them and set alight the fire of their dark minds with a spark of his own brilliance.

With this fire, these men became humankind, a tall race of beings who were soon able to master their world, exerting dominion over the animals and their surroundings. But they did not forget the shining god who had rescued them from their plight, and they raised mighty temples to him, huge buildings where they would gather and praise his name. Their world was called Ahura Azdha.

The King of Heaven saw this and was jealous. His power was great, and so he found a second world, à barren one, and from its dust he created men who were very like those of Ahura Azdha, only they were not so tall or so beautiful as those who worshiped Prince Lucifer. The King of Heaven saw this and was angry that his worshipers should be less great than those who worshiped the god he now saw as his rival.

He offered to trade worshipers with Prince Lucifer, but the Prince refused, for he would not forsake those who praised his name. So the King of Heaven, in a rage, stripped the Prince of his title and his name and forbade him to darken Heaven evermore. This was an insult, for the Prince, who was now nameless, could no more darken Heaven than he could darken the sun, so radiant was his glory. But the Prince, now the Nameless, swallowed his pride and descended upon Ahura Azdha, where he found comfort and solace among his people.

When the angels heard the Prince had abandoned Heaven and that they would be deprived forever of the joy of his glorious light, they became very angry with the King of Heaven. Many of them were so angry that they, too, abandoned Heaven and descended to Ahura Azdha, where they swore allegiance to their Prince. Even some of the Sarim, the thirty angel-princes who were the first and greatest and most majestic of all the angels, turned their backs on the King and swore that the Prince, and the Prince alone, would be their lord and master.

The angels descended upon Ahura Azdha in a glorious white-golden horde, and the reflection of the Prince's brilliant light off the white feathers of their wings was bright enough to blind even the sun. They gathered before the Prince and bowed to him, a thousand thousand angels, begging him to accept them as his servants.

"If thou wilt have it so, then shall it be so," the nameless one answered the multitude of angels. "I will be thy Prince, and I will be thy King, and one day shall We rule again in Heaven. But no more will I be Lucifer, the Morning Star. Instead, thou shalt call Us Adonai Lucere, the Prince of Light, the Bright Shining One."

"All hail the Prince of Light!" a tall warrior-angel shouted.

"Hail the Bright Shining One!" the multitude proclaimed.

The image on the ceiling dissolved into mist, and Christopher blinked as he was pulled out of the mystical realm of the ancient vision. He looked away from the ceiling and stared at the Prince on his glassy throne. No longer nameless, the Bright Shining One now appeared older and wiser than the joyful young god of the vision. It was not only the beard he now wore that made him look less like a prince and more like a king but also the tiny lines that were visible around his eyes and the corners of his mouth, lines born of pain, and loss, and sorrow.

"Thou offereth to serve Us, and so thou shalt," Adonai Lucere told him. "But what We ask of thee is not without risk or danger. These sad events hath taken place many centuries ago, and yet the King of Heaven feareth Us and is jealous of Us still. He is always on his guard and hath raised vast armies of angels against Us. And all this great host shall be arrayed against thee in thy task."

Christopher nodded. He understood that whatever he had to do was not going to be easy. What he didn't understand was how anything he could do would make a difference.

"But what can I do? I'm only sixteen. I mean, I just got my driver's license three weeks ago!"

"Well, we're not asking you to drive Apollo's chariot," said Kaym with a morbid laugh, until a glance from Prince Lucere quieted him.

"The King hath sealed the Gates of Heaven so that no god or angel can open them. But thou, Christopher, thou art the key. The Gates hath been sealed with a spell that only one such as thyself may break."

"How do I do that?"

"When Heaven sleeps and true night falls, thou shalt go to the Twelfth Gate and open it with this key. Open thy hand."

Chistopher obeyed, and the Prince snapped his fingers. Out of nowhere, a small gold key appeared in the air and dropped into Christopher's hand. It was marked with a small inscription consisting of five strange letters that Christopher could not read.

Kaym spat and turned his back on the little piece of metal as the Prince gave his instructions.

"The Gate shall open before thee, and there Our legions shall be waiting. They shall pour in like a raging sea, and all Heaven shall fall before them.

The King will hide in the Eternal City, because he feareth to stand before Us, but it will avail him little, for We shall find him and cast him down. He names Us fallen, but it is he who will soon fall! So shall We keep Our word, and so shall We return to Heaven, to reign forever upon the Throne Eternal!"

The assembled court cheered loudly. Kaym glanced at the Prince, then gave Christopher more detailed instructions.

"Opening the gate will be no problem, just turn the key and your work is done. The real danger, however, is that your true nature will be discovered before you can reach the gate. You'll be disguised as an angel, of course, but the danger is that you'll accidentally give yourself away. That's why we must do more than cast an illusion over you. We must make that illusion a reality."

Christopher made a skeptical face. "It sounds like you're saying I have to become an angel, right? But you can't really do that, can you?"

Kaym shook his head, his eyes darkly serious. "No, I cannot. But with the Prince's permission, I can infuse you with a spark of power, a piece of my own divine spirit that will protect you. Do you remember how the guard at the palace gate commented upon your difference?"

Christopher thought about the silver guard and its eerie, burning gaze. "Yeah, it knew I wasn't like you."

"Yes, because you . . . smelled wrong, might be one way to put it. Your essence is a different substance from ours, so we must mask it with another. Mine."

"Do you mean I'd be able to fly, and do magic,

and read minds like you?" Christopher's heart raced. It sounded way too good to be true, but if this was a dream, he didn't ever want to wake up. "That would be so cool!"

"All of that and more," Kaym promised, his eyes showing amusement at Christopher's excitement. "It will take you far along the Path, toward that knowledge you seek."

The fallen angel placed both hands on Christopher's shoulders and leaned forward so their foreheads were touching. He muttered something, and Christopher felt a warm heat passing through Kaym to himself. The heat rose quickly, and the sensation grew from a pleasing warmth to an uncomfortable burning.

He tried to pull away, but the angel's grip held him tight. The heat continued to rise, and it felt as if a red-hot iron were being burned into his forehead. He tried to scream, but even his voice seemed imprisoned by the angel's iron grasp. His head was ablaze; it seemed as if his very skin were melting before the hellish touch of the fallen angel.

A loud thunderclap sounded in his head, and the hands on his shoulders fell away as he passed through the fire. Christopher's overloaded senses told him he was falling over backward, tumbling heels over head over heels over head, again and again, hurtling through a weightless black void that had suddenly appeared beneath his feet. But all he really cared about was that the terrible burning had stopped. The darkness of the void was blessedly cool, and the empty winds comforted his scalded soul.

Then he found himself standing again in the

Courts of Light, but now he could feel the awesome potential of the angelic power. He looked around the room, and his newly heightened senses provided him with new details about the place and those inhabiting it.

Kaym and the other angels, the courtiers and celebrants, were all wearing disguises of a sort. Whereas before their forms had been as solid and substantial as his own, now their appearances seemed translucent. Only the guards were as before, flaming spirits trapped behind silver. Beneath every angel's hazy figure lurked a large flame, shimmering and dancing to its own rhythm. But to describe them as flames was not quite right, for each flame was distinct, with individual differences that were, to Christopher's newly opened eyes, easily identifiable.

Only the Prince seemed as before, solid and flameless, more human than human as he sat upon his crystal throne, but he seemed to be pleased at what Kaym had done. He smiled at Christopher and made a sweeping gesture with his hand.

"Already thou hast traveled far along thy chosen path. This is the realm of spirit. Enter, and be welcome."

Christopher grinned, but when he blinked his eyes, everything was as before. Kaym's eyes were again encased behind impenetrable black plastic, hiding his golden flame, and the rest of the angels also appeared to be solid. But now he knew otherwise.

"Those flames that you saw are our true selves," Kaym said. "Now that you have eyes to see, you can penetrate through these illusions and many others at your will. What you may not realize, however, is that the fire within you now lends you the same appearance."

"And now art thou ready to face thy task," Prince Lucere said. He rose gracefully from his throne, then reached out to embrace Christopher. His arms were warm and strong, and he gave off a cinnamon scent that reminded Christopher of Melusine.

Christopher returned the princely embrace warmly, feeling exhilarated. The power within him stirred, a chrysalis called to life by the close proximity of the Prince.

"Thank you," he whispered gratefully. "Thank you, thank you so much."

"Be welcome," the Prince said. "Only do not fail Us."

"Never!" Christopher protested hotly. "I will open the gate for you, Prince Lucere. By my soul, I swear it!"

Behind him, he heard Kaym laughing coldly. "You already have, Christopher. You already have."

CHAPTER 5

THE
DARKNESS RISING

THE ANGEL OF THE LORD ENCAMPETH ROUND ABOUT
THEM THAT FEAR HIM, AND DELIVERETH THEM.
—Psalms 34:7

Caught up in the movie, neither Jami nor Holli had any idea that there was an invisible battle being fought just outside the warm safety of their house. But not even Tom Cruise's winning smile could hide the increasing psychic electricity in the air. As the wind howled noisily, the evil presence of the shadows looming outside began to make an impression, however faint, on the two sisters.

Holli frowned suddenly and pressed the button on the remote that paused the VCR.

"Did you hear that?" she asked.

The younger of the twins, she was a sensitive girl, and Jami had learned to pay attention to her sister's feelings, because she often noticed the small things that Jami missed.

"Hear what?" Jami studied her twin's intent face. It was like looking in a mirror or, actually, like an

67

advertisement where she was the Before picture, and Holli was the After. Her twin was slender and pretty, with long, loosely permed blond hair bleached almost white. Holli's features were a little more delicate, and while they both had had their share of boyfriends, Holli's fan club was larger and more dedicated.

Of course, Jami thought ruefully as she toyed with her own wheat-colored ponytail, Holli worked a lot harder at things. They weren't going anywhere this evening, but her twin's eyes were expertly lined and shadowed, and her pale pink lipstick was unsmudged. Jami wasn't jealous, she was just a little envious. There was an important difference, she told herself. And maybe if she quit playing soccer and tried out for the cheerleading squad next year, she could spend more time working on her appearance, too.

Holli interrupted her imaginary plans for a complete makeover before she had decided on whether to bleach her hair or not. "I thought I heard something ... I don't know ... like a howling of some sort." She shivered. "It just feels really, like, heavy in here all of a sudden." Her blue eyes, normally quite pale, were shadowed with worry.

"I didn't hear anything," Jami said doubtfully. "It's probably just the wind."

They sat quietly together for a long minute, listening for an unfamiliar sound, for a noise that didn't belong. It reminded Jami of searching for a word that was lurking just past the tip of her tongue. What finally came to her, though, wasn't a sound at all but a feeling. A horrible feeling, a terror, a sense of being lost in the dark and hearing an unknown something sniffing all around her, and knowing that what it smelled was her.

"I wish Mom and Dad were home," she said suddenly. "It feels . . . I don't know. You know how the sky gets all yellow-green and, like, quiet right before there's a tornado? It feels like that."

Holli didn't say anything. She cocked her head, as if listening for something.

"Where's Christopher?" she asked. With the movie paused, they should have been able to hear the thump of his stereo, or at least the sound of his heavy feet as he paced around his room.

"Who cares?"

Dislike was too strong a word for how Jami felt about their older brother, but it was no secret that she didn't get along with him as well as Holli did. They had fought since they were little, and their fights had grown more and more frequent since she and Holli had entered high school last fall. She figured it was mostly because they were in with the popular crowd, while he was still a social reject even though he was a sophmore now. Only halfway through her freshman year, Jami had already lettered in soccer, had gone out with some of the cuter upperclassmen, and was now barely on speaking terms with Christopher.

He pretended not to see her when he passed her in the halls, so she paid him back by calling him Chris, a nickname she knew he hated. It wasn't exactly the most vicious family war ever but provided just enough fuel to feed a fire that simmered on and on, despite Holli's best efforts to put it out.

"Don't you hear that?" Holli waved her hands excitedly.

"I just told you, I didn't hear anything."

"That's what I mean." Her twin made a gesture that Jami understood to indicate a stereo. "There's no music!"

"So? Maybe Chris had to call somebody?" She laughed cruelly and shook her head. "Oh, wait, why would he do that? He doesn't have any friends to call."

"Shut up, Jami, he does too." Holli's eyes flashed angrily as she defended their brother.

"Okay, but they're all, like, losers." It was harsh but true, and Holli knew it. "Anyhow, he's probably playing games on the Internet or something."

Holli shook her head slowly. A look of sadness crossed her face. She was probably thinking of Christopher and his loser friends. Holli was a soft touch.

"It's not their fault, they just don't know any better." She pushed the stop button and stood up as the frozen image on the TV screen disappeared in a flood of bright blue. "Come on, let's go see what he's up to."

"Go ahead. I'll wait for you." Jami yawned and reached for the almost-empty bowl of popcorn. There were a few kernels left, and she popped one into her mouth, gingerly sucking the butter off the hard little piece of corn.

"Oh, come with me, Jami. I just feel, I don't know, there's something bad going on!"

Jami rolled her eyes, but she, too, had the uneasy feeling that something wasn't quite as it should be.

"You're just imagining things," she insisted, but she dutifully pushed herself off the couch and started to follow Holli out of the room.

But Holli suddenly froze and grabbed her arm so hard that Jami thought Holli's carefully polished nails had pierced her flesh.

"Ouch! What was that for?"

"Ohmigod! What's . . . what are you?" Holli released Jami and cringed, holding her arms in front of her face. "Don't hurt us, please."

"What are who?" Jami looked wildly around the front entryway, but there was nothing there, nor was there anything on the stairs. She grabbed one of Holli's arms and tried to see her face. "Holli, what's the matter?"

Her twin's blue eyes were huge and round with shock. Her pink mouth was gaping wide, a slack-jawed response to something, or someone, that Jami could not see.

"Oh, you scared me," Holli said breathlessly. "I thought, I thought." She laughed suddenly. "I don't even know what I thought."

As Jami watched in disbelief, her twin nodded several times, as if in response to a voice that Jami didn't hear.

"Well, of course you're angels. What else would you be? I'm not afraid, it's just that I was kind of surprised, that's all." Holli shot a look at Jami that was surprisingly sane, considering her bizarre behavior. "She says they're here to protect us!"

"Goody," Jami said sarcastically. She was starting to feel seriously alarmed. Holli wasn't particularly religious, but she went to church just often enough to make Jami worry about her from time to time. "And what are they protecting us from?"

"We're not quite sure yet."

Jami gasped when an unseen male voice unexpectedly answered her question. Her knees buckled, and only Holli's hand on her shoulder kept her from collapsing.

As the room seemed to spin in a circle around her, a tall, lordly angel suddenly appeared right out of thin air. He looked almost like a knight, with a white tunic draped over the silver armor covering his arms and legs. His face was square, his hair was so pale it was nearly white, and a small pair of wings extended slightly past his broad, armored shoulders. He held a sword that appeared to be on fire, but despite the weapon in his hand, his presence was, surprisingly, not frightening at all. He was, quite simply, beautiful. Lose the tunic and the armor, Jami thought irreverently, and he could be a Tommy model.

Beside him was a companion who was smaller but no less fierce. She, too, held a flaming sword and wore armor under her tunic, but her feathery wings were even larger. Her hair was nearly the same wheat-yellow shade of blond as Jami's own hair, but it was cropped off at the shoulders. It framed a face of delicate beauty, but there was nothing delicate about her dark brown eyes or the practiced way she held her sword.

"There seems to be quite a gathering of evil in this area," the female angel said. "Mariel went outside to look, but she hasn't come back, and we haven't heard anything from her."

"Excuse me, but what are you?" Jami demanded, as her agnostic mind reeled in shock. "What are you doing here? Who's Mariel?"

"Didn't you hear what I said? They're angels," Holli said.

"Uh-huh. And I'm Xena Warrior Princess."

The female angel smiled gently.

"Your sister is correct. We are servants of the Most High God. I am called Aliel. I have the honor to be your sister's guardian, just as Paulus here has the honor of serving as yours."

"You're my guardian angel?" Holli breathed. "Ohmigod, that's so great!" She reached out and took the angel's hand, pressing it to her cheek. "I always believed in you. I did! I always knew someone was there, looking out for me. I really did!"

Jami looked on, stunned, as Aliel smiled and enfolded her sister in a warm embrace, as if they'd known each other for ages. She turned and stared at the angel called Paulus, who appeared to be stifling a grin as he stared right back at her. He did not, thank goodness, attempt to hug her.

"Um, hi," she said uncomfortably. "I . . . ah, don't really believe in you, you know."

Her words did sound a little hollow considering that the big angel was standing right in front of her at the foot of the stairwell leading to her bedroom. He had nice eyes, with lashes that were long and surprisingly dark for his coloring. She shook her head. Why was she thinking about his eyes?

"I know." He wasn't stifling the grin any longer.

"So, this is kind of weird, don't you think?"

The grin turned into an outright smile. "I can understand why you would feel that way."

"So, why are you showing yourself to me now?" Jami wasn't sure she liked this angel. Yes, he was completely gorgeous, but he appeared to be kind of a smartass, too. He reminded her of one of the seniors she used to have a crush on, because there was something about his smile that made her think he was laughing at her.

"I'm not sure." His face grew sober. "For reasons that I don't understand, your sister was permitted to see us. After that, well, it didn't seem polite to leave you out of the conversation."

Jami nodded. "Yeah, I was starting to think Holli had lost it there for a second. So, what's up? Are we in trouble or something?"

"It may be so," he replied. "Evil stalks the night, and your brother's guardian fears that Christopher is somehow involved."

"That so does not surprise me!" Jami exclaimed. "What did he do, call up the Devil or something?" She knew her brother had more than a few books on black magic in his library. He'd told her once that he used them to make up cooler-sounding spells for when he played Dungeons and Dragons with his geeky friends. But she wouldn't put it past him to dabble in something even weirder.

"Not to my knowledge," Paulus said, taking her questions literally. "But his guardian has disappeared, and there is something very powerful and very much closer to this place than I would like."

Jami swallowed. Her guardian was tall enough to play basketball, but he was built like a football player. His sword looked as if it could cut a refrigerator in two. And yet he was clearly nervous.

"Powerful?"

"And evil, I should add. Very, very evil."

There was a loud cracking sound from the office, then a huge whoosh, as if every particle of air had been sucked out of the room next to them. The sensation of darkness, vague before, fell upon them with a palpable, crushing weight that threatened to take Jami's breath away. The house lights went out, both inside and out, and the girls could see only by the light of their Guardians' swords.

"What's going on?" Holli cried out, terrified.

"Be brave, child," Aliel urged her. "God will not forsake you!"

But in the flickering light of the flames, Jami saw Holli's angel shoot a concerned glance at Paulus, and she could feel the weight of the darkness growing ever stronger. It surrounded them, it engulfed them, and, worst of all, it called out to them. She crouched beside Holli behind the couch, shivering with fear as hundreds of high-pitched voices chittered like insects in the darkness outside. She could not understand their words, but she knew somehow that they were mocking her, taunting her, and feeding on her fear. They frightened her so badly that she could barely breathe, and yet she felt a terrible urge to scream and run out from under the protection of the angels' swords.

Holli cowered next to her for what felt like forever, squeezing her hand so hard it hurt, although it was only a few minutes before the terrible, overpowering presence abruptly released them from its grasp. The scary voices faded away, the lights came back on, and Jami breathed a sigh of relief as Holli released her hand and sat back on the floor. The awful danger had disappeared, at least for now.

The front door burst open, and both girls screamed, but it was, thank goodness, only another angel, a strawberry-blond angel dressed just like Aliel. But her long hair was all messed up, she didn't have a sword, and what appeared to be

Goth-punk chains dangled discordantly from her wrists.

"Where is Christopher?" the disheveled angel demanded frantically. Jami guessed that the redhead was her brother's guardian, and even though she was still plenty freaked out by the whole situation, she found herself smiling with sympathy. Christopher made her feel like that sometimes, too.

"I don't know," Paulus answered, frowning at the sight of the chains. "Mariel, are you well?"

Mariel ignored him and looked desperately at the girls.

"He's upstairs, in his room," Holli said as she pointed toward the stairs. The strawberry-blonde nodded and rushed past Paulus up the stairs.

Jami saw Paulus glance at Aliel, then he shrugged and followed Mariel up the stairs. As she and Holli trailed behind the three angels, Jami suddenly felt a hot wave of anger flash through her. Something strange and scary and couldn't-be-happening was totally happening before her eyes, and she knew, she just knew, it was all Christopher's fault.

"Perhaps it was one of the Great Lords of the Fallen," Aliel said, with a shaken look on her face. "It must have been strong, for Bloodwinter to humble himself so. His pride is great, and he is not one to be courteous unless he is forced."

"I know," Mariel replied. "I saw the shadow pass over my head, and its aura was so dark that it could have been one of the Averse Sefiroth." The pretty angel shuddered, and tears began to streak her cheeks. "And now it has my charge."

"The fault is not yours, Mariel," Paulus said bitterly. "I should have gone with you." He suddenly stopped talking and held up a hand. His eyes were distant, as if he were listening to something far away. "Hark! Something comes."

The three angels stopped talking and listened. Jami strained her ears, too, but she heard nothing.

"It's bad," Holli said unexpectedly. "Not as bad as that thing that was here, but there's a lot of them. And they stink."

Jami saw the three angels stare at one another, then at Holli. She'd obviously surprised them somehow.

"She smells Mordrim." Paulus spoke first. "Their stench is strong."

"And Malakim, too, I fear," Mariel added. "We must leave here, now."

Jami glanced quizzically at Holli, but her twin only shrugged.

"I don't know, there's just this bad, like, smell in the air." Her white curls bounced as she shook her head. "I can't explain it, it's just, like, there, you know?"

No, I don't know! Jami wanted to scream and shake Holli's shoulders, but that wasn't about to solve anything or answer any of her questions. She looked back at the angels and saw that they were in the middle of an argument. Paulus was pointing his sword toward the door.

"There are too many of them. We have to leave, now!"

"No!" Aliel shouted at Paulus, as she grabbed the big angel's tunic with both fists. "We can't leave the children!"

"Who said anything about leaving the children?"

Mariel snapped at Aliel. "The shadow took Christopher, not me. They are after the children, and if we can't protect them here, then we must take them somewhere we can keep them safe!"

"We're not children," Holli protested, but the angels ignored her. Jami wondered if she should tell Paulus about her father's shotgun, but then he probably knew about it already. And who knew if a shotgun could even hurt an angel, anyhow?

"There is a school nearby," Aliel suggested, her voice calmer now. "On this night, a band of Faithful gather there to praise and worship the Almighty."

"Is it the school Christopher attended as a child?" Jami saw Aliel nod in answer to Mariel's question. "Praise God, that's less than a mile from here!"

"God be praised!" Paulus echoed. He turned toward the two girls. "Jami, Holli, you are in great peril. Do you understand me? You must come with us, for we are outnumbered by the foe, and we cannot protect you here."

Holli nodded. She had already taken one of Christopher's parkas out of the closet and held out a down ski jacket to Jami. "Come on, Jami, hurry up! You heard what they said. We can't stay here."

"Hurry up? But we can't go outside!" Jami protested. "If there's really something out there, that's the last thing we should do!" When the house had gone dark, the evil voices had called her to them, called her outside where they could reach her and rend her with their terrible claws. She didn't really believe they existed, but she had no desire to test that assumption, much less go where something could get her.

Paulus seemed to read her mind. With a sympathetic smile that caressed her like a touch of sunlight, he took her by the hand.

"I know your fear, Jami, but I tell you, the Lord Almighty sent me here to keep you safe. He will not allow you to come to harm." His dark eyes were deep pools of strength and reassurance. "I will keep the shadows from you."

Jami looked away, but she nodded and obediently reached out to take the quilted jacket from Holli. She was sure that Paulus meant well, but Mariel's tear-streaked face seemed to belie his words. As she reluctantly followed Holli down the stairs, she glanced out the window and saw the distant stars looking down on her without pity.

They ran. Jami scanned the skies, hoping not to see the approaching danger, but also afraid to let it sneak up on her. Their little party had left the back of the house, running through the backyard, past the fence, and over the field that led to the railroad tracks. Aliel, her sword drawn and blazing, led the way, while Mariel ran between the two girls, holding their hands. Paulus brought up the rear, his sword drawn, always looking over his shoulder for signs of enemy pursuit.

"Where . . . is . . . it . . . ?" panted Holli, short of breath. Despite her own fear, Jami still managed to worry about her twin. She was a cheerleader, not an athlete, and Jami knew it had been at least a year since Holli had done any running.

"Behind us," Paulus answered curtly.

Jami glanced back, to the south, and saw that the stars in the southern sky had disappeared, swallowed up by an all-devouring blackness. As she

looked, one constellation was slowly engulfed by
the darkness, then another. It was an awful sight,
and she redoubled her efforts.

Her lungs burned as she struggled up a small
rise. She was still in shape from soccer, but it was
hard running through the snow up the rough
series of hills that stood in their path. She knew
their route well, having gone to elementary school
there only five years before. The ground was
uneven, and it was hard to keep from slipping in
the snow. She fell once, tripping over a frozen
chunk of ice, but Mariel quickly hauled her back to
her feet, and Jami marveled at the surprising
strength of the slender angel.

Finally, they reached the top of the last hill, and
she breathed a thankful sigh when she saw the
bright lights of the school in front of them. They half
ran, half slid down the snowy slope and sprinted
past the cars in the parking lot. She dared a quick
glance back and was horrified to see that the sky
behind them was entirely dark. Just as before, the
evil felt as if it were crushing her to the ground, and
she thought she felt its awful claws reaching out to
grab her.

The door to the school was only six feet away
when the shadows reached her. She screamed as
something grabbed the hood of her parka and
jerked her off her feet. She lost her grip on Mariel's
hand as she fell helplessly backward and smacked
her backside on the hard-packed snow of the parking lot. Half stunned by the pain, Jami could barely
make out the shape of her attacker, silhouetted
against the building lights.

It was huge, shaped kind of like a man, but with

bony ridges and giant, crablike claws. It slobbered at her, making a weird screeching sound. As it lunged close to her face, she saw that it had no eyes, only empty hollows where the eyes should have been. She screamed and beat at it with her fists, but it didn't seem to notice. Its wintry blue skin was rough and warty, and its wild, stringy hair stuck out from its skullish head like twisted gray wire.

She screamed again as it tried to grab her with its claws, but before it got a grip on her, Aliel came to her rescue.

"For the Most High!" the angel shouted, and struck a devastating blow with her sword. The demonic being fell back into the darkness, howling, nearly cleaved in two by the burning fury of the blade. Holli's guardian pulled Jami to her feet, then half shoved, half threw her through the open door, all the while brandishing her sword at the onrushing dark. Jami looked desperately for her own angel, but Paulus was nowhere to be seen. Only occasional flashes of flames from the parking lot hinted at his whereabouts, as he struck out against the evil that engulfed him.

As soon as Jami was inside, Mariel slammed the door shut behind her.

"What about Paulus?" Jami gasped in horror. "Aliel's out there, too! She just saved me from that . . . that thing!"

Holli reached out to her, but Jami pushed her twin away and confronted Mariel. "You can't leave them out there!"

"Be quiet, child!" the blond angel commanded, and Jami fell silent before her forceful gaze. Mariel nodded and without explanation led the girls down the steps and into the school gymnasium.

They entered quietly through a back door, and Jami was surprised to see how many people were gathered there. The gym was almost full, and there had to be more than seven hundred people there. She looked around uncomfortably, afraid that someone there might know her, and was relieved when she didn't recognize a single face. The people were sitting on undersized chairs laid out in rows, listening to a middle-aged man speaking from a stage cluttered with abandoned musical instruments. He had curly brown hair and a boyish personality, and he spoke in a rapid-fire, machine-gun manner from behind a lectern that was standing right in front of a big drum set.

"So what I'm saying is, the right approach isn't to be telling God how you want Him to bless you, but how you can best use the blessings that He elects to bless you with. Did you follow me on that one? Because I don't care who you are, God wants to bless you. It's just that everybody gets blessed . . ." He looked up, startled for a moment, and then continued. ". . . in different ways."

He fell silent for a moment, staring fixedly toward the back of the gym. At first, Jami was afraid that the preacher was looking at her, and she looked at the floor, trying to avoid his eyes. She jumped when he suddenly closed his Bible with an audible thump and set it back on the lectern.

"All right, people. I just got something laid on my heart. There's some warfare stuff going on right now, and we're gonna do something about it, right now. Can I get ten volunteers?"

He looked around the room. Ten hands were quickly raised, mostly by people sitting in the first few rows, and he nodded.

"Okay, I'm going to ask you to be our prayer cover, praying protection on this place and on everybody here, all right? But that's just defense, and we need offense." He reached for something in his back pocket. It was a pair of drumsticks, and he brandished them before the crowd as if they were weapons. "Anybody remember how the Israelites went into battle?"

"They went in singing!" a man called out.

"Hey." Jami nudged Holli. "Is that church that you and Mom go to like this?"

"First Lutheran?" Holli had a strange look on her face. "No, not at all. This is different."

"That's right!" the preacher was shouting. "That's how they did it. First the singers, and then the soldiers."

He gestured at a large black man who was already mounting the stage. He was built like a football player, a six-foot-five giant with a shaved head who was followed by a motley group of men and women who began to pick up the instruments scattered about the stage.

"Jeez, he's, like, huge," Holli whispered to Jami.

"What are they going to do, have a concert? That's really going to help. Those things are going to come in here any second!"

"Look, Aliel must have brought us in here for a reason," Holli argued, although she didn't understand why they were here, either. "We can't just keep running."

"So, let's crank it up," the preacher was saying as

the musicians took their places. "You know what the Word tells us, 'not by power, not by might, but by my spirit, says the Lord,' and we need to call upon that Spirit right now!"

Jami watched, her eyes wide, as the entire congregation rose to their feet, and the preacher climbed behind the drums. He began pounding out a furious beat while one of the guitarists, a short fellow with strings of colorful yarn woven into his long dreadlocked hair, joined in with massive power chords that threatened to shake the building's foundation.

"Okay, this is too weird!" Jami told Holli. "Let's get out of here."

"Yeah, you really want to go out and let those things grab you again?" Holli shook her head. "These people are strange, but at least they're not trying to kill us."

"Well, okay, but I don't like it!"

Holli understood why Jami was feeling so uncomfortable. She knew it had to be hard for her twin to suddenly be thrown into the middle of a bunch of people who lived in a world she'd never believed in. Holli herself wasn't quite sure what to think; she went to church every couple of weeks, tried to be a good person, and had always considered herself a Christian. Now, after coming face-to-face with her guardian angel and the passion of the believers surrounding her, she wondered what she was. When was the last time she'd even looked at her Bible? She suddenly felt guilty, as if she was here under false pretenses.

"Hey, look, there's Paulus and Aliel!" Jami interrupted her thoughts. "I wonder what happened with those things outside? Maybe they're gone. Maybe we can go now."

Holli glanced at Mariel, who was singing heartily along with the band.

"I don't know, she doesn't look like she's about to go anywhere." Holli wrinkled her well-groomed eyebrows. "Don't you think we should wait and see what the angels tell us to do? Those things could still be out there."

"I suppose." The music really wasn't bad, but Jami had a trapped look in her eyes.

"Let's just wait and see what's up," Holli insisted. Although she hadn't told Jami, she could still feel the dark presence of the evil lurking outside. Something was holding it at bay, though, for it wasn't coming any closer. Was it Paulus and Aliel, or was it the sheer numbers of the crowd?

Jami nodded in half-hearted agreement, but she kept an eye on the door, desperately wanting to leave and yet afraid that the evil shadows might enter at any moment. Why wouldn't they? There couldn't be anything special about the school that would keep them out. Just then, the bass kicked in, and the giant black man began singing, in a voice that boomed through the room.

You are mighty, you are holy,
You are awesome, in your power . . .

Jami had never heard the song before, but most of the people in the gym seemed to recognize it immediately, for they joined in right away, singing at the tops of their lungs.

You are risen, you are worthy,
You have beaten the power of death . . .

Jami looked over at Mariel. Paulus and Aliel had joined her now, and, like the rest of the crowd, they were singing and clapping along with enthusiasm.

Ha-a-a-lelujah, the angels joined their voices with the roomful of humanity. *We-e will rejoice . . .*

Ha-a-a-lelujah, we-e will rejoice!

As the music crested like a powerful wave, Holli suddenly realized why the shadows had not entered here, for there was power here, too, a power nearly as strong as that first crushing darkness had been earlier. The fiery passion of the crowd was like a light flaming against the evil ones, driving them away, and with them her fear. As her fear faded, her discomfort grew, but unexpectedly, she also felt a secret urge to join in with the rest of the crowd in singing the simple chorus, repeated over and over again. The crowd's enthusiasm did not flag with the repetition. If anything, they were getting even more excited, raising their hands to the ceiling and waving them in the air.

You are awesome, in your power . . .

"Come on, church, raise the roof. Let those demons know whose side you're on!" The black man raised a massive fist and shook it in the air. "Though we walk through the valley of the shadow of death, we will fear nothing, because Jesus won the victory. It's a done deal! We just gotta claim it!"

"These people are nuts," Jami whispered to her sister.

"Yeah ... they're total freaks," Holli agreed, but she was grinning now. "The thing is, you can, like, really feel something here, you know?"

"No, not really," Jami lied. "What do you mean?"

"Well, whatever they're doing seems to be working. I can't feel anything outside anymore."

"Yeah, well, I guess I'm not quite as scared now," Jami admitted. "And like you said, at least they're not trying to kill us."

"I got a verse for you, church," the black man shouted as the preacher hammered out a break-down. "And I know you can tell me what it is!"

"Romans 16:19!" the congregation shouted back, hooting and hollering as the electric guitars kicked back in with a howling vengeance that was as right-eous as it was deafening.

"This is crazy, but it's kind of fun, too!" Holli yelled at Jami over the thunderous din.

But Aliel heard her and shook her head.

"No, this is how we fight our war," the angel said.

And the God of Peace will soon crush Satan.
Yes, God will crush him underneath your feet ...

CHAPTER 6

THE
GATES OF HEAVEN

AND THE KEY OF THE HOUSE OF DAVID WILL I LAY
UPON HIS SHOULDER; SO HE SHALL OPEN, AND NONE
SHALL SHUT

—Isaiah 22:22

The first thing that Christopher noticed about
Heaven was that the Pearly Gates were actually
pearly. Trimmed by a white substance which he
could not identify and hinged with gold, the
famous Gates towered over him, daunting despite
their soft, gleaming appearance.

Fortunately, Christopher was on the right side,
which is to say, he was inside them. How this had
happened, he had no idea, because one moment he'd been standing next to Kaym inside the
Courts of Light, and the next he was standing
here, alone.

He shrugged and in doing so noticed that a pair
of large feathered wings were attached to his back.
He waved them experimentally and was delighted
when he found himself rising from the gold-bricked
street. The sensation of wings was an odd one, but it

was not unpleasant, and he waved them more firmly, until he was nearly one hundred feet from the pavement.

One hundred feet is a long way down, he realized when he made the mistake of looking down. He gulped and almost panicked, but the delightful feeling of flight quickly overwhelmed his fear, and he relaxed, spreading his wings wide to float upon the gentle air currents. He soared toward the Gates, then away from them, building confidence all the while. Once he felt comfortable again, he dared to look down, taking in a bird's-eye view of Heaven. Angel's-eye, he corrected himself, laughing with the sheer joy of it all. Heaven was all right! Best of all, he didn't even have to die in order to get in!

Heaven itself was a large place, a walled city built upon the peak of a massive mountain. It was so big that he could not see its end, but from the position of the sun he guessed that he was near its western edge. The walls were thick, as wide as a football field, and from his vantage point he could see only the single set of gates.

If that's the only gate, I wonder where St. Peter is? he thought. He could see angels moving busily below, but none seemed to notice him or even to look around at the magnificent beauty that surrounded them. I guess you can get used to anything, he thought. How depressing. How long would it take before heavenly perfection itself grew boring? He remembered a trip to Florida he'd taken two years ago. It was a two-week vacation, and by the end of the second week, he'd been quite ready to leave the beaches and the eighty-degree weather for the snowy comforts of home. Then again, why were the angels so busy if there was nothing to do? It was a good question, and he thought about it as he sailed through the cloudless blue sky.

The sun was warm on his face, and he idly considered trying to reach it, like an angelic Icarus. Then he realized that the warmth did not come from the sun but from beneath him, apparently radiating from something toward the center of the city. In fact, despite the bright light all about him, there was actually no sun in the sky at all!

Just as he turned to investigate, a booming voice called out to him. "Who are you? What are you doing here?"

"What?" Forgetting that he was almost a mile above the ground, Christopher whirled around, startled. His wings twisted awkwardly, and he lost control of them. He began to fall, a perilous tumble that quickly turned into an even more dangerous spin.

But strong wings reached out and arrested his fall, holding him fast while he caught his breath. He and his unseen rescuer were suspended in the sky for a long moment together, until his wings began beating again. Sensing the motion, his savior released him from the feathery embrace.

"Thank you," Christopher said in an unsteady voice.

"You are welcome, surely," said the being. It was an angel, but a very strange one, with four sets of brightly colored wings. Set within every feather were several eyes, most of which were focused on him. It was an unpleasant sensation, and when one feathery green eye blinked at him, he shuddered with disgust.

"What were you doing up here, all alone?" it asked.

"I was . . . ah . . . well, I . . ."

"Ah, there you are, little Kristorial! I was searching all over the Temple for you, but you were nowhere to be found. I should have known you'd be trying your wings out and about up here."

Christopher gaped at the newcomer. The interloper was an angel about his size, with a sharp, ferretlike face and an abrupt, impatient manner.

"Your pardon, great Throne, but this one does not know his way about the Eternal City as yet. He was only born yesterday, you see."

The Throne pursed its lips, then made a shrugging motion with its upper set of wings.

"I did not know the King was still creating angels. Since Raduriel fell, I have seen no new creatures in eons."

"Yes, well, we can't have too many angels with those cursed Fallen lurking about outside now, can we?"

While Christopher was glad that he didn't have to try explaining himself, there was something annoying about the newcomer. He wondered if his rescuer shared his feelings, because most of its many eyes appeared somewhat skeptical.

"No, surely not," the Throne agreed. "So this stray is Kristorial, you say? And what is your name, little one?"

"Jeqon, great sir. I have the honor of serving the Lord of Hosts under the command of Ar-Sidriel, first Heaven, seventh Host."

"Sidriel, ah, yes. I know him. An archangel now, is he?"

"Yes, great Throne. Now, if you'll excuse us, we're running late for our duty. If we don't get back to the Gate soon, there'll be Hell to pay!"

The Throne snorted disapprovingly, but his lips twitched. Christopher himself was too startled to laugh.

"Guard your tongue, now, Jeqon. But it was kind of you to look after your fellow. It shall be noted."

Jeqon bowed obsequiously. "You are too kind, gracious sir."

The Throne nodded in farewell. Without further ado, the mighty angel turned away and beat its powerful wings eastward, toward the center of the city.

His new companion grabbed his arm, hard. He was surprised to find that it hurt.

"Ouch!"

"What were you doing up here, fool! You were told to wait at the Gate."

Christopher protested weakly, but he knew he had no real excuse. His new wings were so much fun that he'd almost forgotten why he was in Heaven.

"Curse you!" Jeqon's weasel-like face was red as he vented his fury at Christopher. "Do you know how long I've waited for this moment, fearing all the while I'd be found out for a traitor, knowing they'd cast me beyond the Beyond? Maybe you've had it easy down there, lounging about in the Courts until now, but for the next six hours, you'd better keep your eyes open! You could have ruined everything!"

Christopher blinked several times, surprised to learn that even his accomplice did not know he wasn't an angel. He was surprised, too, at Jeqon's unexpected outburst. Christopher had never thought much about angels before, but even if he had, he never would have imagined that they'd behave like this. There didn't seem to be anything noble, or holy, or beautiful about Jeqon, certainly, and even the great Throne was a little less grand than he would have thought. He felt let down, somehow. If these creatures really were angels, then he didn't see what was so great about them. Well, there was the flying thing, that was pretty cool, of course.

"All right," he said, raising his hand. "Shut up! Just tell me where I'm supposed to go, and what I'm supposed to do."

Jeqon stared at him, taken aback by his sudden change of manner.

"We're scheduled for guard duty tonight at the Twelfth Gate. But I haven't been told what we're supposed to do, other than get the Gate open. I thought that was your job, though I don't see how an angel who can barely fly is going to unseal the Gate. Prince Michael himself sealed it, you know."

"Just leave it to me," Christopher said. Jeqon was really starting to get on his nerves. "Is there anyone else on guard with us?"

"Of course," the angel replied. "There are always twelve guards in every guard detail."

"It figures, I suppose. Twelve gates, twelve guards, one hundred and forty-four ... whatever. Almost makes you think that God is a mathemetician."

"What?"

"Never mind. You wouldn't understand."

Christopher shot a superior look at the traitorous angel. "Have you ever danced on the head of a pin, by the way?"

"What?"

"Oh, forget it, just lead on and show me this gate you've been talking up."

In the three hours it took them to make the long flight to the Twelfth Gate, Christopher learned more about angels than he had in a lifetime of reading. He learned they were indeed immortal but that they could also feel pain and suffering like any other being. They could be petty, greedy, envious, ambitious, and spiteful. In fact, Christopher was prepared to throw Jeqon's name in the hat if anyone was looking for an official Angel of Spite. He learned that there were nine ranks in the angelic hierarchy, ranging from lowly angels like Jeqon at the bottom to the mighty Seraphim at the top. He learned which angels Jeqon liked (there were few enough of these) and the legions he didn't. The leagues passed beneath them as Christopher listened to a long litany of complaints against an endless series of unfamiliar names.

"Ar-Sidriel himself isn't too bad, but, you know, I do think I could do a better job of organizing the guard detail. Of course, Corinthael and Bar-Ezriel are both dumber than rocks, but you always need a few of their sort around in case there's going to be a fight . . ."

Christopher manfully repressed a yawn.

There were a few nuggets of gold amidst the dross of Jeqon's droning, though. Christopher learned that while angels could not be slain, they could be cast out for a time into what Jeqon darkly referred to as beyond the Beyond. It was similar to death, apparently, but it was not the same as mortal death, because the destroyed angels always eventually returned from the darkness. But the experience must be a bad one, because no angel returning from beyond the Beyond ever spoke a word about it.

"How do you get sent Beyond?"

"There's many ways," Jeqon replied. "For some of the great ones, the Thrones and the Cherubim, it is a simple matter of just speaking an angel's true name. I mean, them speaking it, not the other way around. Of course, lesser angels like you and I need a little help, which is why we carry swords."

"Swords?" Christopher looked wildly around his robes and failed to find one. "Shouldn't I have one, then? Where's yours?"

"I left it in the barracks when I went to meet you." Jeqon scowled at him. "I wasn't planning on spending half the afternoon looking for you."

"Yeah, well, sorry about that."

Christopher ignored Jeqon's grumblings and wondered if one of these swords was capable of harming him. It probably would, especially since he now carried the spark of Kaym's angelic power within him. The thought of Kaym made him wonder where the fallen angel ranked in the hierarchy.

"Have you ever heard of an angel named Kaym? Is he one of the great ones?"

Jeqon shook his head. "I've never heard of him, and I know most of the Cherubim and Seraphim, Divine and Fallen. Not personally, you know, but I know who they are, what they look like, all that kind of thing. Now hush, we're getting close to the

Gate. You keep your mouth sealed and let me do all the talking."

"Like I'd have a choice," Christopher muttered to himself. He added self-obsession to his catalog of angelic flaws.

"What?"

"Nothing."

As they began a gentle descent, Christopher began to worry. What if the other angels didn't believe Jeqon? What if the guard detail was split up and he was paired with some other angel than Jeqon? Worst of all, what if he blew the landing and crashed headfirst into the wall?

The other angels of their detail were now in sight, and the sight of swords belted to their sides gave Christopher a new cause for concern. He had no weapon, and he knew Jeqon didn't, either. How were they going to overpower their companions, unless they, too, were secretly in league with the Prince? He was pretty sure they weren't, though, or Jeqon would surely have mentioned it.

Christopher lagged just a little behind Jeqon and watched how the angel spread his wings and flapped gently to slow himself as he came to an easy rest upon his feet. His own landing was a little on the awkward side, but he covered for his clumsiness by pretending to turn his ankle as he came down. The ruse worked, apparently, for aside from a few solicitous questions about his foot, none of the angels seemed suspicious.

He looked up from his faked injury to see a tall, stern-looking angel glaring at him. Not an angel but an Archangel, he corrected himself, noting the silver feathers Jeqon had described to him earlier.

"Who are you, and what are you doing here?" the Archangel asked in a commanding tone of voice. "Jeqon, where is your fellow, Israfel?"

Christopher sighed. It seemed as if Heaven was a giant Swiss clock and he was a little rat scurrying around inside its perfect mechanism, constantly attracting unwanted attention.

"His name is Kristorial, sir, and Israfel is no longer with us," Jeqon answered easily. "There was an attack by the Fallen near the First Gate. Israfel and I happened to be walking nearby at the time . . ."

"An attack, really?" The other angels, most of whom had been ignoring the latecomers, were interested now. "Near the First Gate, you say?"

"What were you doing at the First Gate?" the Archangel demanded, waving the others to silence.

"Did I say the First Gate?" Jeqon coughed. "I'm sorry, I meant the Fifth, of course."

The stern expression on Ar-Sidriel's face vanished, replaced by an interested curiosity.

"The Fifth Gate, then. An attack by the Fallen? What happened?"

"There must have been thirty of them, led by an angel of utter darkness named Belphiel. He wasn't a Great One, but he was big and strong."

"Belphiel . . . hmmm . . . the name sounds familiar," mused Ar-Sidriel. "A Domination once, if my memory serves me correctly."

"Yes, well, it was Belphiel himself who cut Israfel down. A mighty warrior prince, with four arms, each of them bearing a giant blade. I tried to stop him, but he brushed me aside as if I were nothing! It was then that I lost my sword, as it was torn from my grasp after I buried it in the fallen one's leg."

Christopher snickered, and Jeqon looked at him sharply. Christopher only rolled his eyes and tried not to laugh as the traitorous angel continued with his fictitious story of the Fallen raid. A raid that was stopped only by the heroics of the story's teller, who kept his head when all the angels about him were losing theirs and flew to find the great Cherubim, Qamael. And though it was Qamael who finally routed the evil intruders, Jeqon left no doubt about who the real hero had been.

Christopher watched, dumbfounded, as the angels swallowed the ridiculous story, hook, line, and sinker. Only Ar-Sidriel seemed skeptical.

"That's quite a story, Jeqon," he said. He turned to Christopher. "Did you see Lord Qamael battle the fallen one, Kristorial?"

"I saw the Great One, sir," he answered truthfully. "But I did not know his name."

With no reason to doubt his word, the Archangel was reluctantly forced to accept Jeqon's unlikely tale.

"It is not for me to argue with a Great One," Ar-Sidriel pronounced as he ordered his angels to their stations around the Gate. "Jeqon, Kristorial, since you are both weaponless, you will share the first watch with Uzaziel and me in the south tower. I would hear more of today's battle."

And so Christopher was forced to listen to more of Jeqon's extravagant lies. By the time Jeqon finished telling the expanded version of the story, he'd also claimed responsibility for destroying two fallen angels (although he hinted that they might have actually been Archangels), as well as saving Christopher from one of Belphiel's terrible swords.

Christopher soon lost interest in Jeqon's lying fantasies and turned away from the group to look out over the edge of Heaven. The view was spectacular. The rosy golden rays of the fading light spilled out across the clouds beneath him like melted jewels, dripping little splashes of ruby, sapphire, and emerald in an incredible, candy-bright waterfall of light.

As the light at the center of the Eternal City disappeared and the last rays of brilliant color were swept away, the sky darkened but did not fade to black. There was a warm glow circulating through the city that reminded Christopher of a midnight bonfire at summer camp, a soft radiance that engulfed Heaven in a peaceful haze. He did not like it, though. It was smothering, like a wool blanket in summer. It made him feel trapped and uneasy, as if the glow might somehow sense that he did not belong here.

Beyond the walls was only the cold comfort of the dark. It was soothing to look out on a place that the eerie warmth did not touch, could not touch. He could almost feel the army of invisible warriors waiting for him, the legions sworn to a light that did not glow but shined gloriously instead. He grinned suddenly, thinking of the devastation they would wreak upon the sleeping city. The night sky would be lit by flames, lovely red and yellow flames. Kaym's power was growing inside him, swelling, urging him to action. Yes, he thought, oh yes. It was time to act.

Looking over his shoulder, he saw that Ar-Sidriel was arguing with Uzaziel, a stolid, unimaginative

angel, over one of Jeqon's less convincing embell-
ishments. At first, he was not sure how he could
effect his escape, until one of his old Dungeons and
Dragons adventures came to mind.

What was that character's name? Loki, he remembered, Loki the light-fingered. The thief had found
himself trapped in a seedy establishment with two
of the king's guardsmen. Guardsmen who didn't
know that the slight figure in the pale blue cloak
was the very one they sought for the theft of the
queen's necklace. Their ignorance had cost them
dear.

The thief walked past them, idly juggling a brace
of balls that appeared in his left hand as if by magic.
A third ball was added, and a fourth, and soon he
was passing five balls back and forth between his
two hands.

"A jongleur!" the guardsmen cried out with
delight, and after buying him a drink, they were
soon challenging him to juggle more difficult
objects. An apple, and then three. A plate, and then
four. It wasn't long before one of the guards dared
him to juggle something more dangerous, something with a blade.

Christopher stared triumphantly into the surprised eyes of the Archangel, who was undoubtedly
shocked to find himself choking on his own sword.
The gray eyes faded, there was a loud hissing
sound, and the solid forms of Ar-Sidriel and Uzaziel
grew transparent and dispersed in a smoky cloud of
green-and-yellow mist.

"That was easy, now, wasn't it?" He grinned
coldly at Jeqon.

The angel nodded but maintained a cautious distance from Christopher, who was still holding a sword in either hand.

"I was not . . . expecting that," Jeqon confessed, eyeing him warily.

"No, I don't think they were, either. That was kind of the idea, you know."

Jeqon nodded slowly. "Okay, but how will you deal with the others outside? I don't think that trick will work as well on four as it does on two. And I can't juggle."

Christopher laughed as he belted the Archangel's sword to his side.

"You won't have to," he said amiably. "But take this," he added, holding out Uzaziel's sword. "You might need it later."

Christopher was tempted to leap out the open window and fly down to the Gate, but Jeqon convinced him that that would be a bad idea, so instead they walked down the winding stairs of the watchtower together. The angels of the first watch were surprised to see them so early, but far from being suspicious, they were glad for the extra company. Like their captain, they were eager to hear of the action earlier in the day. Jeqon, of course, was eager to tell his tale again. Christopher didn't need to egg him on.

As Jeqon began his story for the fourth time, Christopher slipped away and strolled unnoticed to the sealed doors of the Gate. Like the First Gate, the gleaming doors of the Twelfth were immense, so high that their uppermost limits disappeared unseen into the night sky. He placed a hand beside the gold edges that marked the place where the two doors met and whistled softly to himself as he ran his fingers over their cool, smooth surfaces. The pearly doors were seamless, not, as he had thought before, constructed of stone or timber and covered with enamel. As far as he could tell, they were carved from a single unthinkably gargantuan pearl.

I'd like to see the oyster that made that, he thought, looking back over his shoulder to make sure that no one was looking at him. His wings stroked the air silently, and he flew slowly upward, keeping one hand on the hard metal of the door edges, searching for the mark that sealed them shut.

It wasn't long before he found what felt like a large but simple lock. He could feel the rough edges of the keyhole, which was about the size of his hand. It seemed much too big for the little key tucked away inside his robes. He was surprised when he drew the key out and found that it had magically grown somehow. He inserted it into the lock and breathed a sigh of relief when it slipped snugly inside the hole, as if it had been designed for it.

He twisted it, and the Twelfth Gate of Heaven exploded outward, shattering the darkness with a violent eruption of fire, molten gold, and gleaming shards of pearl. There was a deafening cry from outside, as the waiting legions of fallen angels hailed the long-awaited breach. Trumpets blew, and hordes of winged warriors bearing flaming swords burst suddenly into view as the Prince's captains urged their eager armies forward.

A hand fell upon Christopher's shoulder. He whirled around and saw Jeqon. To his surprise, the traitorous angel suddenly fell back, cringing before his eyes.

"Forgive me, Great One. I did not know you. I did not know you were aught but an angel!" He hurled himself at Christopher's feet, pleading. "Do not hold my disrespectful words against me!"

Christopher blinked, surprised. Great One? Him? He looked down past the groveling angel and saw the Prince's forces sweeping effortlessly past the guards, howling and shrieking as they began their attack. The tiny figures below reminded him of Warhammer miniatures, only this battle was real.

"Don't worry about it, Jeqon. You had a role to play, and so did I. We've done our part." He drew his sword and set it blazing with an effortless flick of his mind. How did he know to do that? He laughed. Did it matter? Not really. "Now, let's have some fun!"

Christopher's smile grew cruel as he spread his wings and hurled himself downward toward the fighting. The power inside him danced and burned, exulting in the feverish glory of battle. He did not know that his snow-white wings had dimmed to an ashy gray color. Nor did he know that when Jeqon had fallen back before his gaze, it was because his green eyes had turned as red as blood.

CHAPTER 7

EVIL COUNSEL

BECAUSE SYRIA, EPHRAIM, AND THE SON OF REMALIAH,
HAVE TAKEN EVIL COUNSEL AGAINST THEE, SAYING, LET
US GO UP AGAINST JUDAH, AND VEX IT, AND LET US MAKE
A BREACH THEREIN FOR US, AND SET A KING IN THE
MIDST OF IT, EVEN THE SON OF TABEAL

—Isaiah 7:5

"You fought well," Kaym told Christopher as he side-stepped a scorched crater in the gold-bricked street. "I saw many falling before your sword."

Christopher nodded, gratified by the praise. Kaym had taken advantage of a brief respite in the battle to survey the front lines and see what kind of force they were facing. Now he sought to find Baal Chanan, the mighty angel-lord to whom he owed allegiance. Exactly where in Heaven they were, Christopher didn't know, although he could tell from the walls still towering over their heads that they weren't very far from the breached Gate.

The fighting had been fierce, like nothing he had ever seen before, wilder and more out of control than any war movie. The Prince's legions had poured into the Eternal City through the shattered

Twelfth Gate like a murderous pack of wolves, but their assault had been blunted by a surprisingly stiff resistance less than a mile inside the breach. Two Great Ones, Cherubim according to what Christopher had heard, had sacrificed themselves in a desperate effort to blunt the force of the attack.

He knew he would never forget the sight of the two mighty angels sweeping down from the midnight sky, blazing with all the furious glory of a thousand angry suns. The shock of their onslaught was unbelievable. It had such force that more than twelve hundred angels had perished in an instant. From his safe vantage point near the broken Gate, Christopher had thought for a moment that the whole attack might fail, as stunned angels reeled and even Archangels began to retreat for the safety of the black void beyond the walls.

But Baal Chanan, the great Lord of Havoc, had stopped the panic with a deafening shout that drowned out the frightened cries of fleeing angels, and revived the Fallen attack by leaping down into the midst of the fray. Surrounded by the shining angels of his bodyguard, Baal Chanan destroyed one Cherub himself even as his guard brought down the other like a pack of wolves killing a moose.

The sacrifice of the Cherubim had not been in vain, though, for the delay had prevented the Prince's army from taking the next series of stately buildings before the Divine reinforcements arrived. A bitter clash ensued before Baal Chanan's trumpeters blew the order to fall back to a defensible position just inside the broken Gate. It was a small foothold, but their most important goal had been achieved; the Fallen were at last again inside the Gates of Heaven.

"Thanks." Christopher warmed to Kaym's praise. "I've played a ton of war games, but I'd never been in a real battle. I'm just glad I didn't blow it."

"Unfortunately, not all of our Host were equally stalwart. Two cohorts of cowards ran away after the Cherubim attacked."

Christopher shrugged. Kaym's voice was full of disgust, but he personally found it hard to blame them. Only his unexpected battle lust had prevented him from freaking out and running away himself.

"I don't know if I would call them cowards. When those big suckers hit, it was like a nuke going off. If I'd been any closer, I think I would have run, too!"

"Nevertheless, they will be held accountable," the fallen angel assured him ominously. Kaym's mood had darkened, and Christopher did not know why. He hadn't seen all that many divine angels during their quick survelliance, although he could have missed seeing a lot of them in the dim glow of Heaven's night, he admitted to himself.

It wasn't just Kaym's attitude that had changed, though. His appearance was harsher, too. He stood taller and was far more massive. The biker jacket was gone, replaced by plated black armor that encased bulging shoulders the size of boulders. His chiseled face seemed broader now, more brutal. His eyes, dark and cynical before, were simply hard now, with a hint of cruelty lurking behind them. The dragon tattoos remained, but they wound their sinuous way down hairless arms now corded with veins and thick with muscle. Only his arrogance and the sense of power that radiated from him were unchanged.

"Didn't they frighten you at all, the Cherubim, I mean?"

"No." There was no bravado in the angel's voice. "They are to be respected but not to be feared. Even the mightiest of the Divine will do nothing more than destroy. They are forbidden to take power from one another, or even from one of us. The King of Heaven brooks no rivals and keeps his angels firmly in check."

"Oh, well, that's good." Christopher frowned, realizing that he'd missed something as a pair of fallen Archangels hurried past them, heading the other way. "What do you mean by taking power?"

Kaym shook his head, then snapped his fingers and caused a scary-looking helmet with a single horn arcing up from the back to appear in his hand. "I don't have the time to explain it to you now." He slammed the helm down over his face. "Just understand that you must stay close to me until I tell you otherwise. The Prince has plans for you, and you cannot be left alone."

Christopher nodded without comprehension as Kaym's trick with the helmet distracted him from pondering the implications of the fallen angel's words. I wonder how he does that, he thought, admiring Kaym's armor as they passed another pile of shattered stone that had once been a building. An outfit like that would make a pretty good Halloween costume for the party at Ground Zero next year.

* * * *

They finally found the Lord of Havoc in a large temple that was only half destroyed, standing amidst white marble scarred with balefire and other signs of angelic battle. He was a giant, red-skinned angel-lord with a brutal, animalistic look to him. Tusks protruded from his lower lip, and his furrowed black brows were thick and hairy. Baal Chanan was angry, punctuating his words with sharp gestures at one of the four commanders surrounding him. It was clear that the situation was dire, and the Fallen foothold was a tenuous one.

"They'll hit us with everything they have as soon as the light comes," the Lord of Havoc said. "Michael isn't as stupid as everyone likes to think. They were expecting us, there's no other explanation for it. Forget the encirclement, we should have been twice as far in by now. No, Im Barku, they were lying in wait for us, I am sure of it!"

"If they were going to attack, they would have done it by now," argued a second commander, who wore an aspect of a crimson-maned lion. Shrouding his rippling, furry shoulders were black, leathery wings. "Maybe they want to parley."

"That's nonsense. They've got us surrounded on four sides, they don't have to hurry. Michael always likes to fight with the light, Verchiel, and that's what he's waiting for."

"I think it's a mistake to assume that we're facing Michael," the lion-angel disagreed. He had an annoying voice. "We don't know that."

"Don't be a fool," Baal Chanan growled. "Who do you think devised this trap? Raphael? Michael isn't the brightest star in the firmament, but he knows how to fight. Unlike some commanders I could name. How could you not see a whole cursed host coming up behind you, Verchiel? The rear guard was your responsibility!"

Lord Verchiel frowned. "That's not fair!" he protested defensively. "When the Cherubim attacked, I saw you needed help. We were nearly overrun by our angels fleeing from the battle, so I brought my cohorts forward. If I hadn't, the front line might have broken."

"Or it might not have," Im Barku muttered to himself.

"No one's questioning your valor, Verchiel," another commander, Belphegor, said viciously. "Just your sense!"

Baal Chanan groaned. It was a sound rich with frustration and long suffering. Christopher almost felt sorry for him.

"What's done is done," the Fallen general pointed out. "Perhaps you were right, Verchiel. It doesn't matter. There will be time for recriminations later. What we have to determine now is what they're going to throw at us and how we're going to handle it."

"Right," said Belphegor. "Great Lord, last night we lost about two thousand, including seventeen Dominations and eight Thrones. Another eight hundred cowards ran away, may the Prince quench their flames with a hand of everlasting ice! That leaves us with just over ten thousand, with only three Seraphim to take on Michael and however many of the Sarim elect to show up."

Baal Chanan glanced around the room and appeared to notice the latecomers for the first time.

"Ah, Kaym. What is your count?"

"I cannot say with surety, Great Lord, but it looked as if there were two full hosts assembled before our lines."

Christopher didn't know how big a host was, but from the reactions on the commanders' faces, it had to be a lot. Either Kaym was lying, or his eyes just weren't as good as Kaym's, and he couldn't imagine why Kaym would lie about this.

"Two hosts!" Verchiel's leonine face blanched to a sickly shade of yellow. "Great Lord, we must retreat! There is only a single host at our back."

"Coward," Christopher heard Belphegor mutter under his breath.

"Retreat? Never. How many times have we tried storming Heaven's gates and failed?" Baal Chanan thumped his armored chest and roared his disapproval. "We're finally inside, and we will not fail. I will not permit it!" He turned again to Belphegor. "So, we are outnumbered, three to one. How many Great Ones are present?"

"Impossible to tell with any certainty, Great Lord."

"Then guess."

Belphegor shrugged. "More than ten, fewer than twenty. There are so many auras out there, it's hard to pick out the stronger ones."

Christopher shook his head, shaken by what he'd heard. He had seen for himself the mighty power of the Cherubim and felt the incredible strength in their majestic wings. If two Cherubim alone had been enough to wipe out a thousand angels, what could ten do? Or twenty! Why, twenty would be more than enough to blast what was left of the Fallen army out of time.

He went over their options in his mind. Retreat was a questionable idea at best. Even if they could force their way through the Divine host that waited outside the Gate behind them, the two hosts at their back were likely to pursue them, and history clearly showed that a retreat turned into a rout quite easily.

Unlike these immortals, Christopher knew that he could die. Unless, of course, death would only lead to . . . whatever death led to. He abandoned that thought. He had no idea what the rules were, and Kaym wouldn't tell him anything. He was already in Heaven, and it was a battlefield. It made you wonder what Hell was like.

He rubbed his eyes, trying to jumpstart his brain, thinking back on the hundreds of battles he'd fought over the same eight-foot piece of green felt. Okay, they'd mostly played with tournament rules, with both sides spending three thousand points per army. But he remembered once when he'd first started playing Warhammer, when Don had teamed him up with another novice and given the two of them six thousand points to his own three thousand.

Despite their two-to-one advantage, Don had beaten them soundly in a defeat as embarrassing as it was complete. Christopher and the other guy, what was his name, Dan, or something like that, had only managed to inflict few casualties, while in return, both of their armies had been wiped out or put to flight. How had Don done it? He tried to picture the setup. Now he had it! Don had focused most of his forces on a single unit on the front, hitting it from three sides and forcing it to run. The fleeing unit had caused the whole allied front to collapse, allowing Don to pick off the allied units one at a time, so that in each little battle within the battle, he had the advantage.

A battle within a battle. The overall numbers didn't come into play if you had the numbers at the point of the attack! He had the answer to Baal Chanan's dilemma! The only problem was, how could the Fallen attack on three sides when they were themselves surrounded?

"We're doomed," Lord Verchiel whispered. His fearsome aspect faded, and in place of the lion-headed monster stood a long-faced Archon, despair written in every line on his face. "There's no hope. We must fight our way back through the Gate, or we will fall here."

Although Baal Chanan and the other commanders refused to submit to Verchiel's pessimistic counsel, they were clearly concerned. Nor did they appear to have any better ideas.

"Ahem ..." Christopher cleared his voice. "Excuse me, but I have an idea, if you want."

The Fallen commanders turned and looked at him as one. It was more than a little intimidating, and Christopher found himself swallowing hard.

"Who is this?" Baal Chanan growled, ignoring Christopher to glare at Kaym.

"He is called Christopher, and he speaks in my name," Kaym answered, unperturbed. "He opened the Gate for us."

Christopher couldn't help grinning as he watched the sharp, disdainful looks quickly fade from the hostile faces surrounding him, replaced by respectful interest and curiosity.

"It was him?" Baal Chanan asked, looking surprised. "I wouldn't have thought he had the power."

"He doesn't," Kaym replied. "But he had the key, you might say."

"Interesting. We must speak more of this later. Unfortunately, we have more pressing needs at the moment." The Fallen general nodded his massive head at Christopher. "Go on, tell me your thoughts."

"Okay, well, when I heard that we were trapped, I got to thinking about how we could get out of this. And I realized that what we need to do is to arrange to attack them from both sides. See, it doesn't matter if they outnumber us, as long as we outnumber them at the point of attack. I read a book on Caesar once, and even though he was almost always outnumbered, he always won."

Baal Chanan looked at Kaym, who shook his head. They didn't understand where he was going, Christopher realized. He spoke faster.

"Okay, well, forget that. The point is, Kaym said we have other legions waiting for us outside the other Gates, right? So what we have to do is to launch a diversionary attack, and at the same time send a force to bust through the lines in front of us. Once they break through, they split off, most of it loops around behind to make a flank attack, and a smaller group runs for the nearest Gate to open it. The flank attack'll get crushed, but it should keep them busy enough to buy the time to get to the Gate and back."

"Are you sure that you can open another gate?" Belphegor sounded as if he was afraid to be hopeful.

Christopher felt inside his robes for the golden key. It was still there.

"Yeah, I can do it." He silently added, *I think*.

Baal Chanan made a strange face that pressed his tusks against his cheeks as he looked up at the devastated dome over their heads.

"I don't like it, but it's worth trying," he growled. "The alternative is to sit and wait for them to run over us, and I like that even less. Kaym, you'll go with him. Take as many fighters as you need. How many do you want for the diversionary attack?"

Christopher nodded eagerly. They didn't need to believe in the plan, they just had to be willing to give it a chance.

"As many as you can spare without leaving your rear undefended. You've got to hit them hard enough to grab their attention. The breakout force shouldn't be very large, just big enough to cut through their lines, and the group going for the Gate should be small enough so they won't notice us breaking away."

"I am forced to wonder how one so young should come to such wisdom, when his elders lack it," Baal Chanan said with a pointed glare at Verchiel, who had resumed his maned aspect.

"Verchiel, you will lead the breakout force, subject to the command of Kaym and this . . . ah, Christopher, I believe was the name." He harrumphed loudly. "I myself will command the diversionary attack. Belphegor and Im Barku, spread the word around your cohorts that we are to attack at once. When the trumpet sounds, we'll hit their left with everything we have except for your cohort, Asmodel. Your job is to keep that other host off our back until we return to our lines."

The Lord of Havoc turned to Christopher and Kaym as his commanders bowed and murmured their assent.

"Now go. Just get him to the Tenth Gate, Kaym, and may the Prince shine His light upon you, for whatever that's worth. By the way, what did you want to see me about?"

"I wanted to put Christopher under your protection," Kaym said.

"Oh, succeed in this, and you'll have it, Christopher. You'll have it and more." Baal Chanan laughed, a deep, unpleasant sound that reminded Christopher of rocks being crushed into gravel. He turned back to his commanders.

As Christopher followed Kaym out into the streets of Heaven, he could hear the Fallen general growling gutturally at his commanders.

"Now tell your accursed cohorts to fall back as soon as they hear the retreat, or I swear I'll eat their souls even if they make it back . . ."

CHAPTER 8

BREATH
OF THE CHERUB

VERE MAGNUM HABERE FRAGILITATUM HOMINUS SECURI-
TATUM DEI.

— Seneca

Christopher ducked under a sweeping two-handed swing, and the angel before him stumbled with the force of the miss. He thrust upward as he moved to the side, and his sword disappeared into the angel's white robes. There was a brief flash of light that blinded him momentarily, and when he opened his eyes, the angel was gone.

"Yaah!" he shouted. He wasn't sure what that meant, but it felt good to shout.

There was a huge explosion behind him and to his left, deafening even at this distance. Christopher winced and looked around as he rubbed at his ear, then realized that they were nearly through the Divine lines. Verchiel was on his right, roaring madly as he dispatched two lesser angels with his claws. Maybe he wasn't such a coward after all. On his left, Kaym had changed aspect

116

again as he grappled mightily with a powerful Archangel.

The Archangel had both hands locked around Kaym's throat and was zapping him with bolt after bolt of furious lightning. But the fallen angel did not clutch at those burning hands with his own; instead, he transformed them into giant crablike pincers. As the stink of ozone filled the air, Kaym's big claws gripped the Archangel by the waist. There was a snap and a flash of yellow, and the Archangel was gone.

Christopher extended a hand, and as the pincers shrank back into their normal appearance, Kaym grabbed it and pulled himself up.

"That's a good trick!" he said.

Kaym grimaced and rubbed his throat. "Good thing, too. He was stronger than I thought. He took me by surprise."

"So use your sword next time, dude," Christopher jeered at him. "Hey, look! We're almost through."

As Kaym advanced on the last two angels standing between them and freedom, Christopher called out to Verchiel.

"Verchiel. Verchiel!"

"Lord Verchiel," the giant winged lion shouted back, with a disdainful look on his face.

"Whatever." Maybe Verchiel wasn't a coward, but he was still a dim-witted jerk. "Look, we're through. Now circle behind them and keep them busy while we make a run for the Gate."

"So Baal Chanan has commanded me. I obey his will."

Yeah, yeah, Christopher thought. Just so you do it.

But before he opened his mouth to yell back at Verchiel, the fallen Archon turned and leaped back into the fray, rending one angel with his claws as another perished before the shock of his bellowing roar.

"Okay, dudes, let's rock!" Christopher shouted to the remnants of his strike force as the second angel fell to Kaym's flaming sword. Fourteen of the warriors chosen by Kaym had fallen already, and there were only six left to accompany them to the Tenth Gate. He just hoped that six would be enough.

They ran as if Lord Michael himself were at their heels, pounding over the streets of gold like terrified horses. Beside him, Kaym blurred and shifted, transforming into the shape of a fleet-footed gazelle.

"Change yourself!" he shouted at Christopher. "We must run faster!"

"I can't! I don't know how!"

"You don't need to. Just feel the force of the power within you. Let it flow into you as you run. It will come to you if you stop fighting it!"

Christopher closed his eyes, picturing a horse in his mind, and tried to feel the spark inside him. It was there, warm and pulsing, and he could sense that it was trying to expand. As his legs churned mechanically, he forced himself to relax, to give in to the fire's inviting heat. At first, it was uncomfortable, but it was not unbearable. It was kind of like jumping into a hot whirlpool after rolling in the snow. His skin burned at first, then itched, and soon the sensation was gone, replaced by a sense of ecstatic well-being.

"You did it!" Kaym shouted at him, and Christopher whinnied with triumph. He was a horse! How cool was that?

He looked down and saw flashing white hooves galloping over the hard metal of the streets, his unshod hooves beating out a fast tat-tat-tat-tat rhythm as they rushed toward the Gate.

Two angels stepped out to bar their way, but despite their drawn swords, neither Kaym nor Christopher hesitated for a moment. They charged recklessly toward the angels, and at the last moment, Christopher unthinkingly lowered his head.

There was a brief shock that staggered him, and the angel was gone, pierced through the heart by the sharp, twisted horn that had appeared on top of his head.

"A unicorn!" Kaym laughed savagely, clearly amused. He had transformed back into his warrior aspect and run the other angel through with his sword. "Well done!"

The fallen angel suddenly unfurled a pair of giant black wings and rose into the air.

"We should be far enough from the fighting that we can fly without attracting too much attention now. Are you up to it?"

"Of course!"

Although the first transformation was tough, the second was much easier, and the pain and itching disappeared almost immediately. Flanked by three angels on either side, Christopher beat his wings furiously, hard on Kaym's heels, determined to reach the Gate.

They were almost there when a hailstorm erupted without warning out of the clear blue sky. Bewildered, Christopher vainly tried to shield his head with his hands. It was a futile effort, though, as the pebble-sized chunks of ice smashed painfully into his arms and body.

"What's going on?" he shouted to Kaym.

"I don't know! I've never seen it storm like this in Heaven!"

Christopher grimaced. He'd been pelted by hail once before when he was a kid, and it wasn't fun. Anything that could dent a car wasn't something he wanted to hit his head. At least Kaym had a helmet.

"Isn't that big thing up ahead the North Wall?"

"Just keep flying. It isn't far now."

But even as Kaym spoke, the hail stopped, and a bolt of lightning arced through the sky, incinerating an angel behind him. The concussion of the following thunder sent a massive shockwave through the air that sent Christopher tumbling, hurtling wildly toward the ground.

"That didn't come from above," one of the angels shouted at him as he regained control of his wings.

"It's behind us!" another screamed in fear.

"Everyone, down to the ground!" Kaym commanded. "We can't fight a Cherub in the air."

Christopher was already nearly on the ground, having pulled out of his crazy tumble barely twenty feet above the shining streets of gold. This probably saved him, because no sooner had the little band of fallen angels begun diving for safety than a giant gust of wind came, catching the two highest-flying angels and sending them somersaulting madly through the sky. In moments, they were out of sight, their outspread wings helpless before the Great One's mighty breath.

"We have to find cover!" Kaym yelled as his feet touched Heaven. "Run for that building over there."

Christopher saw where the angel was pointing. Not a thousand yards away was a large building designed in the shape of a lion's head. A broad series of marble steps led up to an arced double door carved out of dark-grained wood. It was surrounded with a faint golden glow that Christopher didn't like, but there was no time to argue. Christopher ran. At his heels were Kaym and the three remaining angels of their guard.

They didn't make it. They were just reaching the steps when Kaym called out to them.

"Stop! It's no good. We'll have to fight here."

Christopher was tempted to keep running, but he fought down the cowardly urge and turned to join the others.

What he saw nearly caused him to drop his sword in awe. The Cherub was a gargantuan being, much bigger than the two he'd seen the night before. It was a glorious six-winged creature with a wingspan as long as a football field. It floated calmly before them, high in the air, all six wings spread out around its peaceful face. The Cherub didn't appear to be angry, it only looked a little bit sad, as if it regretted what it was about to do.

"Your presence here is forbidden," it stated in a melodious voice. "The Lord Most High has named you exile and banned you from the Gates of Heaven."

"Oh, shut up, Gonael." Christopher was surprised at the familiarity in Kaym's voice. "You know we weren't exiled, we left of our own accord."

"You know, we were just heading for the Gate, actually," Christopher added hopefully. "So if you don't mind, we'll just be on our way."

"You shall not depart by the Gate," said Gonael, unamused. "Release your power, and I shall carry you Beyond on the wind of my breath."

"And if we don't?" asked one of the angels.

"Then I shall send you beyond the Beyond, cast out to join your brethren in the Outer Darkness."

One of the angels made a move as if to step forward, and Kaym whispered to him behind clenched teeth.

"Don't do it," he threatened. "Or I'll send you there myself!"

He raised both hands and made a downward sweeping arc with his arms.

"Grab my hand!" he urged Christopher under his breath.

Christopher took it, and gasped as he felt Kaym draining energy away from him. His vision went red and faded momentarily, and when he recovered he was surprised to find himself still standing on his feet.

"Cursed one! I name you demon, destroyer, denied!" Christopher's head was still spinning, but he understood that the Cherub was furious at Kaym for whatever he'd just done. Come to think of it, he wasn't too sure that he liked it, either, as he tried to find his balance.

"Try me, Gonael," Kaym challenged the Great One. "I am stronger than you think."

The furious Cherub formed its lips into a circle. It blew softly and effortlessly, and though its cheeks did not even bulge, the wind that issued forth from its mouth would have dwarfed even the deadliest hurricane. Howling and shrieking, the gale rushed down upon them, only to be deflected by the invisible shield of Kaym's will.

For a long while, the strange struggle persisted, Gonael blowing steadily and Kaym struggling to stand before its mighty breath. There was a moment when the shield weakened, and Christopher felt a warmly scented breeze ruffle his hair, but Kaym fought back, drawing even deeper upon his own reserves and those of the spirits surrounding him. The breeze grew softer and finally disappeared.

Christopher felt weak and staggered again as the draining suddenly stopped, and the angel on the other side of Kaym collapsed, then disappeared with a bang. As his vision cleared, he looked up and saw a stunned surprise on Gonael's face. Surprise quickly turned to anger, and the middle pair of its wings transformed into muscular arms, each bearing a giant sword.

"The wicked shall not stand before the righteous. Holy, holy, holy, is the Lord God Almighty!"

As the Cherub's words thundered through the sky, it furled its wings and dropped toward them like a stone, both arms upraised to strike.

As Christopher fumbled for his sword, Kaym and the two remaining angels leaped into the air to meet the onrushing giant. Kaym blocked one huge blade with his own peculiar sword, but the second slashed right through the other two Fallen, and they disappeared from Heaven with a wailing cry.

Finally managing to draw his blade, Christopher grimly spread his wings and jumped skyward. He swung his sword with all his might, using both hands, and he groaned with dismay as it bounced right off one white-feathered wing. I'd sure hate to sleep on a feather pillow stuffed with those, he thought ironically as he struck again, but once more the blade bounced away with no effect.

Gonael was now using both swords in an attempt to overpower Kaym, who was being forced back toward the ground by the righteous fury of its assault. The fallen angel was desperately bobbing and weaving in the air, first ducking under one mighty swing, then deflecting another that imperiled his unarmored head.

"Do something!" he shouted at Christopher.

"Like what?"

Lacking any better ideas, he aimed for Gonael's delicate face. He turned a backward somersault in midair, then hurled himself upward with his blade pointed like a spear, coming up from below the Cherub. But as he sped toward his target, a giant wing smashed into his side, a powerful buffet that took his breath away and drove him to the ground.

He managed to spread his wings enough to slow his fall and cushion what might have otherwise been a messy landing on the marble steps, but his weapon was gone. Frantic, he scrabbled on his hands and knees across the hard stone, trying to find his sword. It was nowhere to be found.

Dismayed, he looked up just in time to see Gonael strike Kaym, the huge blade catching one black-armored shoulder and knocking him off balance. Kaym's helmet flew off, and he tumbled backward in a spinning arc that ended with a loud thud at the top of the steps, only a few cubits behind Christopher.

Christopher had no time to see if Kaym was still there, for the Cherub had turned around and was now looking down at him. Its face was cold with anger as it raised one sword and pronounced a judgment upon him.

"See, the storm of the Lord will burst out in wrath, a whirlwind swirling down on the heads of the wicked. The anger of the Lord will not turn back!"

"Yeah, well, your stupid whirlwind wasn't so bad after all, was it?" Christopher sneered in hopeless defiance. Just words, but that was all he had left.

Or was it? He fumbled inside his robes for the little key. It wasn't much of a weapon, but even a Great One might not like getting hit in the eye with it. As the mighty being roared and swooped down upon him, he cocked his arm and threw.

Much to his surprise, as it left his hand, the key was transformed into a shining golden spear. It flew straight and true, piercing the onrushing Cherub directly in its right eye. For a split second, Gonael seemed to hang in the air with its wings outspread, motionless, and Christopher thought he saw a shocked expression on the smooth, androgynous face. Then there was a thunderclap, and the mighty being dissolved in a rosy-gold mist. A faint clink sounded a moment later, as the key struck the ground close to the foot of the steps, no longer a spear, just a simple key again.

Christopher looked up at the empty sky and whistled. One moment, the huge angel was there, and the next, it was gone. Just like that.

"Impressive," Kaym said from behind him. "Now, what in the name of Dante's Seven Hells was that?"

Christopher turned around and saw Kaym slowly getting up off the hard marble steps. He was very bruised and battered, and most of the spikes jutting out from his black armor were broken off, but he was alive.

"Ah, it was the key." Christopher glanced around the ground. "That is, I thought it was a key . . . I mean, it is, but I guess it's a spear, too, of sorts. Who knew?"

"You didn't know it was a spear? How did you know to throw it, then?"

"I didn't."

Kaym looked puzzled. "So why did you throw it?"

"I didn't have anything else to throw," Christopher answered simply. "Good thing there wasn't a rock handy."

He left Kaym standing there, stunned, as he walked forward and stooped to pick up the thing that had saved them. Lying there on the palm of his hand, it looked just the same as before, a little golden key much like any other, except for the five runes scratched upon it. He offered it to Kaym, who still looked dismayed.

"I don't see anything special about it, except for these runes. What do you make of it?"

Kaym took it in his fingers, carefully. There was a hissing sound, and Kaym dropped it, cursing. Christopher wouldn't have thought it possible, but his white face had gone even paler than before.

"Hey, what's the matter?"

"It burns!" Kaym was shaking his hand and glaring furiously at the key. "Dark Angel of the Abyss, I should have looked at it more closely first!"

The fallen angel knelt down and examined the little key, keeping his face a careful distance away. His caution made Christopher laugh at him.

"So, what does it say?"

"I . . . I can't really tell," Kaym said. "But I think you'd better take it now. I don't think I want to touch it, and Baal Chanan's forces will be hard pressed after all this time. These delays have cost us."

Kaym rubbed a hand over his scratched and beaten face, and when he drew it away, the marks were gone. He looked up at Christopher, and as he smiled, the broken spikes of his battered armor magically faded away while the armor was transformed into a spotless white robe. By the time he drew himself up, his black wings were also white, soft and innocent as the feathers of a dove.

"I find the call of battle as glorious as any other demon, but there are times when deception is the better part of valor." Kaym grinned, and a halo appeared above his head. "Hallelujah! Give me a harp, and I'll be ready!"

"Demon?" Christopher was an atheist, or at least he had been until yesterday, but he still didn't like the sound of that. "I thought you were an angel."

"Well, I am, but you heard what he called us, didn't you? Angel, demon, devil, it's all the same to me. They can call us what they like, it's just a name after all. Now, let's get that thrice-cursed Gate open before it's too late!"

Christopher mused thoughtfully as he followed Kaym into the air. Sticks and stones may break my bones, but names will never hurt me, he reminded himself. Still, he was troubled all the same by Kaym's careless words.

CHAPTER 9

THAT WHICH IS DONE

THE THING THAT HATH BEEN, IT IS THAT WHICH SHALL BE; AND THAT WHICH IS DONE IS THAT WHICH SHALL BE DONE: AND THERE IS NO NEW THING UNDER THE SUN.
—Ecclesiastes 1:9

The band was still playing and the people were still singing when a movement to her side caught Jami's attention. She looked over and saw that Paulus had stopped clapping his hands and was craning his handsome head around as if he were looking for something. He apparently found it, because he abruptly stopped searching and indicated that she and Holli should follow him as he made his way toward the exit.

As Mariel closed the door to the gymnasium softly behind them, Jami turned right and followed Holli up the stairs that led to the parking lot behind the school. The sight of the dark sky made her nervous, and she was reluctant to go outside again, but when her sister walked calmly out the big glass door, Jami took a deep breath and followed her. Surely there was nothing waiting for them outside, she told herself. Nothing worse than a little cold weather.

But what she saw when she stepped outside made her freeze with alarm. There were three strange beings greeting Paulus in the parking lot, and while two of the new angels looked pretty much like him, dressed in white robes with big white wings and all, the third angel was really different. He must be a good guy if Paulus knew him, Jami thought, but he was almost as scary as the shadow monsters.

His body was shaped like a man's, but his head was that of a male lion with a long yellow mane. Instead of two wings, he had four, and a second pair of arms as well. In his lower hands, he held a pair of identical swords with deadly looking curved blades. He was massive, more than a foot taller than Paulus, and the guardian seemed to defer to him. Like the others, he wore white robes, but they cast a bright glow that was reflected against the snow.

"What . . . who's that?" she whispered to Aliel. Her voice must have quavered, because Holli's guardian reached over and stroked her hair reassuringly.

"I don't know, but don't worry. He's a Domination, a very high-ranking spirit, so whatever's going on here must be very important. Let's listen to what they're saying."

"Yes, Dominus." Paulus was nodding in agreement with whatever the Domination was saying. "That is in accord with what we witnessed here tonight. Mariel, here, is the boy's guardian, and she cannot sense him anywhere. Do you know where they might have taken him?"

"Or why?" Mariel's worried voice cut in.

Jami found it hard to understand the Domination's reply. His words were clear, but his voice was deep, and it rumbled as if it were coming from a deep cavern far beneath the earth.

"The question is not where, but when. And the answer to that is apparent. There can only be one reason for the Fallen to require the services of such a one, and that is to unmake the events of the beginning."

"The beginning?" Aliel echoed.

"The beginning of this age." The Domination made a growling sound deep in his throat. "The time in which Lucifer fell and sought to overthrow our Lord. The time of the first war in Heaven."

"Is that possible?" Paulus asked skeptically, while Mariel only looked confused.

"The first war?" she asked incredulously.

"How can this be?" Aliel looked a little frightened.

Jami could see that the guardians were shocked and maybe even scared by what the Domination was telling them. She had no idea what he was talking about, but seeing that the angels were frightened struck terror in her heart.

"It's not possible," Paulus repeated, as if trying to convince himself.

"All things are possible for those who serve the Lord," rumbled the Domination. "And much is possible even for those who don't."

"Excuse me, sir." Holli stepped forward to address the awesome being. "But are you saying that the Devil, like, kidnapped my brother and took him to another time?"

The Domination stared at her sister, his big yellow eyes just like a cat. With a start, Jami realized he was looking at her twin with pity.

"Not the one you name the Devil, but one of his servants, yes. That is so."

"Why?"

"Because your brother has been invested with a mighty power that dwarfs that of all the angels assembled here before you." Jami winced as the big angel gestured with a sword that came perilously close to poking Holli. "One that is capable of conquering not only time but death itself. The one you name the Devil seeks to use this power through your brother, since he cannot call on it himself."

"You think Chris has some kind of power?" Jami broke in. Of all the strange things she'd heard and seen tonight, this was the hardest to swallow.

"He does indeed."

"Why Christopher?" Holli asked.

Now, that was a good question, Jami thought. Of all the people in the world, her brother struck her as one of the worst possible people to be given any sort of power. It was just asking for trouble, even if you were God or whoever. This had to be some kind of cosmic joke, assuming it wasn't just a bad, bad dream. Chris was hard enough to take already, she couldn't imagine what he'd be like with godlike powers at his disposal. This wasn't a joke, it was a nightmare!

"I cannot say," the Domination answered. "But tell me this. Would your brother willingly serve the Shadow?"

"No, never," Holli protested vehemently.

But Jami wasn't so sure. She shook her head and

moved a little closer to the Domination, wanting to see into those unearthly yellow eyes, wondering what it wanted to hear. Then she decided to tell the truth.

"I don't know what you mean by that," she said, while keeping a wary eye on the angel's swords. "I don't believe in evil, and Chris doesn't, either. I know he wouldn't do anything just to hurt people, though, he's not like that."

"One who does not believe in evil is likely to end by serving it," Mariel said with helpless bitterness.

The Domination nodded his beastly head. "Oh, yes," he said. "There is little that serves our adversary as well as the belief that he does not exist. And whether he believes or not, the dark ones will make him promises he cannot resist. Whether they keep their promises, now, that is a different question."

"Dominus, what do we do?" asked Aliel.

"We have to go back and find him!" cried Mariel, as Holli nodded in agreement.

"Wait!" the Domination commanded. "One comes."

He pointed, and they turned around to see the curly-haired preacher mounting the stairs, followed by a giant angel whose shirtless chest was covered with scars. The preacher was still carrying his drumsticks, and the sweat dripping down from his forehead started to freeze the moment he stepped outside, but even though he didn't have a coat, he didn't seem to care. A strange aura of flames appeared to dance about his head, and Jami saw his intense eyes blazed with excitement as soon as he saw her standing there. Jami had the odd feeling that he was looking for her.

To her surprise, the angels treated the preacher with great deference, although he didn't seem to see them, and the great Domination actually bowed as the man drew near. The huge angel behind the preacher returned the bow but did not speak, and the man seemed unaware of his presence as well.

"Wait," said the preacher. "I saw you leave. I don't know who you are, or why you were here, but I just had this feeling that I should pray for you. Would you mind?"

Jami looked at Holli, feeling uncomfortable and hoping her twin would sense that. But Holli glanced over at Aliel, who nodded enthusiastically.

"No, um, it's okay with me," Holli told the preacher.

"It can't hurt, I guess," Jami sighed reluctantly. "Go ahead."

Jami closed her eyes and felt a hand on her head. It was warm and sweaty, and she forced herself not to shrink away from the man's clammy touch.

"Lord, empower these young women to hear Your voice, and keep them in Your will to do Your mighty work." He spoke quickly, but his voice was firm. "We thank You for the victory You blessed us with tonight, and for the eternal victory You won for us on the cross."

As he prayed, his voice grew stronger, and Jami felt as if she were falling under a strange kind of spell. "Lord, I ask that You protect them from all evil as they go forth to serve You, in Jesus's name. Let Your will be done, Lord, in Jesus's mighty name. Amen."

"Amen," the angels echoed him.

Jami opened her eyes as the preacher withdrew

his sweaty hands. She still felt uneasy, but she felt strangely comforted by this man's crazy words, and all these crazy people in their crazy church-that-was-a-school. They were somehow in tune with this bizarre world of good and evil that had suddenly forced its way into her life, while she felt completely lost. They were like a lifeline, connecting the real world to this strange new one, and even though she didn't like them, she was glad that they were here all the same.

"Thank you," she told him. And to her surprise, she realized that she meant it.

"You just hang in there," the preacher told her. "And trust God to do the rest."

"Aliel, why did that man have flames around his head?" Holli asked suddenly, as she watched the door close behind the man as he returned to his people.

Her guardian raised her eyebrows and looked at the Domination before answering.

"The child felt the approaching Mordrim as well," Paulus added.

The Domination nodded and studied Holli for a moment before answering her.

"He carries a gift that is also a burden, child. The Spirit has descended upon him, and the flames you saw are the flames of Pentecost, ever burning and ever bright."

"Pentecost?" Holli asked. "That sounds familiar."

It did? Not to Jami. Must be a church thing, she concluded, and made a mental note to ask Holli about it later.

"Pentecost." The Domination nodded, but he

refused to explain any further. "Now, you must not tarry, you must leave here at once."

"Aren't you coming with us?" Jami asked. "I mean, how are we supposed to do anything?"

"I cannot." The massive head shook sadly from side to side. "Nor may the others. It is forbidden."

"No, we can't let them go alone!" Paulus angrily protested.

"But they're just children!" Aliel argued.

But the Domination would not be swayed, despite their pleas. "The Lord will provide," he said, and his words were final. He reached into his glowing robes and drew out a scroll. Two scrolls. He handed one to Holli and gave the other to Jami.

"Eat this," he commanded.

Jami flexed the scroll in her hands. It felt like paper, only it didn't crease when she folded it over. She glanced at Holli, who shrugged helplessly.

"You want me to eat this?" she asked the Domination, incredulous. "It's not even edible!"

"Here, I'll try it," Holli said quickly.

The scroll crackled as Holli crammed it into her mouth. Then she crinkled her eyes and made a face, as if it tasted bitter. She swallowed once, then looked surprised. More chewing was followed by two more swallows, and she was done.

"So, how was it?" Jami asked. It didn't look all that bad, but it didn't look too good, either.

"Actually, it wasn't that bad." Holli grinned. "It was kind of nasty at first, then it was really, like, sweet. It's chewy, though. Kind of like taffy or something."

"Like taffy, right."

Jami eyed the scroll with distaste, then folded it

twice and popped it in her mouth. The initial taste was unpleasant, but not as awful as she'd expected. She swallowed and then blinked with surprise as a rich honey flavor filled her mouth. It warmed her throat and stomach as she swallowed again, and to her surprise, she found herself wanting more.

"That was pretty good," she started to say, but her tongue felt thick. Her vision began to swim, and she felt as if the night sky were dropping toward her. She took a faltering step toward the angels and reached out to try to keep her balance, but her hand grasped at nothing as she was swept away in an overpowering tide of vertigo.

Her face still screwed up from the unpleasant aftertaste of the bittersweet scroll, Holli looked uncertainly at the rocky landscape surrounding her. She was standing on top of a windswept hill, where the grass grew in sparse patches of brown separating large areas of broken rocks and gravel. The sky was a weird shade of yellow interspersed with wide orange stripes, not the golden yellow you might see shooting through the clouds when the sun is setting but the bright yellow that you see on bananas or tie-dyed T-shirts.

There was a mountain range in the distance, a big one from the looks of it, with a rocky majesty that was less purple than blue. Also blue, although a blue both brighter and deeper than the far-off mountains, were the feathery wings and luxurious mane of the large golden lion sitting calmly in front of her.

Compared with the panic of their recent nightmarish run to the church, Holli discovered that standing right next to a winged lion was far less alarming than she would have ever imagined. When the lion greeted her politely, she was pleased to discover that not only did she not have a heart attack, but she actually managed to remember her manners as well.

"I am fine, thank you very much," she replied politely, determined to act calm. "And how are you?"

"I've been better. How would you like it if people rode on your back and pulled at your mane?" The lion's big black eyes narrowed suspiciously. "Weren't there supposed to be two of you?"

Holli nodded and looked around for any sign of her sister, but the rocky ground offered no clues.

"Um, yeah, I guess so. You haven't seen my sister?"

"Does she look like you?"

"Yeah, she does." Holli made a modest gesture. "We're twins." It always embarrassed her to have to tell people. It was too much like bragging.

"Twins, hmmm?" The lion yawned, exposing large white fangs and a very blue tongue. "No, haven't seen her. I haven't seen anyone, to tell you the truth, since Prince Gabriel sent me here."

Holli felt a little annoyed that the lion had dismissed her twin-ness so offhandedly. But perhaps he was just jealous. Then his words struck her. "Prince Gabriel . . . is that, like, Gabriel the angel?"

"Do you know any other Gabriel? I don't. Of course I mean the angel. The one who's always messing about in mortal affairs. It's his job, so I can't say I blame him, but I do think he enjoys it more than he should. But yes, he's an angel, I'm an angel, we're all angels, you know, just doing our angel business."

The lion cleared his throat and glanced guiltily around the hilltop.

"What I mean to say is, of course, the Lord's business, which is really what angel business is, after all."

Holli nodded slowly, finding it difficult to follow the lion's train of thought.

"So, you're an angel, too!" she concluded triumphantly.

"Of course I am," he replied.

"You don't look like Paulus or Mariel. Or Aliel, she's my angel. They look like people, only they're, like, totally beautiful. And they've got wings. Mariel's pretty, and she's got really great hair, but I think I like Aliel better. She's even prettier."

The lion scratched himself absently with a hind leg. He didn't appear to be very interested in her opinions. But perhaps he was, because his next statement led Holli to suspect that he might be just a little bit vain.

"Are you saying I'm not beautiful?"

"Oh, no, not at all." Holli narrowed her eyes and took a critical look. "I mean, yes, you're very beautiful. Your mane is a very nice shade of blue, and it goes very well with your yellow, um, fur, I guess. But it's different, you know?"

"Well, that's really just a matter of perspective, isn't it?"

The lion reared back on his hind legs and was transformed into a tall, handsome youth with black hair streaked with dark blue highlights. His eyes were blue now, precisely the color that his mane had been. He spread his hands and bowed to her, a courtly gesture that made Holli laugh self-consciously.

"Please, do forgive my manners. Taking the form of a beast always has the worst effect on me. I am the Archon Khasaratjofee, at your service."

He was very good-looking, and his attention made Holli blush.

"I'm Holli, Holli Lewis. It's nice to meet you, Khasar . . . Khaserott—"

"Maybe you'd just better call me Khasar," he suggested as she struggled with his name. "It's not a very common name, and if there happen to be more than one of us around, well, I'll just assume you're talking to me. How does that sound, Holli-Holli Lewis?"

"No, silly." Holli laughed at him. "My name is Holli, not Holli-Holli."

The Archon nodded gravely.

"I was wondering about that. I mean, a name like that sort of brings a picture to mind, you know? Not a lot of imagination, if you see what I'm getting at. Repetition, redundancy, and, well, alliteration just isn't what it used to be."

Holli stared at him blankly. She had no idea what he was saying.

Khasar sighed.

"You don't see what I'm getting at?" He nodded mournfully as she shook her head. "People usually don't. I say one thing, and somebody hears something altogether different. That's just how I got stuck with this job. It's not like all the angels in the host were exactly lining up volunteering to carry around a pair of chubby little daughters of Lilith."

"I'm not in the least bit chubby!" She glared at Khasar.

"It's just an expression, you know."

"Oh, is it?" Holli thought for a moment. "Well, why did you call me a daughter of Lilith, then? What's that supposed to mean?"

"That you're a human." Khasar wrinkled his nose. "You are, aren't you? You see, Lilith was the first woman, and so that would make you her daughter, by extension. It's another expression, you see?"

Holli rolled her eyes. "Lilith wasn't the first woman, dummy. That was Eve. You know, Adam's wife?"

Khasar shook his handsome head and smiled. His teeth were very white, and Holli wondered if he used a special toothpaste.

"No, Lilith was the first mortal woman. Trust me on this one. And I don't know who this Adam character is, but I don't think Lilith was ever anyone's wife. She wasn't exactly the marrying kind, as I remember. A most unpleasant woman."

He seemed pretty sure of himself. Holli looked up at the sky. For the first time, she wondered if the yellow sky wasn't just some new kind of pollution or something, and if perhaps she wasn't on Earth after all.

"Khasar, can I ask you a question?"

"Sure, you can ask. But I won't promise that I'll answer it."

Holli stamped her foot. "Be serious for just a second, will you? I was just wondering if this place was, like, Oz or something."

"No, it's not Oz. What an odd name!" He gestured about the hilltop. "Behold Ahura Azdha, as it is called by the humans who live here, but among the Host it's usually called Rahab, after the old name of the great city. Rahab the wicked."

"Now I know how Dorothy felt." She looked back at Khasar, startled. "Did you just say 'the wicked'?"

"Yes."

"Why is it called that?"

The Archon yawned again. Even in his human form, he reminded Holli of a big cat.

"Because this is a very, very bad place, my dear."

CHAPTER 10

CIRCLE OF FIRE

MY SOUL IS AMONG LIONS: AND I LIE EVEN AMONG THEM
THAT ARE SET ON FIRE, EVEN THE SONS OF MEN, WHOSE
TEETH ARE SPEARS AND ARROWS, AND THEIR TONGUE A
SHARP SWORD.

—Psalms 57:4

Heaven belonged to the Dawn Prince. It was a bitter truth to accept, but Michael forced himself to acknowledge it. Although there were fierce pockets of Divine resistance in many parts of the Eternal City, its golden streets were now patrolled by the legions of the Fallen. The shattered remnants of the heavenly hosts now cowered behind the walls of the Arx Dei, the Fortress of Heaven's King that was their only protection against the Prince's legions. The great Archangel thumbed the hilt of his sword angrily, for far too many angels had broken faith with the Almighty and fearfully submitted to the victorious Dawn Prince. Lucifer's victory was close to complete. Or so it seemed.

As to the Lord Most High, there was still no sign. He had not bestirred Himself from His great white throne, and His absence from the battle had done as much as any Fallen feat of arms to contribute to the defeat of the Divine. Though Michael did not doubt that the Almighty would triumph at the moment of His choosing, faltering faith and despair had weakened the will of many lesser angels.

Michael had seen many terrible things over the past few days, but the worst by far was seeing an angel's faith die before his eyes. Oh, that the faithless would only choose destruction and the void instead of blasphemous rebellion against the Highest! One day, he knew, the treacherous ones would regret their damnable decision, but then it would be too late. Michael's heart ached, because he knew that he himself must bear some of the blame.

It was his foolish counterattack that had cost him, and them, so dearly. He thought he had Baal Chanan exactly where he wanted him, and he might even have been right. At first light, Baal Chanan had hurled the Fallen army at his lines in what he thought was an attack of desperation. The attack had easily been beaten back, and although Gabriel had counseled caution, Michael overruled him and led the counterattack himself. Baal Chanan was almost within reach when word came of a surprise assault on his flank by the Archon Verchiel.

Michael closed his eyes and growled deep within his throat. He hadn't thought much about the second attack and was content to send a strong force of Archangels over to contain it. But by the time Verchiel had been driven off and the host was in good order for a final assault on Baal Chanan's lines, a messenger arrived with reports of another Fallen legion entering Heaven through the Tenth Gate.

With his greater numbers, there still shouldn't

have been a problem. Michael remembered a faint feeling of consternation but no great sense of alarm. Undismayed, he'd ordered Jehuel, whose Divine host was positioned outside the walls, to attack Baal Chanan at once and turned his own forces toward the Tenth Gate to meet this latest threat. He knew Jehuel's host was more than large enough to finish off Baal Chanan's decimated forces, and he was eager, perhaps too eager, to settle things with Harab Serap, the leader of the second rebel legion, who had recklessly styled himself the Lord of Destruction.

But he'd forgotten one thing. Jehuel was a jealous and resentful angel. When the Almighty defeated Leviathan, the great king of Chaos, He had done so with Jehuel at His side. Afterward, Jehuel had bound the monster in the bowels of a subterranean prison, a dangerous and thankless task. But when Lucifer fell and began his prideful rebellion, the Lord of Hosts had chosen him, Michael, and not Jehuel, to marshal the Divine forces.

Should he have sent a polite request instead of an order? Should he have gone to Jehuel personally? In hindsight, it was easy to rebuke himself, but how could he have known that an angel-lord would fall over so small a matter? He wished he'd acted differently, although in his heart he knew Jehuel had been honor-bound to obey. It was not his fault that Jehuel was a prideful, petty fool.

With his jealousy goaded beyond endurance, Jehuel changed sides. He gathered his host, bypassed Asmodel and his outnumbered cohort, and launched a savage attack on Michael's unguarded flank. Baal Chanan, ever opportunistic, was quick to take advantage of Jehuel's timely betrayal and threw his forces against Michael's rear just as Harab Serap's legion smashed into its front.

It was more of a rout than a battle. Attacked on three sides and stunned by Jehuel's shocking treachery, many of his angels threw down their swords and fled. Most of them were pursued and quickly sent Beyond; only a small number stayed with Michael and his honor guard as they fought their way past Harab Serap to find sanctuary in the Arx Dei. The first battle for Heaven was over, and with it, it appeared, the war as well.

Michael took a deep breath and looked out over the battlements at the colorful flags and pennants of the besieging legions. It looked like a maddened sea of color, like the coils of a great snake threatening to choke the life from this last Heavenly bastion of the Lord Most High. The thought of a snake reminded him of Lucifer, and his warrior's heart filled with rage. Furious, he raised his white-gloved fist and shouted out a prayer against the Fallen army below.

"Pay them back what they deserve, o Lord, for what their hands have done. Put a veil over their hearts, and may your curse be on them! Pursue them in anger, and destroy them from under the heavens!"

Christopher stood next to Kaym as they waited to be summoned before the Dawn Prince. He wore his new aspect, that of a winged Viking warrior. It wasn't as cool as most of the other angels' aspects, but just having something together made him feel that he fit in a little better. Prince Lucere had flown heavenward from the Courts of Light as soon as he'd received word of his legions' stunning victory, and his first order of business was to reward those who had served him so faithfully and well.

Both Baal Chanan and Harab Serap were honored and titled Dukes of Heaven, while the treacherous Lord Jehuel was named Prince of Aurora and given the honor of ruling a place called Ahura Azdha on the Prince's behalf.

"He'll reward us, too, don't you think?" Christopher asked nervously as he looked around the room. The gathering wasn't anything like the assembly in the Courts of Light. There were many powerful angel-lords here, princely rivals for power, and tense undercurrents filled the massive chamber. He watched uneasily as one giant, four-headed brute pushed a smaller horned angel roughly aside. He made a mental note to remember the monster's faces and stay out of his way.

"Of course he will," Kaym answered, oblivious to Christopher's anxiety. "Unlike the King, the Shining One is no fool. This war would not be over yet had the King given Prince Jehuel his due. Fortunately for us, the King did not, and now Heaven is ours."

"What's this Jehuel like?" Christopher arched his neck and searched the crowd near the front of the room. He wanted to see what he looked like. "Is he cool? Do you like him?"

"No one likes a traitor." Kaym had a contemptuous look on his face. "But I didn't think much of him before, either."

Christopher nodded. Kaym was pretty loyal to the Prince, so his dislike of Jehuel was understandable. "How do you think the Prince will reward us?" he asked. "Will he make you a commander? If he does, maybe I could be, like, your assistant. Or maybe he could make me a commander! My plan worked pretty well, after all. I wish I could tell my dad about it, because he always said I was wasting my time playing war games. Ha!"

Kaym shook his head. "No, you have a talent for war, but it would be a mistake for you to be placed where you should be responsible for commanding angels. Remember that Jehuel came over to us because of his hatred for Michael. You are young and unknown, and there are many who would resent your rise. There are already many who envy you for the glory you have won for opening the Gates."

"That's stupid! The Prince himself said no one else could do it."

Before Kaym could reply, though, four angels clad in the glittering golden armor of the Prince's personal guard approached them.

"Your presence before the Shining One is requested, my lords."

Christopher grinned at Kaym, and the fallen angel smiled faintly back. Kaym walked behind him as he followed the guards up the marble steps and through the silver doors of the chamber that the Prince was using as a makeshift reception hall. It was called the Altar of the Lamb, and the walls were covered with carvings that featured a recurring theme of a shepherd and his sheep. Christopher wondered at the Prince's choice of this place, when there were other, much more impressive buildings to be found.

As he walked into Adonai Lucere's shining presence, the Dawn Prince rose from a crystalline throne and embraced him, then Kaym. The Prince was literally glowing with the pleasure of his long-sought victory, now so nearly in his grasp. His smile was pleased and friendly as he praised them before the crowded hall.

"Well done, Our good and faithful servants!" He placed both hands on Christopher's shoulders. "Ask from Us what thou wilt, and thou shalt receive it."

"Thank you, Your . . . uh, Your Highness." The thought of having a legion to command was still tempting, but when he glanced back at Kaym, the fallen angel shook his head. "But, you know, I guess I don't know what I should ask for. Maybe you could just decide on something for me?"

The Prince stepped back and stroked his bearded chin, weighing Christopher with a measured glance. His golden eyes glinted with amusement. "Shall We then decide for thee?"

Christopher suddenly felt uptight. What if the Prince really was the Devil, after all? He remembered, too, that in most of the fairy tales he'd read as a kid, whoever dealt with the Devil usually got screwed in the end. But, then again, didn't Kaym say that most of what people knew was wrong, anyhow? "Yeah, that'd be cool," he heard himself say.

"Very well, then."

The Dawn Prince clapped his hands, and immediately a score of trumpets sounded. The crowd of angels fell to their knees, abasing themselves before the Shining One, whose raised voice carried clearly across the room.

"Let it be known that Our servant, Christopher,

hath served Us well. As a mark of Our favor, know that Christopher shalt henceforth be known as Phaoton, of the Rose Sefiroth of Sammael."

Right on, Christopher thought. His title sounded cool, whatever it was.

"He's raising you to the rank of Powers," Kaym informed him unobtrusively as the watching angels cheered politely. "That's above the Archangels in the hierarchy, and below the Archons."

"Why Phaoton?"

"It means 'of the sun.' The sun is the sign of the Prince, of course, so it is a mark of His favor."

Christopher nodded. He felt just a little disgruntled, as Phaoton wasn't exactly a name he would have picked for himself. But becoming a Power was awesome, especially considering that he used to think having a twelfth-level mage in D&D was a big deal. Then a jolt of memory struck him like a bolt of lightning. Melusine had called him Phaoton back at First Avenue. How could she have known that the Prince would call him that?

"Let your will be done, o Shining Prince," the assembled crowd intoned as he racked his brain without reaching a conclusion.

The Shining One made a sign to a group of angels standing guard near the door and sank back into his throne. He motioned for Christopher to come closer, and when Christopher did so, the Prince whispered into his ear.

"There is no room for the weak or the stupid in Our courts." His trimmed whiskers tickled Christopher's ear as as he spoke. "Those who are weak are useless to Us, and those who are stupid will overreach themselves until they fall, broken by the weight of their own greed and ambition. Be strong, Phaeton, but be not stupid!"

Christopher was alarmed by the harsh tone of the Prince's warning. Nor did he understand its possible implications until a commotion at the back of the room caught his attention. He turned around and was surprised to see the Archon Verchiel standing behind him in human form with a furious look on his face.

"How can this be, o Prince? It may be that this one has served you well, and thus it is just that he be rewarded. But he is not an angel, nor, even as a named Power, does he have the authority to command the Ben Elohim. He does not have the right!"

"Wretched angel, dost thou think to question Our will?" If the Prince's whispered words had been harsh, they were doubly so now. His azure eyes flared red with fury, and the angels gasped.

"No, Great Prince!" Lord Verchiel, his face blanching, fell to his knees. "I do not question your will, Bright Shining One. I only speak aloud what is secretly in the minds of every angel in these courts, o Prince. I speak the truth! Look into my mind, and see that it is so!"

The Prince leaned forward and looked deep into the Archon's terrified eyes.

"Aye, it is so." He grinned coldly. "And We see thou thinkest thou hast been slighted, that is also so."

Verchiel's eyes opened wide, horrified that his hidden thoughts had so readily betrayed him. He started to protest at first, but then his eyes flashed angrily, and he responded with open indignation.

"Yes, my Prince, I do. I, too, have served you well. Ask Baal Chanan. Ask Lord Kaym. They were there, and they will tell you that without the valor of Verchiel and his cohort, the legions of Harab Serap would never have come in time!"

The Prince glanced over at Kaym, who nodded reluctantly. Despite his dislike for the Archon, Christopher had to admit that Verchiel had a point. He might be stupid and vain, but he had fought well in helping cover their run to the Tenth Gate.

"Let it be so," the Shining One decided quickly. "We shall not revoke Our will, but We give thee leave to challenge Phaoton, if that be thy wish."

What? Christopher couldn't believe that Prince Lucere was going to throw him to the lions like that. The guy had to be kidding! He looked desperately to Kaym for help, hoping the fallen angel would speak up for him, or somehow get him out of this, but Kaym just stood there with his arms calmly folded.

"Yes, Great Prince! Thank you, Great Prince!"

Lord Verchiel bowed deeply before the throne and turned to face Christopher. His jealous eyes were burning with unveiled satisfaction as he looked Christopher over from head to toe.

"You can call yourself whatever you like, *Phaoton*, but it will take more than a name to help you now!"

At the Prince's command, a circle was drawn up in the middle of the chamber. Runes were inscribed at four points around the circle, and Christopher, his stomach starting to tighten, glanced nervously over at Kaym.

"Kaym, what are they doing?" He felt as if an entire herd of butterflies were stampeding around his insides. No, not a herd, a flock. Gaggle? What was the stupid word, anyhow? A swarm, maybe? Christopher desperately tried to think about anything other than the upcoming fight.

"It's part of the challenge ritual. Once you enter the circle, you cannot leave until one of you has submitted to the other. It's similar in some respects to the earthly tradition of the duel."

"Yeah, yeah, I get it. Cute. I didn't think angels were into sumo wrestling."

Kaym laughed. "Don't worry, it's not possible to get thrown out of the circle."

"That isn't what I'm worried about." Christopher grimaced. "What I'm worried about is what happens when I lose. Can he kill me?"

"It is permitted, yes, though you will not die, in the earthly sense. No weapons are allowed, and since he's only an Archon, I doubt Verchiel is strong enough to send you Beyond on his own. He can, of course, drain you of most of your power if he can force you to submit. That is surely his desire."

"My power? You mean the power you gave me?"

"Yes." Kaym didn't look too concerned about it, but Christopher was horrified by the thought.

"But wouldn't that be bad?"

"Very much so," Kaym agreed. "I'm told it's very painful, so don't let him beat you. But remember that he isn't expecting much from you, so you might be able to take him by surprise."

"Okay, I guess." Christopher looked at his opponent across the glowing red line that demarcated the circle. "What's he doing now?"

Thirty feet in front of him, Verchiel was undergoing a series of bizarre transformations. First, he swelled, dropped to all fours, and displayed the aspect Christopher had seen before, the ferocious winged lion of battle. Then his shape flattened, and plated arms extended from his sides as his front legs stretched out and developed large pincers. His tail curved over his head, and a poisonous barb appeared at the tip. The scorpion turned into a monstrous bull-headed human, then back into the form of a tall, ridiculously handsome man. Finished with his display, Verchiel stood there smiling at him, full of malicious intent.

"So what was that all about?"

"It's a taunt, an insult," the fallen angel said. "He's demonstrating to everyone that he can beat you even if he shows you his best tricks beforehand."

"Oh." Christopher raised his left hand to his forehead.

"What was that?"

"The sign of the *L*. I'm demonstrating to everyone that he's a loser."

"Brave words." Kaym laughed approvingly. "Then you are ready?"

"I hope so. I don't want to fight, but if I have to fight somebody, I'm glad it's Verchiel. There's something about him that just pisses me off!" He reached inside his robes and was reassured by the familiar touch of the key. "You said no weapons, right? So, do you think that a certain something-something I might have with me counts as a weapon?"

"I don't know." Kaym looked at him seriously. "I don't know if that little trick will work for you again. I think it would be much better if you didn't use it, not if you can help it. Prince Lucere won't like it."

"Why not?" Christopher felt that he needed any advantage he could get.

But before Kaym could answer him, the trumpets sounded, indicating the start of the contest. Christopher felt hands at his back, pushing him forward, and before he could resist, he stumbled inside the red lines.

He jumped, startled, as a wall of flames erupted behind him. The circle was now a line of blazing fire, but strangely, the heat did not affect him. Nor did it affect his opponent, who had entered the circle wearing his favorite aspect, the lion.

Verchiel roared and leaped at him. Christopher tried to dive sideways, but the speed of the attack took him by surprise, and the Archon's long claws raked his unprotected back. He barely managed to roll clear of the sharp-toothed jaws, and after quickly spinning around, he kept a wary eye on the grinning feline as he rose painfully to his feet. The striped wounds burned beneath Christopher's torn robe, until he remembered his new powers.

With a brief thought, he healed the deep scratches and transformed himself into a Roman gladiator. Suddenly, he was no longer a defenseless Christian waiting to be devoured but a burly warrior armed with a corded net and a trident. When Verchiel leaped again, Christopher was ready. He cast the net directly in the path of the onrushing lion and stepped to the side. The Archon slammed into the net and was ensared, snarling and snapping as he fought desperately to free himself of the thick cords. Christopher laughed triumphantly, raised the trident high over his head with both hands, ready to strike a mortal blow.

But as he struck, Verchiel was transformed. Instead of burying itself in the lion's soft side, the trident's iron barbs were deflected from the hard armored back of a giant scorpion. Armed now with razor-sharp pincers, Verchiel quickly cut himself free of the net and scuttled toward Christopher, waving his poisoned tail. The barbed tail lashed out and pierced Christopher's side, and Christopher gasped as the venom spread throughout his body with a terrible feeling of cold numbness.

Christopher dropped the trident. It disappeared as soon as it fell free of his hand. He fell to the ground, clutching his unfeeling side. With a great effort of will, he managed to force the poison from his body, but the strain left him feeling weak and unfocused. By the time he could lift his head, Verchiel was towering over him in his great bull-demon form, bellowing in triumph. A clawed hand reached down for him and palmed his head like a basketball, its sharp talons jabbing deeply into his scalp. As the pressure grew stronger and the sharp pain became almost unbearable, he could barely understand what the Archon's bestial muzzle was shouting at him.

"Submit, fool! Submit, or I crush your head and send you screaming into the deep!"

It hurt so badly that Christopher would have happily done so, if he could have found his tongue. But the shock of the excruciating pain was so great that he could do little but suffer as Verchiel's powerful grip grew tighter and drops of blood began to trickle down his face. He could see nothing, only a blinding haze of red that was growing darker by the second.

He knew that the key was his only hope, his only chance for salvation. He fought to block out the pain and the increasing darkness as he desperately sought to find the little piece of metal. Finally, his fingers closed upon it and, with the last shards of his flagging will, thrust it blindly upward.

Immediately, the terrible pressure disappeared, and Christopher fell back on the floor, gasping for air. His vision began to clear, and he could just make out the fallen bull-demon only inches away, curled in an awkward ball with both claws clutching at his knee. His ears ringing from Verchiel's agonized howls, Christopher wearily pulled himself upright and saw that the key had embedded itself into the Archon's left leg, in the form of a tiny dagger.

He crawled quickly over and, with one hand gripping the writhing angel's throat, grasped the jeweled haft of the dagger with the other.

"Do you submit?" he demanded.

"Never," hissed Verchiel.

"Are you sure of that?" As he spoke, he twisted the blade, provoking even louder bellows of pain from the wounded Archon.

The bull aspect shimmered and disappeared, replaced by an angelic form as Verchiel's weakened will began to collapse. His handsome, haughty face was now twisted with pain and impotent rage.

"Yes, yes," the Archon wailed. "I submit!"

But it was too late. Christopher knew how to hate; he'd been a reject and an outcast as long as he could remember. In Verchiel's arrogant beauty, he suddenly saw Kent Petersen and Julie Kells. He saw the jocks and the cheerleaders. He saw the face of every boy who'd ever taunted him, every girl who'd ever laughed at him. The dull embers of his helpless, long-held hatred abruptly ignited into a white-hot flame.

"I didn't hear that," Christopher said coldly as he withdrew the toylike blade from Verchiel's leg and drove it into the Archon's heart.

Verchiel abruptly disappeared in a huge flash of red, and the encircling flames climbed higher, until they formed a sphere towering nearly twenty feet over Christopher's head. The jewels in the dagger's handle flashed brightly in response, and he saw that upon each of the five jewels were carved the same runes he had seen before on the key. A moment later, the dagger was again a harmless key, and the flames surrounding him died down enough that he could step carefully over them without being burned.

He closed his hand, hiding the key inside his fist as the watching angels began to cheer him loudly. They seemed surprised but not disappointed by his victory. Only Kaym and the Prince himself were silent as he raised his fist upright in triumph and the assembled angels roared their approval.

"Ave, Phaoton!"

"Thou art mighty!"

"Thou hast conquered!"

He felt like a giant or a conquering king. Now he could understand why the football players at school were always so cocky; it was hard to remember you were only human when people screamed and shouted for you. But he wasn't only human anymore, he was a Power!

Kaym stepped over the flickering remnants of the flames and approached Christopher. His dark eyes were unreadable as he placed an arm on his protégé's shoulder and spoke quietly into his ear.

"You have won a great victory today. Never before has a newly raised Power defeated an Archon in the Circle of Fire, much less sent him Beyond. The gathering demands a sign from you, a symbol of your destiny."

"A symbol? I don't understand, what should I do?"

"Manifest," an angel cried, and soon the crowd joined his call. "Manifest, Phaeton!"

Oh, that was it. He had to show them an aspect. Christopher shook his head, trying to think of an appropriate symbol for himself. He looked at Kaym, hoping for help, but the fallen angel shook his head.

"I cannot help you. This choice is yours alone to make."

As the waiting angels continued their noisy chant, Christopher looked toward the front, and his eyes met those of the Dawn Prince. Adonai Lucere did not look pleased, and the expression on his face frightened Christopher to the depths of his soul. He was extremely aware of the key concealed in his fist, and he hoped against hope that the Prince could not see it. His mind raced frantically, leaping from one image to another, his creativity inspired by his desperate fear of the Prince's wrath.

Hiding the key inside his shredded, bloody robe, he took a deep breath, then assumed a new aspect. His feathered wings disappeared, as did his clothing, and he stood naked before the assembly, tall and beautiful, an unflawed specimen of humanity. His face mirrored the Prince's own, but it was beardless, and the hue of his short golden hair was the exact shade of the Prince's flowing locks. Only the color of his eyes was different, the rose-gold of the morning star instead of the sea's deep blue. Displaying the ultimate embodiment of human perfection, Christopher slowly lowered himself to his knees and abased himself before the Dawn Prince.

The angels abruptly stopped cheering, and he closed his eyes, not daring to look upon the Prince. There was a long, excruciating moment of haunting silence, finally broken by Adonai Lucere himself.

"Rise, Phaoton."

Christopher obeyed at once but did not dare to lift his head.

"Look at Us."

Reluctantly, Christopher lifted his head. He was shocked to see that the Prince was smiling broadly, with genuine amusement dancing in his azure eyes. Then the Prince stepped forward and caressed Christopher's cheek as he spoke quiet words intended for Christopher alone.

"Thou art too clever for thine own good, dear Christopher, dear Phaoton. Too clever by far. But thou art all Kaym hath promised Us and more. It is well that thou knowest thy place. Remember it."

He smiled reassuringly at Christopher, then raised his voice and addressed the assembly.

"The claim of Lord Verchiel hath been settled. Is there any other that disputeth Phaoton's claim to his place in the Order of Sammael?"

This time, there was no protest, only a few scattered cheers.

The Prince nodded, satisfied.

"Then We declare that Phaoton, of the Rose Sefiroth of Sammael, shalt take command of Our legions on Ahura Azdha, where he shall serve as a lieutenant to Our legate, the Lord Matraya. Such is Our will."

"Let it be done, o Shining One."

As Christopher began to step down from the dais and into the adulation of the crowd, he did not see the Prince exchange a glance with Kaym. He did not see the wordless query in Adonai Lucere's shining eyes or Kaym's returning nod of affirmation.

CHAPTER 11

PEOPLE
OF THE DAWN

HOW ART THOU FALLEN FROM HEAVEN, O LUCIFER, SON
OF THE MORNING! HOW ART THOU CUT DOWN TO THE
GROUND, WHICH DIDST WEAKEN THE NATIONS!
                                           —Isaiah 14:12

Rahab was a large world of vast oceans divided by three large continents. It was called Ahura Azdha by its inhabitants, a tall, handsome people who reminded Christopher of his High Elves, only without the pointy ears. The People of the Golden Dawn, as they were known, were a proud, haughty folk, devoted to pleasure above all else, and because they were encouraged in this by their undying ruler, Lord Matraya, they loved him greatly. Lord Matraya was a mortal king whom Adonai Lucere had possessed on this world thousands of years ago, long before his exile from Heaven. Now, there were thousands of temples dedicated to the Son of the Morning, where the People of the Golden Dawn worshiped their shining god-king.

News of their god's great victory over Heaven had reached Ahura Azdha quickly, traveling as it did upon an angel's wings, and had occasioned days of riotous celebration that were only now subsiding.

"What's this Lord Matraya like?" Christopher asked as they walked, in unobtrusive human form, in the general direction of the ruler's palace. "I thought he was just a man, but some of the angels talk about him like he's one of the Great Lords."

They had arrived on the planet in the middle of Aurora, the city that was the capital of Prometheon, the greatest kingdom in all Ahura Azdha. It was here in Aurora that Adonai Lucere had first shown himself to man, and it was here where his most fiercely loyal worshipers were found. Aurora was a vast walled city of stately stone buildings interspersed with grassy parks, where nearly every square was decorated with a light-reflecting fountain, a monument that mirrored the sun, or a beautifully sculpted statue. Its delicate architecture was fantastic, almost to the point of surreality. Christopher liked it very much, except for the strange yellow sky that arced ominously overhead.

"Matraya? Oh, he's human enough. He's the Prince's creature, but now that the Prince has left this place for Heaven, Jehuel guides him. That's what the Prince intended by naming Jehuel his legate. We do not rule openly in the world of men but through mortal instruments, and Matraya is the greatest of these, a powerful vessel of the Prince's light."

Christopher frowned at these words, wondering if he was just an instrument to Kaym. The angel must have read his mind, because he laughed and shook his head although Christopher had said nothing.

"It is a very different thing from the power I gave you. You are more than a man now, while Matraya, for all his greatness, can only call upon the power of the spirit that guides him, he does not wield that power as his own."

Oh. Well, that was different. Christopher was glad. He didn't like the thought of being anyone's instrument or vessel.

"That's Prince Jehuel now, you said?"

"Yes. Jehuel was never intended to lead angels. It's not in his nature. He doesn't realize that it takes more than heroics to make a leader."

"Heroics?" Christopher was surprised. Most of the angels he'd talked to saw Jehuel as a traitor, not a hero.

"You've heard of Leviathan, have you not? And Behemoth?"

"I don't know. They're some kind of monsters or something, right?"

"Oh, yes, but they are more than legend." Kaym made a sweeping gesture with his arm, and the light shining off his tattoos made it look as if blood were running down his wrist. "In the earliest days of angelic memory, Heaven was plagued by great monsters who dwelled amidst the deep of the void. From time to time, they would attack Heaven, for they were mindless, ravenous beasts who tried to devour everything they touched. They were strong, very strong, stronger than the Cherubim, stronger even than most of the mighty Sarim. The Lord of Hosts created the great walls of Heaven in order to protect us from them."

"Geez, they sound bad, dude."

"You have no idea. Think on the terrible strength

of Gonael, that Cherub we faced, and multiply it tenfold. That was how strong most of these monsters were. Then know that Leviathan and Behemoth were their kings."

Christopher whistled, impressed. "So where does Jehuel come in?"

"The King of Heaven decided to do something about these monsters at last. He summoned a great hunt, and all the Sarim joined him in riding the winds of Heaven through the void, laughing and destroying the mindless beasts of Chaos as they rode."

Christopher could almost see the vivid picture Kaym described. He imagined the inky blackness of the void and the explosions of light as the angels hunted down the terrible monsters of the deep.

"But Leviathan and Behemoth were not destroyed," Kaym continued, "though they were forced to bow before the King. Michael, Gabriel, and Prince Lucere together cast down Behemoth and bound it, but Jehuel alone helped the King bind Leviathan. As a reward, the King gave him the key to Leviathan's chains and named him its keeper."

"Doesn't sound like much of a reward to me. No wonder he switched sides. Where is Leviathan bound?"

Kaym smiled and pointed to the bricked street, which became less and less crowded as they approached Matraya's palace. "Underneath your feet."

"What?"

"The King created this world as Leviathan's jail. He formed the planet around the monster, sealing it far below the surface, wrapped in chains, where it burns in an eternal sea of fire." He laughed at Christopher's wide-eyed incredulity. "I told you before, there is always a grain of truth in the old legends. It's not on Earth, but here on Rahab, that the worm writhes underground. As the tales tell, Ourobos devours his own tail, and Iormungandr is steeped in his own poisons."

Christopher frowned, wondering if the fallen angel was pulling his leg. He didn't think so. As far as he could tell, Kaym hadn't told a single joke in all the time he'd known him. Before he could question Kaym further, though, they had reached the high walls that surrounded Lord Matraya's dwelling. Kaym nodded to the spirits standing unseen at the shoulders of the human guards manning the open gate, and Christopher guessed that the spirits blinded the guards' eyes, because the men stared blankly forward as he walked past them, unnoticed.

Unlike the huge marble castle that contained the Courts of Light, Lord Matraya's mansion had clearly never known the threat of war. It was a palatial structure made of wood and stone, delicately rising from an intricate garden of flowers and decorated with dozens of crystal windows placed between sections of light-colored wood. The angular roof was stacked in an unusual manner remniscent of a Japanese pagoda. A winding path of rosy gravel took them through the gardens, until at last they approached the red-painted doors of the mansion.

They did not enter, though. For no sooner had Christopher followed Kaym up the stone steps leading to the painted doors than both doors were flung open wide. A tall, angry man stalked out, followed by a pair of lesser angels. He would have been handsome were it not for the rage that contorted his narrow face and the wild fury that filled his eyes. Christopher wisely slipped behind Kaym, for when the possessed man spotted them, he immediately rushed toward them and grabbed the front of Kaym's robe. Kaym tried to bow politely, but the man's firm grip did not give him the chance.

"Lord Matraya—"

"Did you do this, Kaym? Are you with them?" Flecks of spittle flew from the god-king's mouth. "Answer me, curse you!"

Kaym, taken by surprise, tried to push the angry man away from him, but Lord Matraya would not let go. Jehuel's possessing spirit gave the god-king great strength, for he shook the fallen angel like a helpless rag doll.

"Who did this to me?" he demanded. "Asrael didn't do this on his own! Was it Gabriel? Or Barakael, maybe?"

Kaym looked as confused as Christopher felt. Christopher winced as Matraya again shook Kaym roughly.

"Who else has turned against me? Does Baal Chanan resent me? Do you, Kaym?"

Comprehension dawned in the fallen angel's face. He addressed not the man but the angry spirit within.

"Prince Jehuel, I have nothing to do with Asrael. I have not seen him in ages." His dark brows wrinkled, concerned. "What has he done? Has he betrayed the Prince?"

Matraya-Jehuel abruptly shoved Kaym away, throwing him to the ground, but his face remained agitated. "Im Barku told me. The host was corrupted and has turned against me."

"Im Barku did what?" Christopher made the mistake of asking.

"Who are you?" Matraya glared at him. "No, not Im Barku, Asrael! May his halo rot with his head! He seduced the host that was to be mine."

Christopher saw a look of dismay flash across Kaym's customarily cool face as he was dusting the pinkish gravel off his ash-gray robes.

"Seduced the host! Does he mean to rebel against the Prince?"

"He rebels against me!" Matraya shouted. "He means to rejoin the Divine cause."

"He's not rebelling against you, Jehuel!" Kaym spat bitterly. He pointed past the yellow Azdhan sky, toward Heaven. "This has nothing to do with you. Asrael's betraying the Prince. With a host at his command, he could break the siege of Heaven! You have to stop him!"

"With what? Lucifer only left me with two legions here. Twelve thousand angels against a host? It can't be done."

"That's Prince Lucere, Jehuel, and don't forget it again. Who commands the legions?"

"Ra'shiel and Asmodel." The angelic god-king looked unrepentant.

"Oh, by the Pit, that's even worse." Kaym looked as if he were going to be sick.

"Why do you say that?"

"Because Asrael has long been friends with Ra'shiel, and Ra'shiel's loyalties are weaker than the good will of a Chaos spawn. That's why the Prince kept Ra'shiel here, away from Heaven. No, we can't depend on Ra'shiel's legion, either. But Asmodel will stay loyal to the Shining One, even if all the others fall away."

Kaym waved his hand, sending one of angels hovering behind Matraya off to do his bidding. "Go and find Lord Asmodel. Tell him to come to me at once."

Christopher watched as the angel hurriedly flew away, then bent over to pluck a pale red flower and brought it curiously to his nose. Its smell was pleasant but unfamiliar. As he looked over the rows and rows of flowers in the elegant garden, he could feel a thought teetering on the tip of his mind. It had something to do with ... something to do with ... he wasn't sure yet. He turned back to Kaym and Matraya and saw that the possessed god-king was calmer now, sobered by the seriousness of the situation.

"If you are right, then Asrael will have forty-eight thousand to our six. Even if Ra'shiel holds fast, we face three warriors for every one of ours. They have no Great Ones or any of high rank, but that won't be enough. We still have no hope of defeating them. We need a miracle."

A miracle. Now he had it. It wasn't the flowers, exactly, but the rows. Rows and rows of warriors, growing from the ground. The children of the dragon.

"We could make our own," Christopher broke in, daring to speak again.

The possessed god-king of Prometheon regarded him sourly and ignored his words.

"What is this, Kaym, that project of yours I've heard about?"

"He's a who, not a what. His name is Phaeton, of Sammael's order."

"Strong for a mortal," Jehuel-Matraya commented as he looked Christopher over. "I'd hardly call him a Power, though. His aura has the strength of an Archangel, perhaps."

"He defeated Verchiel in the Circle, my lord. Sent him beyond the Beyond."

"Did you now?" The god-king looked impressed. "No wonder the night stars were weeping red. The Lion mourned for his master."

Christopher shrugged and tried to assume an aggressive tone. He could see that this angel-lord only respected strength. "Yeah, well, it was no big deal, Highness. And look, you can do the same thing to this Asrael."

"In the Circle? There is no doubt!" Matraya scoffed at the idea. "But even in this mortal body, Asrael would not be fool enough to enter the flames with me! I am a prince of the Sarim, Lord of the Sword—"

"Excuse me, but with all due respect, Highness, you're missing the point. What I mean to say is, you've only got six thousand angels, right? So look around you, and what do you see?"

Christopher grinned as the possessed god-king glanced around the grounds of his palace with a baffled look on his face. The impeccable gardens grew lush and thick on either side of the groomed walkway, and beyond them were a geometric series of high hedges. There was nothing that looked like a weapon capable of defeating an army of fifty thousand angels.

"Flowers?" he suggested doubtfully.

Christopher laughed. "I didn't mean that literally, Your Highness. What I meant is that there's plenty of people, or mortals, like you say, right here on Ahura Azdha, right? Is there any reason why you couldn't have your six thousand angels do to them what Kaym did to me?"

Lord Matraya raised his eyebrows and glanced at Kaym, who, by the approving look on his face, had already guessed what Christopher was suggesting. When the fallen angel nodded, the god-king of Prometheon pursed his lips and looked up thoughtfully at the cloudless saffron sky before speaking.

"It is possible. If this one could defeat a Zodiac lord, then beings created by lesser spirits might well have strength enough to war against Asrael's angels. But such congress between mortals and angels is forbidden, of course."

"Forbidden by Heaven," Kaym answered quickly. "Not by Prince Lucere, who is the only authority you must answer to. Do you wish to face His anger if Asrael relieves Heaven? I don't!"

Lord Matraya pursed his lips, clearly not liking that idea any better than Kaym did. The look on his aristocratic face showed Christopher that the Dawn Prince was capable of using a stick as well as a carrot. Then Matraya shrugged.

"In that case, shall we not release Leviathan as well? It's no worse to be thrice damned than twice. Even if our legion were defeated, Asrael would not be able to use his host to relieve Heaven, for he'd be compelled to wrestle with Leviathan first."

"An excellent idea!" Kaym praised Matraya heartily. "I myself would like to see the beast."

Christopher smiled. Ourobos and Iormungandr, it

sounded as if Leviathan were a giant snake of sorts. Now they had the dragon, too, and the mythic image was complete. The odds were looking better by the moment.

He was surprised, though, when Lord Matraya shook his head.

"No, Kaym, I would have you here. None can release Leviathan but me, and since I must go, you must rule this body in my stead. Asmodel is loyal, but his temper is too fierce, and he is a poor general besides. Our forces are small, and we must husband them carefully if we are to prevent Asrael from reaching Heaven."

Christopher was impressed by the wisdom of the angel-lord's words and wondered if perhaps he had misjudged Prince Jehuel. At first, Matraya had seemed almost psychotic, but then, lots of people didn't make sense under pressure. Even Holli got a little crazy when she was really mad.

"It will be as you say," Kaym told Jehuel-Matraya, bowing. "Will you inform Lord Asmodel, before you go? He may be displeased with the burden of serving under my command."

Matraya's possessed eyes glinted dangerously. "I will tell Asmodel. He will obey."

Kaym nodded, satisfied. "In your word, Highness, I have great faith. But is it not true that it will take some time for your angels to empower the mortals of this city?" He pointed to Christopher. "When I blessed Phaoton with my power, it was an arduous task. It will not take long for your angels to recover, but they will need some time. You must take care that Leviathan is not released too soon."

"It won't them take as long as you think, Kaym,"

Matraya insisted. "It is not needful to raise these mortals to such heights as you've done for this one. A small measure, only, of the fire should be quite enough for our purposes."

"Will your angels be willing to serve you in this way?" Kaym appeared to have some doubts. "Won't some shrink before the task?"

Matraya's lips twisted up into a smile for the first time since they had arrived at his doors.

"They will not find the task unpleasant. Have no fear, Kaym. They will obey."

Christopher did not understand the god-king's amusement, and he looked questioningly at Kaym. Kaym, too, looked puzzled for a moment, then his expression changed as awareness dawned upon him. He grinned salaciously at Christopher.

"Too bad you'll have to miss this one, my dear Phaoton." He laughed. "It would be a most educational experience for you."

"You would send him with me?" Matraya asked, surprised.

"With your permission, yes. It seems only wise, for if anything goes wrong with you, Phaoton may have the strength to return and bring word of your fall. If we're creating our own host of mortals, we'll need every angel to lend, shall we say, a hand, while Phaoton, being mortal himself, can do us no good here."

"But I want to stay with you, Kaym!" Christopher objected strongly. And if he had guessed the angels' intentions correctly, he really didn't want to miss the upcoming soiree.

But the fallen angel shook his head, refusing even to listen to his protests. He had his own reasons, and he knew well what he was about. It did not take long for Lord Matraya to affirm Kaym's wish, and the matter was settled.

Christopher sighed, disappointed. In this way, at least, the spiritual world was just like the real world. He never got invited to the good parties.

Aurora was erupting into a single, massive celebration when Prince Jehuel and Christopher began their descent into the bowels of Rahab. As the angel-prince had said, his angels were quite willing to favor the mortals of the city with their beings, and the Aurorans themselves were ecstatic at the prospect of becoming more like the godlike one they worshiped.

A few early experiments had shown that although this method of transferring spiritual powers to mortals was not as effective as the more difficult process Kaym had used, it worked nonetheless. The newly uplifted Auroran mortals did not have a tenth of Christopher's awesome strength, but the angelic flame was definitely there. To Christopher's now-practiced eye, though, their flames were different, darker, colored by a greenish tinge that was somewhat ominous.

Matraya-Kaym was pleased with the results, though, and cheerfully presented the task of building up his new host of ur-mortals to Lord Asmodel, one of the eleven remaining Zodiac lords. The Archon approached his responsibility with all the bullish vigor of his sign and promised Kaym that he would swell the ranks of their Fallen army by one hundred thousand by the following sunrise, in plenty of time for the coming battle.

"The mortals will not be as strong as Asrael's angels, but they will outnumber them more than two-to-one," Prince Jehuel commented with satisfaction as he snapped his fingers, causing a giant, rune-inscribed rock to roll away from the cave mouth it concealed. "That should be enough to account for whatever remnants of the host survive Leviathan."

"The real question is, will we survive him ourselves?" Christopher said under his breath, looking nervously into the gaping darkness of the cave. His stomach fluttered anxiously as he followed the fallen angel-prince into the the darkness, desperately hoping that the keeper of Leviathan was its master as well.

Was it right to pray? he wondered. And if it was, whom would he pray to? His fear was threatening to bloom into full-grown terror, and in the past, in moments of fear, he'd prayed to the God he didn't believe in. Now he knew that God existed, but as Heaven's fall showed, He didn't seem to care too much about anything.

The Prince cared, though. He cared a lot, Christopher had seen. Even though he was supposed to be the Devil, Kaym had showed him that things weren't always what they were supposed to be. The Bible might say that Satan and Lucifer were one and the same, but Christopher knew differently now. The fictitious, pitchfork-bearing figure of evil had nothing in common with the great angel-prince he knew, the beautiful lord of light he now served. If any god would hear his prayers, it would be Adonai Lucere.

"Great Prince of Light, please protect me now!"

he prayed silently, and the thought of the Dawn Prince was a comfort to him, the certainty that he bore the sign of his godly favor burned away the doubt and fear inside him. He only hoped that favor would be enough to protect him against Leviathan as well. He strongly suspected that the beast was not going to be in a very good mood.

About thirty yards into the cave, Jehuel stopped, bringing Christopher's nervous reverie to an abrupt end. The angel-prince pointed down, and Christopher saw that they were standing on the lip of a huge precipice descending as far as the eye could see. Toward the bottom was an orange glow that might indicate volcanic activity of some sort.

"You don't mean to tell me that we're going down there, do you?" Christopher asked, knowing what the answer was.

"Peace, Phaeton, you still think like a mortal." Prince Jehuel shook his head, and his lack of concern was comforting. "You are not in the material plane here, nothing can hurt you, not even the molten fire at Rahab's core. Just don't slip back into the material, or you will burn up in an instant."

"Did you have to tell me that?" Christopher protested, but the angel's words did make him feel better. "Now I'm going to be thinking about it the whole time we're down there!"

Jehuel laughed. Having left Matraya's body to Kaym, he now looked like the mighty angel-prince he truly was. As he spoke, his form blurred for a moment as he shifted completely outside the material.

"No, you won't," he said. "You'll forget all else once you see Leviathan. Truly, you are most fortunate, for never before have mortal eyes feasted on such a being."

Christopher smiled wanly. He felt a little steadier now, but his nerves reached a fever pitch as Jehuel furled his large wings and leaped into the abyss. Fearing the fall, but even more afraid of being left behind, Christopher shifted into the spiritual realm himself, closed his eyes, and jumped.

His fall was rapid, but in his nonmaterial form, there was none of the discomfort he expected. Christopher opened his eyes cautiously at first, then, as nothing disastrous happened and he grew accustomed to the downward motion, he began to look around. The walls of the huge chasm were not jagged as he'd expected but smooth and unnaturally flat. He shuddered. Someone had obviously made the huge pit, someone with unthinkable power at their disposal. He hoped it wasn't Leviathan.

He imagined falling faster, and immediately his speed increased. Soon he caught up to the Seraph, who was calmly plunging downward. The orange glow was growing closer, and he started to feel heat pressing against his skin. It's just your imagination, he told himself, but the burning sensation became harder to deny as he hurtled ever closer to the bubbling magma.

As he fought to ignore the heat, a voice whispered into his ear, urging him to shift back into the material. It was deep and pleasant, the subterranean rumbling of an earth elemental.

"Release thyself," it urged. "Open thy heart, and all that troubles thee shall be gone, the Hellfire quenched by the cool darkness of the void."

Christopher started at the sound of the voice and looked frantically around, but all he saw were the glowing walls of the chasm as he shot past them, plunging ever deeper. The heat was more intense now, more painful, and when he looked at himself, he saw that his arms were afire.

"Highness, help me!" he screamed in panic, but the angel-prince did not hear him as they fell ever closer to the burning lake of fire.

"Open thyself to me, and I will take away thy pain," the deep voice promised. *"Thou dost not want to enter the lake, the lake, the lake of Hell!"*

As the fiery pain wholly engulfed him, he was about to give in when another voice called to him, a soft, seductive voice that was hauntingly familiar. It sounded like a woman, and she calmed him with her caressing tones.

"The pain isn't real. The fire cannot touch you, golden Phaoton. You are stronger than the fire!"

The bubbling orange-red lava was only a hundred yards below him, and he was falling fast. It felt like a white-hot furnace reaching out to devour him, eating away at his face and peeling his black, scorched skin away from his bones. He felt his will weakening against the whispers of the first voice and began to relax, starting to slip back into the material. It would be the end of him, but that seemed the lesser of two evils now.

"No, think only on the Light, the Great Light of the Shining One!"

The soft whisper was urgent, as the speaker refused to let Christopher give up. He tried to picture the pure light that surrounded the Dawn Prince, but it was impossible. The white light turned hot and red in his mind, and he was filled with the incandescent heat and pain.

"The lake, the lake!" the first voice sobbed. *"Thou shalt not enter the lake!"*

"Trust in yourself!" the second voice whispered in reply. *"Trust in your strength. You are stronger than the fire!"*

"Give in! Submit! Obey!"

The suffering was terrible, worse than any he had ever known. The first voice hammered deeply in his skull, urging him to submit, but buoyed by the cool whispers and his faith in the Dawn Prince, Christopher's will remained strong enough to resist.

"No!" he screamed in agony as his nonmaterial form plunged into the magma with a gigantic, thickly liquid splash.

CHAPTER 12

JAWS OF THE WICKED

AND I BROKE THE JAWS OF THE WICKED, AND PLUCKED
THE SPOIL OUT OF HIS TEETH.

—Job 29:17

Jami was just recovering her senses when she
noticed the good-looking young man standing
next to Holli. She shook her head ruefully. Holli
acquired boyfriends nearly as fast as Chris could
scare girls away.

"Jami!" Holli screamed happily as she threw her
arms around her sister. "I'm so glad to see you!
Khasar didn't know where you were, and I was
worried that something bad happened to you."

Jami gave her twin a quick squeeze before disen-
tangling herself from Holli's embrace. As she
stepped back, she noticed the sky was yellow, of all
things. Either the pollution was really bad, or, she
suspected, they weren't on Earth at all.

"Khasar?" she asked.

"Yes, he's kind of weird, but he's really nice."
Uh-oh. Whenever Holli stressed *really* like that,

she had a crush on somebody. "Here, I'll introduce you."

"Wait a minute, where are we?"

"I don't know. It's not our world. It's called, like, Ahurra Ozda or something."

Her twin stepped back and indicated the handsome Archon.

"This is Khasar. He's a lion, but he's really an angel."

Jami didn't understand just what her sister meant by that, but she blushed as the Archon bowed to her and kissed her hand. He did it smoothly, in a flattering way that made her feel very grown-up. Okay, so maybe having a crush on the guy was understandable.

"I am the Archon Khasaratjofee, at your service. Your sister has informed me that my name is somewhat difficult for your kind, so please call me Khasar. I understand that you are the Lady Jami?"

"Uh, yeah, I'm Jami." Augh! That sounded so stupid! She couldn't come up with something better than that?

"Excellent." Khasar smiled. It was a ridiculously charming smile. "Well, now that you are both here, perhaps we could get under way. I have been commanded to bring you to the Tower of Qawah."

"Qawah?" Holli asked. "That's a funny name."

"Is it? You'll have to tell the Lady of the Tower that."

"Who told you to bring us there?" Jami asked.

Was it the Lady? Was the Lady human, and could she just order angels around? Jami wondered about that. Since she'd never gone to church or believed in angels, she had no idea what the rules were. She didn't think angels were just there to take orders, but then, the sky wasn't supposed to be yellow, either.

"The Lady of the Tower, of course. I can't tell you why, because I'm just the transportation service. The Lady does not tell me her secrets."

"The transportation service?" Jami said, puzzled.

"I told you he was a lion," Holli replied, as Jami jumped, startled. Khasar was transforming himself back into his leonine aspect.

"Wow, that's pretty cool," she said.

"I like him better the other way, though," Holli whispered in her ear.

"He is pretty cute," Jami agreed. But he made a handsome lion, too.

Khasar stretched out his forelegs and lowered his chest to the ground, extending his wings to their full span as he yawned loudly.

"Forgive me," he apologized. "For some reason, I always feel like I need a nap when I switch into this form. Well, we'd best be going. Hang on tight. There are some loathsome creatures lurking about, and I'm afraid that some of them aren't too happy about your presence here."

Jami didn't like the sound of that, but she obediently climbed on top of Khasar's broad, muscular back. Holli clambered on behind her. She took a firm grip on Khasar's thick blue mane and felt Holli wrap both arms around her waist.

"Don't pull, child! That mane is attached, you know."

"Sorry," Jami apologized, then she stifled a scream as the big Archon leaped into the sky, his blue wings beating strongly against the air. In a matter of moments, they were high over the stony hills, looking down across the striking landscape of Ahura Azdha.

It was a breathtaking sight. Although the hills were stony and bleak, the snowcapped mountains were beautiful, a tall and majestic range that erupted against the yellow sky like a dark, haughty challenge. It was as if earth and sky were fighting, and the earth was winning. The sky seemed subdued and quiet, for little wind ruffled her ponytail despite the speed of their passage.

It was not long before they approached the mountaintops, and the temperature grew colder as Khasar's shoulders worked powerfully, carrying them steadily ever higher. A thin mist surrounded them as they passed through wispy, reddish clouds, and their damp moisture chilled her to the bone.

She could feel Holli shivering against her as she snuggled closer, trying to stay warm. Jami curled over herself and pressed her chest against Khasar's shoulders, warming herself with the heat that was steaming away from the Archon's laboring body.

"Not long now until we're past the mountains, ladies," the angel told them. "Not long now."

"Good, 'c-cause we're freezing back here," Jami said, her teeth chattering.

"It is not an enjoyable experience for me, either. Why didn't you tell me that you're heavier than you look?"

"Are you c-calling me fat?"

"I don't think you're in a position to dispute it just at the moment, my dear. Next time, you can take turns carrying me on your back, and we'll see just how you feel."

"I didn't know angels were so whiny," Holli whispered as Khasar continued to complain. For some reason, that cracked Jami up.

"Me neither," she finally managed to get out as she looked down at the mountains passing below them. It was a little scary, but they were not too high above the icy peaks, and she could see quite a bit as they passed by. The mountaintops seemed totally lifeless. Above the treeline, there were no signs of life, either plant or animal, only jagged piles of ice, rock, and snow.

Khasar was true to his word, because it was not long before they were finally past the last mountaintop, and Jami felt her stomach drop as the ground suddenly seemed to fall away beneath her. Even as her vision whirled, though, she caught a glimpse of movement behind her. She glanced back quickly over her shoulder and saw a large white thing that blended into the whiteness of the snowy slope. For a second, she thought her mind was playing tricks on her, until it moved again.

"Khasar, what's that?" she shouted into the Archon's furry ear. Whatever it was didn't look too friendly.

"What's—oh!"

A forceful blast of freezing air hit Khasar's right side, forcing one wing up and sending him lurching into an awkward, downward path. The wing passed just over Jami, crouched behind Khasar's mane, but it smashed into Holli's shoulder. Jami heard her cry out in pain. She herself was hurting as Khasar's head, jerking abruptly upward, had smacked her right in the face.

"Holli, are you all right?" Jami tried to turn

around. "Khasar, what happened? Did that thing just attack us?"

"I'm okay, kind of," Holli insisted, but Jami could tell from the looseness of her grip that she was hurting. She wished desperately for a piece of rope or something she could tie them together with.

"It attacked us," Khasar told her. "I could not tell if it was an ice *wyrm* or a mountain *dreki*. They're both very dangerous. Still, I hope it was just a *wyrm*."

"Why's that?"

"Because *drekis* can fly."

Jami looked over her shoulder. Below them, the barren mountains were being replaced by steep, tree-covered hills, but there were still no signs of life or movement. She scanned the misty skies on all sides but saw no winged white monsters.

"I don't see anything," she started to say, but Khasar interrupted her.

"Hold fast," he said. "It was a *dreki*."

Khasar suddenly banked his wings and angled sharply to the left. Jami felt a chill as a subzero blast just missed her head, and she ducked down, burying her bleeding face in Khasar's mane. They circled around in a tight turn, then the Archon was beating his wings backward as he pulled up into a vertical position.

Jami squeezed her legs tightly, holding her position against gravity's frightening pull as the *dreki* came into view in front of them. It was big and ugly, with wings nearly twice Khasar's wingspan and a fat, gray-and-white mottled snake's body. Jutting out from the body were four stumpy legs. On either side of the wide, triangular head were set pitiless emerald-green eyes. Jami could see they were not the eyes of an animal, though, for they gleamed with alien, evil intelligence.

"Back away, snake!" roared Khasar in a voice like thunder. "Back away before I burn you with the fire you fear!"

The *dreki* didn't react, it simply stared back at them, and the horned ridges over its eyes made its hooded gaze seem even more malevolent. It flapped its giant leathery wings lazily, keeping pace with Khasar as he rose ever higher through the red mists.

"I know you, little lionheart," its sibilant voice whispered harshly. "Khasaratjofee. Do you not know me? You were of my host once."

Jami felt Khasar's wings miss a beat, then the mighty strokes resumed.

"Bilethel? Is that you?"

"Bile, now," the snake pronounced. "Lord Bile. The Son of the Morning knows how to reward those who are loyal to him. You should have stayed with me. I would have made you my lieutenant, and we could have ruled the Mountains of the North together."

"You are mistaken, *Lord* Bile." The Archon's voice was level, but Jami could feel Khasar's suppressed anger. "You have chosen your way, and I have chosen mine. Now, for the sake of the friendship that was once ours, get out of my way."

The heavy rattlesnake's head moved slowly from side to side.

"It is only for the sake of that friendship that I do not destroy you now. I was always stronger than you, Khasar, and now I am stronger than you would believe possible. I am warning you, you cannot stand before me; do not put me to the test. Give me the children, and I will let you go."

"Khasar!" Jami breathed urgently into the Archon's ear. "Don't listen to him."

"Silence, child!" Khasar commanded roughly.

"Is this what you have come down to?" he chastised the fallen angel. "Is this how far you have fallen? To prey on the innocent? Did your heart rot? Is it as ugly as your face is now, Bilethel? If there is a glimmer of conscience left in you, if a single shard of the pure and holy being you once were remains intact, it will bury itself in your heart like a poisoned blade! I am warning you, do not do this thing!"

For a moment, the demon seemed to regard Khasar's plea seriously. Jami held her breath, hoping against hope that the Archon's words would soften Bilethel's heart, hoping he would let them go. She watched anxiously as the snake's green eyes stared at them, its forked tongue flicking in and out of its broad mouth.

Then Lord Bile dashed her hopes with a short burst of cruel laughter.

"You seem troubled by my appearance, Khasar. Is that the problem? That you see me as ugly? I tell you, there is nothing ugly or beautiful, nothing good or evil, but for our minds that make it so. If my appearance troubles you, then I shall give you another!"

The air about him blurred momentarily, and in the place where the snake-demon had been was a stunningly beautiful angel, with silver iridescent wings and the body of a Venus model. Her long red hair spilled across a tight white dress like a sacrificial offering, and she wore a golden torque emblazoned with a sunburst around her neck. A bright aura surrounded her, a shining ruby glow. Only the eyes were the same, green orbs that were colder and harder than any jewel.

"Is this better, Khasar? Now do you find me easier to look on?"

"You blaspheme against your nature, Bilethel. It is forbidden."

"Nothing is forbidden to me anymore, Khasar." Lord Bile's voice was still the same, and it was particularly creepy coming out of the gorgeous angel's mouth. "What is forbidden is your passage here! You may not take the children, Khasar, not if you would leave here. My patience is at an end, so make your choice. Are you with me or against me?"

"I gave you your answer a thousand years ago!" the angry Archon roared.

Jami gripped Khasar's mane tightly as he opened his jaws again and belched forth a burst of blazing fire. The blast engulfed the beautiful demoness, and her silver wings crumbled away to ash before the heat of the inferno. As Bile howled in pain, Khasar dived below, flying eastward as fast as he could.

"Nice shot," Jami praised him. "That had to hurt."

"Way to go, Khasar," Holli cheered. But her voice was weak, and that worried Jami.

"Not enough to stop him, curse the luck. He just wasn't expecting the attack. Now he's angry, and if I know Bilethel, he'll chase us to the Gates of Heaven and back."

Jami looked back. Sure enough, Lord Bile was back in his snake-demon form and was in full pursuit, the great mottled wings beating the air as if every stroke were a lash laid to Khasar's naked back. Even at this distance, she could feel his hateful fury.

"Khasar, I think he's gaining on us."

"I know, I know."

"Isn't there anything we can do?"

"Pray," Khasar said, his voice already sounding strained with the effort he was making. "That's all I can think of at the moment."

Jami sighed. She could hear Holli murmuring something behind her, but her own lips were sealed. Praying made her feel uncomfortable, mostly because until a few hours ago, she hadn't believed in God, the Devil, or any of these stupid supernatural creatures surrounding her now. They weren't supposed to exist at all! No. She shook her head. She hadn't prayed in fifteen years, and didn't see any reason to start now.

She turned her head to look back at the snake-demon, and a blast of cold air brushed past her right ear. Her ponytail suddenly felt very heavy, and when she reached back, she could feel that a chunk of it had been frozen solid by the blast. Suddenly, she realized that it didn't matter if she believed God existed or not; they needed help, and they needed it now. Swallowing hard, she closed her eyes and began to pray.

"Okay, God, I think we're in, like, a lot of trouble here. You know what I'm saying? They say you're supposed to be so great and powerful, and so I'm thinking you should be able to get us out of this situation. I don't know if you can make Khasar fly faster or what, but I'd really, you know, like, appreciate it if you'd do something."

When she finished her prayer, she opened her eyes and was deeply disappointed to see that the demon was still gaining on them. Khasar was straining mightily now, and she could feel his fur growing damp as he gave his all. But Lord Bile was flying closer, ever closer, and it was obvious to her that the Archon's effort would not be enough.

"O Lord, be with your servant now!" Khasar cried suddenly. "Save us, Almighty One!"

"There is nothing that can save you. Save your voice to cry the Prince his mercy, the King of Heaven does not care!"

Lord Bile mocked Khasar, then paralyzed the Archon's left wing with a freezing blast that caught him squarely from behind. A second paralyzed his front legs. With one wing locked into position, Khasar was forced to extend the other and begin a gentle downward glide that would leave them helpless on the ground, completely in the demon's power.

"Khasar!" Jami shouted at him. "Don't stop!"

"I can't move my wing!"

They continued to glide lower and lower, and Jami could see that Khasar was aiming for an open field of grass between a large clump of trees and a steep hill. Behind them, Lord Bile floated easily like a monstrous, evil shepherd, guiding his sheep into the slaughtering house. There was a look of cruel satisfaction in the emerald eyes, and Jami shivered before them. She wondered fearfully what the demon had in mind for her and Holli. It couldn't be good if he'd gone to such lengths to get them.

"Get ready! This is going to be difficult!" Khasar yelled at them as they lurched toward the ground.

But as Khasar tried to steady himself for an awk-

ward, two-legged landing, Jami heard the sound of
trumpets blaring. There was a sharp crack of thunder, and she heard a wail of pain and fear behind
her. She looked back and saw that Lord Bile had
been struck by a bolt of lightning that had burned a
large hole through one of his leathery wings.

"Where did that come from?" Jami tried to ignore
the field of green rushing up at them.

"Hold on," she heard Khasar cry just as his rear
paws touched the ground. He was trying to keep
himself upright, running on two legs, but he could
not keep his balance and tumbled over on his side,
sending her flying off his back.

Jami felt the unpleasant sensation of the earth
becoming sky as she somersaulted through the air
and saw the yellow turn to green and back again,
before the breath was knocked out of her body. Her
vision went red as she slammed into the ground. It
felt almost like a car crash. The redness quickly
faded, although she found it hard to breathe. She
carefully wiggled one part of her body at a time.
Everything was still there. Nothing seemed broken.

Flat on her back, she stared up at the sky in
stunned disbelief as twelve angels riding raging
steeds of fire swept across her vision. Did she get
knocked unconscious? Was she dreaming them?
The angels rode headlong through the air, bearing
lances. They charged the wounded snake-demon.

Lord Bile snapped and bit at the white riders,
but to little effect. They stabbed at the monster
with their lances, piercing his massive torso as
they rode past, then circled around to attack again.
Lord Bile roared in pain. Although no single

wound appeared to do him much damage, he was losing the battle.

Jami was just beginning to regain her wind when the demon roared his angry disappointment one final time, then turned and retreated toward his mountain stronghold. The trumpets blew a second time, and the riders halted their fiery steeds, abandoning the pursuit.

"Are you all right?"

Jami winced as she tried to take a deep breath before answering Khasar. The handsome Archon was in his human form, leaning over her with a look that showed only concern for her despite a left arm that was dangling awkwardly from his side.

"Holli!" she gasped painfully, worried about her sister.

"She's here," he reassured her. "Lie still, she's being attended to."

"Is she okay? Your arm . . ."

"Don't worry about me." He grinned and gently squeezed her shoulder. "We're safe, and I'll be fine."

Jami tried to sit up, but a wave of nausea passed over her, and she was forced to lie back upon the prickly green grass.

"Relax, child. Close your eyes. All will be well."

The voice was not Khasar's but that of a woman. As her eyes obediently closed, Jami caught a glimpse of a kindly wrinkled face, and she felt a soft hand tenderly stroke her brow. She smiled as she sank thankfully into unthinking darkness, soothed by the woman's gentle touch.

CHAPTER 13

THE
KING OF CHAOS

WHEN DID YOU SAY THE EARTH WOULD STOP TURNING?
WHEN DID YOU SAY WE WOULD ALL START BURNING?
WHEN SHOULD I MAKE A PLEDGE?
SHOULD I LISTEN TO THE VOICES IN MY HEAD?
             —Ministry ("Burning Inside")

In an instant, the voice, the heat, the pain, and even the lake itself were gone, and Christopher found himself standing beside Prince Jehuel in a large, dark cavern. He was still in his spiritual form, unscarred by the fall. He looked curiously at his arms, surprised and happy to find them whole.

"Are you unwell?" the Seraph asked, eyeing him strangely.

"No, I'm . . . I'm fine." Christopher looked at his arms again. They were still there. "I thought I was just about all burned up there, while we were coming down. Why didn't you . . . I mean, what were those voices?"

"Voices?" Prince Jehuel looked surprised for a moment. "Oh, just a trick of the mind. Leviathan is not a mindless monster and has had no visitors in a long, long time. No doubt he would prefer to be left undisturbed."

"Well, if that was him, he can't be mindless," Christopher agreed. "But I heard a second voice, too."

The angel-prince shrugged his robed shoulders, clearly uninterested. "I heard nothing. But there's bound to be strange things happening this close to the King of Chaos." He walked over to the far wall, where a set of keys magically appeared in his hand, then began unlocking the first of seven silver locks attached to a large stone door.

"Beyond that door is Leviathan," he said as he unlocked the second lock. "Pray that I still hold the means to its mastery!"

"You got it, dude!" Christopher had absolutely no desire to face a primordial King of Chaos pissed off from a millennium of imprisonment. "But just in case you can't control it, what should I do?"

"Then you shall discover what lies beyond the Beyond," said the prideful Seraph solemnly. A surprisingly ironic smile flashed across his haughty face. "Are you curious?"

"Well, I'm not, actually," Christopher said, honestly enough. "I hope you're not, either."

The last lock was finally opened, and Prince Jehuel drew himself to his full height. He glanced quickly back at Christopher, and Christopher realized that Leviathan's keeper was not quite as confident as he wanted to appear.

"Behold the King of Chaos!" Jehuel said dramatically as he hurled open the stone door.

Behind it was a massive lake of fire, a huge, bubbling pool of magma that looked a lot like the illusion Christopher had seen during his descent. In fact, it was the same. The main difference, though, was that there was a giant black object floating in the middle of the lava, half the size of a football field.

"It's so . . . big!" Christopher gasped.

The huge structures of Heaven had been impressive, but if this monstrous creature stood up, it would dwarf the buildings lining the streets of gold. It kind of reminded him of Godzilla towering over the skyscrapers of Tokyo. Then the giant thing moved, and Christopher realized that what he thought was Leviathan's body was only its head.

"Holy—!" he blasphemed incredulously.

The dragon, for Leviathan was indeed a dragon, glared at them with all six of its yellow eyes. It had three heads, each attached to a long neck encrusted with hardened scaly armor. Christopher shook his head in awe as he saw molten lava drip from its thick snaky necks, but the lava did not even seem to burn the dragon. He ducked when the colossus noticed them, lifted two mighty wings, and flapped them forward, spraying a huge torrent of magma over them.

"I know thee!" its angry voice hissed, so loud and deep that the rocks of the chamber shook with the force of its fury. The magnificence of its anger was truly breathtaking.

Prince Jehuel bowed politely, as he brandished a small silver object in front of him.

"I am honored by your recollection, great King of Chaos."

Christopher thought he heard sarcasm in the angel's voice, and Leviathan's angry response proved him right.

"It is no honor, Prince of Heaven! I have sworn to destroy thee, and so I shall!"

"One day, maybe," the angel-prince agreed. "But not today, Great King. Not while I bear this talisman. Your heart is in my hand, and with but a single squeeze I can end you for all time."

"Dost thou think I know it not? Long have I thought on thy talisman, Prince Jehuel, and thou knowest I will not try thy strength! Speak, then, of thy purpose here. Surely thou hast greater concern than to mock thy prisoner?"

"Perhaps, or perhaps not." Jehuel smiled cruelly. "Truly, it gives me great pleasure to see you bound. And maybe I will come again one day, simply to scoff at you."

Leviathan roared, a wordless cry of sheer and impotent hate that echoed off the rocky walls of the prison.

Jehuel laughed, then relented. "But you are correct, Great King, and such is not my purpose today. I have need of you."

"Is it so?"

"It is so. There is war in Heaven, and angel battles angel as the Divine Host has been riven apart."

"Thy news gladdens mine ears!" the beast exulted. "Which side hast thou chosen?"

"I have cast my lot with the Son of the Morning, whom you may remember as Lucifer, the Shining One. He seeks to overthrow the King, whose rule has grown heavy on our shoulders."

"Lucifer, yes, I remember him." The three heads bobbed up and down. "He was strong. But not so strong as the King of Heaven."

Christopher snorted. Prince Lucere had conquered almost all of Heaven, and the King still hadn't lifted a finger in his own defense. But then, it wasn't fair to expect Leviathan to be up on current events, considering he'd been locked up in here for centuries.

"Times change," Jehuel informed the monster. "Heaven has already fallen to Prince Lucere's hand. But on this mortal plane, our angels are outnumbered by the hosts of Heaven, and I would not trouble Prince Lucere with the issue."

The dragon chuckled, making a rumbling sound like an avalanche of rock. "Thou wouldst have me cover for thine own mistakes, mayhap."

"Even so," Jehuel admitted freely. "Your hatred for me is great, I know, but not so great as that you harbor for another."

The three great heads nodded slowly. "As thou sayest, even so. A day of reckoning will one day come for thee, but first I would break the King of Heaven in these jaws. An thou provideth me the way, I shall postpone thine own deserved reward. Set me free!"

"Do you take me for a fool?" Prince Jehuel shook his head. "You will be set free, but for a brief time only. First you shall swear to bind yourself to my will."

"Never!" The great beast was stubborn.

"No? Then you may stew in your own hatred until I come again to you, a time that may never come. Will you forgo the chance to wreak vengeance on your greatest enemy because you would not serve a lesser foe? Then your foolishness surpasses your hate."

Christopher watched, breathless, as the great

dragon contemplated the matter, weighing its hatreds in the balance. Its three heads moved slowly in a rhythmic pattern, and Christopher wondered if they were debating the choice among themselves. Did the monster have one brain or three? Was it possible that the second voice he'd heard might have belonged to Leviathan itself?

But even as the thought crossed his mind, a hint of cinnamon wafted past his nose. Suddenly, he realized who the second voice belonged to, and it wasn't Leviathan.

"Melusine?" he whispered in astonishment. "Is that you?"

"Shhh," she urged him. "I'm here, right behind you. I'm invisible. But you don't need to talk aloud, we can speak through your mind."

"How? Like this?"

"That's it! Just think at me. It was strange, but I could hear your thoughts right after you defeated Lord Verchiel in the Circle. I . . . well, I followed you to this world. Lord Kaym found me out, but instead of getting angry with me, he told me to follow you."

"I . . . okay. Listen, if Kaym told you to follow me, then it's cool." Christopher didn't know why Kaym would have sent Melusine after him, but he was glad he had. Without her, he would have surely burned up in coming here, and besides, he understood more of what was happening, better than the seductive little angel did herself. Melusine, he knew, would one day become his guardian angel, even though she couldn't possibly know that now. And apparently they shared a bond that was much deeper than he'd realized. "Does Prince Jehuel know you're here?"

"I don't think so. Lord Kaym told me to keep myself hidden from him. But listen to me. He told me to give you this command."

Christopher raised his eyebrows. Command? That was new. "Yeah, I'm listening."

"You are to take the talisman from Prince Jehuel. Lord Kaym says you're stronger than the prince thinks, so he won't be expecting it. Then you will be Leviathan's master!"

"Yeah, and I'll have a pissed-off Seraph going after my head in the Circle, too!" What was Kaym thinking?

"Don't you understand? Lord Kaym told me that Leviathan hates Jehuel! So give him Jehuel."

Christopher laughed. While the thought of such a callous betrayal might have bothered him before, he had seen too much of the spiritual world to flinch at treachery now. He had learned, too, that the lure of power was sweet, much too compelling to resist. Besides, Kaym had ordered him to do this, and he didn't like the idea of crossing his mentor.

"You're not making this up, are you?"

"Me!" Melusine sounded indignant. "Of course not! I wouldn't dare."

"Okay, okay, I believe you!" She was probably telling the truth. "Anyhow, like Jehuel himself said, might as well be three times damned as twice. But won't the Prince mind? I mean the Dawn Prince, not Prince Jehuel."

"Oh, he's always hated Jehuel. Lord Kaym knows what he's doing. Prince Lucere will be pleased."

Okay, well, if Kaym thought the Prince would like it, then that was that. Christopher took a deep breath and turned his attention to Prince Jehuel, steeling himself for the confrontation. The angel-prince was threatening the monster, shouting and waving the talisman around as if he were going to destroy it at any moment. The dragon wasn't giving in, though. Christopher tried to act casual, pretending he was getting bored, as he moved carefully into position behind Jehuel. He took one surreptitious step forward, then another, until he was within a few feet of the angel-prince.

"That's it, you can do it!" Melusine encouraged him.

Well, here goes, Christopher thought. Gathering himself together, he leaped into the air and smashed his shoulder into the Seraph's side, knocking them both into the lake of fire. The lava hissed and burned, but it was as harmless as water to his supernatural form. When he struck, he'd managed to grab the talisman with his left hand, while his right hand was locked in a death grip around Jehuel's wrist. As they tumbled through the lava, he pulled and twisted at the small object, desperately trying to yank it out of the angel-prince's hand.

But Jehuel was strong, and though taken off-guard by Christopher's treacherous attack, he hung onto the talisman. They rolled over twice, then the angel-prince spread his mighty wings and hurled himself upward, erupting from the lava and dragging Christopher with him. They flew through the air, and just as they were about to strike the roof of the giant cavern, Jehuel twisted, forcing Christopher between the angel's body and the jagged rocks.

"Uff-da!" Christopher grunted. He smashed into the sharp edges so hard that the cavern shook, and stalactites and other stony debris fell into the giant pool of magma. His supernatural strength and angelic form allowed him to survive the blow, but

even so, it hurt badly. He dared not shift into full immateriality lest he lose his grip on the talisman.

"I'll eat your soul for this, Phaoton!" Jehuel snarled.

They were nose-to-nose, and for one dreadful moment Christopher thought the angel was going to bite him in the face.

He didn't have the breath to spit back an answering threat but made a violent reply by turning his teeth into fangs and sinking them into the angel-prince's fingers. Jehuel howled, and his grip loosened for a second, but when he transformed the talisman into a small dagger with the blade cutting into Christopher's fingers, the angel-prince regained any advantage that had been lost. Christopher started to lose his own grip as, moments later, Jehuel hammered him down into the rocky floor near the stone entrance.

Okay, this is not good, he thought as pain exploded through his body again. I can't take much more of this.

But Melusine threw her sparse weight into the conflict, wrapping her arms around Jehuel's wings at their base and preventing the prince from leaping toward the ceiling again. Jehuel flexed his shoulders, and the great wings sent her flying, but the brief respite was all Christopher needed to get the grip he had been seeking on Jehuel's right arm.

He pulled the talisman one way, while his forearm, locked behind the angel-prince's elbow, forced Jehuel's arm into a painfully straight position. The prince's greater strength was useless against Christopher's leverage. Christopher threw everything he had left into exerting even more pressure on the prince's arm. Jehuel was able to resist the pain for an inhumanly long time, but at last even his will failed, and he was forced to shift into full immateriality, leaving the talisman in Christopher's possession.

Jehuel was back in seconds with his sword drawn, ready to continue the battle, but Christopher was already diving deep into the lava, speeding directly toward Leviathan's massive jaws.

"Who art thou?" the deep voice thundered inside his skull.

"Do you want him?" Christopher screamed as the furious angel-prince hurtled toward him through the magma like a winged torpedo of wrath. It was a matter of seconds before Jehuel would be close enough to strike.

The three-headed dragon roared in wordless affirmation.

"Then take him!"

One of the great horned heads abruptly dipped down into the lava, seizing the powerful angel-prince in its dripping jaws like a dog catching a squirrel. Jehuel screamed, more in outrage than in alarm, but as the dragon shook him, the look of fury on his face quickly changed to amazement and then panic. Christopher realized that there was a powerful magic about the Chaos monster that prevented the Seraph from shifting to the spiritual plane and escaping.

Leviathan's two outer heads roared in triumph, bobbing up and down in some kind of serpentine dance of celebration as the beast threw its middle head back, opened its great maw, and swallowed Prince Jehuel whole. Seconds later, there was a mighty detonation from within the torso of the dragon, and the beast belched forth a massive fireball against the far side of the cavern.

It exploded on impact, and white-hot phosphorus was splattered all over the huge grotto, burning away the surface of the rocks it struck and hissing angrily as it rained down upon the lake of fire. Of the princely Lord of the Sword, there was no sign except his namesake weapon, buried to its hilt in the rock of the cavern wall.

Christopher and Melusine quickly shifted into the nonmaterial to avoid the burning rain, but Leviathan could not, and its roars of pain were deafening even to their angelic ears. It finally fell silent when the liquid remnants of the Seraph stopped burning. Christopher watched uneasily as its three pairs of yellow eyes raked the cavern from side to side, searching for him.

"I think someone wants to talk to you, Phaoton," Melusine said, satisfaction mixed with anxiety in her voice. "You'd better show yourself."

"We should just get . . . uh, I'm right here, uh, Your Beastliness."

Christopher tried not to flinch or appear uncertain as a massive head suddenly dropped down to within a few feet of his face. Apparently, sneaking out wasn't going to be an option.

"What dost thou ask of me?"

Christopher stared into Leviathan's huge yellow eyes, but they were impossible to read. Without any clues about what the dragon was thinking, he decided that honesty was the safest path. "Well, I kind of hate to say it, but it's pretty much the same thing Jehuel wanted. You know, slay a couple thousand angels, then help us torch what's left of Heaven while we overthrow the old King and put the Dawn Prince in his place. Sounds like fun, don't you think?"

"Why should I help thee? Wouldst thou threaten me, as Prince Jehuel was wont to do?"

Christopher considered his answer carefully. As much as he wanted Leviathan's help, it seemed stupid, not to mention suicidal, to try to make the monster do anything it didn't want to do. "No, I won't," he said decisively. "See, I'd rather work out some kind of deal that would work for both of us, you know? A win-win situation where I'm not having to, you know, keep an eye out to make sure you're not going to eat me or whatever."

The great beast snorted. It almost sounded amused. *"I would be free, released from this cursed place to roam the universe, riding where I choose upon the winds of Chaos. Canst thou do that?"*

Christopher eyed the talisman. "I think I can, maybe. What is this thing, anyhow?" He turned the talisman over in his hand. It was no longer a dagger but had returned to its original form, a dark, curved object shaped rather like a shark's tooth, only larger. A lot larger. "Is it one of your teeth?"

"It is. Lord Jehuel hath stolen it from me long ago. My dominion lies outside the bounds of Order. Once Order is imposed, however slight the imposition, my reign is curtailed, and I am bound. To be free again, I must be complete. Until then, I will serve him who beareth that part of me."

"Hmm. That's interesting. I would have thought it worked the other way around. You know, a little Chaos creeps in, and then everything goes to Hell."

"Mayhap it works that way, too. Give me one of thy teeth, and we'll see."

Christopher laughed. It was pretty awesome that this huge beast had a sense of humor. "I don't think so, dude." He spread his hands and made a suggestion. "What do you think about this? You help me out, and we can beat the King of Heaven. You can even eat him, too, but if it's going to be like that indigestion you had with Jehuel, you'd better warn me so I can get the heck out of Dodge. Then, after we win the war, I set you free, as long as you promise not to ever attack me, my friends, or anybody serving the Dawn Prince."

"What if thy friends choose to attack me?"

"Then the deal's off, and you can go after anybody who attacks you first, me included. Look, I'm not dumb enough to try taking you on, okay? It's a big universe out there, and there's plenty of room for both of us. What do you think?"

All three heads bobbed slowly. *"We are agreed."*

Christopher exhaled, relieved. "Okay, well, we can't really shake on it. Do you swear?"

"By my everlasting hatred of Heaven and its King."

"Good enough for me." He looked back and saw Melusine smiling at him. She had extricated Jehuel's sword from the cavern wall and was offering it to him. "Thanks, I could probably use that. But first, how do we get out of here?"

"Thou shalt ride, but first thou shalt free me." Leviathan lowered two of its giant heads. *"It will be most comfortable for thee if thou sittest behind mine ears."*

"Okay, ears it is. How do I free you, then?"

As the dragon informed him, Christopher looked

back at Melusine, looking for confirmation that he was doing the right thing. Melusine smiled and shrugged, as she waved one of Leviathan's heads away from her. She had no further instructions from Kaym, and Christopher outranked her. For better or for worse, he was on his own.

The scales on the neck of Leviathan's middle head were harder than rock, and Christopher made a mental note to see about getting a saddle in the future. In the meantime, he shifted back into the spiritual plane, because he had an idea how the dragon intended to free them from this subterranean prison. As Melusine settled in behind him and wrapped her slender arms around his waist, Christopher took a deep breath and looked at the tooth in his hand.

> Thy will is mine, my will is thine
> Meshakhrer kan, lehaba lesharat
> Amen, selah, fiat

When Christopher completed the spell, the great dragon, freed at last, rose from the burning lava, and the hot molten rock dripped from its mighty wings like the last remnants of a cocoon falling away from a newly wakened butterfly. With a triumphant bellow of victory, the great beast of Chaos flew up toward the unsuspecting rock, eager to shatter the last vestige of its primordial prison.

CHAPTER 14

LADY OF THE TOWER

HONOUR AND MAJESTY ARE BEFORE HIM: STRENGTH AND
BEAUTY ARE IN HIS SANCTUARY.

—Psalms 96:6

"**I**'m glad to see you're feeling better."

Jami whirled around, alarmed at the sound of a woman's voice. She thought she was alone in the gardens that surrounded the Tower of Qawah. Except for a large purplish bruise on her back, Khasar's crash landing had left her unharmed. But Holli had not woken up yet, and Jami was worried sick about her sister, because she'd been unconscious for two days now.

She turned around and saw a young woman standing behind her.

"I'm all right, thank you," she replied politely. "But I'm worried about Holli. She's my sister, you see, and she hasn't woken up since she got hit on the head a couple days ago. I'm Jami, by the way. Are you one of the angels who rescued us?"

The young woman smiled unself-consciously. She

was rather plain, with medium-length brown hair, but she had a friendly smile and a pleasant way about her. Her eyes were attractive, large and colored an unusual shade of purple-gray.

"No, I am no angel, just a woman like yourself. But you need not fear for your sister. She will be well and will awaken when the time is right."

"How do you know that?" Jami asked sharply. No one could, and it wasn't fair to raise her hopes like that.

"Because I say it will be so." The woman shook her head. "Is not my word enough for you?"

"No!" Jami snapped angrily. Then, as she realized what she'd said, she covered her mouth, mortified.

"I thought not." Fortunately, the woman did not seem offended. "I remember when I was young and needed to know everything. But take this to heart. It is not always for us to know why things must be, it is only for us to know what we should do, and then to do it. Understanding is good, but obedience is better."

"Um, okay, I guess."

"Good, then enough is said." She turned away from Jami and gestured toward the lush garden in front of them. "Do you like my flowers?"

"Oh, totally." She was glad to change the subject, and the flowers really were beautiful. The roses were bigger than any she'd ever seen before, and the tulips were pretty, too. She'd never even seen blue ones before!

"My favorites are the lemon trees, except I don't get how they can grow so close to the mountains. Isn't it too cold for them?"

The woman's violet eyes sparkled with pleasure

at Jami's words. "Not in this place. I am glad you enjoy my garden. It reminds me of how beautiful life can be, and how fragile."

She reached out and delicately snapped a leafy twig off a nearby lemon tree. The twig was bare, but, as Jami watched, a small yellow bud appeared and quickly grew into a firm, full-sized lemon.

"Here, try this," she said as she offered the fruit to Jami.

Jami stared at her for a moment before accepting it. Was she some kind of witch or something? She must be, if she wasn't an angel. Was it safe to eat? There was no way of knowing. Of course, if she was a witch, not eating the thing might be worse.

Jami shrugged and peeled the yellow rind, which tore easily away from the juicy orange-yellow fruit inside. She hesitated momentarily before popping a section into her mouth, anticipating the familiar sourness of lemon. But she was pleased to discover that instead of tasting sour, the fruit was sugar-sweet, and the lemon taste was flavored with lime and orange as well.

"It tastes like Juicy Fruit!" she exclaimed. Her blue eyes narrowed. "If you're not an angel, then how did you do that? You're a witch, aren't you? I bet you're the Lady that Khasar told us about. The Lady of the tower."

"I am," the Lady admitted. "But I am no witch. I must confess, though, this is not my true form. I wear this one at times, when I wish to forget my cares and come to play, here in my garden."

"Then why didn't you tell me right away?"

"I cannot say." The Lady looked away for a moment before explaining. "I think sometimes one grows tired of the burden of always being something rather than someone at times. I don't suppose you understand what I mean."

"But I do!" Jami did understand, and she liked the Lady better for it. "Like, when I go over to the Thompsons', I'm always Jami the baby-sitter, not just me. It's, like, the kids think I live there, and I only come out of the closet when their parents leave."

"Exactly." The Lady laughed, a warm and pleasant sound. Jami laughed, too, until she remembered Holli.

"You say you're not a witch, but how do you know my sister is going to be okay?"

"I know because of a dream I had."

"A dream?" It was hard, but Jami managed not to scoff.

"Yes, and I will tell you of it. It was three months ago, at a time when I was feeling despair. The armies of Lord Matraya, whose evil arm reaches to the ends of the earth, were on the march again, and for almost a week my nights were sleepless. Finally, worn out by exhaustion and fear, I fell asleep at last.

"In my dream, I found myself standing in the sand before the ocean. I stood before a castle of sand such as the children will build. As the tide swelled, mighty waters threatened the castle, only to fail inches from the ramparts. This happened many times, and I heard a voice say, 'Be strong in thy faith, daughter, even unto the End of Time.' Then, in the distance, I saw two seabirds flying low over the water, and out of the sea rose a terrible serpent, which tried to devour them. It failed, but in the attempt it struck one bird. The wounded bird fell to the earth beside the sandcastle, its wing broken.

"When I approached it, I could see that the birds were not normal seabirds, for they were gold, not white. When the wounded bird touched the sand, its wing was miraculously healed, and just in time, for another serpent rose out of the sea, this one even more terrible than the first. This second serpent crawled upon the sand, though whether it came in pursuit of the birds or sought the destruction of the sand castle, I do not know. When it came upon the land, though, the birds flew at it, pecked out its eyes, and the serpent fell back into the sea."

Jami frowned, thinking about the vision. "So, are you saying that this Tower is the sand castle and that Holli and I could be, like, the birds?"

"That is my thinking, yes."

Jami nodded. That made sense, sort of. "Okay, so the first serpent is the snake-thing that attacked us, Lord Bile or whatever, right?"

"It seems likely."

"But here's the problem. How could Holli and I hurt something like that? We're just two girls, and even Khasar couldn't fight that thing."

"I cannot say. I do know this, that the Lord will provide."

Jami sighed. "You know, the angels are always saying things like that."

"In my experience, I have always found it to be so. You asked how I could cause the lemon to grow, remember? I have no power, except that I am an instrument of the Lord. Despite the wisdom of my years, I have found that when I attempt to predict the future and control my destiny, I am usually wrong, and my plans often fail."

A look of sadness crossed her face. "Even now, I

can see the evil seeds of my greatest failure coming to fruition, and yet I have confidence that all will be well in the end."

"Your greatest failure?"

The Lady smiled. "It is a long story."

Jami snorted. "Well, I'm not going anywhere. Not 'til Holli gets better."

"I will not tell you now. Some secrets I must keep for the future. For the present, how would you like a cup of tea?"

Over the next three days, the Lady told Jami many things. She told her about the angels, about the demons, and how the fate of humanity was intertwined with both. She told her about Ahura Azdha, its history, and how the Dawn Prince had won over the soul of Lord Matraya and the hearts of nearly all of his people. And she told her about her own life and how she had become the Lady of the Crystal Tower so many years ago. Late on the third night, as the dancing flames on the hearth died down to glowing embers, she even told Jami of the failure that still haunted her sleepless nights.

Of one thing only she did not speak, and that was the end of her vision of the birds. For at the very moment the golden birds had leaped into the sky, striking at the second serpent, a mighty wave had swept in from the sea, washing away the little sand castle. As the serpent fell back, wounded, the birds returned to the beach only to find it empty, devoid of any sign that children had once played there.

* * *

Holli woke with a start, and the sudden movement made her head hurt. She winced and ran a hand through her tangled curls as her other hand fumbled blindly for the curtain pull, trying to shut out the bright sunlight that had woken her. The sun was uncomfortably warm, and she realized that her legs were sweating as she kicked off the heavy blankets that covered her.

Eewww, how nasty was that, she thought, completely grossed out.

"Mom!" she shouted. "What time is it?"

Then she froze as she looked past the foot of the bed. In the place where her bedroom door should have been was a giant picture window. Or, rather, as she saw when she looked more closely, the window itself was a wall, constructed of clear glass. Wherever she was, it wasn't home.

Since her head was still aching, she climbed carefully out of bed and walked over to the window. The scene below her was quite pretty, as a wide blue river wandered lazily through the green grass that covered a series of gentle hills. She realized that her room was high above the ground, and from the curve of the glass walls, it was obvious that she was in a tower of some sort.

She pushed away the silk curtains that covered the rest of the room and discovered that not only were the inside walls also made of glass, but there didn't seem to be a way out. For some reason this discovery seemed kind of funny, and she started to laugh, but laughing made her head hurt, so she stopped. The pain recalled her fearful flight from the house with Jami and the angels. She also remembered meeting Khasar and riding on his back with Jami, but though she tried to recall more, she simply couldn't figure out how she had come to be here, in this pleasant, pretty little prison.

"I hope they didn't lock you away, too," she told her absent twin as she walked back toward the window and looked down at the river.

She felt a little like Rapunzel, like a princess locked in a tower, when she saw a rider on a white horse approaching the river. The man was riding hard, and even from this great distance, his mount looked as if it was almost finished.

"Someday my prince will come," Holli sang to herself as she watched the rider, although his plain green cloak and huddled posture made her think that he was probably a delivery boy, not a prince.

But it was more romantic to think of him as royalty in disguise, perhaps the crown prince of a great kingdom who would boldly sneak into her glassy prison and rescue her. They would ride madly away, racing to reach his royal castle before the evil witch even realized she was gone. He would be handsome, of course, and kind and loving, and would even have a younger brother only slightly less handsome than her prince, who would himself fall in love with Jami and marry her.

Swept away by her little fairy tale, she gasped as her imagined prince did not hesitate at the river's edge but urged his horse directly into the flowing waters. For a moment, she feared for them both as the tired horse fought against the current, with the river rising almost to its muscled chest. But as the horse reached the midpoint, she saw that its rider knew what he was doing, because the water didn't get any deeper.

Then, behind her, she heard a grinding sound. She whirled around, frightened. But the hand that pushed away the hanging silks was a familiar one, and the face that followed was a very welcome sight.

"Jami," she exclaimed joyfully, and this time her sister returned the exuberant embrace.

"Holli, you're up! Ohmigod! You have no idea how worried I was."

But Holli could see the relief in her sister's eyes. It surprised her, because she didn't feel that bad. Why was Jami so upset?

"How long was I sleeping? It doesn't look that late."

Jami shook her head, still holding Holli's arms. "You've been unconscious for three days, ever since we were attacked by Lord Bile."

"Ever since what?" She had no idea what Jami was talking about.

"You don't remember being hit on the head? No, I don't suppose you would. Well, I'll explain later, because Lady Tiphereth wants me to bring you to her. She knew you'd be awake."

"Who's Lady Teefer?"

"The Lady Tiphereth. She's the Lady of the Crystal Tower, which is this, obviously."

Holli tapped the thick walls with her fingertips. Even though her nail polish had mostly flaked away, her nails still evoked a soft *chunk-chunk* sound.

"Wow. I thought we were going to the Tower of Qawah."

Her twin smiled. "It's, like, the same thing. Anyhow, the Lady is really, really nice. She's the protector of the whole land or something, and she's so pretty. She dresses like a queen, and everything in her court is just like something out of the movies."

Holli eyed the expensive white silk of the dress Jami was wearing and fingered her simple shift.

"I can't go out in this!" she protested. "Especially not if she's, like, a queen."

"No, it's okay," Jami insisted. "I brought some stuff. The Lady said it was for you. It's out in the hall. She even gave me a brush, so we can do something about that hair of yours."

"We'd better," Holli agreed ruefully, as she worked at the mass of curls knotted behind her head.

As Jami helped Holli make herself presentable, she gave her twin a quick rundown of the events of the last few days, starting with their escape from the night shadows. Between Khasar and the Lady, she had learned much about the struggle that had begun for this strange and wonderful land of Ahura Azdha, which the Lady had told her meant the Deathless Kingdom.

"But the Lady says that the land is dying because most of the people are so bad now," Jami grunted as she finally managed to jerk the brush through a particularly recalcitrant knot of hair.

"The land is dying?" Holli repeated absently as she reviewed the results of their hasty labor in the little mirror her sister had supplied. "Hmmm. I wish I had some lip gloss. And I can't believe how chippy my nails are. If I don't find some polish soon, I'll have to cut them."

Jami gave her a quick kiss on the cheek. "Oh, what a tragedy! Anyhow, you look fine, especially for a girl who nearly had her brains splattered on the rocks. It's just a good thing you don't have any!"

"Like you do?" Holli stuck her tongue out. Jami laughed. It was so good to see Holli back to herself again, it made her want to cry. She pinched Holli instead.

"Ow!" Holli glared at her. "What was that for?"

"Oh, nothing. The Lady said I'm supposed to bring you down to her right away, and you don't want to keep her waiting. She's a queen, after all. Let's go!"

CHAPTER 15

THE GREEN RIDER

DO NOT ACT AS IF THOU WERT GOING TO LIVE TEN
THOUSAND YEARS. DEATH HANGS OVER THEE. WHILE
THOU LIVEST, WHILE IT IS IN THY POWER, BE GOOD.
—M. Aurelius (IV, 17)

Jami held Holli's hand as she rushed her down the twisting spiral staircase of the tower. They couldn't go too fast, though, because, like Holli's chamber, the rest of the castle was made of clear, unflawed crystal, and the steps were slippery. The tower was a marvelous building. Jami wished she'd thought to ask the Lady how it was built, when a squad of guardsmen appeared at the bottom of the staircase.

"Please follow me, Lady Jami, Lady Holli," the captain of the Tower Guards said, bowing gallantly. Jami had met him before, and he was a handsome man, although she really didn't like his thick brown mustache. "The Lady will see you now."

"Of course, sir," Holli replied, favoring him with a charming smile. Jami coughed and covered her mouth with her hand. She knew Holli wasn't about to tell the young captain that they didn't merit the title.

The captain didn't seem to notice Holli's play for attention, though, and Jami thought his eyes looked distant and troubled as they swept unseeing across her sister's face.

"I wonder what's bugging him," Holli whispered in her ear. Even at fifteen, Holli was used to being appreciated, and she did not enjoy being ignored.

Something was obviously wrong. Not only had the man looked past the two of them as if they'd been a pair of wrinkled old ladies, but he set a pace that was uncomfortably fast for a pair of girls wearing gowns. That was really weird. Jami knew that the captain normally had excellent manners. His rudeness did not offend her, it only worried her.

"Maybe the rider," Holli said suddenly.

"The what?" Jami had no idea what she was talking about.

"The rider," her twin repeated. "Before you came in, I woke up and looked out the window, and I saw a man riding across the river. He seemed to be in a hurry."

"Maybe that's it."

"Think we'll get to meet him?" Holli's eyes danced.

"Oh, Holli, can't you think of anything but boys?"

"Got anything better to think about?"

Before Jami, exasperated, could come up with a good retort, the massive silk curtains that covered the entrance to the reception hall were drawn apart, and they heard their names announced to their waiting audience.

"My Lady, the Ladies Jami and Holli Lewis, of Mount Arden."

"Mount Arden?" Holli hissed under her breath as she took in the small crowd of courtiers, ladies-in-waiting, and guardsmen. She looked for a green cloak but did not see her rider anywhere. Khasar wasn't there, either, as far as she could tell, not in any of his forms.

"Well, it sounded better than Arden Hills, don't you think?" Jami sounded miffed. "We're supposed to be ladies, after all."

Holli did not reply, though, for her gaze was arrested by one of the most spectacularly beautiful women she had ever seen. Not even the most gorgeous movie star could have rivaled her, and only the angelic perfection of Ariel and Mariel surpassed her. She was neither old nor young but somewhere in the middle, at that timeless age that combines the best of April and September. There was effortless grace in her every gesture, and Holli marveled that not a single dark strand of the complex, upswept coiffure that supported a circlet of silver was out of place. She decided she would have to hate her.

But unlike most of the beautiful women Holli had encountered, the Lady did not use her appearance to intimidate or unsettle them. Her violet eyes were friendly, even kindly, as she indicated that they should come closer to her glassy throne.

"I bid you welcome to the Tower of Qawah. I am the Lady Tiphereth."

Holli nodded. She was indeed a queen.

Her voice was a rich contralto that was pleasing to the ear. Holli made a polite curtsy, and the people of the Tower applauded warmly, echoing their Lady's sentiments.

"Thank you, Lady," she heard Jami say. "Thank you for the hospitality you've shown us for the last three days. And thank you for taking such good care of my sister."

The Lady smiled, and tiny lines appeared at the corners of her upturned lips, the only imperfections on her otherwise flawless face. How was that possible? Holli wondered. She had to be at least thirty, but she had almost no wrinkles. Did she have a special skin cream, perhaps? And if she did, would she let Holli have some of it? Wrinkles, she thought, shuddering, had to be the worst.

"There is no debt, Lady Jami, for it was at my command that you were brought here. If there is an obligation, then it is mine, for I should have foreseen the attack that injured you, Lady Holli. It was only thanks to the Almighty and His brave angels, however, that my mistake did not cost you your life."

Holli flushed, embarrassed by Lady Tiphereth's use of her false title. Letting it slide past a nice-looking young guardsman was one thing, but here, in front of the real thing, well, it was just asking for trouble.

"Um, that's okay, Lady Tiphereth," she said awkwardly. "I mean, I had a little bit of a headache for a while, but I'm fine now. And we're not really ladies, we're just two girls, you know?"

"What she means, Lady Tiphereth, is that you should probably just call us Jami and Holli," Jami explained.

The audience tittered, but the Lady quelled them

with a reproving glance before replying. "I would be honored to address you so." She smiled reassuringly. "Jami, you may recall that when you asked me before to tell you why the two of you had been summoned here, I told you that I would tell you later. Now that Holli is awake, the time has come."

The Lady leaned back in her throne and raised her face toward the great chandelier that hung suspended from the high, transparent ceiling. As she lifted her arms, she raised her voice that she might be more easily heard by all those present in the hall.

"For many years, I have ruled here, in the most holy name of our Lord God, who lives and reigns forever."

"Hallowed be His name," the audience replied.

"I was here when the mighty angel of the Lord caused this place to be. I was but a maiden of some thirteen summers, and I watched, hidden behind a tree, as this castle was constructed. It was not built by the hand of man, as some have foolishly insisted in the past, but by the spoken command of a great and wondrous spirit. He was a fearsome being of flame and mist, and when he spoke, the ground shook and trembled, and the river tried to hide inside its banks."

The Lady waved her hand, and Holli felt as if she were there, as if she were the young girl hiding in the woods, watching awestruck as the elements themselves obeyed the spirit of God.

"I was frightened, but despite my fear, I found that I was curious, too. I thought perhaps I should run, but where can one hide when the world itself is quaking? Then the spirit gave a great shout, and out of nothing, nothing at all, this Tower appeared, on this very hill. It was as if the air had suddenly become solid, for the Tower was pure crystal, in all aspects complete, just as it is today. I was so surprised by this miracle that I forgot my fear. I wandered out from the woods in a daze of disbelief and awe.

"I wanted to touch the glass, to know that it was real and not a fevered summer daydream. Then, from behind me, I heard the spirit speak. My heart was seized with fear. 'Don't be afraid,' he said, and as he addressed me, he was transformed into the appearance of a gentle old man, with a beard that was as white as snow. 'Are you a magician?' I asked. 'Surely you must be one of the great Mages of the East, of whom it is written that even the angels bow before them. Will this be your great tower of sorcery, and shall I be your acolyte?' "

The Lady paused a moment to reflect, and her gaze dropped from the ceiling to meet Holli's eyes.

"What you must understand is that I knew nothing of the true Lord, for my parents were followers of the Dawn Prince and his unholy ways. I had never heard of God, or of Heaven, or of the life beyond death that awaits the faithful," she explained before continuing with her story.

"His wrinkled face was red with anger, but it was not with me that he was wroth, for he turned west, toward the great city of Aurora, and pronounced a terrible vengeance upon it. Then he told me of the True God, of the world beyond this one, and of the life to follow. I took his words into my heart, and when he saw that I believed, he gave the Tower into my care and said that I should live as long as it would stand, clear and incorruptible, a light in the darkness pointing the way toward Heaven.

"I thanked him, for I accepted his charge and I believed his promise, and you can see that he spoke true, for last year did I not celebrate my four hundred and ninetieth summer?"

Holli's eyes narrowed in disbelief, but when she elbowed Jami, the sharp purple-gray eyes of the Lady caught the movement.

"You do not believe me? Ah, well. Ages pass and cities fall, but people never change."

She smiled and continued.

"When I asked what purpose this Tower should have, he answered me strangely indeed. He raised his voice and sang a little song:

This world has no explanation
For the wonders in Creation
And lo, forsooth, in Beauty, Truth
In Truth, Beauty, there thy duty
'til this Tower of Strength shall fall
The End of Days awaits thy call

"Of course, I did not understand at the time, but as centuries pass, my knowledge deepens, and now I do. In a world of darkness, ugliness, and sin, there is no way for the People of the Dawn to explain away the existence of this Tower and its people. You all know how they avoid it and us and deny our existence. Their golden temples are but castles made of sand in comparison, their artistic masterpieces are seen for lies, and their claims of power are exposed for falsehood, for they can never hope to compare with the splendor and majesty of the Lord, not even with us, the least of His creations."

The Lady's voice grew stronger as she dismissed the shining world surrounding her Tower, but even as she reached a crescendo, her eyes fell, and a grim look crossed her face.

"But I have failed in my duty, for corruption has entered this place, through your complacency and my own misdeeds. As time passed and Matraya's armies learned to pass us by thanks to the strength of our walls and the swords of our men, we ceased to live by faith, trusting instead in our own strength. We became soft as we sought pleasures to fill our worldly desires and decadent as we turned the wealth with which the Lord blessed us toward our own selfish purposes rather than His."

She bowed her head and cleared her throat. Then she looked up, and her honest gaze swept firmly across the assembled gathering.

"Many of you know my son, Bel Mavor. He has been my joy and my heart for twenty years. But he is also the lasting sign of my sin, the capstone of the corruption into which we have slowly fallen. You know that I married his father thirty years ago to secure an alliance with the people of Sepharvaim when we felt threatened by Matraya's waxing power. What you do not know is that I disobeyed the angel of the Lord when I did so, refusing to trust in the Lord to protect us instead of the arms of mortal men."

"Lady, you have done no wrong," Holli heard a man protest from the rear of the room.

"You know not of what you speak," the Lady rebuked him. "When my son was born, an angel came to me in my chambers and told me that because of my sin, his father would fall before the shattered walls of Sepharvaim within the week. This would be a foreshadowing, he said, of our own fall. Ten days later, word came that Sepharvaim had been taken by Matraya and that my husband was dead."

Holli swallowed hard. She did not like stories without happy endings, and this one did not sound promising. She felt the pressure of tears threatening to spill and wiped irritably at her eyes. She was not going to cry, not in front of all these people, but it was so hard not to feel sorry for the kindly, beautiful Lady.

"Long ago, I was given a key to the doors of this place," Holli heard the Lady say as she reached into the bodice of her purple robe and withdrew a large key suspended from a silver chain. "And on that day it was as pure and crystal-clear as the Tower itself."

As the Lady lowered her head and slipped the chain off her neck, candlelight from the chandelier sparkled golden-red from the key's glassy surface. But when she raised her hand and held it aloft, Holli saw that it was not a trick of the light, that the key itself was now a deep shade of red. No longer clear, it was as if the key had been carved from a giant ruby.

There were many gasps of shock and dismay as the Lady's demonstration provoked much whispering amongst the people in the hall. Their murmured conversations were quickly stilled, though, as the Lady rose from her throne and slipped the chain back around her neck.

"This is the sign that the Lord will no longer

withhold His judgment from Ahura Azdha and all its people. On that day, which comes even as I speak, the Almighty will cleanse this world with the righteous fire of His wrath. But be brave, my children, for are we not His people? And though we have been unfaithful, He is true and His promise still remains. Though we shall perish with the rest of this world, we will live forever before His eternal throne. We are fortunate, indeed, the most fortunate of mortals, for we have lived to see His victory!"

Holli blinked, and the tears that were pressing at her eyes began to slide down her cheeks, despite her best efforts to resist. She was not ready to die, and she didn't belong to the Lady's God. And even if she did, it didn't sound as if that would make any difference anyhow.

"Blessed be the name of the Most High God," she was surprised to hear a man's voice call, and his cry was echoed by others shouting praises to the Lord. A woman's voice lifted in song, and soon the hall resounded with a simple hymn that was mournful but, to Holli's surprise, seemed at the same time joyful, a cry for help that was also victorious.

> Oh, God
> Oh, God
> As we pray
> As we pray

The singing reminded Holli of the school that saved them from the first attack of evil. There were no guitars, no drums, no instruments at all, but she could feel the same powerful electricity in the air, binding the people together as if they were a choir, or an army. It made her feel a little better, but not that much.

The people of the Crystal Tower sang with determination. Their voices echoed from the crystal walls. They repeated the same refrain over and over again. Holli turned away, unable to look at them, and saw a familiar figure part the thick curtains at the end of the hall. He entered cautiously, a travel-stained man wearing a green cloak.

Oh, God
As we pray

The people did not react, but the Lady saw the man and raised her hand, quieting the people. Holli drew in a sharp breath as she realized that the man was no Prince Charming come to rescue her. As he walked slowly toward her and she saw the narrow features of his drawn face, she knew that he brought bad news. His eyes were bleak, promising not love and life but suffering and death.

"Hail, Bel Mavor," the Lady called out. "Hail, Stormcrow."

Holli started. Bel Mavor? She'd heard that name just a second ago. Why, it was the Lady's son. Why wasn't she glad to see him, then?

The green rider seemed to be surprised himself. He stopped dead in his tracks.

"I am not your enemy, Lady," he insisted. "I know you must think me a traitor, Mother, but I promise you, that is not the case."

"Do not call me Lady, or Mother, for you are no longer mine. I know that you have sold yourself to another, to the one who hungers to grind this Tower into the ground."

Holli winced at the Lady's harsh words. Beside her, she felt Jami shift uncomfortably.

"The King of Prometheon does not desire your destruction, Lady. I have spoken with him, face-to-face. He assured me that he is deeply concerned for the Tower, for its own fate and the fate of its people. Lord Matraya will protect you from the coming storm you fear, if only you will submit yourself to his protection."

"Words," spat the Lady. Holli could tell she didn't believe him.

"Not words," the rider insisted. "I told him that you would doubt me, and so he agreed to offer his surety under the sanctity of his seal. Look!"

He withdrew his right hand from the long sleeves of his cloak and extended it toward the throne. He held his hand upright, exposing a symbol branded upon his palm.

Holli couldn't quite make it out from where she was standing but thought she saw what looked like an eye or perhaps a sun branded in the scar tissue marking the man's hand. It was clear, though, from the Lady's angry reaction that she knew very well what it was and what it represented.

Her nostrils flared, and a steely edge of fury glinted from her eyes as she pointed a slender finger at her son. Her anger was breathtaking. It made Holli feel like cowering herself. Her voice was colder than death as she shouted at him.

"Close thy hand ere I have it stricken from thee, nameless one!"

"Lady, I only thought to save..." Bel Mavor stammered. "Lord Matraya—"

"The king of this world would do well to look to his own, for we have no need of his aid. Tell him so, for he shall no more protect Ahura Azdha from the doom that is foretold than the doe protects her yearlings from the lion."

Her son bowed his head, cowed by his mother's fury. Holli didn't know why the Lady was so mad and couldn't help feeling sorry for him. He wasn't particularly handsome, but the misery in his eyes was somehow appealing.

"I will tell him, Lady," she heard him say.

"And as for you," his mother stated with clenched teeth, "whose name I will not utter, I have only this to say. When the ocean burns away into the night, when the very stones shatter before the terror in the air, when the sky itself falls down upon you, look into your heart, and face the truth at last. Perhaps it will not be too late for you, I cannot say. Now go!"

Holli thought Bel Mavor looked sick as he turned away from the Lady. His narrow face was nearly as green as his cloak, and his shoulders slumped like someone carrying a heavy weight on his back. She watched as he walked slowly toward the end of the hall, his head down to avoid meeting anyone's eyes. But when he reached the heavy curtains at the entrance, his back straightened with a sudden jerk, and he turned around.

"There are no ears so deaf as those that will not hear," he shouted in a deep, scary voice that was different from before. "The Auroran levies are in the field. They march this way, avowing your destruction, only hours behind me. The Sons of Pride are born, Leviathan is free, and the Gates of Heaven have fallen before the Son of the Morning. Fight or fly, as you will, but you will not stop this new dawn, nor can you stop the sun from rising!"

Alarmed, Holli looked at Jami. Her sister's face was white with shock and fear, and Holli's heart sank. She had no idea what was going on, but it sure didn't look as if it was going to have a happy ending. Not for her. Not for anyone.

CHAPTER 16

SHATTERED CRYSTAL, BROKEN GLASS

THE VIRGIN OF ISRAEL IS FALLEN; SHE SHALL NO MORE
RISE: SHE IS FORSAKEN UPON HER LAND; THERE IS NONE
TO RAISE HER UP.

—Amos 5:2

Jami watched the curtains close behind the green cloak of the Lady's son with a feeling of despair. She didn't know a lot about Ahura Azdha, but she had learned enough in three days to know that they were in trouble. The king of Prometheon, Lord Matraya, was as strong as he was evil, and the Lady's doom-filled prophecy left her with no doubt that they were dead.

At Lady Tiphereth's command, the hall was quickly emptied as the people of the Tower hurried to prepare their defenses. Only she and her sister remained with the Lady, but the Lady did not speak to them. She was silent, and her eyes were closed, and Jami thought maybe she was praying. Maybe it would even do them some good, Jami hoped. But considering her earlier words, that didn't seem too likely.

Her heart leaped when the angels appeared. Khasar was first, wearing his handsome human form as he flickered into sudden visibility. He was followed by three others, then by a fourth, a tall and beautiful angel with muscles that rippled like molten bronze. His glowing radiance cast even the Lady Tiphereth into shadow, and Jami found it hard to take her eyes off him.

"Khasar!" Holli cried upon seeing the Archon. She rushed to greet him and embraced him warmly.

Jami was really happy to see him, too. The enemy was on its way to the Tower, but maybe they could get out of this mess on Khasar's back.

"I am sorry, Lady Holli," Jami heard Khasar apologize as he extricated himself and made a formal bow. "I failed to protect you from Bilethel."

"Oh, Khasar, it's all right. It was just, like, a bump on the head."

"Might have actually done her some good," Jami teased.

Holli shot her a dirty look, but she didn't get the chance to respond, as the Lady raised her voice and addressed the angels.

"Servants of the Most High God, I thank you for your faithful service over these many years. But all things mortal must come finally to their end, and for this Tower and its people, that time is at hand. Our purpose here is done, and soon we shall go joyfully before the throne of the King."

The beautiful bronze angel stepped forward. "Lady, shall we not fight for you?"

"Ah, Lokhael, how I shall miss you, my fearless champion, until we meet again in Heaven." The Lady took his hand and pressed it against her cheek. "But this battle is not yours." She gracefully indicated the two girls at her side. "Stand by them as you have stood by me, that is the last charge I lay upon you."

Lokhael bowed his head slowly. His radiance was undimmed, but his shining face was full of grief.

"It shall be so, even as you command, Lady."

The Lady glanced at the other angels. "Nor is this charge yours alone, my friend, it is for all of you. The young ones are in great danger, though they know it not, and they face an evil that is beyond my power to rebuke. Khasaratjofee has no doubt told you that Lord Matraya seeks to capture them and sends great spirits, such as the fallen Bilethel, forth to hunt them."

Lokhael nodded solemnly, as did his companions.

"Lady, can't you come with us?" Jami asked. It looked as if they were going to escape after all. She felt really sorry for the people of the Tower, but it was a huge relief that they weren't going to have to stay here and die with them.

"That I cannot do. My place is here, with my people."

"But you can't stay here! You said they're going to kill you, all of you," Holli cried, her eyes brimming with tears. "There's five of them, and Khasar can carry us just by himself!"

The Lady only smiled, and Jami shook her head, amazed by her calmness in the face of approaching death.

"Are you sure, Lady?" she asked. "I know you said that it was kind of your fault and all, but what good will it do if you just get killed?"

"What good will it serve?" Lady Tiphereth sounded almost amused. "It will serve the highest purpose of all, Jami. There is no higher call that I could answer than this, to lay down my life for God. I do not fear my death, I welcome it. You see, in this fragile flesh I cannot approach my God face-to-face."

She gently stretched out a hand to wipe away a tear from Holli's face.

"Believe me, child, I know whereof I speak. I have seen spirits in their fiery realm, and they are terrible indeed. How much greater, then, is the glory of the Almighty? No, if my heart bleeds, it is for you, who are left behind, to carry on the struggle against the shadow."

"But we don't know what to do, Lady," Jami protested. "We don't even know where to run!"

The Lady did not answer her directly; instead, she turned first toward the angels. "In my dream, the second serpent rose out of the sea before the rising sun. Take them east, toward golden Aurora. Children, do not trouble yourselves overmuch, because God will guide you. But I can give you these, the gifts that the angel of the Lord gave to me so long ago."

The Lady gently placed her hands on Holli's shoulders, which shook as she tried to stop crying.

"I have not known you long, lovely child, but I see that your heart is good and kind. I give you the eyes that the fiery spirit once gave me, that you should be able to see spirits and see as well into the hearts of men. This gift is a hard one, for you will see not only angels but devils and the lies that lurk behind many smiles. And yet you must not judge; you may find that to be the hardest part of all."

"Thank you, Lady," Holli tearfully replied. "I will, I mean . . . I'll try not to."

Jami stared at the floor, envious and relieved at the same time. The Lady's gift sounded pretty cool, but that whole not-judging thing? Even when you knew for sure that somebody was lying to you? She shrugged. It was probably a good thing Holli was stuck with it, not her.

She held her breath as Lady Tiphereth turned her violet eyes toward her.

"You, my dear Jami, have a lion's heart and a lion's pride. Two sides of the same coin, perhaps, but one path leads to light while the other ends in darkness. Humble yourself before the Lord, and all will be well with you, for the fear of the Lord is truly the beginning of all knowledge." The Lady reached out and touched her forehead lightly. "My gift to you is this, the word of command that spirits of good and ill must needs obey. Use it wisely, and always remember that this authority comes not from me but from the Lord."

Jami bent down and kissed the Lady's ring, as she had seen the guardsmen do. When she straightened up, she was glad to see that the Lady looked pleased.

"I'll remember what you told me," she promised solemnly.

"My blessing upon you both," the Lady said softly. "Now, go quickly, for there is little time!"

"We can't leave by ground," Khasar growled as he released his grip on Jami's arm. Jami rubbed at it gingerly, wondering if she had a bruise that would show. The Archon was in a huge hurry and had half dragged her up the central staircase. "Bel Mavor lied. Matraya's army already has the Tower surrounded."

They had reached the top of the staircase and were standing in a small hallway that led to several small rooms. Khasar led them into the easternmost room and, once safely past the doorframe, transformed himself back into his lion form. The Lady's bronze champion, Lokhael, walked past him to the far side of the room and threw open a large window. Jami stared at him, confused. It was big, but it was definitely not big enough for the Archon to pass through.

"Get on my back," Khasar told Holli. "Jami, you ride with Jhoforael."

Holli meekly complied, but Jami protested, even as the big angel beside her blurred and shifted form into another blue-winged lion. He looked a lot like Khasar, but his fur was white instead of golden-yellow.

"You can't get through there! It's too small!"

"Get on!" Khasar roared, and Jami, startled into obedience, climbed quickly onto Jhoforael's back.

She winced and held her breath as Khasar hurled himself at the open window with her sister aboard. Holli screamed, and there was a massive crack as the Archon struck the sides of the window. Then glass exploded outward like a crystal waterfall as the force of his leap smashed a huge hole in the side of the Tower.

Thousands of razor-sharp shards of glass rained down. Khasar spread his wings wide. He flew in a tight circle, turning about to face them. Jami finally exhaled. Khasar was clearly unharmed, and her idiot sister was grinning cheerfully at her.

"Come on, Jami!" she shouted. "I double-dare you!"

Jami ignored her.

"Hey, you might want to watch your wings, huh?" she murmured to Jhoforael. "That hole's big enough, no need to add on to it."

"Keep your head down," the Archon replied in a deep voice as he gathered himself on his haunches.

Jami ducked down as far as she could, but the jagged edges of glass came way too close to her head for her comfort. But they were safe, or at least as safe as you could be flying high up in the air without an airplane around you. She felt the wind blowing her hair and steadfastly refused to look down as they began their flight to the east.

"Oh, no!" she heard Holli cry as the angels found their rhythm. "The Lady! The Tower!"

She craned her neck around and looked back to the west. Wow, she thought. These guys fly really fast! They were already more than a mile away from the Tower but were close enough to see that the enemy army had crossed the river and was already attacking. The enemy warriors looked like ants as they swarmed up the glassy building in such numbers that it seemed the whole thing would crack and crumble before their weight.

What was happening inside the Tower? The thought sickened her, and she was thankful that they were too far away to see the last bitter struggles of the Lady and her people.

Then she slammed her head into the back of Jho-for's big, blue-maned skull as he abruptly turned his wings up and came to an unexpected stop in the sky.

"Ow!" she complained, rubbing at the side of her head. These angels flew rough. At least it wasn't her nose again. "Why did you stop?"

"Shhh!" the Archon commanded as Lokhael began to sing in a deep bass.

When the Enemy presses you hard, do not fear!

The other angels replied with voices that rumbled through the clouds like thunder.

The battle belongs to the Lord.
Take courage, my friends, your redemption is near!
The battle belongs to the Lord.

Lokhael raised something high above his head as the three angels raised their voices in a triumphant chorus.

We sing glory, honor,
Power and strength to the Lord
We sing glory, honor,
Power and strength to the Lord . . .

As she stared at the warrior angel, wondering why in the world he was stopping to sing, Jami realized that Lokhael was holding the key to the Tower in his bronze hands. It was bright red now, glowing hot like a fiery coal. As the angels finished their chorus, he snapped the key in two.

The snap was echoed by the distant sound of cracking glass mixed with the unmistakable wail of human screaming. Jami whipped her head around just in time to see that the clear crystal of the Tower had turned blood red and was splintering into millions of pieces. The cries came from the enemy troops climbing its sides. The soldiers screamed with fear as they realized that the Tower was about to collapse.

But before the Tower fell, one of the angels withdrew a trumpet from his robes, and its brassy cry was echoed moments later by a mighty blast that shook the earth. Even the sky seemed to shake. Jami clung to Jhoforael's mane, stunned speechless, as the splintered Tower exploded, hurling thousands of glass fragments in all directions, slicing through the attackers. In a single heartbeat, there was not an enemy soul left standing. It was amazing. Moments before, there was a tower and an army, and the next moment there was . . . nothing. Nothing but a few fluttering shadows, circling in confusion above the terrible ruin of the battlefield.

"Oh, Jami, I think I'm going to be sick!" Holli cried, and a moment later, she noisily proved herself right.

That didn't help. Jami had to swallow hard a few times herself to avoid following suit.

"Our God is mighty," Jhoforael said solemnly. "Blessed be the name of the Lord."

"Oh, but how can you say that?" Holli asked, looking more than a little devastated herself. "It's so terrible, so terrible."

Lokhael heard and answered Holli. "He did this

so that all the peoples of the Earth might know that the hand of the Lord is powerful, and so that you might always fear the Lord your God."

"But I thought God was supposed to be, like, a loving God," Holli protested.

"He is. But He is also just, and this shall be a warning to the Son of the Morning, and to Matraya, his slave."

"A warning?" Jami closed her eyes, hoping to forget what she had seen. Some warning.

"The Lord is merciful and slow to anger, but when His anger comes, it is sudden, like the whirlwind," Lokhael said.

"The Son of the Morning must repent of his rebellion," added Khasar. "Or he will drink the bitter wine of the wrath of the Almighty. As will those who follow him."

Jami saw her sister shake her head. She looked sad and miserable, but Jami thought she got some of what the angels were telling them. She felt a jerk as Jhoforael started moving his wings again.

"Maybe that's what the Lady meant," she said out loud as they resumed their journey.

"What the Lady meant?" Jhoforael asked.

"About the fear of the Lord being the beginning. Of knowledge, or whatever."

"Wisdom."

"Okay, well, wisdom then." She started to glance back at where the Tower had been, then stopped herself. She had already seen what God could do. Fear of the Lord wasn't going to be a problem in her book. "Is there a difference?"

"There is. Wisdom is supreme, therefore seek it. Though it cost you all you have, seek understanding. Esteem her, and she will exalt you. Embrace her, and she will honor you."

It was the first long statement she had heard from the white Archon in the short time that she'd known him. He didn't seem to be very talkative, so she thought about his words as they flew, riding the wind, toward the dangers waiting unknown in the East.

CHAPTER 17

SONS OF PRIDE

WE HAVE HEARD OF THE PRIDE OF MOAB; HE IS VERY
PROUD: EVEN OF HIS HAUGHTINESS, AND HIS PRIDE, AND
HIS WRATH.

—Isaiah 16:6

Through Lord Matraya's mortal eyes, Kaym surveyed Asmodel's newly manufactured legions of ur-mortals with satisfaction. The Anakhim, or Sons of Pride, as Asmodel proudly named them, stood in row after row of red-clad warriors, their lines stretching out as far as the eye could see. The rosy rays of the rising sun cast a bloody hue upon their unsheathed weapons, a favorable omen before battle. The ur-mortals were eager to fight, their blood fired by the angelic power coursing within them, and they slavered after his promise of the divinity that would be bestowed upon them after the battle.

Each group of twenty was captained by a real angel, most of whom were exhausted after the carnal activities of the previous day. The preparations had gone on until the wee hours of the morning, when the last of one hundred thousand mortals had been infused with the angelic flame of the eternal.

Lord Asmodel had favored the last mortal himself, an attractive woman with red hair whose features reminded Kaym of the lovely Seraph Raphael. Kaym had suspected that the Zodiac Lord had gone too far, given her too much in his bullish enthusiasm, and now he watched as her exotic features were distorted with pain as she fought to keep the Bull's chaotic power from shifting her form again. Already she had taken on some of the aspects of Asmodel's sign, as horns curved outward from her forehead and her boots were split by the cloven toes that peeked out from the ruptured leather. Godhood, Kaym decided, was not an easy task for mortals.

The fallen angel shrugged indifferently and turned away from Asmodel's creations. He did not like them, but he had need of them, two for every angel in Asrael's host, and that was all that mattered. All that mattered until the battle actually started. He had no doubt that the true spirits of the Divine Host would brush aside the Anakhim like a flood uprooting a newgrown sapling, but Asmodel had done his part, and Kaym had what he needed. He would do his part, and if Christopher could help him by removing that narcissistic fool Jehuel, then this makeshift legion might stand a decent chance of winning.

The sun had risen less than an hour before, an auspicious time for an army that fought in the name of the Son of the Morning. The yellow sky was clear, and the winds were still, but Kaym knew that the respite was only momentary. Sure enough, trumpet blasts echoing from the nearby hills gave the first sign of the approaching Divine Host. Soon Asrael's vanguard was within sight, speeding high over the southern plains, a vast array of white wings beating together in a rhythm that sent a sweet-smelling breeze cascading over Kaym's waiting army. Kaym wrinkled his nose and spat. Moments later, the rest of the host appeared, an incendiary cavalcade of fiery chariots, flaming swords, and flashing wings.

It was an awesome sight, but Kaym was pleased to see that the Anakhim did not flinch before the Divine display of force. With weapons held ready and nostrils flaring with anticipation, they waited for his command. He did not give it, though, even as a trumpet blew three notes and a thousand Archangels began to hurl thunderbolts down at his unshielded army.

He watched impassively as the deadly bolts of lightning exploded within his ranks and five thousand Anakhim were blown to pieces, their mortal frames too weak to withstand the power of the spiritual bombardment. The ground shook under the massive detonations, and the surviving ur-mortals wailed as they were spattered with the gory remnants of their companions.

"He's not mixing his ranks, Lord Kaym," Asmodel told him, wearing a fierce aspect of a fearsome four-armed, bull-headed minotaur with wings. "All his Archangels are on the right."

"There were only a thousand in that last blast. He should have twice that," Kaym pointed out. "Let's wait and see if he'll try again. He's already confused, because he thought we'd only have one legion."

"Do you think that's wise?" The Bull was no coward, but passive endurance was not his way. "If the Anakhim break, we're finished, and there's no sign of Prince Jehuel yet."

Kaym smiled to himself. If things went well, there never would be. But Asmodel didn't need to know that.

"That's why I need to wait. Even with our numbers, we're not going to win this battle without Leviathan. The longer we can wait before my hand is forced, the better off we'll be."

The Bull grumbled, but he had no counterargument ready at hand. He stood beside Kaym, and together they watched the flaming skies in silence. The Divine trumpet sounded, and again the host cast forth a terrible bombardment. This time, two thousand bolts of lightning fell, accompanied by five hundred massive fireballs launched from the left side of the host.

This second attack was far deadlier than the first. The huge balls of fire, hurled by Asrael's mighty Powers, blasted deep craters into the earth, sending shards of rocky shrapnel hurtling through the Fallen ranks. Twenty thousand more ur-mortals were slain in one horrid moment of thunder, screams, and bloodshed, and eighty of their angelic captains perished with them. Weak from exhaustion, their flames were snuffed out by the righteous wrath of the Divine.

Now the Sons of Pride truly quailed, as they began to understand that their godlike strength was not enough to withstand the power of the Beni Elohim. Shouts of fear and panic filled the air, and as Asmodel feared, the ranks toward the rear of the

Fallen army began to break away. They ran toward the protection of Aurora's high stone walls.

But even as thousands of ur-mortals ran and tens of thousands more considered the possibility, Kaym refused to change his plans. As he expected, just moments later, two towering walls of flames appeared between the panic-stricken Anakhim and the city, cutting off the deserters' escape route. The Archon Mahalidael was stationed with the rear guard, and the zodiacal Lord of the Ram had done his duty exactly as instructed.

Kaym grinned at Asmodel as one deserter, more desperate than the rest, dared to essay the fire. He burst through the first wall with his skin ablaze and stumbled into the second, the flames of which quickly enveloped him in their fatal embrace. His piercing screams of soul-searing agony were enough to convince the rest of the deserters that they had no choice but to return, met by a small force of angels who quickly directed them back into fighting ranks.

"There, you see?" He pointed. "They will not run."

"No, they won't," Asmodel agreed, shaking his horned head ruefully. "Good, you were ready for that. But what are you waiting for?"

Kaym didn't bother to reply, preferring instead to watch Mahalidael's angels efficiently restore the shocked rear guard to good order. In the main body, his captains were trying to do the same. Their angry shouts and curses drowned out the cries of dying Anakhim as they repaired the gaping holes in their ranks created by the Divine onslaught.

"It's time!" Asmodel bellowed at him, his red eyes swirling angrily. "They won't stand another strike! They're ready, curse you, now let them loose!"

Kaym nodded slowly, noting the Divine formation. The Bull was right. It was time.

"Hit their middle, but if you manage to break their line, try to move through to the right," he commanded. "Stay as far from their Powers as you can, and I'll try to keep their Archangels from flanking you."

"Selah!" Asmodel roared. "What about Jehuel?"

"Mahalidael knows what to do if he shows up. Go, thou, and slay, in the name of the Shining One."

"Fiat!"

The bull-headed Archon nodded and spread his wings, hungry to lead the Fallen attack. He lifted a gilded ram's horn from his belt and blew a short series of angry notes. As if in response, a rumbling sound seemed to come from somewhere deep within the earth. The ground began to shake violently. The very rocks undulated beneath the Fallen army, causing more than a few ur-mortals to lose their balance and fall, as the Auroran plain imitated an uncertain sea.

But Asmodel's belligerent call gave heart to the embattled Anakhim, who were hard-pressed just to maintain their ranks as the ground beneath their feet continued to roll and shake. They roared their defiance of Heaven as the Bull leaped into the air and hurled a blue-tinged fireball up toward the waiting enemy lines. It was the sign that the Fallen army had been waiting for.

As Kaym watched, Asmodel sped toward the enemy, with the Anakhim right behind him, seventy-five thousand strong, swarming up from the ground like a huge flock of deadly black-winged birds. Kaym was pleased to see that the ur-mortals did not shrink from the imminent conflict; indeed, they seemed relieved to abandon the treacherous ground where they were helpless before the Divine thunderbolts. Released into action at last, they howled with fury, eager to avenge themselves upon the angelic forms of their Divine foe.

As they saw that his army was finally moving to attack, Asrael's Powers and Archangels launched another barrage of lightning and thunder. But this time, Kaym had no intention of allowing them to shred his forces. He drew upon the massed power of the thousand angels he'd been holding in reserve and unleashed a prepared spell. The stars of Taurus glowed red hot as a vast inky net shot across the sky, filling the gap between the rapidly closing armies for a brief moment and absorbing the full force of the Divine assault. Then, without a sound, it disappeared again, as quickly as it had come. But Kaym was satisfied, for the spell had served his purpose.

A few thunderbolts had found their way through his dark net, and several Fallen warriors, stricken, dropped from the sky like stones. But before their tumbling bodies even hit the ground, Asmodel and the first of the Anakhim were already engaging Asrael's vanguard. They smashed into the Divine lines like a black blade slashing through white silk.

The struggle in the sky was a fierce one. The very presence of the Anakhim had upset Asrael's plans, while their greedy lust for battle made them strong, stronger even than Kaym had hoped. The savagery of Asmodel's initial assault had come close to breaking the Divine middle, but Asrael's rear guard stiffened, and Kaym realized that the breakthrough he had planned for was not going to happen. It was not long before the greater strength of the Divine angels began to tell, and inexorably, as the Anakhim weakened, the tide of battle began to turn against the Fallen.

Kaym frowned and cursed himself for a fool as he saw Ra'shiel, the twice-traitorous Archon, lead five thousand flaming chariots away from the Divine right, moving in a swift arc that would send them hammering into Asmodel's unguarded left flank. Ra'shiel was trying to divide the Fallen force in two, panicking the rear half into retreat while engulfing the rest, trapping them for wholesale slaughter. Kaym knew he should have placed his reserve force between Ra'shiel and his target, but the angels were still weak from his great spell, and the Divine Archon had moved faster than he'd expected.

Kaym folded his arms and thought upon which would be the worse of his two apparent options: perishing in battle or reporting failure to the Dawn Prince. His chances were better in battle, he decided, when he realized that the ground was still shaking, even more violently than before. It seemed to be coming from the south. Sure enough, there was a hill ten stadia away, one that had not been there when he'd surveyed the ground that morning.

Mahalidael rushed toward him, and the Ram's face was filled with wonder and fear. "What is that?" he asked Kaym, pointing unsteadily at the ever-growing hill.

"It's the King of Heaven!" a nearby angel cried. "Come to curse us and send us all Beyond!"

Kaym threw back his head and began to laugh. Whether it was Christopher or Jehuel, their timing could not be better. Ignoring the battle in the sky, he pointed to the bulging ground, as the giant mound grew wider and higher before his angels' amazed eyes. Filled with joy at the thought of the coming victory, he triumphantly shook his fist at them.

"Your salvation, fools. I mistake it not!" he declared, enthusiastically slipping back into the archaic tongue. "Spirits of small faith, unleash thy swords, for in Chaos is thy salvation found!"

Before him, the hill swelled into a mountain, pregnant with the awful expectance of an uneasy volcano. Before the stunned eyes of the Fallen rear guard, it erupted, vomiting forth a huge black monster amidst a boiling shower of shattered rocks and magma.

Christopher felt as if he were riding a rollercoaster, as Leviathan rose ever higher into the sky, lifted by the powerful blast of the eruption. The force of the blast was an unsteady support. He could feel the dragon straining with all of his mighty strength to keep from tumbling tail over three heads. It was terrifying, but exciting, too, and he didn't even have to pay for admission!

Melusine shrieked and clung to his waist so tightly he could hardly breathe, which was just as well given the ash and poisonous gases that surrounded them in a dark gray cloud of death. Fortunately, his mostly nonmaterial state rendered it harmless to him, while Melusine, of course, was immortal.

They finally reached a height at which the deadly cloud stopped rising with them. Christopher was able to see the battlefield, if that was the right word for the chaos that filled the sky before him. They were nearly half a mile away from the action, which was mostly below them, but Christopher's game-practiced eye saw immediately that the Fallen army was in serious trouble.

His idea of using the Auroran mortals must have worked, because the Fallen army was clearly larger than the Divine Host. But its main wedge was buried in the Divine center, and its advance had stalled, while a small reserve guard waited uselessly on the ground. Meanwhile, the Divine forces were advancing on both sides in a pincer movement. A large detachment was moving openly toward the wedge's left flank, as a smaller group advanced on the right, using the huge Fallen wedge as cover. From his vantage point in the sky, Christopher could see that the second detachment's target was the unsuspecting Fallen rear guard, which had to be protecting Kaym and the Fallen command.

The two Divine detachments were advancing quickly. Christopher knew he had only seconds to make up his mind. Both targets were terribly vulnerable, but he could only aid one. He knew that military history called for saving the main body of troops, but in Warhammer and other games, a hero was worth more than a whole regiment of troops. The question was, what was true nature of this warfare? Was it fantasy or history that applied here?

Let's see, he thought. I'm riding on a dragon's back with a gorgeous devil-girl hanging on behind me. It was definitely fantasy, he decided, and he urged Leviathan to intercept the second group, the one stalking the rear guard.

"Melusine, get off now," he ordered.

"No, I have to protect you," she protested.

"Come on, I'm with Leviathan, for God's sake!" he swore unthinkingly. "I need you to tell Kaym about that group of angels, there." He pointed to the larger Divine detachment. "He can't see them coming from there, and I'll need his help if Leviathan and I can't take these guys on ourselves."

It was a lie, of course. Kaym wasn't a complete idiot. There was no way he hadn't seen the Divine force heading toward him. Christopher just hoped Kaym would hurl his reserve into the gap in time and keep the larger detachment from flanking the Fallen wedge.

"I understand. Be careful."

He felt a soft pair of lips lightly caress his ear, then Melusine's slender arms released his waist. He looked down and saw her diving speedily with her wings furled down toward Kaym's position. Her body was exquisite, and despite the battle looming only seconds away, it was with some reluctance that he turned his eyes away from her and toward the enemy below.

He lifted Jehuel's sword and easily transformed it into a giant lance.

"It's too bad you're not an ostrich," he told Leviathan. "Or an emu."

"What?"

"It's a joke, dude." He laughed, couching the silver weapon under his arm. They were dropping rapidly now. Christopher was pleased to see that the Divine angels seemed totally unaware of their impending doom. In only seconds he was upon them.

Leviathan breathed three large bursts of orange-red flame as Christopher's lance impaled two white-winged angels. They weren't regular angels, he realized at once, but even the great strength of the stricken Powers was not enough to resist the terrible force of the blow, and they vanished in brilliant bursts of purple light. Shouts of surprise and dismay filled the air. Christopher transformed the lance back into a great two-handed broadsword.

He struck down three more Powers before the angels seemed to realize that they were in danger. Thanks to Leviathan, another thirty or so were discovering what lay beyond the Beyond, but there still remained hundreds of angels who were even now regrouping for a counterattack. Twenty fireballs suddenly arced his way, but Leviathan turned one head and breathed again. The greater fury of its fire blotted out the Divine assault.

Leviathan had eliminated all the angels within reach, so Christopher pointed his sword at the massed Powers and willed a score of thunderbolts into existence. He was pleased to see twenty silver bolts arc through the sky and obliterate fifteen angels. He blinked, shocked that his weapon had worked so well, and did it again. The second blast vaporized ten more Powers.

"The Lord of the Sword!" a white-robed angel wailed. He had just turned to flee when a third blast evaporated him and several of his fellows.

"Almighty One, save us from the fury of the Foe!" another Power cried aloud.

As others took up the fear-filled cry, the Archon

leading them realized that his Powers were not strong enough to face the combined might of Leviathan and what seemed to be a ranking Seraph. Though four hundred Powers yet remained to him, he lifted a trumpet to his lips and blew the retreat. Christopher laughed when he heard the horn and watched, pleased with himself, as the survivors obeyed with glad alacrity, speeding back toward the Divine lines.

"We have them now!" Leviathan bellowed with deafening glee. *"Slay them all!"*

"No, wait!" Christopher exerted his will and forced the great dragon to wait. It was hard reining in the ravenous beast, but he did it. "Look there!"

Miraculously, Kaym had managed to disengage the rear half of the main Fallen wedge. It was moving now in a path that would cut off the fleeing Powers' line of retreat. His rear guard of one thousand angels, meanwhile, had flown up to defend this new detachment's rear and was desperately battling a Divine force of charioteers that outnumbered them five-to-one.

"That's where we go!" Christopher shouted, pointing toward the vicious fighting with his sword.

Leviathan resisted, though, as the great monster's instincts urged him to chase his routed foes.

"You will obey me!"

Christopher cursed at his monstrous mount, throwing the whole force of his will behind the command, knowing that the battle might hang in the balance. At last, one of the dragon's heads stopped straining forward and turned to the left.

"There will be a reckoning!" Leviathan hissed angrily.

"No, there will be a victory! For both of us."

"We shall discuss this anon!"

"I'll be happy to explain it to you later," Christopher promised, hoping that the great beast would be in a mood to listen then. "Now, go shred some white robes!"

Kaym's rear guard was decimated by the time they arrived, but Leviathan unleashed his ungodly fury on the Divine chariots, smashing flaming wheels with his great wings and tearing apart the angelic charioteers with his terrible claws. Christopher wielded Jehuel's silver sword to lethal effect. It was not long before the chariots were fleeing, too, reduced to less than half their original number.

"Who art thou?" shouted the ram-headed Archon who'd been commanding the tattered rear guard.

"Just call me Ishmael, Goat-boy!" Christopher shouted at him. Leviathan's bloodlust was contagious, and at this point, he didn't care who he was insulting or who he killed.

As he glanced past the Fallen captain, he realized that victory was close at hand. Kaym's new detachment of mortals had smashed through the routed Powers, then curved around to strike the main Divine flank, and Asrael's angels, outnumbered and outwitted, lost heart and began to flee. Christopher began to laugh, giddy with murderous glee, as his spirit burned with an insane lust for battle.

As the Divine angels fled desperately away from the skies over the city of Aurora, a huge black shadow slashed again and again through the retreating host, like a giant three-headed eagle wreaking havoc on a flock of helpless doves. The battle for Rahab was over, and though Asrael himself survived the day, his army was reduced to fewer than twenty thousand shattered spirits. The siege of Heaven would not be lifted, and the King of Chaos was free to soar through the darkening yellow skies.

CHAPTER 18

FALSE GODS

THEREFORE PRIDE COMPASSETH THEM ABOUT AS A CHAIN;
VIOLENCE COVERETH THEM AS A GARMENT.

—Psalms 73:6

Holli had finally stopped crying, but she could still feel the taut track of dried tears on her face. Even though she hadn't known any of the Lady's people, the thought of their deaths hurt her deeply. She still couldn't quite believe that they were all gone. It was not something she wanted to remember, but the sight of the Lord's righteous fury was impossible to forget, no matter how hard she tried.

She shifted uncomfortably on Khasar's broad back, trying to find a position that would put less strain on her aching legs. No matter how she moved, though, it hurt. Lions just were not built for riding, not even winged angel-lions, and she didn't think Khasar would want to wear a saddle, not even if she asked him nicely.

"How long until we get there?" she couldn't

help asking, even though she already knew the answer.

"I don't know," Khasar replied patiently. "We'll know when we arrive. It's another hour to Prometheon, if that's where we're meant to go."

"How will you know?"

"The Lord will make His will known. Trust me. When I was young and foolish, I often questioned the Lord, thinking that my understanding a task was needful if I was to perform it. But I have learned that while it's good to understand, it's better to obey."

Holli looked down. They were past the rolling hills now and were flying over a patchwork of golden meadows broken up by a farm every now and then. Up ahead was a big patch of green that looked like a forest or something. Once, they flew past a small village, and Holli saw people walking between the tiny buildings below her. She waved, but no one was looking up at the sky.

"Isn't it, like, important to understand why you're doing something?" she asked.

"Not if you've already been told what to do." She felt Khasar shake his blue mane. "The *why* is not important, only the *what*."

"The *what?*"

"Of course, the *where* and *when* can be important, too. But not the *how*, that's where faith comes in."

"What?"

"No, the *how!*"

"Oh, shut up." Holli laughed for the first time since leaving the Tower. "You're just being silly."

"I am," Khasar admitted freely. "But though I am

a fool, there is truth in what I say. Understanding can mean many things." Her sore legs twinged a little as he shrugged. "To know the difference between right and wrong, between truth and falsehood, well, those kinds of understanding are important indeed. But, you see, it's not important to know where we're going right now, because the knowing won't get us there any sooner."

Holli frowned and blew a stray curl out of her face. "But it would still be nice to know how much longer it will be. I mean, I'm kind of sore."

Khasar snorted. "Flying one daughter of the King on your back is much easier than two, but I do pray that the Most High will soon find some other way for me to serve Him."

"I'll bet!" Holli looked over at her sister, who was riding the white Archon in uncharacteristic silence. Jami was playing with the end of her ponytail, which usually meant that she was thinking about something. "Do you think Jhofor . . . Jhofor—"

"Jhofor," Khasar cut her off.

"Okay, Jhofor then. Does he mind flying Jami, too?"

"Probably not," Khasar replied sadly, sounding put-upon. "You're much heavier."

"Did you say—I am not!" Holli cried, mortified. "Take that, you stupid cat-bird!"

"Ouch! My mane is no plaything, child!" Khasar yowled. "And do not even ponder tugging at my ears."

"Oh, yeah?" Holli tugged at his little ears again. "Take it back!"

"I relent!"

"I'm not heavy!"

"No, no, not at all," he hastily agreed. "Light as a feather, one might say."

"And . . . hey, what's that?"

Holli leaned over Khasar's shoulder, peering down at a flash of movement that caught her eye. They were high above the forest, and while it was hard for her to see anything past the thick blue-green mass of leaves that covered the tall elmlike trees, something was definitely there.

"There's something down there, Khasar. Can you see it?"

The big Archon sniffed the wind, then glanced back at Lokhael.

"There is something foul down below, but I don't recognize it."

"Nor I," the bronze angel replied as he drew his sword. "Let us descend, that we not fly into the arms of our enemies."

Khasar pulled his wings in, and they dropped so quickly that Holli's eyes teared up. They plunged toward the treetops as she wondered if her heart would stop on its own before they smacked into a tree. But Khasar slipped through the trees without crashing, located a small clearing, and brought them safely to the ground without injury. Holli slid off his back with a weak smile and a tremendous feeling of relief. The others landed only moments later, and Jami rushed to Holli's side.

"What did you see? What did you see?"

Holli didn't answer; instead, she clutched gratefully at the hands that were holding her upright. Her legs were weak, and not just from the flying.

"Oh, that was just a bit too much! Can we please,

please, pretty please trade next time?" she appealed to Jami.

Jami laughed at her but put an arm around her and helped her stand up. Khasar and Lokhael were arguing about who would stay with them and who would go out to see what was hiding in the woods. Apparently, Lokhael won, because she heard him mutter a hurried prayer before he ran into the forest. She tried to keep an eye on him, but he quickly faded into the blue-green darkness.

Lokhael had not been gone for more than a minute or two, and Khasar was still complaining to Jhofor, when there was a sudden shimmer of light and a glowing blue disc appeared in front of them. Holli jumped. Khasar quickly transformed into his human form and stepped between her and the light. But before anyone did anything, the newcomer materialized more fully, and the blue glow disappeared to reveal a short, sturdy-looking angel holding a pair of short swords. He seemed tired, and Holli thought he looked a little bit beat-up for an angel.

"I know this one," Khasar reassured her. "He is a friend, I believe."

"Greetings, Rhamiel," Jhofor called. "Is it well with you?"

"It is well, Archon Jhoforael, though it is my sorrow to tell you that this day our host was defeated by the rebel armies. Although the Adversary himself was absent, we were routed before the gates of Aurora. Many were sent Beyond, and the rest now flee, scattered to the winds."

"How can this be?" Khasar growled. "Didn't Asrael join us?"

"They did, but we were outnumbered nevertheless. Matraya committed a foul blasphemy, ordering his minions to pollute themselves and endow countless humans with their immortal powers. They call themselves the Sons of Pride, and they are proud and mighty warriors."

"No!" Khasar exclaimed, disgust on his face. Holli wondered what had grossed him out so much, especially since the whole Tower blowing up didn't seem to disturb him. She shivered. If it was worse than that, she didn't want to know.

"There is worse news. Leviathan, too, is free. Despite the Anakhim, we were winning the day when Leviathan appeared, bearing on its back a terrible warrior-prince who bore a lance of black fire. None could stand before him, not even the Cherubim."

"Who was this warrior?" Jhofor asked gruffly.

"As we fled, we heard the armies of darkness cheering. The names were three; Prince Lucere, the Lord Matraya, and one unknown to me, called Baal Phaoton."

"I do not know the name."

"Nor I," Rhamiel said. "We have heard word, though, that he comes this way. Now that the Crystal Tower has fallen, there is only one group of the Faithful left in all Ahura Azdha. They are nearby, in the city of Chasah."

Khasar turned to Holli and nodded his head. "You see, my dear, how the Lord guides us even now. We go east, but not to Aurora." His blue eyes narrowed. "I have a feeling we will learn why the Most High sent you here when we reach Chasah."

Holli nodded, but when she turned to look at her sister, Jami's face was pale.

"What's the matter?" she said.

"The snake," Jami said slowly. "The second snake."

"The what?"

But Jami only shook her head. Her silence upset Holli, but not as much as the look on Khasar's face as he spoke quietly with Rhamiel. She looked away from him and stared into the dark woods, wishing with all her might that this was just a very bad dream.

Unseen and unheard, Lokhael was praying cheerfully to the Most High as he intercepted the path of five shadow-beings that appeared to be stalking the two young ladies in his charge.

"O Lord, my God, may Thy servant be of use to Thee here tonight. Make of me a weapon against the foe, that all glory and honor should be Thine. Amen."

The demons seemed oddly unaware of his presence, so he allowed his weapon to flare, and they started as if surprised, blinking their beady eyes as if the sword's flames were too bright to bear. Strangely, they did not seem in the least alarmed; instead, they looked at him like wolves eyeing a helpless lamb. Their confidence puzzled the guardian, who had sent hundreds, if not thousands, of evil spirits fleeing before him.

"Who art thou?" he challenged boldly.

The largest of the group, a horned beast-man with a brutish goatlike head, sneered at him. He held a heavy iron mace, and his shoulder was covered by what looked like a human skull.

"Stay out of our way, angel-boy, or we'll have your guts for breakfast tomorrow. We know all about you, and you pathetic little spirits aren't any match for us."

Lokhael felt anger rise within his breath. The beast was wholly material, but inside the massive, muscled flesh of the monster burned an eternal flame that, to the best of the angel's understanding, should not have been there. Such a thing was unheard of, and yet there it was, flickering mysteriously with an eerie green-blue flame. He glanced at the other four, and they, too, bore the marks of the fire, though not so strongly as their leader.

"There is something . . . different . . . about you. What are you?"

The beast-man drew back his black lips to reveal yellowed, twisted tusks. It took Lokhael a moment to realize it was smiling.

"We're immortals, you moron. Gods!"

With a loud roar, it launched itself at the angel, oversized jaws yawning dangerously wide. But Lokhael easily side-stepped the airborne monster and slashed his sword horizontally across its body, cutting through both the carnal body and the spirit of flame it housed. The flame was immediately extinguished, and as it disappeared, the mass of flesh landed heavily in a lifeless heap on the ground.

Without looking back at the fallen beast, Lokhael had already turned his attention to two of the other false angels, striking them down with a forehand-backhand combination that was lighting-quick and deadly. As he spun around, he saw one of the two survivors had already taken to its heels, but the other was standing frozen in place, its bestial jaws gaping wide in stunned disbelief.

The warrior-angel leveled his sword at the imposter's furred throat as its companion disappeared into the dark shadows of the woods.

"There are many who pretend to godhood who do not have the right. So tell me, if you will, in whose name do you make this claim?"

CHAPTER 19

LAST DAYS
OF THE FAITHFUL

THAT BE FAR FROM THEE TO DO AFTER THIS MANNER, TO
SLAY THE RIGHTEOUS WITH THE WICKED: AND THAT THE
RIGHTEOUS SHOULD BE AS THE WICKED, THAT BE FAR
FROM THEE: SHALL NOT THE JUDGE OF ALL THE EARTH
DO RIGHT?

—Genesis 18:25

Jami was worn out from their long flight, and she was amazed when Khasar pointed out it was only noon. She preferred riding with him instead of with Jhoforael, who could only be persuaded to talk about serious things. As the sun reached its peak, a small city appeared on the horizon. It was basically a walled village, but it wasn't the limestone walls or the tall spires of its temple that caught Jami's eye. What grabbed her attention was an army of men that surrounded those walls, a large army nearly twice the size of the one she'd seen destroyed at the Crystal Tower. Khasar muttered something about the demons that accompanied it, and though she couldn't see them, she could feel their invisible, oppressive presence like a heavy weight on her chest. It was a feeling she was really learning to hate.

"Can you see them, Holli?" she shouted over her shoulder.

"Oh, Jami, there's so many of them, so many!" Sure enough, the Lady's gift was real. "And they're ugly, just so ugly. I hate them, I hate them!"

"Hold tight," Khasar said abruptly, and Jami alertly grabbed a firm hold on his mane.

"What are you—*ulp!*"

She didn't finish her sentence as the Archon pulled in his wings and dove toward the ground. A hail of arrows arced through the air, passing just over her. Horrified, she whipped her head around and was relieved to see that Jhofor and Holli had evaded the attack.

"Khasar, where did that come from?" she shouted.

"Matraya's men," Khasar growled shortly. "Shooting at us."

"So make us invisible or something!"

"I can't."

"What?" Jami didn't believe him. "Of course you can. You're an angel!"

"Prince Gabriel told me not to. It isn't in the prophecy."

The prophecy? What prophecy? She would have asked him, but he banked suddenly to the right, taking her breath away and nearly throwing her out of her seat. Three arrows flew past her ear, inches wide of the mark, but one slammed into the Archon's left shoulder with a meaty *thunk*.

"Grrraauuuwlll!" Khasar snarled, but Jami saw the embedded shaft didn't slow him down as he kept flying toward the city. Because of his dive, they were flying very low now, below the level of the city's thirty-foot-high stone walls, but as they came closer, the Archon redoubled his efforts and began climbing higher into the sky.

They were close enough now that Jami could see the hurried activity of soldiers rushing about behind the walls, and she suddenly realized that the arrow that had hit Khasar came from the city, not the enemy army. She watched with horror as an archer wearing a conical helm lifted his weapon and drew the bowstring back to his cheek. She saw him close one eye as he took aim at her chest, and knew he was too close to miss.

"Khasar, watch out! He's gonna shoot me!"

"Just hold on," came the terse reply.

Jami screamed hopelessly as the archer released his shaft, but before it flew off the bow, Khasar threw himself upward, placing his body between Jami and the arrow. She could feel his body shudder as the arrow buried itself deep within him, but his wings didn't stop beating for a second.

Ohmigod! That was too close. She concentrated on breathing, on hanging on to Khasar's mane as he howled in pain.

"Khasar!" Jami wailed to herself, suddenly realizing that falling to the ground from this height would kill her as surely as any arrow. "Don't die on me now!"

But Khasar was an immortal angel after all, and it took more than a mortal arrow to finish him off. They were nearly at the wall when she heard the brassy call of a trumpet blowing. There was a short blast, then a second, and with the third the sun went dark. The sky was suddenly darker than midnight, a frightening shadow broken only by the distant stars. It was as if an eclipse appeared out of nowhere, a huge object obscuring all Ahura Azdha in its massive shadow.

Jami breathed a sigh of relief as she heard the blinded archers shouting and milling about in confusion. She realized that she was safe, at least for the moment. Despite his terrible wounds, Khasar seemed to be all right. She guessed his divine nature was somehow protecting him. She looked around for Holli and Jhofor but couldn't find either of them in the unnatural darkness.

Torches were just being lighted to the south as they sailed silently over the walls of Chasah. Jami still couldn't see much, but Khasar's eyes were better than hers, and he landed easily on the ground just inside the south gate of the city. Moments later, she heard a flutter of feathers, then the deep patter of large paws landing heavily nearby.

"Jami, are you there?" she heard her sister whisper.

"Yeah, I'm all right. Khasar got hit by an arrow, though. Are you okay?"

"Oh, no!" Holli gasped. "I'm fine, but did you just say Khasar got shot?"

"Hush, girls," Khasar hissed. "I'm fine, now be quiet."

"Who's there?" an unfamiliar voice called, and Jami shut her mouth, hoping the darkness would conceal them.

The unseen stranger sounded suspicious, even afraid, and Jami didn't blame him. With an enemy army surrounding the city, giant winged lions flying into it, and the day turning unexpectedly into night, fear was the only reasonable response. Of course, a scared dog was more likely to bite, but even so, she couldn't help feeling something in common with the poor guy.

"Show yourselves!" she heard another voice command.

From all the footsteps and clanking weapons, she could hear that there were a lot more than two people surrounding them now. She wasn't sure what she should do, but it seemed that staying motionless and keeping her mouth shut was her best option. At least she wouldn't give herself away by bumping into someone.

Then, just as abruptly as it had gone dark, the sun reappeared. Jami blinked. It was a cloudless sky, and the sudden brilliance dazzled her eyes so much that she dropped to her knees and buried her face in her hands.

"*Fiat lux*," she heard Khasar say, chuckling, but she didn't know why. "Be brave, little one."

Then he was gone.

"Khasar!" she yelled. "Where are you going? Get back here, you jerk!"

It only took a few moments for her vision to readjust, but by the time she was able to open her squinting eyes wide enough to see anything, a group of armored men were gathered in a circle around her, pointing wicked-looking spearheads at her. She didn't see Holli anywhere, and Khasar was gone, too. She was completely alone.

Except, of course, for the guys with the spears.

"I—" she started to say, but they would not let her speak.

"Silence!" a thin-faced, angry-looking soldier yelled at her, his face twisting with fury. "You be quiet now! Don't let her speak, or she'll cast a spell on us!"

Spell? Ha! I wish.

"What should we do, then, Safek?" another man asked, jabbing his spear uncomfortably near her face.

"Koser's got another one right over there," the thin-faced man said. "Bring her over there... Matraya's manhood! Will you look at that! Koser, look at this. They're just the same!"

Jami saw another group of men surrounding her sister. Holli was standing in the shadow of the walls on a small, dusty street, right in front of a group of small brick houses built into the walls. Chasah was bigger than the Crystal Tower, but it seemed to be more poor and violent. She shook her head, wondering why Khasar had disappeared so suddenly and what in the world she was supposed to do now.

She watched, alarmed, as a tall man with a thick black beard left the group surrounding Holli and walked confidently toward her. Two of his men forced Holli to follow him, holding her arms pinned behind her back. One of the men was angrily rubbing a fresh bruise under his left eye, and the other's face was scratched. Despite the lousy situation, Jami grinned. Kittens had claws, and so did her sister. It's just that Holli's were painted a pretty shade of pink.

"Look, Koser, she looks just like the other one!"

"Do I look blind to you, Safek?"

The thin-faced man cringed before the other's acid tone. He looked so much like a weasel that Jami almost laughed.

"N-no, Koser," he stammered. "I was just saying—"

"Yes, I heard it the first time." The bearded man

turned his attention back to her. "You do look just like the other—"

"You can't let her speak, Koser!" Safek protested. "She's a witch!"

His cry was echoed by the crowd.

"She's a shapeshifter!"

"A demon come to destroy us!"

Koser ignored the surrounding soldiers and turned a withering look on Safek. "Hold your foolish tongue!"

"But—"

"I will send you on a one-man sortie before nightfall if you interrupt me again. I swear I will, Safek. Do you understand me?"

Safek nodded miserably. The bearded man glared at him a second longer, then turned back to face Jami again. He jabbed a thumb over his shoulder at Holli.

"You look just like her. Is it some kind of magic trick? Are you here to help our attackers? No, don't answer me, just nod your head, yes or no."

Jami frowned and shook her head. If he wasn't going to let her talk, one question at a time would be nice.

"Are you witches? Demons?"

She shook her head again.

"Then how did you get inside the walls? My men tell me that they saw you flying from the west on some kind of winged beasts. Was it your doing that turned day into night?"

Jami didn't know how she was supposed to answer him without talking, but it was pretty clear from all of the white knuckles gripping the spears pointed at her that this was not a good time to argue. She shook her head.

The bearded man shrugged and drew a knife from his belt. "I don't know why I'm even bothering to ask you anything. Maybe you're not one of Matraya's witches, but there's only one way to be sure..."

Jami stepped away from him and tried to scream, but a soldier grabbed her from behind and shoved a thick wad of cloth into her mouth. She heard Holli cry out, but with her arms pinned, that was all she could do. The curved blade arced back, and she saw the corded muscles in Koser's arms bulge as he started to bring it slashing back toward her exposed throat.

"Drop that blade, Koser Vadout, you accursed fool!" she heard someone shout. "Would you destroy our very deliverers?"

Jami held her breath as the forward motion of the blade suddenly stopped. It seemed to hang in the very air for an agonizing, endless moment. She felt as if her heart had stopped beating. Then a querulous old man leaning on a twisted staff marched stiffly up to the big bearded man and pushed the blade away from her. Her rescuer pointed an accusing finger at the bigger man and began to lecture him.

"How blind you are! Can you not see salvation when it drops from the heavens right before your eyes? Have the Faithful grown so sick with fear that we snap like dogs at those who come to save us? Praise the Lord, friends, let us all praise the Most High, for I tell you the deliverance for which you have prayed is before your very eyes!"

The big soldier was stunned speechless. Even the unsettled crowd was hushed for a moment, taken aback by the fervor of the old man. But their silence did not last long, and their mood quickly turned to anger at his interference.

"Get out of here, Havtah!"

"Forget him, Captain, kill the witch!"

"Kill them both, and stone the charlatan!"

But Koser had already returned his dagger to his belt. Thank God for that! He raised a commanding hand, and the crowd again was quiet.

"Your wisdom is well known, Father Havtah, and I honor you in the memory of my own father, may God rest his soul. But you say these are our saviors . . . tell me, how can two girls save us from the army camped outside our walls? Matraya's men outnumber us twenty-to-one, and even as we speak, another army attacks the Crystal Tower. There will be no help from the west this time."

He sounded like a reasonable man, and Jami almost found herself sympathizing with the difficult position he was in. She and Holli didn't exactly look like warriors. Considering the bizarre means of their arrival, she couldn't blame the people for their suspicions.

Father Havtah, however, didn't see things her way. "Have you forgotten the prophecy, you dolt?" he lambasted the captain.

"What prophecy?"

"From the book of *Hatsallah Anshei!*"

"Um, yes, of course, but . . ." Koser paused uncertainly. "Which one would that be?"

"The only prophecy that has not yet been fulfilled!" Havtah rolled his eyes, as if unable to believe the depth of the ignorance that surrounded him. "Regarding the last days!"

The old man turned to the crowd and lifted his staff, waving it dramatically in a wide circle about him. He looked up to the skies, and, despite his aged voice, his words resonated with a power that was rich and deep.

The morning sun shall fail
And shadowed sky unveil
Hark! The trump shall blow three times
In the last days

Two alike as one shall ride
Upon the wings of angels' pride
One shall be fair and pure in light
One shall be fair and shining bright
In the last days

In those days the Foe will quake
Before My wrath the earth will break
Rocks will shatter, mountains fall
The void shall triumph over all
Silent witness to the power
And the glory of the Lord

There was a respectful silence as Father Havtah finished, and many people jumped in startlement when the old man punctuated the prophecy with a loud crack of his staff on a nearby brick. Jami felt the soldier release her, and with her hands now free, she quickly removed the foul-tasting cloth from her mouth before it made her gag again. Holli rushed to her side and hugged her.

"Oh, Jami, Jami! I thought ... I thought they might ..." She couldn't finish the thought. "I saw them. It was the bad spirits whispering to them, trying to get them to hurt you."

"They were just scared," Jami reassurred her, although she was still pretty shaken herself. The bad spirits? She stopped and stared. "You mean you can see the angels? Then where are Lokhael and Khasar?"

"I couldn't see them, just the bad ones. Wait, there they are!"

Jami stared at Holli as she put her hands on her hips and glared at a wall. There was nothing there, and then, a moment later, Khasar, Jhofor, and Lokhael suddenly appeared. They didn't look very upset, and their apparent lack of concern infuriated Jami. She was just about to lay into them when Holli beat her to it.

"So where were you while that guy with the beard was about to chop Jami up?" she demanded.

"We never left," Khasar protested. "Except for Lokhael, we were at your side, but we had to conceal ourselves so the dark ones would not know we were here."

"You left me, Lokhael?" Jami accused the bronze angel. "Nice! I'm surprised the Lady lasted so long with you protecting her. I'll be lucky to make it a week!"

The handsome Archangel stared back at her, unperturbed.

"Who do you think fetched Father Havtah?" he said.

Oh. "Uh, thanks," she muttered, blushing as Khasar grinned mockingly at her.

The old man, meanwhile, was staring at her as if she'd suddenly grown ten feet tall.

"Who are you talking to?" he asked. "Do you see them?"

"See who?" Jami asked.

"The angels! Was it the angels that brought you here?"

"Well, yeah. Oh, that's right, you can't see them now, I'll bet." She turned to Khasar. "Would you do me a favor and show yourself to this guy? I guess he saved my life, so I figure I owe him, you know?"

Instead, Khasar grinned mischievously and caused glowing halos to appear around her and Holli, bathing them in a pure and holy light.

Jami stepped back as the crowd of people again began to point at her, but this time in awe and wonder rather than fear.

"They are angels!" they cried.

"Save us, Holy Ones!"

"Yes, save us!"

"Save us from the fury of the Foe!"

Koser approached her warily. His face was full of wonder, but his dark eyes were guarded, as if he feared their retribution.

"I, *ahem*, apologize." He would not meet her eyes. "I should not have lifted my hand against you, Divine One. I only beg that you not hold my people responsible and let your anger fall on me. Do not leave them without hope because of me."

"It's okay. I mean, don't worry about it," Jami reassured him. "The only thing is, though, we're not really angels."

"You're not?" Koser and Havtah cried together in a chorus of astonishment, and Jami saw dismay fill the faces of the people crowding around them.

"Then how are you going to save us?" the old man demanded.

"There's an army of ten thousand men just outside the walls," the captain said angrily. "What are you going to do about that?"

"I don't know," Holli replied, glancing worriedly at her.

"Me, neither. But, um, we're working on it," Jami added in what she hoped was a reassuring manner.

Koser threw up his hands.

"This is crazy!" he said angrily, and the crowd noisily agreed with his conclusion.

Even Father Havtah seemed disappointed that they weren't angels. He was about to say something when a runner came sprinting around the corner, shouting out a warning.

"Matraya's army ... comes ... north and west gates!"

The crowd reacted immediately, as officers waved their arms and gathered their troops, and townspeople hurried to their assigned posts. It was clear from their speedy response that they'd been preparing for this attack for quite some time.

Jami gulped as Koser turned and glared first and her, then at Father Havtah, as if trying to decide who was more at fault. He finally settled on the familiar, wrinkled face of the old man.

"If your prophecy will not defend us, then we shall defend ourselves, just as we always have!"

"The prophecy is not mine but the Lord's," she heard the Father respond mildly, but the captain's back was already turned, and he was running, sword in hand, toward the north gate.

The old man shrugged and turned back to the

girls, scratching his bony chin with an age-spotted hand. To Jami's relief, he seemed disappointed but not angry.

"If you cannot save the Faithful of your own power, then perhaps you will help us call upon a higher one. Come with me, and together we shall pray for the salvation of this city."

Jami shot a questioning look at Khasar, who nodded his approval. As the clashing sounds of battle began to ring in the distance, they followed Father Havtah away from the walls, into the center of the city.

By the time night fell, Jami's knees were aching from the unpadded stones of the temple floor. But she knew from the blowing horns that her prayers and the Father's sacrifices must have been effective, because they were still alive. A messenger arrived, bringing the good news that the brave men of Chasah had forced Lord Matraya's mighty army away from their walls, inflicting great losses upon the attackers.

She saw Holli weeping, but she was too spent to cry herself as he told them of a bitter, hard-fought victory. The Promethean plan was to storm the walls using ladders and grappling hooks, but the Chasahan discipline held, and they braved the hailstorm of enemy arrows to hurl back the assailants' ladders and slash their climbing ropes. More of the attackers were killed by falling to the stony ground below than to Chasahan swords, and the deadly aim of the city archers accounted for hundreds more of the enemy.

"It is a miracle!" Father Havtah raised his hands

toward the domed ceiling of the temple before warmly embracing the bearer of the good news. The weary young soldier smiled grimly and returned the embrace, but he knew better than to share the giddy joy of the others in the chamber.

"It's not over yet, good Father. This was just their first try, to see if they could beat us without putting any real effort into it. No siege engines, no war machines, not even any fire arrows. This was just the first test, and the next one will be worse. That's what the Captain says."

"I'm sure Koser is right, my young warrior." The old man smiled beatifically. "But it is better to pass the first test than not to pass it. And if God will answer one prayer, shall we not hope He will answer a second, too?"

"I do hope you are right, Father." The soldier bowed respectfully and left the temple.

"Go with God, my son," Havtah called after him.

Jami was glad they'd won, but she was too exhausted to celebrate. She glanced at Holli and saw that her sister was even worse off. Her eyes were red and puffy, and her curls drooped loose and flat around her face. Father Havtah must have noticed, too, for he placed a withered hand on Holli's shoulder.

"Rest now, the two of you. In the outer chamber, you will find food and a place to sleep. Place your trust in the Lord. What tomorrow will bring, only He can tell."

CHAPTER 20

A
MOMENT OF TRUTH

FOR WHATSOEVER IS BORN OF GOD OVERCOMETH THE
WORLD: AND THIS IS THE VICTORY THAT OVERCOMETH
THE WORLD, EVEN OUR FAITH.

—1 John 5:4

Tomorrow came far too soon. Jami felt a hand
shake her shoulder, and she batted feebly at it,
hoping she was dreaming it. But it was all too real,
and she groaned when she realized her tormentor
was not going to leave her alone. Her back was sore
from sleeping on the hard wooden slats of the cottage floor, and her knees ached, too, from yesterday's marathon prayer session.

"Ohhhh, what time is it?" she moaned, rubbing
her eyes. She opened them cautiously and discovered it was almost pitch black, except for a faint
radiance surrounding Khasar, who'd released her
but was still kneeling by her side.

"The sun is not yet risen," the Archon said quietly. "But it is time."

He looked pretty serious, so Jami swallowed the
protests that were running through her mind. She

grasped the hand he held out to her, and he drew her to her feet.

"Come with me. We must hurry to the east gate."

"Why?"

"Now is the time," Khasar repeated.

"Where's Holli?"

"Right here," her sister said from behind her. Jami turned around and saw her standing next to a strange male angel. "Jhofor woke me."

"You're Jhofor?" Jami said incredulously. She hadn't really thought about what the grim, quiet Archon would look like in human form, but if she had, she wouldn't have imagined a slender artist who looked as if he'd rather be reading poetry in a coffeehouse.

"I am," Jhofor answered simply as he walked past her and opened the cottage's wooden door.

"If you want to talk, do it as we walk," Khasar said. "You did well yesterday, by the way."

"We did?" Holli said, sounding pleased. "But where were you?"

"You saw the dark ones yesterday, did you not?" Khasar asked her.

"Well, yeah, if you mean the things that were flying over the bad guys."

"We prevented them from interceding in the battle on Matraya's behalf. Prince Gabriel wished me to thank you, for we could not have done it without your prayers."

"I don't get it," Jami said. She hadn't seen the evil spirits, and it made her feel a little left out. "We were just, you know, saying what the old man told us to."

"Prayer matters," Jhofor said, and Khasar agreed.

"The more you pray, the more power God per-

mits Himself to unleash His will through us. You
saw the vast size of the shadow, Holli, and yet we
were triumphant."

God permits Himself? Jami knew the Archon had
just told her something important, but her mind
was too groggy even to start thinking about the
implications. She filed the thought away for future
reference and concentrated on following the angels
as they reached the end of the street and turned a
corner. She could see that they were getting closer to
the walls and wondered what the gate would look
like. They were still surrounded by darkness,
although the lower edges of the gray horizon were
beginning to glow with a pinkish tinge that
promised the sun's rise.

Jami suddenly felt angry. "You know, nobody's
told us what's going on," she declared furiously.
"You just tell us, trust in the Lord, trust in the Lord,
but nothing happens! The Lady trusted in the Lord,
the people in the Tower trusted in the Lord, and
what good did it do them?"

The two Archons looked at each other. Khasar,
standing between her and Holli, reached out and
put a strong arm around each of them.

"In time, you will understand. All I can tell you
now is that we are not allowed to intercede."

"What?" Jami caught her breath. "Oh, that's just
great! You can't get us out of this? Why not?"

"It is not permitted," Jhofor said grimly, in a
somber tone that filled both girls with fear.

Khasar nodded. "There is a very powerful . . .
spirit, we believe, coming here. It is strong in this
Fallen world, a spirit before which even Prince
Gabriel cannot stand."

"Oh, jeez." Jami closed her eyes. Even though her stomach was empty, she felt like getting sick. "So what are we supposed to do?"

"Trust in the Lord," Jhofor said, with a wry smile on his face.

Jami punched him in the chest. "Would you shut up with that?" she snapped angrily, cradling her bruised hand. "That's easy for you to say! You can't get killed. Trust in the Lord? I don't see Him anywhere. I don't even know if He exists!"

"Hey, Jami," Holli interrupted, placing a gentle hand on her wrist. "You can't see, like, gravity, but it's dumb to think it doesn't exist, right? So maybe God really does exist. I mean, we didn't see angels before, either, you know."

Holli pointed toward the city walls and mournfully ran a hand through her long, tangled curls. "There's nowhere else to go. Even if we were going to, like, run away, where would we run?"

Jami's mind was whirling, spinning with fear, and she couldn't think of anything to say. Still furious and filled with doubt, she nodded mutely, consenting to follow the angels to the east gate.

It did not take them long to reach it. The gate was closed, with a thick iron bar supporting its massive timbers. There were many angels standing before it in two rows on either side of the earthen street. Human soldiers stood there, too, staring curiously at her and Holli but ignoring all of the Divine ones. Jami was pretty sure they weren't being allowed to see the angels. She stared at the gate, knowing, just knowing, that she was going to have to walk out through it. Considering what was out there, it would probably be the last thing she did.

"Girls, you do have a choice," Khasar said unexpectedly. "There is always a choice. If you truly fear to confront this evil, you can choose to ignore it. It may even spare you, if it feels merciful this morning. But the day will come that it will come for you, in a time and a place that will not be of your choosing, when you will not have a city supporting you with its prayers."

As he spoke, a bell rang in the heart of the city, and its deep gongs resonated seven times throughout Chasah.

"That is the temple bell, summoning the people to pray for you," Khasar explained. "Lokhael has spoken with Father Havtah, and even now he storms Heaven, interceding for you and calling on the Lord for your protection." The Archon smiled tenderly, and his voice softened. "I know how terrible your fears are, Jami, but I also know that God will not allow you to come to harm. Trust in His promise, child, and all will be well."

Jami swallowed hard and looked at the angels around her. Although they were outnumbered by the shadows waiting in the darkness outside, there was no fear on any of their faces. They knew more about this strange world than she did, so much more that the unfairness of it all made her want to scream. Obviously, they knew something that she didn't know, and whatever it was kept them from being afraid. She wished she had it herself. But at least she did have her pride, and she was determined not to be a coward in front of everyone.

"All right, I'll do it," she said firmly, trying to keep her teeth from chattering. "But Holli stays here, with you."

"No way!" her sister protested. "If you're in it, I'm in it!"

"But—"

"No!" Holli put her hands over her ears. "I'm not listening to you! You were the one who told me about the dream, right? There were two birds! So we're in it together."

Jami closed her eyes. She didn't want to face this by herself, but she really didn't want anything to happen to her baby sister. It was like Holli to want to share the terror, but it just wasn't necessary. Why should both of them go out into the shadow when one would be enough?

"I can't . . . I can't let you!" she insisted.

"It's not up to you!" Holli said, looking to the Archons for support. She reached out and hugged Jami, so hard that it brought tears to Jami's eyes. "I know you're trying to do this for me, but I won't let you sacrifice yourself for me."

"I don't want anything to happen to you," Jami whispered, fighting to keep herself from crying. "I'm just so scared!"

"I'm scared, too, but it'll be okay." Holli squeezed her. "I don't think angels are supposed to, like, lie, you know? So we'll be all right."

Jami couldn't help shaking her head at her twin's ridiculous logic, but before she could say anything, there was an ear-splitting crash of thunder, and Lokhael appeared before the gate. His sword was blazing in his hand, his eyes were fierce, and his bronze face was shining so bright that it hurt her eyes to look directly at him.

"The time is now, daughters of the King! Fear no evil, for the Lord of All Creation is with you!"

Lokhael pointed his sword at the gate, and the giant timbers, hewn from solid two-hundred-year-old oaks, were blasted outward in ten thousand splintered pieces. The nearby soldiers gasped and cried out with dismay, thinking an evil magic was at work. Horns blew, and men shouted as they hastened to reinforce the gaping breach in their defenses.

But Jami paid them no attention, for just as the gate was torn apart, the morning sun rose in splendor above the horizon. As its warm, golden rays spilled over them, Matraya's army was inspired by its appearance, clashing swords upon shields and shouting skyward to salute the chosen symbol of their master. It was a terrible and fearful noise, but it was not the army that filled her body with a crazed feeling of panic. She felt Holli's hand creep into her own and squeezed it in a feeble attempt at reassurance.

From the heart of the rising sun, a shadow appeared, growing larger as it swept over the hills and down into the valley. It was huge, an awesome prince of the air. Silhouetted against the brightness of the sun, it was impossible to make out any details or even to see what it was. Only its vast wingspread was apparent, so wide that it seemed it would obscure the sun.

"What . . . is . . . that . . . thing?" she heard Holli breathe in amazement. "It's so . . . big!"

"I'm thinking maybe it's that second serpent the Lady told me about," Jami said, her voice cracking with dryness.

"And what did she say we should do?" Holli knitted her eyebrows and looked crossly at her sister. "Like, turn into birds or something?"

"I think that was a simile or an analogy or something. You know, it's like we aren't really supposed to do it."

"Oh, great," Holli sighed, her eyes never leaving the looming shadow. "So what are we supposed to do?"

"I have no idea."

"Think we can still choose not to, like, do whatever?"

Jami looked back at the shattered gate. The soldiers of Chasah were gathering there, but there was nothing they could do about their broken defenses. "I think it's too late for that," she said.

They watched, still holding hands, as the monster flew closer, soaring high over Matraya's army. The Prometheans hailed it with a rousing chorus, gleefully anticipating its attack on the defenseless city. As the monster reached the battle standards marking Lord Matraya's front lines, it banked its wings and bellowed out an answering salute, then made a slow, effortless circle above the cheering army.

Jami saw the sun glinting off the armored scales of a giant dragon. It looked a lot like the metal figures that her brother collected. But it dwarfed those in the way that an airliner dwarfs a mosquito. It had three separate heads extending from the massive torso on three thick, snaky necks. It had four legs which it curled underneath its body, and a barbed tail that was twice as long as its necks. Its scales were like a rainbow, mostly red but with a scattering of blues and greens, purples and yellows mixed in randomly. The huge wings were a lighter, almost pinkish shade traced with a darker band of black. It was both beautiful and terrible.

As it completed the circle and sailed toward them again, she saw that upon each head were set three horns, with several more ringing each neck. Its six yellow eyes were hard and cruel but, like Lord Bile's, gleamed with an active intelligence. A lone golden whisker jutted out from behind the unarmored ears of the middle head, but when the whisker moved and pointed itself at her, she realized the dragon had a rider on it.

He was seated behind the neck horns, and what she'd mistaken for a whisker was actually a very long spear. He was a big man, without armor or shield, and his bare chest heaved with the effort of directing the fifty-foot lance he was holding in both hands. His long brown hair flowed from under a horned helm, and his square-jawed face would have been handsome if it hadn't been twisted into an angry battle cry. Jami was suddenly struck by the surprising thought that he looked kind of familiar.

Under his direction, the dragon was diving toward them now, with its jaws gaping wide to swallow anything the rider's wicked lance might miss. The thunderous noise of its violent descent was deafening, and Jami closed her eyes, not wanting to see anymore.

"Christopher!" she heard Holli cry over the onrushing wind, and Jami, surprised, opened her eyes. Her sister was jumping up and down like a nut, waving both her arms and shouting at the rider. "Christopher, it's us!"

Still the dragon dove toward them, bellowing even louder as if trying to drown out the sound of Holli's voice. The rider himself was still snarling, and his eyes were wild with a greedy appetite for destruction. She knew those eyes. Jami almost fell down in shock when she realized that Holli was right. Despite the impossible steroid-stud body, it was her brother bearing down on them.

Ignoring her mind's complaints about the illogic of it all, Jami started shouting, too, waving her arms and screaming so hard she thought she would sear her throat.

"Chris, knock it off!"

"Christopher, it's us! It's me, it's Holli!"

"Chris, pull up!"

It was useless, Jami thought. Even if it was their brother, Chris couldn't possibly hear their cries. She wondered, too, if it would make any difference if he did. How far into the Shadow had he gone, and what had they done to him? Was he still her brother anymore?

The point of the lance was only twenty feet away. The terrible stink of the dragon was overpowering when the snarl suddenly disappeared from the rider's face. His eyes went wide with horror, and he screamed an urgent command as the golden lance magically disappeared. The huge beast roared in protest but obeyed, spreading its wings as it swept to the left, and one snapping head missed the girls by only a few feet.

The force of its passage was tremendous and hurled both girls to the ground. Their fall was a blessing in disguise, though, for the huge beast lashed out with one clawed foot that would have torn them to pieces if they had not been lying flat on their backs. Jami watched, breathless, as the terrible warrior who was her brother forced the great beast away from the city, toward the east and into the rising sun.

Still flat on her back, Jami looked over at Holli, who was already sitting up and trying to run her fingers through her disheveled white curls.

"That wasn't really Christopher, was it?"

"Yeah, it was." Holli looked haunted and sad. "There's something really, like, wrong with him."

"He sure looked different." She shook her head. "How did you know it was him?"

"I don't know." Holli shrugged. "When he was yelling, you know, when he was coming at us?"

"Yeah?"

"Well, I just thought to myself, you know, that looks just like Christopher when he's playing those games. When he's really into it, you know, yelling and all. Once I thought that, I kind of looked closer, and I was, like, wow, it really is him! Weird, huh?"

Jami sat up and hugged her. "Too weird. But I'm glad you noticed," she said, laughing with relief. When she looked up, she saw that their angels had gathered in a circle around them.

"Glory to the Most High!" Khasar said triumphantly. "Praise His holy name! Our prayers have been answered." He cleared his throat and grinned at Jami. "In rather dramatic fashion, I might add. It was, perhaps, a little close for my liking."

"Our God is mighty," Lokhael declared. "Leviathan is overcome, and who could have foreseen it!"

"Who's Leviathan?" Holli asked as the Archangel lifted her up and gently placed her on Jhofor's leonine back. "That dragon thing?"

"It's a long story," Khasar said as he, too, transformed back into a lion. "But yes, that was Leviathan."

"So where did Chris find a pet like that?"

"I told you, it's a long story. You must come with us now."

"Where are we going?"

"You'll see."

"What about Father Havtah and the people in the city?" Jami asked as she climbed behind Khasar's shoulders. She looked back and saw that a group of unarmored men and women holding spears were forming a small, pathetic line in a desperate attempt to fill in the gap left by the destroyed gate. "Don't they need help? That army is totally going to wipe them out if you don't do something!"

Khasar only laughed, surprisingly unconcerned despite the blowing horns and ominous movement beginning to take place amidst the ranks of Matraya's army.

"Have you learned nothing, daughter of the King?" The cheerful tone of Lokhael's voice took the sting out of his words. "What happens today in this place will happen as the Lord wills it."

"Praise the King of Heaven, for there is none like Him!" Jhofor added.

Jami looked at Holli, who shrugged as if to remind her that some things were simply beyond their understanding. The Lady's vision had miraculously come to pass, and if God would bother to save the two of them, then surely He would want to do something for the faithful people of Chasah, too.

"All right," she said finally, hoping that the angels' trust was not misplaced. "I guess . . . I guess after everything . . . I guess I've got to believe you."

The two Archons roared their approval, and Lokhael drew his sword, pointing it at the sky. Jami watched, transfixed, as the ground fell suddenly away, fading into a misty haze as they rose toward Heaven. But despite her words, she watched anxiously as the enemy army began its deadly march toward Chasah, like a column of ants swarming over an unwatched picnic basket.

Christopher's mind was still reeling from his surprise encounter with his sisters. Leviathan's silent voice was raining curses down upon his mind, furiously demanding a return to the battlefield, but Christopher barely noticed. For the first time in the three months since he'd come to Ahura Azdha, he felt something that reminded him of his hateful former life. He was feeling embarrassed.

With a shudder, he blinked and caused his fearsome battle horns to disappear. Boy, oh boy, he thought, would Jami give him a hard time about them. He could just hear her voice now, calling him a cheesy Conan wanna-be, and in response, his oversized muscles shrank to slightly less heroic proportions. He shook his head. What in the shining name of Adonai Lucere were his sisters doing on Ahura Azdha? It wasn't fair. It wasn't possible!

He commanded a nearby cloud to scry the battlefield, and it obeyed him immediately. He saw the army of Anakhim marching unopposed toward the defenseless city, accompanied by the usual cloud of petty demons. He did not see his sisters, though, not on the ground where he had seen them last or anywhere among the people of the city or its defenders. They were gone as if they had never existed, and he smiled grimly when he realized that he'd been had. It was the only answer. Some angel with a talent for visions had read his mind and made him see the one thing that would stop him from attacking.

Now that he knew his sisters hadn't been real, the cowardly part of his mind urged him to stop thinking about them, but he ruthlessly suppressed it as he forced himself to confront his feelings. No, if he was brutally honest, what he had felt for a moment was not embarrassment, exactly, but shame. Seeing Holli and Jami forced him to recall the young girl at Hamath, who could not have been any older than his sisters. He could still see her, slender and pretty, black eyes wide with terror as he dropped from the clouds above her. He had not spared her, though, any more than he had spared the rest of city for its refusal to join in what Kaym called Illumination. He winced at the thought, glad that Holli had only been an image, for he would not have liked her to hear about what he had done.

Since his own Illumination, he hadn't really thought about the consequences of his actions, he'd simply been too intoxicated by the heady realization of his own power and the knowledge that he was practically a god. Now the Gates of Heaven were broken, Leviathan was free, and soon all Ahura Azdha as well as Heaven itself would belong to the Dawn Prince, and the whole universe would bow before its new King. Yes, there were consequences to everything, and he was going to have to start thinking about them.

But not now. He idly pointed his finger at a nearby copse of trees topping a ridge and effortlessly unleashed a bolt of lightning, scorching the ground and blasting five trees into splinters. Yes, he thought, the Dawn Prince did know how to reward a loyal servant. He forced Leviathan to circle the ridge and surveyed the damage with satisfaction. His power had grown considerably since Hamath, swelled by the sacrifice of twelve thousand lives, to the point that even Matraya-Mahalidael now showed him respect. It was good to be favored by the gods, but it was even better to become a god yourself.

Something pricked his collarbone as he turned his head and startled him. It was only his gold key, though, which had now become almost useless to him. It had broken the Gate, taken out the Cherub, and banished Verchiel for him, but now, with Jehuel's sword and his own swelling power, he knew he was strong enough to overcome a hundred Archons single-handed. Even without Leviathan.

"Ouch!"

"*What's the matter now?*" Leviathan grumbled. It was still bitter about missing the battle at Chasah.

"This stupid thing burned me!"

Outraged, he glared at the little key in his palm. It was glowing now, getting hotter by the moment. Christopher could banish the pain, of course, but not the sense of betrayal. He had been through a lot with this little key, and now it was turning on him!

"Knock it off!" he commanded, but still it glowed defiantly, so hot now that the metal felt as if it were melting in his hand.

"Well, forget you, then! It's not like I need you anymore!"

He drew his arm back and cast it from him, watching as it tumbled down toward the ground until it disappeared from sight. He spat a curse after it, and the dark spirit leaped eagerly from his lips, arching downward like an arrow as it hurried to bury the key a thousand feet beneath the earth. Christopher knew what a dangerous weapon it could be, and even though he was pretty sure it couldn't do him much harm, he had no desire to test his theory.

He felt suddenly free, as if an oppressive weight had been lifted off his shoulders. The thought of his sisters no longer bothered him, and he grinned savagely as he wished his deadly horns back into place and added a third, curving up from behind his skull, for good measure.

Leviathan, sensing his change of mood, turned its left head around to look at him. The yellow eyes were darkly hopeful, yearning for more chaos and bloodshed. *"Where to, o Master mine?"*

"Asrael's host is shattered, and if Mahalidael can't take that city with its doors blasted off, I'll come back and eat his soul myself. I think it's time to return to Heaven, don't you? I want to be there for the final action. It's not often you get to see a new King of All Creation crowned." He grinned to himself. "And it would be nice to see Melusine." He hadn't seen her since Kaym took her back to Heaven with him forty days ago.

"What about the girls, the twain who haunted thee so?"

"I don't think they were actually there. It was just a vision one of the defenders cast upon my mind, a glamour or something. I looked for them, and they're not there anymore. It's time to return to Heaven."

"Then shall we storm Paradise, Master!"

Leviathan roared and hurled itself toward the distant stars, as Christopher howled with joy at the feeling of power pulsing within him. He called out to the Anakhim, summoning six thousand of them to serve as an honor guard. Followed by the legion of ur-mortals, Christopher hurtled triumphantly through the empty darkness of space, flying toward the conquered realm of Heaven.

CHAPTER 21

RIVER OF FIRE

JOHN ANSWERED, SAYING UNTO THEM ALL, I INDEED
BAPTIZE YOU WITH WATER; BUT ONE MIGHTIER THAN I
COMETH, THE LATCHET OF WHOSE SHOES I AM NOT
WORTHY TO UNLOOSE: HE SHALL BAPTIZE YOU WITH
THE HOLY GHOST AND WITH FIRE.

—Luke 3:16

Jami climbed off Khasar's back and joined Holli by
the side of a large marble pool as the Archons
shifted back into their angelic form. Together, they
watched Lokhael as he glanced about the grassy
courtyard that surrounded the pool. It looked as if
he were expecting someone, so Jami, her curiosity
aroused, walked up to him.

"Who are you looking for?"

"Someone very important."

"Can you tell me?"

"Yes."

Jami waited, but Lokhael didn't say anything. She
rolled her eyes. "Okay, then, *will* you?"

"No."

Jami growled under her breath and returned to
Holli's side. Stupid angels. They were worse than
her English teacher! But if she'd learned anything

from them, it was that understanding sometimes took time, and it wasn't always important to get your answers right away.

"So, is this, like, Heaven?" she heard Holli asking Khasar.

"It is indeed."

"Really? Wow!" Holli exclaimed, but then she frowned. "I don't know, it's not all that, like, impressive. I guess I was expecting more than blue sky and green grass, you know? I mean, the Lunstads have a bigger pool than this one. But it's nice to see blue over your head instead of all that ugly yellow."

"And there's some nice flowers over there," Jami pointed out.

"Yeah, and those carvings in the sides of the pool are kinda cool, but they're a little too *Lifestyles of the Rich and Famous*, you know?"

There was a sudden rustling of feathers, and Jami turned around to see Khasar, Jhofor, and Lokhael dropping to their knees before a man in white robes. He was tall and broad-shouldered but rather plain in appearance, with an unremarkable dark-tanned face and callused hands. He had no wings, nor did he give off a radiant glow like the angels before him. As far as she could tell, he was just a man, nothing more.

Then the man looked at her, and Jami started, for his eyes were alarmingly, intensely red. They were not blood-shot, it was the irises themselves that were unmistakably red. It unsettled her, and for one frightening moment she wondered if the angels she'd come to trust were really on her side.

She grew even more worried when the strange

man nodded to Lokhael, Khasar, and Jhofor, and the three angels abruptly disappeared. Alone with the girls now, he spread his hands and smiled at them. It was a genuine smile, warm and friendly, and Jami relaxed a little.

"You are welcome here, Jami. You are welcome here, Holli."

His voice was surprisingly soft, a mellow baritone that was rich and pleasing to the ear. His hair was long and white and just a little bit unkempt.

"Thanks, um, sir," Jami said. "You seem to know who we are. Who are you?"

"Who do you say I am?"

Jami shrugged. How should she know? "I have no idea," she said.

"Well, the angels were bowing to you," Holli observed. "So I think you must be, like, a king or something. Only you don't look very much like a king."

"Holli!" Jami blurted out, appalled, hoping the man with the red eyes didn't take offense at her sister's words.

But the man only chuckled softly, not insulted at all. "What is lovely on the outside may conceal a monster within," he said. "And a common face may hide a royal heart. But I am indeed a king. I am the Son of the King of Heaven, and on the world you recently left I am known as Kherev Elohai."

"Okay. Kherev Elohai." Holli tested the sound of it out loud. "I think I can remember that. But would Kherev be all right? Just for short, that is."

"If you call me Kherev, Holli, I will know to listen," he promised solemnly. He smiled at Jami. "But you seem doubtful, Jami."

"So are you saying you're the Son of God?"

"I am."

Jami snorted. "And you think we're just going to believe you? Okay, if you are, like, God, then how come you let that Matraya guy wipe out the Lady? And why did Chris turn into a monster? And look at your eyes. I mean, you say monsters can look nice, but they can be ugly, too. Maybe you just tricked Lokhael and Khasar into leaving us here with you!"

"Jami!" Holli protested. "He's not a monster, he's good inside. I can feel it. You're wrong."

"Then let him prove it!"

Kherev didn't reply. Instead, he reached out and placed one large hand on each girl's shoulder. Jami shrank from his touch, but his grip was strong. He did not let her pull away. He drew them to him, turned them gently around, and began to walk with his arms around them, toward a path that led away from the pool.

"I understand your anger, Jami, and your lack of faith as well. Let me tell you a story about My Father's kingdom, and perhaps you will understand Me better."

Jami struggled against the forceful arm around her, but Kherev held her tightly. She had no choice but to accompany him as he led them through the courtyard toward a small wooded path.

"The Kingdom of Heaven is like a man who planted good wheat in his field. But while everyone was sleeping, his enemy came and planted weeds among the wheat. When the wheat grew up, then the weeds appeared, too. The man's servants came to him and said, 'Sir, didn't you plant good seed in your field? Where, then, did the weeds come from?'

" 'An enemy did this,' he replied.

"The servants asked him, 'Do you want us to go and pull them up?'

" 'No,' he answered, 'because while you are pulling up the weeds, you may pull up the wheat with them. Let them both grow together until the harvest. At that time, I will tell the harvesters: First collect the weeds and tie them in bundles to be burned; then gather the wheat and bring it into my barn.' "

"You're the man," Holli said confidently. "Are we the wheat, or are we the weeds?"

"The field is the world, and the good seed stands for the sons of the Kingdom. The weeds are the sons of the Evil One, and the enemy who sows them is the Devil. The harvest is the end of the age, and the harvesters are angels."

"That makes sense," Holli said, nodding her head. "But you didn't answer my question."

Jami didn't say anything. She had a bad feeling about this. Her life suddenly looked, in retrospect, alarmingly weedlike.

"As the weeds are pulled up and burned in the fire, so it will be at the end of the age. I will send out My angels, and they will weed out of My Kingdom everything that causes sin and all who do evil. They will throw them into a fiery furnace. Then the righteous will shine like the sun in the Kingdom of their Father."

"Okay," Holli said slowly. It was an answer, of sorts, but she clearly didn't like it.

"So you're planning to end the evil, but you haven't done it yet?" Jami asked hopefully.

"That is so."

"And when you do, people like Chris and Lord Matraya will get burned, right?" And me, probably, she added to herself.

"Yes." Kherev's voice was sad but resolute.

"How can you do that?" Holli wailed. "Don't you care about them?"

"I do care, very much. My Father is a loving God, but He is also a just and holy God. His hatred for sin runs every bit as deep as His love for you, and that love is deeper than the oceans. There is no place in My Kingdom for sin or any kind of evil."

"Wait a minute," Jami said. "What's the difference between the good seed and the bad seed? How do the angels know who is what?"

"The wheat is like the flower that turns its face toward the sun that gives it life. Even so will the good seed turn toward the Son, and My angels will see this and know that they are Mine."

"Can I be wheat?" Holli asked hopefully. "I don't want to be a weed."

"You can indeed, Holli."

"But that doesn't seem fair," Jami protested. "What if someone's never heard of you or doesn't know to look for you? What about them?"

Kherev stopped walking and released her. He turned to face her, then bent down and took her hands, so that her eyes were level with his own.

"Look at Me, Jami. Look into My eyes, and tell Me how people might know to look for Me."

Jami stared into the strange red eyes. They were a window into the universe, a glimpse into an encyclopedia that contained all the wisdom and knowledge that had ever existed, that ever would exist.

She saw compassion, and caring, and love, as well as righteousness, perfection, and power. She suddenly knew that to call this divine being with the modest appearance of a man unfair was like calling a hurricane a cheater. The concept just did not apply.

"I'm . . . sorry," she said, hanging her head. "I didn't understand."

Kherev hugged her, enfolding her in his strong arms.

"But I do. And I forgive you. But now you haven't answered my question."

Jami frowned and thought, but her mind was a blank. Then she remembered hearing a voice whispering to her, a voice that spoke to her without words from a place deep inside her. It was a voice she knew well, the voice of her conscience. And with that insight, she understood.

"You, I don't know, talk inside them. Like, in their hearts or something."

"Yes, that is My Spirit, whom I have poured out over the nations. I did this so that none might say they have not heard Me calling."

"Did you do that for us? On our world, I mean?" Holli also seemed to grasp the concept.

"I did. And I can do more than that as well. How would you like for My Spirit to fill you, so that you could call upon the fullness of My power anytime you need it?"

Holli clasped her hands together, delighted. "Oh, I'd like that!"

Jami didn't say anything at first, but after thinking about it, she shook her head. "I don't know. I . . . just don't know."

"There is no hurry. Come and walk with Me."

He extended his hands to them, and Jami took the left as Holli took the right. They walked with him to the path's end, beyond which was a clearing. There was a bright glow that became stronger as they approached the open ground, and Jami thought she heard a faint crackling noise that grew louder as they approached its source. Kherev stopped as they passed the last tree, and Jami stared, dismayed, at a roaring river of silvery-red fire that burned its way through the middle of the green grass of the clearing.

The fire was clearly supernatural, for its strangely colored flames were not fed by any visible source. It wasn't like the melted lava that flowed down the sides of volcanoes, more like a wildfire, leaping and swirling down its course like a forest fire running before the wind. The heat came off it in waves, and Jami could feel her cheeks flushing and tiny beads of sweat appearing on her forehead. The fiery river was so hot that the earthen slopes of its banks had been baked into hardened clay, interspersed with little glassy pebbles of what had once been sand.

"Now, go and bathe in the river."

Jami looked at Kherev in disbelief. He was smiling, and his strange eyes were glowing red as they reflected the howling silver flames that danced nearby. He pointed to the fire, and she fancied that his fingers had grown just a little longer, with nails that ended in sharpened points.

She backed slowly away as smoke began to billow from the river, a thick foul-smelling haze that threatened to choke her. Was it her imagination, or did Kherev suddenly throw back his head and laugh, a horrible cackling sound of triumphant evil. He wasn't the Son of God! How ridiculous! Maybe he was a clever shadow of evil that was trying to trick her into burning herself! Where was Khasar, and why had he left her here with this lying spirit?

Jami was about to scream when Holli's voice suddenly broke through the fear that was paralyzing her.

"Jami, take three steps sideways! No, to your left! That's it, now just one more."

Suddenly, the smoke and the evil smell were gone, and Kherev was again a simple man in white, his hands callused but otherwise normal, and a gentle smile on his face instead of the demonic leer, though his eyes were still red.

"Tell Shannis to show herself, Jami," he suggested. "Remember the Lady's gift. Command her, and she will obey."

"Um, okay," she replied uncertainly. "Thelael, show yourself!"

A female angel obediently materialized right in front of her, standing between her and Kherev. She was an arrogant spirit, wearing what looked like a bikini made of smoke that coiled and roiled strategically, just barely keeping her decently covered.

She snarled at Kherev, exposing small fangs and a forked, snaky tongue before turning toward Jami.

"Heaven falls, and all the Earth is ours. Join us, Jami, or risk destruction with the dotard King and this, his poor, mad Son. Your brother already has. Will you let this Kherev burn you in the River of Death? He seeks to destroy you now rather than see you serve the Prince who is the true King of Heaven."

"She's lying, Jami," Holli yelled.

"Who are you?" Jami asked the angel, whose fangs had disappeared, replaced by a reassuring, white-toothed smile.

"I am an angel, sent by the Prince of Light to save you. This one you call Kherev is a great devil. He wants to burn you, for he is doomed to burn himself one day."

Jami looked at her. There was something in Shannis's eyes that troubled her. There was nothing of Lokhael's nobility about her, of Khasar's amusing good nature or Jhofor's sober responsibility. She reminded Jami of one of her friends, Kristie, who was always getting into trouble and whose lies had dragged Jami into that trouble with her more than once. She made her decision.

"Go away, Shannis," Jami commanded. "Leave me alone!" The temptress wailed in protest but reluctantly obeyed and disappeared in a sulfuric yellow-gray flash.

Then, before she could think better of it, Jami rushed toward the silver flames. The furious blast of the fire hit her painfully hard, but she didn't slow down despite the scorching heat, and when her toes touched the hard-baked clay of the riverbank, she dove into the River of Death as if it were a swimming pool.

She found herself in a gentle pool of water, clear and blue as the sky. After the blast-furnace heat of the fire, it was as refreshing as a cone of frozen yogurt on a hot summer day. She opened her mouth to taste the water and was delighted to find that it was not only drinkable but delicious.

"Holli, jump in! It's great!" she yelled, and then sputtered as water splashed over her face.

"I already did." Holli surfaced nearby, shook her drenched curls, and smiled happily. "Isn't it wonderful?"

"It's amazing," Jami tried to say, but it came out in an unintelligible burble of nonsense syllables. She started laughing and found that she could not stop. Never had she felt so alive.

Holli was laughing, too, and they splashed in the shallow water like happy children, giggling and babbling with joy.

"Come out, daughters of the King," they heard Kherev calling, and they hastened to obey. When they clambered out of the water, they found their hair and clothes were miraculously dry.

"Well done, My children," Kherev said, and he embraced them, first Holli and then Jami. "When you tasted the River of Life, My Spirit entered your heart, and He will never, ever leave you."

Jami smiled with relief. Now she knew, beyond a shadow of a doubt, that she wasn't a weed anymore. But she wasn't just wheat, either, she was a daughter of the King. She wasn't exactly sure what that meant, but it sure sounded good. Like a princess, almost.

She was surprised to see that Holli was crying.

"What's the matter?" Jami asked.

"I'm so happy, I'm just so happy." Holli threw her arms around Kherev and squeezed him. "Oh, thank you, thank you so much!"

Kherev returned the hug, then gently pushed her back, still holding her shoulders. "With fire and water you have been baptized, and you are sealed to Me forever. I rejoice in the knowledge of your salvation, and I promise that one day you shall return here, to dwell in glory with Me. But there is still much to do."

"What about Chris?" Jami asked suddenly. "Can we see him? That, ah, Shannis said that Chris was with them already, you know, and I don't think she was lying about that."

Kherev nodded. "She did not lie. Your brother has fallen into darkness, but do not despair. You will see your brother again, before the end of days. I promise."

He clapped his hands, and Jami was delighted to see Lokhael, Khasar, and Jhofor appear, accompanied by thousands of white-robed warrior-angels, all armed with swords and spears and slings. The angels gave a great shout, so loud that it seemed as if the sky would crack before it. As Khasar, in his lion form, kneeled and lowered his shoulder so she could mount, a black-skinned angel with a copper horn flew into the sky and blew a mighty trumpet blast.

CHAPTER 22

THE KING COMES BACK

BE YE THEREFORE READY ALSO: FOR THE SON OF MAN
COMETH AT AN HOUR WHEN YE THINK NOT.

Luke 12:40

Koser Vadout was not a coward. For thirty-six
years, he had struggled against the overwhelming might of Lord Matraya and his false god, and he
had never given up hope, not even once. But when
word came to him that the Tower of Qawah had
fallen, and with it its deathless Lady, Koser learned
what it was to despair.

Despite the siege of the city, the appearance of the
two strange twins had lifted his hopes for a little
while, and at the end of that first day's victory, he'd
felt almost confident. He remembered his father's
last words to him, spoken seven years ago, just
before the battle in which he'd fallen before a royal
Promethean charioteer: "Matraya's men are like the
sands scattered 'round the sea. We'll never match
their numbers, Koser, never. If victory depended
upon the strength of our arms, we would surely

lose. But the Lord promised us victory, and He is faithful. The victory will be ours if we are faithful to Him. And then, one day, the sea will come in like a tide, and wash all that sand away."

The aging war leader had gripped his shoulders, smiled fiercely, then turned to walk away, to the field where his death lay waiting for him. But before he joined his bodyguard, he looked back one last time.

"Be strong, my son, and wait for the sea."

But what good was the Lord's promise to the Faithful of Qawah? They waited, but their promised sea never came, and the Dawn Prince had won in the end, just as he always did. The girls had frightened off the huge sky-beast, a miracle for which he was indeed grateful, but then had disappeared before his very eyes. Matraya's army, forty thousand strong, remained, against which he had three thousand men, women, and boys defending a defenseless, broken wall.

The fanfare of trumpets jerked him from his despairing thoughts. He saw a single rider, cloaked in green, slowly approaching the broken gates of the city. He held a long lance upright, to which a flag of truce was attached above a red pennon with Matraya's yellow sun stitched upon it. As the green rider came closer, Koser waved off his archers and stalked out to hear what the man had to say.

"Who are you?" he demanded.

"I myself am of no account. I speak with the voice of Lord Matraya, the priest-king of Prometheon, whose armies stand before you. Do you speak for the people of Chasah?"

"I do."

"This is what the King of Prometheon says: Make peace with me, and come out with me. Then I will take you to a land of grain and new wine, a land of bread and vineyards, a land of olive trees and honey. Choose life and not death! Do not listen to your old men, for they mislead you when they say your god will deliver you."

The rider spoke loudly to be sure that the people inside the broken walls could hear him.

"Has the god of any nation ever saved his land from the hand of Lord Matraya? Where are the gods of Hamath and Arpad? Where are the gods of Sepharvaim, Henah, and Ivvah? Did they rescue their people from his mighty hand? Did they stand against the God of Fortresses? People of Chasah, your gates are broken, and your walls lie open before the armies of the sun. Submit, and you shall be saved. Refuse, and be destroyed!"

He nodded and folded his arms confidently, awaiting Koser's response.

Koser knew that what the rider said was true. All the world had fallen before the Dawn Prince, and with the recent fall of Qawah, only Chasah remained. With the gates shattered, there was no hope of resisting the massive Promethean army, and his refusal would only guarantee the death of every man, woman, and child in the city.

No one would blame him for surrendering now. They had fought a brave fight, and he knew no man could have done more to defend his people. What was the price, then, of his faith? His own life was of no account, but what about the lives of his wife and his children? What about five thousand others who would have to die for his faith, his pride? And yet, could he so easily abandon the god of his fathers, the god his father had died fighting for?

Koser stared at the huge army in front of him. It waited, motionless, for his reply, as the rising sun reflected brightly off countless metal helmets and spear tips. Too many to count, he thought, too many to count. Just like the sands of the sea.

From the ramparts of the walls, Father Havtah listened to Matraya's envoy. As the green rider threatened the city, then tempted its people with the sweet promise of life at the expense of their souls, the old man burned with indignation. Nearly choking on his rage, he fell to his knees and angrily called out to the King of Heaven.

"O Lord God, enthroned among the Cherubim, You alone are God over all the kingdoms of the Earth. You have made Heaven and Earth. Give ear, o Lord, and hear; open Your eyes, o Lord, and see; listen to the words Matraya has sent to insult you, the living God. O Lord our God, deliver us from his hand, so that all kingdoms on Earth may know that You alone, o Lord, are God!"

"That is your final answer?"

"It is." Koser replied shortly. The die was cast. O God, he prayed silently, please defend Your people, because I cannot.

The green rider nodded grimly. "Then hear the words of Lord Matraya: Because you reject me, and in me all the mighty glory of the Son of the Morning, you, o people of Chasah, shall not see tomorrow's dawn. My hand is against your city, and not one stone shall be left standing on another. Every living being shall die, and neither woman nor child shall be spared my wrath. I have spoken."

Koser's face was calm, although his heart was painfully heavy as he thought of his wife, whom he loved dearly. "So be it," he replied steadily. "May God have mercy on your soul."

The green rider shook his head. He did not look pleased. "You can ask him about that soon enough, you arrogant idiot," he spat contemptuously, then wheeled his horse and cantered back to the waving flags of the Promethean front lines.

Koser watched him ride away, then took a deep breath and ran back toward the makeshift defenses at the ruins of the east gate. It was not long before he heard the sound of distant trumpets and a guardsman's voice crying out with fear, "They march!"

Koser chewed his dirt-stained nails, disappointed, as he watched the Promethean general send his armored levies forward in conjunction with two large detachments of Auroran archers. His unknown opponent was not in a hurry despite the tempting target presented by the breach, and Koser's unlikely hopes that his own archers might keep the levies at bay were dashed. The enemy was still five stadia away, but the battle was already over. In only minutes, he knew, he would be dead. He drew his sword and held it over his heart as he commended his soul to God.

But no sooner had the first Chasahan archer loosed an arrow toward the approaching enemy than a horn sounded somewhere over his head, much closer and louder than the Promethean trumpets. Koser watched in stunned disbelief as the slender arrow stopped in the air and hung there, motionless and unsupported, but did not fall. The enemy also seemed taken aback, for their advance abruptly halted, and it wasn't until Koser shook his head and forced his disbelieving eyes away from the shaft hanging in midair that he realized it was not surprise that had halted the enemy approach.

The world itself had stopped, he realized, but not for him. At the sound of a great cheer from the city behind him, he realized that he was not alone, caught outside time. All the people of Chasah were alive with him, and out of the sky a vast host of angels was descending, singing and clapping and blowing horns in rampant celebration.

"*He is come,*" the angels sang in voices that rang like celestial bells. "*Praise the Lord, He is come!*"

Koser dropped his sword and fell to his knees as tears began to flow from his eyes. He raised his hands in worshipful relief and saw that the angels were rejoicing, wildly, exuberantly. They flew ecstatic circles in the sky around the glorious figure of a man who was more than a man, the long-promised Son of God who was come for His faithful people at last.

> *He is come, He is come, and the victory is won!*
> *Sons and daughters of the King*
> *Lift your voices now and sing*
> *He is come, He is come,*
> *And the victory is won!*

Koser suddenly started laughing as he realized old man Havtah had been right all along. Not far from the shining Son of God were two pretty girls riding on the backs of winged lions, the very twins who had saved Chasah from the dragon. As Koser rose joyfully into the air, he opened his mouth and began to sing his own praises to the King. He did not even notice as his earthly body was miraculously transformed into a glorious, godly vessel of the Light.

CHAPTER 23

SILENCE
IN DARKNESS

THOU HAST BROKEN RAHAB IN PIECES, AS ONE THAT IS
SLAIN; THOU HAST SCATTERED THINE ENEMIES WITH THY
STRONG ARM.

—Psalms 89:10

The mood in the Fallen camp when Christopher
arrived was full of unruly anticipation. Legions
of armored angels flew patrols around the high
walls of the Arx Dei, making sure that the remnants
of Asrael's shattered host could not come to the aid
of their besieged king. The legions were brimming
with confidence, swollen with power stolen from
thousands of angels sent Beyond, and eager to begin
the final assault that would break this last bastion of
Heaven and mark the dawn of the new era.

Melusine was the first to greet him, embracing
him warmly and pressing her luscious lips against
his with a greedy fervor. She was as sensual as ever,
and for a moment Christopher nearly forgot that he
was looking for Kaym.

"Phaoton! Everyone in Heaven is talking about
you," Melusine informed him, as she took his arm

possessively. Her hand was tiny compared to his massive arms, but he was quite willing to go wherever she wanted to lead him. "There's rumor that you're to be raised to the Principalities, maybe even the Teraphim!"

Right on, he thought. "Is Kaym around?" he asked.

"Lord Kaym? Oh, yes, he's here. I haven't seen him around the camp, but I've heard that he's often conferring with the Prince. He is much in favor now, so much so that I heard Lord Belial complaining to Baal Phaleg about him just the other day."

"What is Kaym's title, anyhow? I can never keep all these ranks straight."

Melusine shrugged. "I think he's maybe a Domination. But rank means nothing compared to the favor of the Prince."

Christopher grinned. "Yeah, I noticed that. Do thou what the Prince wilt, for that is the whole of the law."

She grinned knowingly at him, and he patted her perfect little bottom, which lacked a tail now. He wondered why she wasn't wearing it or the little horns he'd seen. He shrugged and abandoned that line of thought, for that way lay madness, or at least a mondo headache. The whole thing was impossible anyhow, the rational part of his mind insisted again. He happily ignored it. *Carpe diem*, he thought with savage pleasure. Seize the day, and the devil-girl, too!

The appearance of Leviathan must have caused a stir in the Fallen camp, because he hadn't walked far with Melusine before Kaym appeared. The fallen angel stood out like a sore thumb amidst the robed and bejeweled angels, since he was back in the aspect of the Raybans-wearing biker. His eyes were unreadable behind the dark lenses, but his twisted grin was still the same.

"Welcome back, Christopher."

"His name is Phaoton!" Melusine protested hotly, but Christopher waved her off.

"Kaym can call me whatever he likes." He peered at his mentor's face. "What's wrong? Are you angry with me?"

The fallen angel gazed levelly at him, with his arms folded and his pale face impassive.

"No," he said quietly. "Not at all. I am surprised, again, at your unforeseen power. I was not strong enough to stand before Leviathan, while you mastered it. I will confess to a certain amount of dismay, for it is always unsettling to see one's protégé surpass one, particularly in such a spectacular manner. But I am not displeased."

Christopher was relieved. He was strong now, certainly. But he found it hard to believe Kaym's humble words.

"Is the Prince going to raise Phaoton to the Teraphim?" Melusine asked hopefully. "I heard He might."

"I cannot speak for the Prince, Melusine. But He is pleased, I think, that the rebellious hosts were put to rout. Now He does not have to fight a war on two fronts, and all of our resources can be thrown against the King. Leviathan will no doubt play some part in His plans for the final battle, as will Leviathan's master."

He gracefully indicated Christopher, who grinned widely and nudged Melusine with his elbow.

"Someone told me once that his lord was a generous one, and I've always found him to speak the truth."

Kaym's wry smile became even more twisted. "Perhaps that is true. You will find out soon enough. The Prince sent me to find you and bring you to Him."

"Is He here?"

"Yes, He's in the Courts of Light."

"The Courts of Light?" Christopher was confused. "I thought that was back on . . . I don't know, Rahab or whatever. It's in Heaven now?"

Kaym smiled and shook his head.

"You may be strong, but you have much to learn. There is no here or there where Adonai Lucere is concerned."

The Shining Prince Himself was feeling rather well. He had the assurance of His generals that they could indeed find a way past the daunting walls of the Arx Dei, while Mahalidael now had the world of Ahura Azdha under the control of his iron fist. There had been losses, to be sure, there always were, but one Seraphim, a few angels, and countless mortal deaths were an excellent trade for Leviathan tamed, the Host shattered, and the Crystal Tower broken. Surely the King of Heaven was growing desperate, He imagined. His shining noose wound ever tighter around the King's almighty throat!

The Lady of the Tower had been a thorn in His own shining side for centuries, ever since He had first revealed His Godhead to the People of the Golden Dawn, those favored mortals who were rightfully proud to bear His name. How dared she scorn Him, when even the rocks and mountains bowed before His radiance! Well, it was no matter now. She was dead at last, finally, gone the way of all mortals as her accursed gift of life had finally fallen, like the Tower of Qawah itself, before His servants.

Three angels entered the throne room, and He chuckled as He saw His own beautiful face staring back at him. It was that useful mortal from the Adamite future, of course, accompanied by Kaym and another angel, one of the nameless multitudes of His legions.

The mortal and the third angel immediately covered their eyes and fell to their knees, blinded by His radiance. Only Kaym seemed unaffected by the brilliant sight, though whether it was the dark lenses he wore or just simple familiarity, the Shining One could not tell. He nodded with approval, though, as Kaym joined the others, kneeling out of respect and duty, if not awe.

"Rise and approach Us, Adon Christopher, who art called Phaoton!"

The voice echoing from within the blinding brightness had the silvered melody of a church bell, and Christopher blinked painfully as he tried to face the light. He couldn't see, but he hurried to obey and approached the throne with both hands over his eyes.

"Prince, ah, Prince Lucere, forgive me, but the light . . . it's too much!"

The burning radiance faded a little, to a level that was almost bearable.

"We are pleased with thee, Phaoton. Thou hast served Us well, far better than others in whom Our trust hath been ill placed. Now all shalt know the favor in which We hold thee. Two legions shalt thou commandeth, subject only to the advice and counsel of thy mentor, Kaym."

"Two legions!"

It was what Christopher had hoped for but hadn't dared to ask. Command, he'd learned, was the only way to power, command of yourself and those around you.

"Yes, thou shalt take command of the legion that routed Michael's host before the Gate of Heaven, according to thy plan. Kaym hath told me of this, and also of the Sons of Pride. It is meet that a legion of the Anakhim, too, shall be thine."

"You shower me with blessings, Great Shining Lord," Christopher replied carefully. "But will the angels listen to me? The Anakhim were mortal once, and I think they'll obey me all right. But I don't know about the angels."

"Obey the Master of Leviathan? Obey one who holds authority at Our command? Doubt Us not. But to place thy fears at rest, We give thee this as a mark of Our favor."

There was a flash, and Christopher felt a wave of heat pass quickly over him. His skin tingled, kind of painfully, as if he'd just been sunburned.

"Go now, Baal Phaoton, and taketh command of thy legions," the Shining Prince commanded. "Thine is the honor of leading Our assault on the fortress of the King."

"Thank you, Majestic King!"

Very cool! Christopher bowed as low as he could, then backed down slowly from the dais. When he turned around to face Kaym and Melusine, the devil-girl gasped and raised a hand to her mouth.

"Phaoton, you . . . your skin! You shine like the Shining Prince!"

Christopher looked down at his hand. Melusine was right. It was gleaming with a familiar metallic shine, and Christopher had to stifle a laugh. While he understood that the Prince was paying him a compliment, he felt as if he'd suddenly turned into C-3PO.

He whistled three notes. "Wheet-whoo-wheet!"

"What?" Melusine stared at him.

"Oh, never mind, you wouldn't get it." He grinned at Kaym. "Hey, I guess Melusine was right. I've been promoted. We get to command the two legions that will lead the assault on the city walls tomorrow."

Kaym nodded, and Christopher saw him raise an eyebrow. Was he pleased or not? It was hard to tell. "Which legions?" he asked.

"Um, one of Baal Chanan's, I think. And we keep the Anakhim, too."

But even as he answered Kaym, Christopher felt a sudden wave of weakness pass over him. His skin cracked painfully, and when he looked at his hands, he saw they'd turned a deep shade of red. He sank to his knees as Melusine was struck by the same unknown force, collapsing wordlessly into an unconscious pile of slender arms and legs. Only Kaym remained standing, though he swayed back and forth as he fought to stay on his feet.

"Great Prince, what is happening?" he heard the fallen angel shouting toward the dais.

The blinding light from the dais had disappeared completely, and Christopher could see that the Son of the Morning was breathing hard and clutching the engraved arms of his throne with knuckles that were white with effort. His handsome face was stricken, as if someone had punched Him in the stomach, and two ugly purple veins protruded on either side of His forehead. As Christopher looked on with horror, the Prince's skin was suddenly transformed, from supple gold to a horny red substance that looked like painted pottery.

"Ahura . . ." the Prince was moaning. "The world . . . My temple . . ."

The Shining One pointed to the ceiling, to the alabaster dome that had once shown Christopher his first images of Heaven. As He whispered a painful word of command, the dome flared brightly and came to life, presenting a clear picture of the Fallen world of Ahura Azdha and its great, golden capital, Aurora.

Aurora was tranquil, with the commotion of the last few days replaced by the People of the Golden Dawn going about their everyday business. The temples were packed with the Prince's worshipers practicing their epicurean rites, the prosperous streets were filled with tradesmen and their customers, and the only sign of the supernatural was the occasional strutting Anakhim, walking through the city with lofty, godlike arrogance. All in all, it was a pretty, prideful picture of wealth and decadence that would have put Nero's Rome to shame.

Christopher, sprawled uncomfortably on the marble floor, watched as the white clouds floating slowly across the yellow Azdhan sky were parted with a mighty trumpet blast. A giant Divine angel appeared in the gap, holding a great scale aloft in one of his powerful hands.

"Gabriel," he heard Kaym mutter as they watched the far-off events unfold.

On either side of the scale lay a single object. On the right was a sword, and on the left was a live white bird that looked like a dove. The angel of the Lord flicked the restraints away with his free hand and watched closely as the scale began to right itself. First the sword dropped lower, then the dove, but after two bounces back and forth, the scale came to a rest with the sword very much lower than the bird.

Prince Gabriel raised his voice so that it could be heard throughout all the world, and the judgment rang down from the skies like thunder.

"Wicked men of Rahab, the stink of your corruption has risen to the very heights of Heaven. You have been judged by the Most High and found wanting. You have chosen to follow a false sun instead of the true Light of the World, and your treacherous hearts have embraced the wickedness of the Dawn Prince. I say to you now, the sentence of death is upon this world."

The angel lifted the dove from the scale, and it disappeared in his mighty hand. He squeezed, once, crushing the dove, and a black rain began to fall from his fist down upon the city and the surrounding plains. It engulfed everything as far as the horizon. Wherever the rain touched, men began to sicken and die in agonizing torment.

"This is the mercy of the Lord, which you rejected in your pride, refusing to repent of your unholy ways."

The cries of the afflicted were terrible, and the very mountains rang with their suffering. Only the immortals were unaffected, although even the greatest among the Fallen trembled before the righteous wrath of the Lord. They trembled and shook with fear but were too full of pride to humble themselves, even as thousands of Aurorans died in awful torment all around them. But it did not take them long to realize that the black rain did not affect them, and with that realization their haughty confidence returned.

Christopher heard the Fallen begin to curse the angel of the Lord, shouting terrible threats as they vowed to see him utterly destroyed, sent beyond the Beyond for all eternity. Those few humans who survived did not repent but instead blasphemed the King of Heaven, swearing their undying hatred. And the howling of the Anakhim echoed from the mountains, drowning out the cries of their dying mortal brothers. It sounded as if the rocks themselves were slavering for Gabriel's spirit.

But the mighty Archangel was unfazed by their threats, though his face was grim with purpose as he lifted the sword from its place on the scale. He held it high, as if saluting Heaven, before hurling it like a lance down toward the heart of the wicked city.

"Behold, wicked ones, the judgment of the Lord!"

Thunder boomed three times as the blade hurtled toward the great Temple of Light at the very center of Aurora. There was a mighty blast as it pierced the great golden dome, sending huge chunks of metal and marble flying in all directions. The force of the blow sent shivers through the foundation of the massive building, and hundreds of cracks began to appear throughout the structure like many rivers carving out new channels through a barren land.

The cracks spread and widened, until they covered the whole edifice like a giant spider's web. Then, with an earth-shaking roar, the great Temple of Light collapsed, burying alive the thousands of Auroran mortals who had taken shelter from the deadly rain of judgment. For a moment, all was still, and Christopher thought everything was over.

But the King of Heaven's wrath was not ended; indeed, it was just beginning. Only moments after the last remaining temple stone had fallen, the ground itself began to quake. From the mountains to the valleys, from the central streets of wicked Aurora to the farthest reaches of the globe, from the deserts to the seas, Rahab began to shake. It shook and shook, until every building had collapsed and fallen, and there remained not one stone standing upon another. The mountains crumbled into the seas, and the mighty forests thundered with the splintering sound of great trees falling.

High above the stricken world, in the hands of the angel of the Lord, the empty scale was transformed into a great ram's horn. As the last mountain fell, Gabriel lifted the horn to his lips and blew. It was a great and terrible sounding, and even though he was safe, watching from afar in Heaven, the blast echoed in Christopher's heart like the final trump of doom.

And with that mighty blast, Rahab the wicked was shattered, broken into millions and millions of pieces, a mighty stone smashed into dust and pebbles. Its yellow sky boiled away into the pitiless blackness of space with a mournful sound, weeping for the world it no longer embraced. Where a world had once been, there was nothing but the void.

"It is finished," he heard Gabriel intone with solemnity, and even as Ahura Azdha perished, a second cataclysmic shock rocked the Hall of the Morning. He tried to roll over and get up, but the effort was too much for him, and he gave in to the cool temptation of the marble floor against his cheek. His eyes closed, and the Courts of Light disappeared.

CHAPTER 24

THE
LIGHT OF TRUTH

AND JORAM TURNED HIS HANDS, AND FLED, AND SAID TO
AHAZIAH, THERE IS TREACHERY, O AHAZIAH.
—2 Kings 9:23

When Cristopher came to, he found himself still
lying facedown on the marble floor. He rolled
over and looked up to see that the dome over his
head was cracked and ruined. Large chunks of marble had been gouged out of it, and when he turned
his head, he saw a large piece had fallen right next
to him, nearly crushing his skull. He shuddered at
his near escape as he stiffly, painfully struggled to
his feet.

The first thing to meet his eyes was the Dawn
Prince, and he cried out with horror when he
looked up and saw the terrible changes in the Son of
the Morning. The Dawn Prince didn't look like a
golden king anymore, he was scary, like a demon on
a Megadeth cover. His reddened eyes blazed with
an insane fury that was frightening to see, and his
cracked, bleeding face was filled with rage.

329

"I will tear Heaven down to its foundations, then I will smash the foundations! I will drain the fire from every angel who still stands against me, then vomit it forth that I not be polluted with their feeble spirits! I will destroy everything He has created, everything, and not until all Creation is shattered and scattered upon the winds of Chaos will I begin to build a new world, a new universe, a new creation without the stink of the Ancient of Days!"

Christopher blinked and wished he had a place to hide as the Prince shook his fist at the shattered dome and turned to Kaym.

"How dare He? How dare He!"

"I do not know," the fallen angel said slowly, choosing his words carefully. "But I know this. He is a fool to choose You as His adversary, Great Prince."

Adonai Lucere nodded, mollified, but only for a moment. Then He raised His hands and felt the broken, hardened leather of His ruined face. It was almost too painful to watch. His long fingers probed the deep furrows of His lined cheeks and the bestial thickness of His jutting chin. He softly stroked one of the curved horns that had burst through the skin of His forehead, leaving two trails of blood oozing down the sides of His face. Then, as He fell back on His throne, dark tears welled up in His suffering eyes as He howled at Heaven.

"Thou hast destroyed My world and broken My temple, but why didst Thou need to steal My beauty!"

The Prince's wail of anguish was so loud that it caused the Courts to shake. Christopher's ears were ringing, and the sentries outside the Hall of the Morning rushed in, thinking He was under attack.

"Go now, all of thee, go!" the Prince commanded between heart-rending sobs.

"But where shall we go?" Kaym asked, his brow furrowed with concern. "We cannot leave Thee!"

"Leave Me!" the Prince howled, crazed with grief and fury, and white flames erupted from His mouth, enveloping Kaym in a scorching blanket of fire.

"No!" Christopher screamed, appalled beyond belief. "Kaym!"

His face seared black with horrible burns, Kaym stumbled back, and he would have fallen if Christopher hadn't caught him. He shouted for Melusine and, with her assistance, helped the stricken angel out of the Hall of the Morning, now lit by a different kind of dawn. As they hurried from the destruction of the Hall, Christopher heard the Son of the Morning crying bitter tears of rage and sorrow for the shining beauty that was His no more.

The Fallen army was a great and terrible sight. Well over half a million angels were gathered together, each filled with enough power to make the foundations of Heaven shake and tremble. They were arrayed before the walls of the Arx Dei in a vast panoply of wings and weapons, auras and aspects, more colorful than any rainbow.

But all their glittering array was outshined by the Shining One. He appeared in all the brightness of His former glory, as if that terrible moment in the Hall of the Morning had never happened. His face was pure and white, unmarred by a single line or wrinkle, much less a scar, and His golden eyes were bright with pride and confidence as He surveyed his mighty legions.

"Spirits of Air, Spirits of Fire, I welcome thee here! Spirits of Earth and Water, thee art well come! Know that on this day, We are as one, for We are angels of a new age, spirits of a new day dawning!"

The cheer that answered Him was wordless, but it was approving, and Heaven shook before the thunder of hundreds of thousands of angels lifting their voices in praise of the Dawn Prince. It was awesome, and Christopher himself yelled so loud he thought his lungs would burst.

"Know that on this very day, thou hath a new God. Heaven is fallen, and soon the King of Heaven shall also fall from His mighty throne. And though it falls to Us, as thy head, to claim that throne and bear its awful weight upon Our shoulders, know that We are but a symbol. Know thou, when thou bowest before Us, the God thou worshipeth is thee!"

Again, the legions roared their approval.

"We say to thee now, look on Us and tremble, for We are all that thou art and all thou shalt someday be. Are We not beautiful? Are We not glorious? So shalt thou be, if thou wilt only will it so. The King of Heaven hath said to thee, thou art the Bene Elohim, the sons of God. So doth he claim thee! But We say to thee, thou shalt be called El Zahavim, the golden gods! Only thyself shall thou worship, and do what thou wilt shall be the whole of the Law!"

The Shining One spread his arms, and a spectral radiance began to glow between them. It was a miracle of sorts, for Christopher saw his own face reflected there, his true face, but shining in the fullness of a perfected glory. It startled him, until he realized that each angel was seeing a different vision, a picture of his own idealized self.

"Bow down and worship Us, thou who would be gods!"

And Christopher, like every other angel in the Army of Light, bowed before the Son of the Morning. He worshiped his own image as he worshiped the great and lordly prince of angels who promised him perfection even as He Himself was perfect.

The mass ecstasy was incandescent, and it was not long before a Seraph, intoxicated by the vision of his own godhead, lifted up his voice and sang.

> Who can compare to Thee
> O shining Lord
> What can compare
> To Thy promised Word

> Thy glory and majesty
> Always shall be
> Golden embodiment
> Of Thy beauty

Other, lesser voices joined in with the singer as he chanted a mantra of praise and thanksgiving to the Dawn Prince. Soon the whole assembly was singing, the angelic army suddenly transformed into a heavenly chorus of voices filled with power.

> We praise Thee
> O Shining One
> We glorify Thee
> Great Golden King

Adonai Lucere closed his eyes and threw His head back in a divine rapture. This was the moment

He had been waiting for, to have His Godhood acknowledged by all the angels of Heaven. It was the pinnacle of his existence, one that would be surpassed only at the moment He took His place upon the majestic throne of Heaven.

And, He thought with satisfaction, that moment was at hand. Surely the King of Heaven could see that His beautiful Light-bringer was now truly a god, proclaimed and acknowledged by nearly all the angels in Creation. Even he would call Him Adonai Lucere, a Bright, Shining God wholly worthy of all praise, glory, and honor.

"You have not the right, Lucifer!" He heard a voice break in on His exultant reverie.

Blasphemy! Adonai Lucere's disbelieving eyes snapped open and took in a small, slender figure standing before the open gates of the Arx Dei. He did not recognize the angel, which confused Him, for He knew the face of every angel who existed, who ever had existed, in Heaven.

The strange angel's skin was dark, a deep bronze, and his hair was long and white. He did not have wings, and he was not beautiful. His features were broad and indelicate. However, his eyes were intense, flashing with all the fiery scarlet of the setting sun. Nevertheless, he held his head high. He showed no fear despite the vast army standing before him.

"You have not the right," he blasphemed again.

"We are the Shining One, the Prince of the Courts of Light and the Son of the Morning! We claim the Eternal Throne in Our holy name, and Our claim hath been witnessed by all the hosts of Heaven!" Adonai Lucere sputtered.

The strange angel didn't seem impressed, though, and pointed a slim finger at Him as he flayed Him with a barrage of withering scorn.

"I said that you do not have the right, Lucifer. You are less than a jest, you are three-in-one: a charade, a myth, and a lie. And you delude yourself, o Prince of Vanity, because you were the first to believe your own foolish, prideful lies."

Adonai Lucere gasped. The unbelievable effrontery, the sheer rudeness, left Him speechless. Fortunately, before His silence had time to linger, Baal Chanan stepped forward and spoke for Him.

"Who are you, who dares to speak so to the Son of the Morning?" he demanded.

"I am the Way, the Truth, and the Life. I am not created, but I am the great I AM. I am the truth just as he is the lie, for while he is the Son of the Morning, I am the Son of God, the Lion of Judah, the bright Morning Star. And I tell you truly, one day I will sit at the right hand of the Father."

"No! Thou art nothing!" Adonai Lucere lost His temper, and the air about Him began to crackle with angry electricity. "Look at thee! Thou art small and ugly and dark and . . . and nothing! We are the Shining One! Do you see this host? To Us the host hath bowed, to Us the world hath bent its knee! I am the Son of God, not thee! Is there even one who would bow before thee?"

"Oh, you will, Lucifer," came the confident reply. "One day, you will indeed."

With this impudent assertion, anger rippled like a tide through His loyal legions. The wingless one's words sparked angry whispers and impassioned murmurs that grew louder with each repetition.

Soon the whispers rose into loud, hate-filled shouts, as angel after angel howled for Him to punish this lowly blasphemer.

With great difficulty, Adonai Lucere controlled Himself. Should He respond, He wondered, or would it be better to act as if these ridiculous and reprehensible accusations were beneath Him?

But before He made up His mind, there was a commotion near the front of the legions as a huge black figure forced itself through the ranks. It was Abaddon, armored in his terrible rune-inscribed carapace, wearing the fearsome aspect of the Destroyer. The Dawn Prince smiled. Abaddon towered over the little angel like a massive god of destruction. His giant sword, Soulthirster, with its ivory handle of chaosbone and eerie, flickering ebon flames, looked as if it could account for the wingless one all by itself.

"Name yourself," He heard Abaddon thunder. "I am Abaddon, the Destroyer, and I would know what you are called before I send you Beyond in the name of Adonai Lucere, the Shining Lord of Heaven."

The legions cheered lustily, and He raised His hand, casting a ray of light that illuminated the giant warrior and demonstrated His favor. He caused the golden light to dance and whirl with abandon, lighting first one dark sigil, then another.

He frowned when He saw that the wingless one was still not impressed, either by His champion or His artistry.

"I have many names, Gog Sheklah. But for the present, Kherev Elohai will suffice."

The Sword of the Lord? Adonai Lucere almost

laughed. Kherev Elohai didn't look like a weapon so much as a mortal's dining tool, especially compared to Abaddon. Still, He did not like that this Kherev knew Abaddon's real name.

"Sword of the Lord?" Abaddon echoed His disdainful thoughts. "Are you the champion of the King, then?"

"In a manner of speaking, yes."

"Then where is your weapon?"

"I need none."

Abaddon flourished Soulthirster, and the dark flames leaped with hungry anticipation. "That's true. I'm told one can visit the Beyond emptyhanded just as easily as not."

The legions roared with laughter, and Adonai Lucere Himself had to grin, though not for the same reason. Abaddon did not have a way with words, and He knew that His champion was completely serious. Any humor on the Destroyer's part was wholly inadvertent.

Abaddon's opponent didn't see it, though.

"I warn you, Gog Sheklah, you come against me with a dark aspect and a darker blade, but I come against you in the name of my Father, the Almighty God. Repent of your pride and your false god, and you shall be spared the flames of your destruction."

"Destruction? I am the Lord of Destruction! Let the Circle be joined!"

Abaddon spat, and a circle of fire erupted immediately around the two champions, great and small. The unholy blaze burned blue and green with the hot force of the Destroyer's anger.

But even through the hissing of the flames, the Prince heard Kherev laughing softly.

"There is no circle that could contain Me, Gog Sheklah. I am the beginning and the end." He glanced at the flames leaping madly about Him, licking at Him, eager to taste His soul. "Be still."

The flames disappeared almost as fast as the smile from Adonai Lucere's face. The cheering legions fell abruptly silent.

The silence was broken by Abaddon's rage-filled shout, as, goaded beyond reason by Kherev's casual exhibition of power, he leaped toward the wingless one, bringing Soulthirster down in a brutal stroke that looked as if it would cleave Kherev in two.

But Kherev calmly raised His hand, and the mighty weapon was deflected away with such force that it was buried to the hilt in the golden streets of Heaven. The dark flames flickered feebly, as if in protest, then winked out.

Adonai Lucere saw Abaddon stare in disbelief at his empty hand, then at his extinguished sword. It was beyond understanding! With His help, Abaddon had made Soulthirster from the power-laden bones of one of the great lords of Chaos. It was an awesome artifact, with all the incendiary power of more than a score of suns. Yet Kherev had parried it with nothing more than an empty-handed gesture.

"Who are you?" Abaddon whispered, as he stared into the intense red eyes of his enemy. "How can this be?"

"I honor My Father, and you dishonor Me," came the quiet answer. "But you have no power over Me."

Abaddon wavered, and for a moment, the Prince feared his champion would humiliate Him by submitting to the enemy. Don't do it, he silently urged the Destroyer. Strike him now. Strike him now!

Kherev Elohai must have heard His thoughts, for he shook his head sadly.

"Amen," he said, just as Abaddon hurled a black thunderbolt at His midsection.

Even when he replayed the memory in his mind, Christopher was never able to figure out just what exactly had happened that day before the Fortress of God. He didn't see the one called Kherev move, but Abaddon's thunderbolt didn't seem to hurt him at all. He did see the Destroyer pause, though, as if surprised that his opponent was still there.

But Abaddon never got a third chance, because as Kherev pointed at the golden bricks beneath the Destroyer's feet, the street burst open with a Heaven-shaking crack. The mighty fallen angel spread his dark wings and tried to fly upward, but to no avail, as the yawning chasm sucked him down into the depths. Christopher heard him bellow once, angrily, then the chasm closed and the Prince's champion was gone, banished in a heartbeat by a simple gesture.

A groan of shock and dismay went up from the watching legions, but it was quickly drowned out by the melodious harmonies of angels singing. It was the Choir Invisible, unseen but not unheard. They sang a song without words, conveying an air of victory that was ominous and frightening in the aftermath of Abaddon's fall.

"Save us, Great Prince!" he heard angels calling out to the Dawn Prince.

"Fools," Adonai Lucere replied angrily. "Cowards! Canst thou not see that he lies? He is alone. Thou art legion, and he is but one. Attack him now! Destroy him!"

"But he destroyed the Destroyer, the mightiest of

us all," Baal Phaleg shouted in protest. He was clearly shaken by Abaddon's untimely demise.

"It was a trick." Adonai Lucere's voice was sharp, and Christopher wondered if the Dawn Prince was afraid, too. "We command thee, now, in Our shining name, attack that accursed pretender!"

But the cause of all this commotion smiled and raised His hands above His head, and lifted His voice in a joyful chant that blended magically with the wordless tune of the unseen singers.

> Open their eyes, Lord
> O let them see
> Thy power, Thy glory
> Thy eternal majesty

As Christopher watched, worried, Kherev Elohai began to glow as if someone had switched Him on. His dusky face brightened, slowly changing from bronze to gold to a bright white light that was as pure as it was impossible to look at. Christopher could feel the glow rushing over him, but it was a heat that warmed instead of burning, it was a warm embrace, not a scorching assault. It was terrible, smothering, and he felt as if he were being sucked in against his will.

In desperation, he glanced back at the Dawn Prince, and for the first time, he saw the Shining One outshone by another. The Dawn Prince looked duller by comparison, smaller somehow, and uglier in the white light that engulfed him. His shadow cast a form over the legions that was deformed and twisted, wrong. It was like the golden rose of morning being overwhelmed by the bright radiance of high noon.

"No!" the Son of the Morning screamed. "No! No!"

As the Dawn Prince shrieked his protest, Christopher watched the self-proclaimed Son of God draw Himself up before them. He grew taller and broader, getting bigger and bigger until He dwarfed Baal Chanan, Baal Phaleg, Lord Belial, and all the greatest lords of the Fallen.

"Begone, false Light-bringer!" He commanded loudly. "The darkness of thy shadow shall not touch Heaven again except by permission of My Father. As thou wert bright before, so now will thy spirit be one of darkness. Now begone, Satan, and all thine host with thee!"

The Son of God raised His glowing hand, and a beam of white light shot out and illuminated Lucifer like a spotlight, stripping away all his pretense, demonstrating the ugly nature of his twisted spirit for all to see. Christopher retched, and even Kaym quailed momentarily at the hideous sight.

The humiliation was more than Lucifer could bear. Christopher saw that although the light didn't harm the Prince, he seemed to feel its touch like an inferno. Shattered by this single deadly stroke, Lucifer leaped upon Leviathan's massive back and fled from Heaven upon the wings of Chaos.

"Wait . . . Leviathan, get back here!" he yelled, but the great dragon either didn't hear him or ignored him. He felt about himself for the tooth that would give him command of the beast, but it was gone. He stared at the retreating figure, wondering if the Dawn Prince had taken it from him.

The legions were stirring fearfully with Adonai Lucere's flight, and Christopher, sensing panic in the ranks of his Anakhim, turned desperately to Kaym, hoping that the fallen angel might have some idea of how to salvage the situation. After a heart-stopping moment when he thought Kaym had run away, too, he saw him in the middle of a hasty conference with Baal Phaleg and Lord Belial.

"Kaym!" he shouted, relieved.

Kaym looked up and gestured for him to join them, but before Christopher could fight his way through the frightened Anakhim, a noise captured his attention. It sounded like a strong wind blowing through a forest, except there were no trees around. A burst of light drew his eyes up to the sky, and he caught his breath when he saw hundreds of thousands of white-robed angels suddenly appear out of thin air.

They were armed and ready for battle, confident, and eager to unleash their flaming swords upon their rebellious brethren. They rushed down upon the disorganized legions like an avalanche of fire, and the overwhelmed Fallen were quick to fly before them. Incredibly, impossibly, they seemed to outnumber the combined force of the six hundred and sixty-six legions.

"What is this?" Christopher screamed at Kaym as he saw his Anakhim melting away before the fury of the Divine assault.

It was like watching a hot knife slicing its way through soft butter, so quickly did the ur-mortals fall before the angelic swords of fire. He tried to think of something, anything, that would blunt the force of the attack, but his mind was blank. The confusion was beyond his control, and it was all he could do to defend himself.

"What?" Kaym couldn't hear him over the din of the battle. He ducked one flaming blade and struck down its wielder.

"I thought you said most of the angels were on our side!" he shouted as he parried two attackers at once.

"They are!" Kaym was hard-pressed himself. "They were!"

"Then where are all these angels coming from?" Slash, parry, thrust. Two more down, only a million more to go.

"I don't know!"

Well, that really helps, Christopher thought acidly as the battle surged away from him, giving him a chance to survey the situation. His legion of angels was holding up somewhat better than the Anakhim, but despite their ferocity, they were still being forced back. Christopher looked back at the Anakhim and came to a quick decision. They couldn't be saved no matter what he did, so he might as well use them to save the rest of his angels.

"Kaym, we can't stay here!"

"I know!"

He saw the fallen angel duck under a burly Archangel's swing, then rise and bury one of his spiked fists into the other's throat. The Archangel choked out a strangled cry, then disappeared in a red burst of light.

"Take the legion and retreat to that hall near the Courts," he ordered. "You know what I mean?"

"I remember. Will you stay with the Anakhim?"

"Forget it, they're toast. Hurry, and I'll meet you there."

"Okay." The fallen angel met Christopher's eyes

for a second, but his emotion was unreadable. "Then I'll see you there."

It took a little time, but as soon as Kaym had successfully extricated the remnants of his legion from the deadly chaos of the battlefield, Christopher turned his mind toward getting out of there himself. Thunderbolts and massive fireballs were landing indiscriminately all around him, and the deafening sound of their detonations made it impossible to think clearly.

He looked around and shook his head. Only a fourth of his Anakhim were left, but the Divine angels were pressing them hard, and they couldn't last long. The path to the west was clear, for the moment, but a force of Divine chariots were galloping hard to cut off that line of retreat. If he was going to get out, it had to be now.

His decision made, he started to run, but a large hand caught his shoulder and stopped him in his tracks.

"Are you leaving us, Baal Phaoton?"

It was one of his Anakhim, a giant ur-mortal with two piggish eyes set deep within a broad, flat face. Christopher had talked to him once before, and this was not one of his brighter warriors. Reason, he knew, would be useless.

"Let go of me, you idiot!"

"You can't leave us, Baal Phaoton! We'll be destroyed without you. They said we would be gods—"

"Shut up!" He looked over his shoulder and saw the chariots quickly closing the gap. In minutes, they would be surrounded.

"They didn't say we could die. They promised us!"

"Shut up, you moron! Let me go!"

Frantic with fear, knowing he had little time left, Christopher drew his blade and slashed at the heavy hand still holding him fast. The ur-mortal howled and stepped back, his face bewildered with pain and the knowledge of betrayal. At that moment, a random bolt of lightning fell from the sky, transfixing the monster, and the ur-mortal fell dead at Christopher's feet, his bloody, wounded hand stretched out in supplication.

Christopher stared at the lifeless hand for a moment, then turned his back and ran.

CHAPTER 25

CITADEL OF THE KING

BLESSED IS THE MAN WHOM THOU CHOOSEST, AND
CAUSEST TO APPROACH UNTO THEE, THAT HE MAY DWELL
IN THY COURTS: WE SHALL BE SATISFIED WITH THE
GOODNESS OF THY HOUSE, EVEN OF THY HOLY TEMPLE.
—Psalms 65:4

It was just the coolest place, Jami thought, as she
looked around the lovely garden, inside the
fortress that Khasar called the Arx Dei. What could
you say? It was beautiful, of course, with classic
architecture that reminded her of that storybook
castle in Germany, or was it Austria? She frowned,
trying to remember. Lichtenstein, maybe? Well,
whatever. But even though the Arx Dei looked like a
walled castle from the outside, inside it was, well,
hard to say.

The room that had been a cozy little library complete with books and a fireplace one day would, the
next day, be a pretty flower garden that was, as far
as she could tell, totally outside. It was weird, but
inside and outside didn't matter anymore. Size
didn't seem to enter into the equation, nor did
anything else, apparently. So much for finishing

that book about the Chaos Lords, she thought with a shrug. She leaned over and smelled a yellow tulip.

Holli said this place reminded her of the Laura Ashley store at the mall, where everything always looked just the way you thought it really should. Not that the Divine decorator, whoever she was, was particularly fond of floral prints and paisley, although there was a pretty tapestry with blue-and-yellow flowers in the room she shared with Holli and a very nice angel named Daliel. She wasn't sure how long they'd been there, but every day, Lokhael and Khasar came to visit, and Daliel instructed them in the Path of Righteousness. The stuff about the path was too much like school for her liking, but Khasar made up for it, telling story after story of the creation of Ahura Azdha, Lucifer's rebellion, and how a beautiful world was corrupted and became Rahab the Wicked.

Neither she nor Holli had spoken to Kherev since the miraculous rescue of the people of Chasah, but Jami had caught a glimpse of a woman who looked like the Lady Tiphereth and later learned from Lokhael that it had indeed been the Lady. Holli returned joyfully from a walk one morning, excited to report that she'd run into Father Havtah, who was now happily employed as an assistant to the Archangel Rhamiel, who was one of the scribes in Heaven's great Scriptorium.

"Excuse me, but you are the Lady Jami, are you not?"

Jami looked up, surprised to see Koser Vadout, the captain of Chasah who'd almost killed her. He apologized to her, at great length, until Jami finally made him stop.

"So what are you doing now?" she asked him, curious.

The black-bearded warrior smiled at her, his face no longer grim but filled with the same kind of light she'd often seen in the faces of the angels.

"I serve my Lord much as I did before," he said, fingering the sword at his side. "But my faith is all the greater now, because I have seen Him face-to-face."

"As you did before?"

"Once a warrior, always a warrior," a tall young man in a white robe who looked almost like Koser's twin said as he joined them in the garden. He gripped the captain's shoulder and smiled proudly.

"My father," Koser explained, grinning. "He always told me that the Lord would come as He promised, and he was right! And we serve Him gladly, for in these bodies of light we fight against the Evil One himself, rather than his minions. Now that the wicked world of our birth is gone, we shall fight for Him here in Heaven."

"The world . . . is gone? What do you mean?"

"Had you not heard, Lady Jami? Ahura Azdha is no more. Not long after His Son came for us, the Lord destroyed it in His wrath."

Jami did not know what to say, because for the first time in a long time, she felt a deep pang of concern for Chris. What had become of him? Had he been blown away with the rest of that wicked world? Somehow, she didn't think so. Most likely, he was with the doomed legions that surrounded her right now.

* * *

Lokhael was gone when Jami returned to the room, but Khasar was there, helping Holli and Daliel make perfume out of some flowers. Jami laughed at the Archon and threw a tulip at him. Moments later, the heavy tapestry that covered the entrance to the room was pushed aside, and in walked Kherev Elohai, followed by seven royal Seraphim wearing the form of simple Archangels. They were in full armor, and only their many-eyed wings indicated their lofty rank.

Khasar and Daliel immediately fell to their knees, and Jami quickly followed their example, as did Holli. But the Son of God smiled gently and extended His hands to raise them, two by two, to their feet again.

"It is time now to bring these matters to a close," He announced softly. "Soon I will rid Heaven of this wicked rebellion. Be strong of heart, and fear not, for we are no longer outnumbered. My Father has raised a new host, stronger and more loyal than the first."

"Praise be to the Almighty!" Khasar exclaimed, clenching a fist. "That'll confuse the foe!"

"Indeed it will," Kherev replied. "They shall be utterly defeated, cast upon the winds of Chaos and dispersed throughout Creation."

"But they'll be around to cause trouble later," Jami predicted.

Kherev glanced at her and arched an eyebrow. "Yes, they will." He smiled again, a confident smile that would have made the most cowardly soul feel brave and unafraid. "But I believe My Father has a plan for that as well."

"Well, I'm sure it's a good one, then," Holli said.

Her innocent certainty made the Seraphim laugh. They sounded like thunder rumbling at a distance.

"You have the gift of faith indeed, my dear," Kherev praised her. "And you will need faith, both of you, for what I am asking you to do."

"What's that?" Jami asked.

"As I recall, Jami, you asked if I would give your brother a chance to repent of the evil path he has chosen. I promised you that I would, and I am here to keep My promise. Will you go to him and tell him that he must turn from his evil ways and repent?"

"So he's alive," Jami breathed with relief. "And yeah, of course I'll go."

"Can I go, too?" Holli asked hopefully. "You said both of us, didn't you?"

"Yes, you shall go together. But I must warn you both, your brother is not the same person you knew before. He has walked deeply into the shadows, and his soul is stained with the darkness of his deeds. His power is now great, and he will not, I think, be eager to give it up."

"You make it sound hopeless."

"Nothing is hopeless, Jami, not ever. But listen to Me well. You are not to fight him, so do not enter into battle on his terms. If you would save him, you must be willing to forgive him as I have forgiven you, to love him as I have loved you. There is no other way. Are you still willing to go to him? The task is a hard one, and there is danger, that I promise you as well."

Jami looked at Holli. "Well, what do you think?"

"What do I think? Of course we go. If we don't

try to save him, then who will?" Holli put her hands on her hips.

Khasar cleared his throat. "I'll go with them, Lord, if it is Your will."

"As will I," added Daliel.

Kherev nodded approvingly. "I thought as much. It is well. Go with them, and take My blessing with you." He placed one hand on Jami's head, the other on Holli's, and prayed aloud. "Father, protect these two, as they go to do Thy will. Be with them, even unto the end. Amen."

As Kherev prayed over her, Jami felt a warm, glowing sensation flow through her body, an electric tingle that swept away her lingering fears. All would be well, she thought. No matter what happened, God would be with them. That was all that mattered.

CHAPTER 26

RUINS
OF RIGHTEOUSNESS

YOU CANNOT BUILD A SCIENCE TO ALLAY DESPAIR,
THERE IS NO ATHEISM, GOD IS EVERYWHERE.
SO WILL YOU BUILD A TEMPLE TO THE RACE OF MAN?
THERE IS NO SEPARATION, CAN'T YOU UNDERSTAND?
　　　　　　　　　—Psykosonik ("I Am God")

Christopher entered the dark sanctuary of the empty building with caution and a blade in either hand. He knew he hadn't been followed, but he wasn't certain of what to expect. Where was the legion? Where was Kaym? He had to be careful. Many among the Fallen, maddened by fear, were indiscriminately attacking anyone that came near them, regardless of their loyalties. Divine or Fallen, Christopher had no desire to get run through by anyone's sword.

"Kaym?" he called, but an echo was the only reply. "Kaym, are you here?"

The palatial building had once housed many thousands of scripts, of one sort or another. There were lists of angels and their duties, paeans of praise to the Almighty, essays on the nature of Creation, and creative works of angelic inspiration.

They were still there, but many had unfortunately been destroyed by one of Baal Phaleg's rampaging legions, which had made use of the building for the past fortnight. Now it stank, literally, to high heaven, and there was hardly a single wall that was not covered by some form of blasphemous graffiti or other vile pollution.

"Baal Phaoton," he heard Kaym whisper quietly behind him.

Christopher whirled around to see the fallen angel standing in the shadows, shrouded by black wings, with a warning finger over his lips.

Heeding the warning, Christopher stepped closer and spread his hands in a questioning manner. The fallen angel pointed down the hall where Christopher had been heading and made a sign that indicated danger.

Christopher nodded and gestured with his sword that Kaym should precede him, but his mentor shook his head. Kaym pulled his gray robe aside, and Christopher gasped at the sight of the grievous wound that marred the white skin of the angel's chest. Clearly, Kaym was too drained by the battle to heal himself, and he was in no shape to fight. Christopher reached out to him, thinking perhaps he could heal the angel, but Kaym shook his head and urgently indicated the hall again. Okay, dude, whatever you say, Christopher thought. He bowed his head obediently and began to walk carefully in the direction Kaym had pointed.

He walked down one carpeted corridor and up a wide marble stairway that led to the great hall that was the heart of the Scriptorium. It was a vast room, with a domed ceiling arching over three floors, several sets of stairs, and row upon row of shelves covered with the shredded papyrus that was all that remained of many priceless scrolls. In the center of the room was a platform, upon which rested the blasted shards of a destroyed statue, but it was not the statue that caught his attention, it was the four figures, angels all, sitting as if they'd been waiting for him on the square base of the platform.

He saw the four Divines rise and begin to move toward him. He could see that the biggest one was an Archon, large and powerful and full of leonine grace. The other three were lesser angels, and he dismissed them for the moment as he focused on the Archon.

He dropped into a fighting crouch and stepped toward the right, toward the winged lion, making sure that the others could not circle behind him. His blades flared to life with a dark purplish light, and he whispered a spell that would deflect anything hurled at him.

"Ohmigod, is that thing Chris?"

"It is! Christopher, it's me. Put your sword down!"

The figures stopped their approach, as they realized that he was no weak and easy prey. He sensed the tables turning, for he could see they felt his power. Now he was the stalker, the predator, the hunter-killer. He moved closer, almost ready to strike.

"Christopher, what are you doing?"

The voice sounded fearful, almost hysterical. He fed on the fear, savoring it, a tasty treat that only whetted his appetite for blood and fire.

"Don't you recognize us, Chris?"

"Get back," a third voice commanded. It was the big Archon, and he was moving to place himself between Christopher and the other three. "He is swallowed in his sin. He does not know you anymore."

The Archon growled at him, warning him off, and Christopher laughed out loud. It seemed a lifetime ago since he had destroyed Verchiel in the Circle of Fire, and he'd only grown in power since that day. He needed this, a fight, a battle, a little taste of victory to take away the bitter sting of the Prince's humiliating defeat.

"If you run away now, I might let you live," he promised the Archon.

It was even possible that he meant it. But the question was moot.

"I stand before you with the blessing of my Lord." The Archon bared his claws and roared, exposing long white teeth. "In whose name do you come against me?"

"My own," said Christopher, and he struck like lightning.

"Khasar!" he heard the others scream as the Archon fell, slashed into three pieces by Christopher's flashing blades. There was a sound of rushing wind, a flash of blue light, and the winged lion was gone.

"And that, you see, is all I need!" he shouted at the departed spirit of the vanquished Archon.

A second angel launched herself at him with a shout, brandishing a flaming sword. He parried the attack with one dark blade and riposted with the other, running his assailant through the midsection. The light this time was pinkish instead of blue, but the result was the same. Then there were two.

One angel backed away, but the other fell down on her knees before him, as if she wanted to pray to him.

"Will you worship me?" he asked, surprised. He didn't think slaying an Archon or two was reason to compel such devotion, but perhaps she had heard of his mastery of Leviathan.

The angel looked up with a confused look on her face. It was a pretty face, and recognition came almost as an electric shock as he stared down at her. It was Holli's face, his sister's face, stolen from his mind again and used against him.

"Worship you? Christopher, I'm trying to save you! I know you're in there, somewhere. Listen to me! You've got to give up! Don't you understand that Kherev and His Father weren't even trying? You can't win!"

He was angry as he realized that she expected him to fall for the same trick twice. It had worked once, before the gates of Chasah, but he was no fool. It would not work again now.

"I cannot win? Do you know who I am?"

"Of course I do, I'm your sister!"

The voice was familiar, too much so. It haunted him from within, from a place deep within his soul. A place he did not dare to look.

"I have no sister," he shouted harshly. "I am Baal Phaoton, the Master of Leviathan, a Captain of the Fallen, and I bear the favor of the Dawn Prince Himself. See this!"

He pointed to his golden face, a shining inhuman visage.

"I am Baal Phaoton!"

"No, your name isn't Ball whatever, it's Christopher Lewis, and you're not an angel. You're my brother, and you're human, just like me."

"Shut up!" he shouted at the pretty angel kneeling before him. She was really starting to anger him. "Don't you talk that way to me!"

"But—"

"Shut up!"

His blade slashed downward, and the haunting voice was stilled. Unlike the others, though, there was no flash, and the third angel collapsed before him, clutching at the terrible wound cleaving her shoulder.

"Christopher, no!" she moaned faintly.

Christopher had just drawn back his dripping blade to finish the wounded angel when a mist seemed to pass from his eyes. Suddenly, the stricken angel was transformed into Holli, his little sister, his favorite. Her pretty face was now twisted into a tightly drawn mask of pain, but her soft blue eyes held the same look of concern for him that he had seen many times before. And then she was gone, in a pale flash of white light that left him dazzled and confused.

Somewhere, he thought he heard a dark voice laughing in the back of his mind, but he did not know who it belonged to. He hoped, almost, he prayed, that that dark voice was not his own.

Jami watched in shocked dismay as the hulking warrior that just could not be Chris stalked into the ruined Hall of Righteousness. There was, she could see, very little that remained of her geeky, loser brother anymore. He was taller, built like an NFL linebacker, and covered with dark spiked armor that looked as if it was permanently welded onto him.

His face was not a face at all but a death mask, a lifeless metal parody that reminded her of King Tut. Except in the pictures she'd seen, King Tut was sort of smiling, and this evil imitation of her brother didn't look capable of cracking a grin. But he moved with a careful, catlike grace, and he carried two darkly glowing swords as if he knew how to use them.

She called out to him. He didn't respond. When he ignored Holli, too, Jami felt her stomach drawing together in one huge knot. Something bad was going to happen, she could feel it in the air, and there was nothing she could do about it. As Khasar moved to intercept the monster, she backed away, her fear escalating into terror.

Surely, Khasar would protect them, she thought. He'd done okay against Lord Bile, at least for a time, and she couldn't imagine that Chris was stronger than the Archon. At least, she sure hoped he wasn't. She felt a momentary pang of remorse for cheering against her brother, but after all, he'd made his choice.

But when Chris struck down Khasar and then Daliel with effortless ease, Jami realized they were completely at the mercy of this killing machine that was once her brother. She felt the loss of the angels like a knife in her heart, but it was nothing compared to the icy hand of dread that gripped her whole being when she saw Holli kneeling before the one called Baal Phaoton.

Even before it happened, she saw it coming.

Once, when Chris was ten, a neighbor's puppy had nipped at his face, drawing blood as its needle-sharp puppy teeth unexpectedly pierced his nose. The puppy had leaped away, its tail wagging, intent on play and completely unaware of the rage it had inspired. Her brother, angry, his nose bleeding, had smashed the little dog to the ground with his fist and was just about to kick it when Holli, her eyes full of tears, managed to intercede and take the puppy safely home.

Jami saw the whole thing happen, and that face of rage, just before he struck the puppy, had imprinted itself forever on her mind. Now, she saw it again, in an inhuman mask of gold.

"Chris, no!" she cried, as if her words could stop what an Archon couldn't.

She rushed to Holli's side, but her stricken twin vanished before she got there. Her world reeled, and everything went red. Hate and rage and grief and horror swept through her soul, and a sword appeared in her hand as if by magic, burning with a darkly raging light.

"I hate you!" she screamed. "I hate you! You should be in Hell!"

She slashed wildly at him, and he stepped back from the clumsy stroke. Twice more, she swung, and both times, he easily evaded her attacks. Panting hard, and finding it hard to see past the tears that blinded her eyes, she suddenly remembered Kherev's words.

"*Forgive him as I have forgiven you. Love him as I have loved you.*"

No! She hated him. She hated him more than she even knew she could hate. He'd just stolen her bet-

ter half away from her, and she would never forgive
him for that. Never, never, ever! It was not possible,
not now, and not ever. She would hate him until he
died, horribly, she hoped, and then she would hate
him even more as he burned forever in Hell.

She tried to run him through, but he parried her
blade and for the first time struck back. The blow
was heavy, but she blocked it, though its force was
strong enough to make her stagger.

*"Forgive him as I have forgiven you. Love him as I
have loved you."*

"Shut up, Kherev," she snarled at the voice inside
her head. "Where were You when I needed You?
Why didn't You save Holli?"

*"Have you learned nothing, daughter of the King? I
am with her now, just as I am with you."*

A picture suddenly filled her mind. It was as if
she stepped outside herself and watched, from a
distance, as a sister fought her brother. It was a
scene that had been played time and time again,
over fifteen years, over two short lifetimes. They
fought with words, they fought with fists. Now
they fought with swords burning black with
hatred.

But then the terrible gold-faced warrior seemed to
shrink before her eyes. She saw he was not so terrible, not so mighty, just a wounded spirit that had
learned to lash out at everything around it, like an
unloved, mistreated pet. It was as if his heart were
open before her, and she saw each unhealed scar,
each bleeding wound. She stared at the heart and
was filled with shame when she saw that many of
those wounds had been inflicted by her own hand,
by her own tongue.

"Forgive him as I have forgiven you. Love him as I have loved you."

Now she knew what she had to do. She dropped her weapon and spread her arms wide, as if to embrace him.

"I forgive you, Christopher," she heard herself say. "I love you, Christopher."

And she smiled victoriously as his dark blade entered her heart.

CHAPTER 27

THE
SHAME OF CHEMOSH

AS FOR ME, I WILL BEHOLD THY FACE IN RIGHTEOUSNESS.
—Psalms 17:15

"Well done, Baal Phaoton," Kaym told him as he limped into the hall.

Christopher nodded absently and turned back to look at where his false sisters had fallen. He wondered why the second angel, the one that looked like Jami, had suddenly quit fighting. Her unexpected smile now haunted him, because it was not the smile of a victim, it was the smile of a victor, of someone who knew something he didn't. It gnawed at his confidence, but also, he thought with relief, confirmed that she'd been a fake, because his real sister didn't even know how to stop fighting. He turned back to the fallen angel.

"So what do we do now?" he asked. "Where's the legion?"

"Asmodel is taking it to the second planet. He thinks the Prince might be there. Which leads to your first question, and what we do is we find the Prince, gather our forces, and continue the war. That is what I will do." A spasm of disgust flashed over Kaym's face, and his eyes grew cold. "Though if you wish, you may join the cowards who have submitted to Heaven's King and be a slave again."

"No, of course not," Christopher protested. "I'll go with you. But, you know, the Prince kind of, well, ran away, didn't He?"

Kaym stared levelly at him. "Yes?"

"Well, I didn't really think that was cool, you know."

He choked as the fallen angel grabbed him by the throat. Kaym's hand felt like a metal vise around his neck, and despite his power, he couldn't break free.

"Never mention that again! Not to me, not to yourself!" But then Kaym sighed and released him. "Though I agree with you. Still, what you must keep in mind is that if you would claim the power you desire, you have no choice but to serve the Shining One. When He claims the throne of Heaven, then we who have been loyal shall finally claim the godhood that will otherwise be denied us. Heaven's King will never allow that, because he is—"

"A jealous God, and He will have no other gods before Him," a stranger interrupted.

Christopher was surprised to see the King's champion, Kherev Elohai, walking into the defiled hall. He was alone and unarmed, but he wore a crown of fire, and his quiet confidence made Christopher feel very uneasy. Knowing how easily he had beaten Abaddon, Christopher decided that discretion was the better part of valor and returned his blades to their scabbards. He inclined his head respectfully and waited to see what Kaym was going to do.

"The Lord has accomplished His fury," Kherev told them. "He has poured out His fierce anger and kindled a fire that has devoured the foundations."

Christopher glanced at Kaym and saw that the fallen angel had gone even whiter than normal and was shaking with fear before the unarmed intruder.

"What do you want with me, Son of the Most High God?"

Kherev pointed at the fallen angel, who shrank before him. "Woe be unto you, Chemosh, you are undone," He said with an air of finality.

Kaym bowed as he firmly grasped Christopher's arm. "Do not torture me with your flames, Lord Jesus. We will depart this place . . ."

Kherev shook His white head. "That is enough, Chemosh," He commanded, and His voice was like a bullwhip cracking. "Release him."

"Please, Lord, he is mine. He is all I have left." Kaym protested from behind gritted teeth.

"He is not yours. Take only that which is yours to take, damned one. To the rest you have no claim. Now begone, and join your master in the place of darkness."

"This war is not over."

"It was over before it began, Chemosh. Did you not understand when I told Gog Sheklah, I am the beginning and the end? Now leave this place before My Spirit flays you with the holy fire."

Kherev's voice deepened and echoed against the stones of the empty hall as silver flames began to erupt from His blazing red eyes. Christopher cringed, and Kaym fell humbly prostrate before the

Son of God, defiant no more. Then, with a rose-gold flash, the fallen angel abruptly disappeared.

Christopher was not sure what he should do or say, so he waited for Kherev to break the silence. But the Son of the Most High did not seem inclined to initiate a conversation, though He seemed calmer, and the terrible silver fire stopped leaping from His face. He simply stared at Christopher with those frightening red eyes, and Christopher had the sinking feeling he was being judged and found wanting. He stood that terrible feeling as long as he could, but when he couldn't take the silence any longer, he cleared his throat and addressed God's Son.

"I, um, noticed that Kaym . . . You know, the one You called Chemosh . . . I noticed he called You Lord, ah, Jesus, actually."

"He did."

Christopher looked closely at Kherev's plain bronze face. It was hard to read any emotion there, any feelings hiding behind the intensity of the strange red eyes.

"Would that happen to be the same Jesus that's mentioned in, ah, the Bible?" He tried to assume an airy, intellectual tone. "You know, Jesus of Nazareth and all that?"

"I am."

"Oh." There was a long pause. "I thought, You know, You were more, like, the peace and love dude. Not so much the warrior sort. I just thought . . ." His voice trailed off.

Lord Jesus laughed, not unkindly. "I am the Lamb of God, it is true. But I am also the Lion of Judah."

"I see." Christopher took a deep breath and went directly to the point. "So, I'm pretty much going straight to Hell now, aren't I? Do not pass Go, do not collect two hundred dollars, right? Just turn and burn."

"That, Christopher Lewis, depends entirely on you."

"On me? But what about..." His head whipped around, seeing the defiled hall as if it were the ruin he'd made of his soul. "I mean, I've done some bad things. Really bad things, you know?"

"Yes, I know. You have murdered and lied, you have blasphemed, you have cheated and stolen and shown disrespect to your parents. You have had congress with demons, you have warred against God, and you have worshiped at the false idol of your own desires."

Put that way, it sure sounded a lot worse than it had felt at the time. Christopher felt sick to his stomach.

"I think You got everything except cheating on that algebra test last week... So, is there really a Hell after all? But You said... well, what do I do now? I suppose I can't change what I did."

Lord Jesus smiled. "Yes, there is a Lake of Fire. And you cannot change what you have done. But you can change who you are."

"Change who I am? What do you mean? How can I do that?"

"Follow Me."

"Follow You? Where?"

"I speak not of a place but a Way."

"A way? What way?"

"The Way to the Father. The Way out of bondage, death, and sin. It goes through Me. I am the Way, the Truth, and the Life."

"I don't understand. How can following Your Way change who I am?"

"What is made may be unmade." His voice was soft and caring. "You see, Christopher, one day, you will stand before the throne of My Father's judgment. And on that day, you will be judged. Every word, every thought, and every deed must be deemed pure and right and holy in order for you to be deemed worthy of entering into the glory of My Father's house."

"But I'm already doomed, then."

"You are, because you have sinned and fallen short of the glory of God. The glory of God is perfect, Christopher, and even one small sin in an otherwise saintly lifetime of righteousness would render one unworthy of His radiant glory."

"That seems a little harsh."

"Can you be just a little dead and yet be alive? No!" Christopher jumped at His sudden vehemence. "Nor can you be a little stained by sin. My Father is pure and holy, and He demands like purity and holiness from all those who would enter into His presence. This is right and just. But My Father is also merciful, and He knows that you are weak. That is why He will one day send Me to your world, to die, so that you may live forever in the Light."

"Yeah, the cross thing. But even if it were true, or will be true, I should say, how does Your death help me?"

"Because My Father has promised Me that when He judges those who have pledged themselves to Me, those who have repented of their sin and walk in My Way, that on the Day of Judgment, He will look at Me in their place and judge them as if My life had been theirs. And I am without sin, Christopher. Mine is the only life that can be deemed worthy."

"So what do I have to do?"

"Give up all that you have, and follow Me."

"Everything?" He looked down at the mighty body of the powerful being he had become. "Do you mean even all of . . . this?"

"Everything."

Christopher thought about it for a moment. The Son of God was clearly powerful and pretty cool to boot. And the thought of serving Him had some appeal, but he hated the idea of losing everything he had fought for. Before the light-filled presence of Jesus, he could see that, like the Prince, it was the darkness that had changed him, but he could not truly say that he disliked what he'd become. Whether he was, as Kaym had told him, beyond good and evil, or if he was just evil now, was hard to say. But he knew that he loved what he'd become, whatever it was, and that he could not, would not, throw it all away.

To be a slave of the King might be no bad thing. But he would still be a slave. No, he would be his own master, he decided, no matter what the cost.

"No," he said finally. "I will not serve anyone but myself. I don't want to set myself against You, but I won't be your slave, either."

"If you are not for Me, Christopher, you are against Me."

Christopher nodded. "I know. I'm sorry, but I guess that's the way it's going to be."

Jesus nodded, as if He understood.

"Can I ask You one thing, though?" Christopher

asked quickly. "Before You came, I fought some angels. Two of them looked kind of like my sisters. Would You know if it was them or not?"

Jesus only shook his head. "What is that to you, Christopher? Look to your own soul."

Then the Son of the Most High God reached out and placed a small object in Christopher's hand. He closed Christopher's hand around it and raised a finger in warning.

"You are going to have the light just a little while longer. Walk while you have the light, before darkness overtakes you."

CHAPTER 28

A LION ROARS

A LION ROARS IN THE DARKNESS
ONLY HE HOLDS THE KEY
A LIGHT TO FREE ME FROM MY BURDEN
AND GRANT ME LIFE ETERNALLY
—Creed ("My Own Prison")

Jami lost her balance as the blinding light that surrounded her faded into a dark haze. As she stumbled, she reached out and felt something soft. She squeezed experimentally and was rewarded by a squeal of pain.

"Ow! What did you do that for?"

"Holli?"

"Yeah? Jami, is that you?"

"Uh-huh. Are you all right?"

As her vision adjusted, Jami saw Holli standing in front of her, unharmed but with a puzzled look on her face. She was no longer wearing the white robes that she'd worn in Heaven but was dressed instead in the green sweatshirt and jeans she'd been wearing six weeks ago, when the power had first gone out in their home.

"I'm fine, I think. Where are we?"

Jami ran her hands over her chest. She couldn't feel any signs of a wound under her T-shirt and breathed a thankful prayer of gratitude to God. Again, He had saved them. "I don't know, but I'm pretty sure it isn't Heaven. Or Hell, for that matter."

There was something familiar about the low ceilings and thin, raspberry-colored carpeting. The coat racks were absurdly low, as if constructed for dwarves or, as Jami realized was actually the case, young children. There was a large glass window to one side, and behind them was an entrance to what appeared to be a library. It was hard to make out any details, though, for it was dark outside, and the only light in the room was cast by the red glow of the exit signs.

"Holli, this is the same school we were in before. You know, Chris's elementary school, the one that those church people were meeting in."

"Wow, you're right!" Holli agreed. "We must be in a different part of the building, then."

As Jami looked around, she saw Holli's face grow serious.

"That was Christopher we saw, wasn't it?"

"I . . . I don't know. I thought so. But I also thought we were, like, dead, you know? And we're not."

"He hit me with his sword." Holli spoke slowly, as if she couldn't believe what she was saying.

"I know. I saw it. He stabbed me, too."

Holli glanced down at her shoulder, then back at her sister. "So how come we aren't dead?"

"Maybe we couldn't be killed there." Jami laughed. "You're not supposed to die in Heaven. Or maybe if you die there, you come here!"

Holli nodded, and a faint smile crossed her lips. "Well, at least we know there's life after death, right?"

"Sure, but who would ever believe us? Do you think it's like the *Chronicles of Narnia*, and only a few minutes have passed?"

"I don't think so. Those church people were pretty loud before, and it's really quiet in here now."

"Yeah." Holli tilted her head and frowned. "Actually, I hear something."

"Where?"

"That way." She pointed toward a ramp that was barely visible in the dark library, leading past another large window to an unknown destination.

"Wait a minute." Jami grabbed her sister's arm as Holli led her toward the ramp. "What if those demons are still around?"

"They can't be. Remember, we were outside, and they'd run away from the angels."

"Maybe they came back."

Evan as she spoke, a ghastly face loomed in toward the glass. Its beastly head was twice the size of a human, and its dripping teeth were long and sharp. The grotesque thing leered at them for a second, then turned away and howled, as if calling to others.

"Run, Holli!" Jami shouted as she jumped back from the window.

"Where?" Holli screamed, frozen in fear.

"This way, children," they heard a deep male voice urging them from somewhere past the bottom of the ramp. "Hurry!"

They hastened to obey, but Jami's heart nearly stopped beating when she heard the loud thud of something crashing into the thick glass of the library window. The two girls sprinted down the ramp, past a bathroom and a corridor of offices, then turned the corner and were nearly spitted on the drawn swords of Mariel, Aliel, and Paulus.

"Jami! You're safe!" her Guardian exclaimed, throwing his muscular arms around her. "Oh, praise the Lord, how we've prayed for you!"

"I don't really think we're, like, safe, Paulus," Jami corrected him. "There's something big and nasty outside trying to break in." There was a loud crashing noise from above as the big window finally gave way and shattered. "Did you hear that! It's after us!"

And there was a loud noise like an onrushing train passing by, except that it did not stop. Instead, it continued to come closer, growing ever louder and more menacing as it approached, a hurricane of evil intent on their destruction.

Mariel uttered a little cry, then turned and ran. The girls started to follow her, but they were prevented by Paulus and Aliel, who grasped their charges and prevented them from fleeing.

"Shouldn't we run?" Holli cried out.

"From this shadow you cannot flee," Paulus said, his eyes blazing with determination.

Jami grabbed her sister's arm and pulled her from Aliel's protective embrace. "This is like the city and the dragon, remember. We've got to pray! That's how we fight them."

Paulus nodded in surprised approval. Then he wrinkled his forehead suspiciously. "When this is over, you must tell me where you girls have been. I rejoice to hear it, Jami, but since when did you believe in prayer?"

"Since Kherev told me how important it is!"

"Kherev?" Paulus and Aliel looked at each other, and Jami's big Guardian shrugged. "Later."

"Just pray, my dears," Aliel urged. "We'll circle you and protect you, and the Lord will surely defend us."

Jami fell to her knees and tried to pray, but the words would not come. She stared, paralyzed by fear, as an ominous dark presence slowly made its way around the corner, unseen but palpable. It gave off an oppressive sense of power that Jami had felt before. It was, she realized, the same spirit of evil that had come to the house on that first awful night.

"Oh, it's ugly, it's so ugly," Holli cried.

The fear and repulsion in her sister's voice reminded her, unexpectedly, of Kherev Elohai. She could almost hear his voice, speaking those gentle words of encouragement to her.

"It's not hopeless, Jami, not ever."

She grabbed Holli's hand and squeezed it reassuringly. Then she closed her eyes, turned her mind away from the approaching darkness, and fervently began to pray.

As the light faded away, Christopher found himself lost in the dark. He could see, but only with difficulty, and he could not determine where he was. He still wore his golden aspect of Phaeton, but it was uncomfortable, like wearing a jacket that didn't fit quite right. He shrugged and shifted easily into the form of a normal angel with metallic wings of gold. It felt better somehow.

He looked down, and in his hand was the little key the Shining Prince had given him to break the

Gates of Heaven. Now, how did Kherev, or Jesus, whoever He really was, ever get His hands on that? When Ahura Azdha was blown to bits? Talk about a needle in a haystack! But as he thought about the impossibility of the coincidence, a noise came to his ears, and he realized that there were spirits nearby.

He tucked the key away and walked down a flight of stairs, then turned a corner and walked down another flight. As he strode past an empty gymnasium, he suddenly stopped, for in the corridor before him stood a lowly Divine angel, a Guardian by the look of it, holding her sword drawn before him. She was the loveliest creature he'd ever seen, and he caught his breath in surprised appreciation, though he kept a wary eye on her weapon.

"Who art thou, pretty one?" he asked, mimicking the speech he'd heard in the Courts of Light, hoping to impress her.

"One who would like to see you walk out from that shadow wrapped around you," she replied sadly. "I am Mariel, your Guardian, Christopher, and I see that I have failed you."

Christopher laughed. "My Guardian? That's funny. Just how many of you do I have?"

"One, and that is me. Melusine is not your Guardian, Christopher. She is a Temptress in service to the Adversary, and she has led you into great evil, I fear."

"Melusine is pretty tempting," Christopher admitted with a smile. "But that's all right, you know?"

The pretty angel shook her head, and tears

appeared in her eyes. "No, it isn't. I fear your conscience is already dead."

"Well, it wasn't much to start with." He shrugged.

Shouting voices broke into their conversation, and Christopher felt a disturbance in his soul as a strong spirit wielded its power not very far away from them.

"What's that?" he said, looking around.

"A Great Lord of the Fallen comes, to kill your sisters, Jami and Holli. They have been away for hours, and where we could not tell."

"They're alive? You mean—where are they?"

"Yes, and their Guardians are with them, but—"

"Guardians? Ha! A lot of good that'll do them!"

Christopher's dark blades were drawn in an instant, and he ran past Mariel before she tried to stop him. He ran down the hall, turned a corner, then came to a halt as he saw two angels in white standing protectively over his kneeling sisters. They were alive! Mariel was right, he hadn't killed them after all! But he quickly swallowed his joyful impulse to call out to them when he saw the four beings standing beyond them.

Two of them he did not recognize, but the others Christopher knew well. The black-jacketed, Raybans-wearing figure in the lead was Kaym, and behind him was Melusine, her devilish tail swishing as seductively as ever. Without thinking, he drew upon his powers and made himself invisible, hoping Kaym and Melusine hadn't noticed his presence. As he watched, Mariel approached him from behind and, laying a small hand upon his shoulder, began to whisper in his ear.

* * *

"Stand aside for Lord Kaym." Jami looked on as the devil-girl standing beside the angel wearing shades tried to order her Guardian around. "If you oppose him, he will destroy you."

"They are under our protection, and we will not abandon them." Paulus was nearly as pale as the one called Lord Kaym, but his voice did not waver.

"Your protection is meaningless," Lord Kaym told him. The evil one was handsome, Jami thought, but there was something cruel and ruthless about him, too, as he pointed at her and Holli.

"Now, stand aside, for I will have these here. They are young, but they are no innocents, for they have seen things they should not have seen, and My Lord, the God of this age, has ordained they shall not live. This is His right, and I am here to carry out His will."

"We may oppose you. It is permitted by the Law."

Lord Kaym shrugged indifferently. "As you wish. It does not matter."

The evil one gestured, and the flames that leaped and hissed from the Guardians' swords were extinguished without a sound. Another gesture, and the blades went flying in separate directions and were buried to the hilt into the plastered concrete walls. He raised his hand a third time, and Paulus and Aliel were hurled back by an invisible force that held them, helpless, pinned up against the wall like smashed bugs.

Aliel shrieked once, and Jami could only hope she hadn't been hurt too badly. As Lord Kaym took a step toward them, Holli rose to her feet, pulling Jami up with her. Her sister was surprisingly calm, and she didn't seem scared at all as she stared into her reflection in the dark glasses.

"God just told me that you can't touch me or my sister. I just thought I should, like, tell you that."

Lord Kaym's laughter was echoed by his three demonic followers. "He did, did He? Very well, then, we must see to it that your God keeps His word. I won't touch you, that I promise."

He pointed both his tattoo-covered hands at the carpeted floor, and the red dragons that covered them came to life, hissing and writhing their way down past his fingers until they fell freely to the floor and began to glide toward the two girls. The serpentine creatures were small, less than two feet long, but their curved teeth were long, glinting with bright green poison, and their yellow eyes were filled with hate.

Jami didn't dare to move a muscle as the snakes approached them, sinuous and sinister. She saw Lord Kaym raise his now-unmarked hand, and the dragon-snakes stopped, one in front of her and one in front of Holli, each within easy striking distance.

"I will give you one chance to save yourselves," Kaym said. "Kneel before me, and I will spare you, in my Master's name. You are young and have long lives before you if you will but serve Him. I can tell you that the rewards are great when one swears service to my Master. Your brother would tell you the same."

A golden blade suddenly slashed downward, beheading both serpents in a single stroke. They vanished in a cloud of stinking green smoke so acrid that it brought tears to Jami's eyes.

"Their brother would like you to leave them alone, Kaym," she heard Chris say.

"Christopher!" Holli shouted gladly.

But Chris ignored both her and Jami. He stood with his back to them, facing the Lord Kaym. How did he know the evil one's name? Jami found herself wondering. She knew that Chris had been on Ahura Azdha. Had this Lord Kaym been there as well?

"Will you oppose me now, Phaoton?" Lord Kaym said, with an odd smile twisting his narrow lips. "For the sake of those you have yourself slain? All that you have, all that you are, I have made you. You are mine, now and forever."

"You made nothing, Kaym," Chris denied. "I wouldn't be Kherev's slave, but I'm not yours, either."

"You pathetic fool!" Kaym barked angrily. "What do you know? Do you think you have a choice? You made that choice a long time ago, when you sold your soul for my power."

"Then come and get it." Christ brandished his golden blade, and it began to burn with a white silvery fire. "If you think you can."

"Indeed." Kaym appeared nonchalant, but Jami thought she sensed concern lurking behind the angel's dark glasses. "And what is this weapon, with which you dare to stand against me?"

Chris said nothing, but a quiet voice whispered to Jami from a place deep inside her, and she knew the answer, although her brother didn't.

"It is the sword of the Spirit, which is the Word of God!" she shouted at Kaym.

"In the beginning was the Word, and the Word

was with God, and the Word was God!" Holli giggled as she spoke, and Jami saw her sister's head was now wreathed in the silvery-red flames of Kherev's holy river. As His promised Spirit filled them both, they began to laugh uncontrollably, fearlessly, in the face of the demon-lord.

The devil-girl began to back away from them, and the two lesser demons cringed fearfully before the flickering light of the holy flames, but Lord Kaym stood fast.

"What is this talk of words and gods to me!" he spat angrily. "I, too, am a god, and you will burn in my fire, not His!"

In a fit of rage, Kaym transformed instantly into his fearsome aspect of the Dark Warrior. A crack of thunder exploded just above the building. The two girls fell to their knees. But Kaym's indignant fury only sent Jami into another fit, and as she rolled on the floor, still laughing helplessly, she saw his terrible image gradually become transparent. The fire of the Spirit stripped away the Dark Warrior and revealed a small, hunched being glaring balefully, but impotently, at her.

Christopher was shocked when he saw his mentor's true nature. Kaym was not truly a great spirit of arrogance and proud rebellion but a cruel, ugly thing, twisted by eons of hatred and self-loathing. The fallen angel was not more than a man but less, far less, and Christopher couldn't keep the contempt from his voice as he pointed his sword at the remnants of the being he had once sought to imitate.

"They don't fear your fire, Kaym. Neither do I.

There's something here, and it's a lot bigger than you or me."

The shrunken creature pursed its thin, bluish lips, and then it was again Kaym who stood before him, transformed back into the shaded biker, though his hands were still bare of dragons. The fallen angel cracked his knuckles thoughtfully as he stared balefully at the silver flames dancing victoriously above the heads of Christopher's laughing sisters.

"You may be right," Kaym admitted at last. "I know that one from a long, long time ago, and I will not test Him again." The dark shades were black, impenetrable. "You are giving up everything, you know. Riches, power, women, fame . . ."

"So?" Christopher pretended not to care, but the enormity of what he'd just done made him feel suddenly sad. Was he to go back to his old life now, back to the rejection and isolation of the helpless outcast?

"You will regret it."

"Maybe." Christopher looked away, fearing Kaym was right. "We'll see."

"We shall. I will not say goodbye, Christopher Lewis, because we shall meet again."

Christopher nodded coolly. "Not if I see you first. Go away, Kaym."

There was no flash, no sudden roar of thunder. Instead, Kaym simply faded into insubstantiality, like a Cheshire Cat without a smile.

As the fallen angel disappeared, Christopher lowered his head, though whether in relief or regret he did not know. He swallowed hard and desperately tried to master his emotions. Challenging a demon lord was one thing, but the idea of turning around filled him with terror, because he did not know how to face his sisters.

The joyful spirit left Jami without warning, the flame over her head winking out just as she felt the strange but comforting warmth flushing out of her body. Her mind was blank, but her fear was gone, as if the overwhelming joy had burned it out of her. There was a faint aftertaste that reminded her of Kherev, but why that was she couldn't say. She looked around and saw that the demons were gone, even the great demon-lord that had cast Paulus and Aliel aside as if they'd been ragdolls instead of angels.

Two scorched marks on the floor were all that remained of the Lord Kaym's evil dragon-snakes, and she knew that if Christopher hadn't killed them, they would have killed her. She was glad that he had, of course, but she didn't understand why, when he hadn't held back from striking her himself. She was still a little unclear about what had happened at the end, when he'd struck her down. Had he really tried to kill them? Could it have been some kind of vision, sent by their demonic enemies to scare her?

"Oh, Christopher, it is you!" She watched Holli rush forward to embrace their brother.

His eyes were still dark and shadowed, but Chris appeared otherwise to be himself. The warrior with the golden face was gone, replaced by a familiar, lanky teenager with his too-long hair falling into his eyes.

"Holli . . . oh, Holli . . . I'm so sorry."

When she heard his halting apology, Jami realized

that the vision of death in the defiled hall wasn't hers alone. It had been real somehow, somewhere.

"Forgive us our sins, as we forgive those who sin against us," she whispered Kherev's words, reminding herself.

Jami stared at Chris, still being hugged by Holli. He was crying openly, which was an odd thing for Chris, who usually tried not to show his feelings. Though she'd known him all her life, Chris was still in many ways a stranger to her, a stand-offish, bitter stranger with whom she shared a roof and a last name, and little more. For the last four years, they'd lived in an uneasy truce broken only by moments of anger and vicious name-calling. Always, she had blamed him for their poor relationship, although, if she were honest with herself, she was maybe a little jealous of the way he liked Holli better.

Now, she could see through the transparent shell of his feigned indifference, and she realized that Chris wasn't the only one to blame. There were times when she could have helped him with his problems and she'd hindered him instead, and times when she could have made a difference but looked the other way instead. If he hated her, she admitted to herself, she'd given him some pretty good reasons.

Jami froze as Chris squeezed Holli one more time, then turned and looked at her. He took a deep breath and wiped angrily at his reddened eyes, then exhaled and folded his arms.

"Jami, I, ah, know we don't get along too well. And I'm sorry, I really am. Not just for what, um, what happened in that other place, but for all that stuff I've said to you before. I know I'm not a very good brother for you, you know, and I'm sorry." He looked away for a moment, then back at her. "Do you think you can forgive me?"

Jami bowed her head and bit her lip. They were in the real world now, not Heaven. She thought again of all the nasty comments, the malicious put-downs, and the insults. She remembered how he'd taunted her and made fun of her proudest accomplishments. She still felt the scars of hurtful words that had seared insecurity deep within her soul. And she could still see the terrible look on his face when he'd stabbed her right through the heart.

"Nobody's perfect, Christopher," she found herself saying, incredibly. "Not you, and not me, either. Can I forgive you?" She smiled tightly and fought back the tears that threatened to run from her eyes. "A week ago, probably not. But a lot's happened, and now, you know, I guess I can. And I will, I mean, I do."

Chris reached out and hugged her, and she could feel the dampness of his tears against her cheek. She hugged him back, and as she did, she felt something inside her suddenly snap and disappear. It was as if a dam of hate was suddenly broken, and a flood of peace and joy and love rushed in to wash away the bitter scars of yesterday.

Something wickedly sharp brushed her thigh, and she jumped, alarmed. When she saw what it was, she laughed and drew away from her brother.

"You'll have to do something about that sword, you know. I don't think Mom and Dad are going to be too psyched about you having that."

Chris nodded as he ran his sleeve across his face. "Actually, that won't be a problem."

He held the golden sword upside-down, and it shrank into a simple little cross of the kind often seen dangling from gold chains.

"That's weird. I thought it was a key." He peered at it curiously. "Hmm. It's still got those letters on it. See?"

Both girls examined it.

"I—X—O—Y—E," Jami read.

"What does it mean?"

"Iesou Christos Theo Yios Soter. It means Jesus Christ, God's Son, the Savior," Mariel answered from behind them, and all three Lewis children whirled around. In her emotional confrontation with Chris, Jami had forgotten the angels, but she was relieved to see that Paulus and Aliel were now free from whatever the demon-lord had done to them.

"There you are." Chris addressed Mariel as he held up the little cross. "This was a good idea, you know. You were right, Kaym was afraid of it. But you're saying that this is a symbol of Jesus? Not the cross, I know that. I mean the letters."

"Without a doubt," Mariel told him, and Paulus agreed.

"You can look it up when you get a chance, if you like. It's Greek, the language of the New Testament."

"Oh, man," her brother sighed. "I don't get it. I mean, well, let me tell you that there's power in this thing, okay? It may not look like much, but it's, I don't know, like, powerful. But if it means what you say, then the power must come from Jesus, right, Mariel?"

"Certainly."

"Then why could I use it to, you know, help the other side?" Chris frowned at Paulus. "Why are you laughing at me?"

"Because I know who you are," said the big Guardian. "You are the one who opened the Gates of Heaven to the Foe! I fought in the battle that followed the breaking of the Gate, and one thing we never learned was how Lucifer managed to make his way inside. So that's how he did it!"

"Did what?" Jami demanded, echoed by Holli, Mariel, and Aliel.

"Lucifer! Oh, what a sly snake he is. Don't you see? He needed a human to break the Gate! It couldn't be an angel because even the Sarim lack that kind of power, and only the sons and daughters of Adam may claim authority to call upon the name above all names!"

"I see," murmured Mariel. Jami didn't.

"I have the authority to call on that kind of power?" Chris asked. "Just because of this cross . . . or whatever?"

"You do. You all do! You don't need the cross, it's just a symbol. The power is within you, a gift from the Son of Man to every son of Adam and daughter of Eve. He said Himself that He has given you all authority on Heaven and on Earth." The big Guardian frowned at him. "It is unfortunate that you chose to do so in the service of the Adversary. I don't understand how that could happen."

"There is precedent," Aliel pointed out. "It was also so in Ephesus, once. The power is in the Name, not the one who wields it."

"It was Him, then," Jami heard Chris whisper. "From the time this whole thing started, it was Him!"

He glanced at Holli, then at her.

"You follow Him now, don't you? Those flames... I saw Kaym react that way only once before, in the hall. He didn't want to fight Lord Jesus, he was afraid."

"You saw Him?" Mariel and the angels were astonished. "Did you speak with Him, too?"

Chris nodded and held the little cross out to Mariel.

"Yeah, He told me I should serve Him, but when I turned Him down, He warned me about walking in shadows or something. So what do I do? What if I want to do what you said, you know, and walk out of the shadow? Is it too late?"

Jami watched, holding her breath, as Mariel closed Chris's fist around the cross, then took that hand in both of hers and gazed deeply into his eyes.

"It is never too late. If it was not too late for a thief dying on a cross, it cannot be too late for you, Christopher. Another man once asked the Son of God how he could have eternal life, and Jesus told him: 'Love the Lord your God with all your heart and with all your soul and with all your strength and with all your mind'; and 'Love your neighbor as yourself.' That is what you must do."

"He also said that He will acknowledge whoever acknowledges Him before men, and that whoever disowns Him before men will be disowned before the angels of God," Paulus added. "Do you understand this truth?"

"Yeah, I do." Christopher cleared his throat. "You said before men. Would, ah, my sisters count?"

"Certainly," Paulus confirmed.

"Well, I should think so!" Jami snorted.

"Good. Well, then, of my own free will, I acknowledge Jesus Christ as my Lord, before my sisters, Jami and Holli Lewis. I will serve Him in His battle against evil, darkness, and Adonai Lucere."

"Amen!" cried the angels, and their approval was echoed by the sound of trumpets blowing, accompanied by a slow roll of thunder booming outside. There were three flashes of blinding light, and suddenly, a mighty Prince of Heaven stood before them, flanked on either side by two lordly Archons, both in the form of winged lions.

"Khasar!" the girls cried. "Jhofor!"

"Welcome, Prince Michael," Paulus hailed the Archangel warmly. "What brings you to this place?"

"These children," Michael answered gravely. "I have been sent with a message for them."

The three Lewis children glanced at one another.

"Don't tell me this is the part where we have to forget everything," Jami muttered under her breath to Holli. "Those kids in the *Narnia* books didn't have to. We can keep our mouths shut."

"You shall forget nothing," Michael answered. "Nor shall you hold your tongue. The time is not far off when the Son of Man shall return in splendor and rule this Earth as its rightful King. But until that day, darkness shall cover the land, and evil shall take root and harden many a heart. The Son of Man has need of warriors, who shall be a light in the darkness and war in His name against the spiritual forces of evil in the heavenly realms. Will you serve Him in this way?"

"Of course," Jami agreed instantly, as did Holli and Chris.

"Sure."

"We will."

"Then, I say to you, in addition to the gifts of the Spirit you now bear, I have been commissioned to give you three more gifts, in the most holy name of the Son of God, the Lord Jesus Christ of Nazareth."

The lordly angel placed his hand upon Holli's head.

"To you, lovely child, the gift of hope. Though the night grows dark, you shall not know despair."

Still touching Holli, he placed his other hand on Christopher's head.

"To you, o wayward son, the gift of faith. Knowledge of the Truth shall be yours, and mountains shall move at your command."

Jami bowed her head as Michael released the other two and turned to her, placing both hands upon her head.

"To you, daughter, the greatest gift, the gift of love. To love another person is to see the face of God, and you shall see Him everywhere you look."

She felt a strange tingle as the angel spoke these words and stumbled back when a spark of electricity jolted her, as if she'd been walking across carpet in her socks and touched something metallic.

The angelic prince released her and raised his hands. His parting words were addressed to all three of them.

"Already you bear within you the gift of eternal life. Be now warriors of eternity, in service to the Son of God, standing fast for Him against the foe. Dark days lie ahead, but you are not alone and shall not be overcome, not by all the hosts of Hell. Farewell!"

The two Archons roared their affirming witness,

then vanished with Michael as unseen trumpets blared a goodbye salute.

"Wait, Khasar, I want to ask you . . ."

"He's gone," Holli said sadly.

Jami looked around and realized that not only had the big Archon disappeared, but Paulus, Aliel, and Mariel had as well.

"Oh, no! They're all gone!" she cried.

All three of the Lewis children looked around the empty room, wondering where their angels had gone, until Chris started laughing.

"Great! We get a new job, but no one can tell us what we're supposed to do!"

"So what do we do?"

"I . . . don't know," Jami answered. She glanced at her watch. "I know one thing, though. I mean, do you think it's still Saturday night?"

"Why's that?" Holli asked.

"Well, if it is, I thought we might want to get home before Mom and Dad do. Their movie got out ten minutes ago!"

CHAPTER 29

I'LL BE WATCHING YOU

FOR DO I NOW PERSUADE MEN, OR GOD? OR DO I SEEK
TO PLEASE MEN? FOR IF I YET PLEASED MEN, I SHOULD
NOT BE THE SERVANT OF CHRIST.

—Galatians 1:10

Christopher had remembered to pull down his window shades before going to bed the previous night, so the unexpected knocking on his door was the first sign of morning he was forced to deal with. He rolled over and put a pillow over his head, hoping that the unwanted visitor would give up and go away, but they were persistent, until he finally gave in himself and called out in surrender.

"What?"

The doorknob turned, and Jami poked her face around the door's edge.

"Hey!"

"Hey, what?" He glanced at his alarm clock. It was only nine o'clock, far too early for any reasonable person to get up on a Sunday morning. Football wouldn't even start for another three hours.

"Do you want to go to church with us? Holli

391

thought we could go to that place that meets in the school."

"Are you kidding? Go to church? Come on, that's ridiculous!"

Jami didn't tell him off or anything, but the grin on her face vanished, and he got the vague impression that she was disappointed in him.

"So, maybe you can think about coming with us next week, then." Her words were surprisingly soft, at least for Jami, anyway.

"Um, all right. Look, I just need some time to get, you know, used to all this. I mean, what are Mom and Dad going to say if we start going to church? It'd be too weird, you know?"

Jami shook her head. "Since when did you care what Mom and Dad think?" She sighed and blew a stray hair out of her eyes. "Well, never mind. Holli and I have to get going if we're gonna make it on time. Go back to sleep."

"Yeah, okay. See you later."

" 'Bye."

The door closed softly, and he slumped back onto his pillow, feeling relieved but left with a nebulous sense of disquiet. Not a strong one, though, for it was not long before he was sleeping again, dreaming crazy dreams of dragons and devil-girls.

As he drifted in that gray haze that lies somewhere between sleep and consciousness, he felt a hand gently caress his forehead. It lightly traced the lines of his face, the profile of his nose, then lingered for a moment on his lips. He caught the scent of cinnamon and vanilla, and as a soft pair of lips pressed slowly against his, he started and sat bolt upright.

"Melusine!" he breathed, his pulse suddenly pounding.

"Hello, my darling Phaeton." She smiled at him from her seat at the foot of the bed.

She looked a little different from how she had before, wearing less revealing robes than what she usually wore, though her wings were as black as Kaym's shades. But her cute little horns still poked through the mass of her crimson hair, and her curves were still seductive, covered as they were.

"Why are you here?" he demanded. He was angry, but he was glad to see her, too. Maybe too glad.

"Why shouldn't I be?"

"Well, because we're on different sides. We should be enemies."

Melusine smiled sadly. "We may be on different sides, for now. But you know I'm not your enemy, and everyone's entitled to a mistake or two. Lord Kaym was disappointed in you, and Prince Lucere was very angry, but they have not forgotten what you have done for them. Nor have I."

She leaned forward, and he discovered that her scent was as intoxicating as ever.

"Have you forgotten what it was like to be a god, Phaeton? Will you really be content to be mortal again? To be nothing more than the unhappy boy that was Christopher Lewis? What a waste, all that talent, intelligence, and power, doomed to death in the mortal world."

"That's not—"

"To be a slave of the King . . ."

Christopher's eyes narrowed. Finally, he began to understand what Melusine was and why she was here. And he remembered, too, the King he served. To be His slave, well, that was no insult. It was an honor, a noble title he wasn't even worthy to hold.

"Get out of here, Melusine."

"No!"

He gritted his teeth and steeled himself. "Don't make me throw you out!"

"You don't have the power, Christopher," she taunted him. "Not anymore. Not without Kaym. Not without me."

"Maybe not, but I know who does." He looked up at the ceiling. "Lord Jesus, would You help me out here, please?"

In immediate answer to his prayer, Mariel materialized, and the flames of her sword were like a candle compared to the righteous bonfire burning in her eyes. Melusine fell back before Mariel's furious onslaught, spitting and cursing but clearly overmatched. Unable to stand before the angry Guardian, Melusine shot Christopher a disgusted look, then spread her dark wings and flew through the glass of the closed window.

"Hey, thanks," Christopher said, delighted to see his beautiful Guardian.

"You're welcome," Mariel replied, but her level gaze made it clear that at least some of her anger was reserved for him. "She'll be back, you know, and if you're going to serve Lord Jesus as you promised, you need to arm yourself against her and the rest of the Fallen."

"How do I do that?"

"Read His Word. Surround yourself with believers. Learn from others who serve the Lord. Exercise your gifts, that you may serve Him better than before." She frowned. "And you cannot do any of these things if you're consumed with worry about what others think of you."

Christopher bowed his head, ashamed. "I understand. I'm sorry."

She kissed the top of his head, then rumpled his hair and laughed. "If you mean that, then you've taken another step on the pathway to righteousness, Christopher."

Mariel began to glow, and as the glow brightened, her outline began to shimmer and fade.

"Wait, where are you going? You can't leave me!"

He could already see burgundy-and-blue wallpaper through her increasingly translucent form, but the white flash of her smile was unmistakable.

"Don't be afraid, Christopher. You may not always see me, but I'll be with you, always."

Beaded sweat was gleaming from the big music leader's shaved head, and the church band was well into its fourth or fifth song when Jami felt someone nudge her side.

"Hey, got any room here?"

"Christopher!" Jami impulsively reached out and hugged her brother. Surprisingly, he did not stiffen uncomfortably or push her away. "You came after all!"

"Yeah, well, it's hard to be a warrior all by yourself, don't you think?"

Jami's heart was too full of joy to speak, so she only smiled back at him.

"Hey, look, you guys!" Holli exclaimed happily. "There's, like, an army of angels all around this place!"

Jami glanced around the huge space of the gymnasium. Without her sister's gift of sight, she did not see anything at first, but then a flicker of flames and white feathers caught the corner of her eye, and for a moment she glimpsed Paulus, Aliel, Khasar, Jhofor, Mariel, and hundreds of other angels, all clapping their hands, dancing, and singing in joyful harmony with the human worshipers.

Paulus met her eyes and winked at her, once, then he and the rest of the Divine Host disappeared from her sight. But she had seen, and she understood that Prince Michael had spoken true; they were not alone, and they would not be overcome.

Blessed be the Name of the Lord
Blessed be the Name of the Lord
Blessed be the Name of the Lord
Most High

Jesus is the Name of the Lord
Jesus is the Name of the Lord
Jesus is the Name of the Lord
Most High

SELAH

AUTHOR'S NOTE

Although the events depicted in *The War in Heaven* are fictional, the invisible world of spirits it describes is not. We cannot see the spiritual forces that affect our lives any more than we can see the four forces that dictate the physical world, and yet the good and evil that result from their influences are as readily apparent as gravity.

The question of evil and our response to it is one of the central themes of this book. The problem is that a rational, post-Enlightenment world has a difficult time admitting evil's reality, despite its omnipresence in the modern age. Here, at the beginning of a new millennium, we have a tendency to avert our eyes and label those whose dreams reflect our nightmares as lunatics and madmen, instead of seeing them for what they truly are: conscious agents of evil.

And evil, it should be noted, does not consist solely of the horrific or the criminal. It is simply sin, or violating the perfect will of God. Sin can be beautiful, it can be entertaining, and it is always, always seductive. The Reverend Billy Graham said it best when he remarked that if you don't think sin is fun, you haven't been committing the right sins. Because sin is so attractive, it is easy to understand how we have all sinned and, in doing so, fallen short of the glory of God.

The reason I have concentrated here on the question of evil is that for many years, I was one of those who wholeheartedly embraced it as a way of life. Until four years ago, I was not a Christian and was living what the world considers to be an ideal lifestyle. Sadly, success today seems to be defined by Hollywood and is largely a matter of the car you drive, the appearance of the people you date, and how happy you happen to feel. Those were my standards, too, and I thought I was on top of the world, or near enough, anyhow.

But sin always find a way to enslave and corrupt you. After a while, I started to get bored. The everyday sin that filled my life was no longer enough, and I craved more excitement, more thrills, more of everything. I could feel my mind slipping away with the shards of my morality as I became less and less interested in anything but sin, until finally, I reached a point where I had to admit that I was heading straight for self-destruction. And when I contrasted my life with those of my friends who had become Christians, and when I thought about the positive changes I had seen in their lives, I knew that I had to make a decision between following my own way and following the Way, the Truth, and the Life.

A friend of mine once told me that he did not believe in God or Jesus because he did not understand how a loving God could send anyone to Hell. But in my experience, I have seen that it is not God who sends us there. Hell is our natural destination. Each of us is already drowning in a sea of self-destruction, and God has thrown us His Son as a rescue line. It is up to the individual to make his own decision to grab on to that line by acknowledging Jesus Christ as Lord and finding safety in His promise of salvation and eternal life. It is my hope and prayer that everyone who reads this book will one day make that same decison.

However, it is not enough simply to accept Jesus Christ's gift of salvation and then sit back to live happily ever after. Jesus did not shrug His shoulders in the face of this world's evil; instead, He fough actively against the spiritual forces behind it. Those of us who worship Him must follow His example and do the same. The Earth is a battlefield between the Most High God and the god of this world, and it is my hope that this book will inspire its Christian readers to realize this and take a more active part in fighting the forces of evil.

For those nonbelievers who are skeptical but are interested in learning more about Jesus Christ and what it means to follow Him, I recommend *Letters from a Skeptic* by Dr. Greg Boyd, whose sermons on spiritual warfare helped inspire this novel, or *Mere Christianity* by C. S. Lewis, the author of the brilliant Narnia novels. You can also visit the Eternal Warriors Web site at www.eternalwarriors.com, which features teachings by Dr. Boyd and other Christian writers. Above all, I recommend going directly to the source, the eternal Word of God, the Bible. The New International Version is the translation that I favor.

May God bless and protect you,

THEODORE BEALE
SHOREVIEW, MINNESOTA
JULY 22, 1999